GENERATION APOCALYPSE

BOOK TWO OF 1000 SOULS
PECTOPAHBOOKS.COM

MICHAEL ANDRE MCPHERSON

First Paperback Edition, October, 2014

Published by: Pectopah Productions Inc.

ISBN: 0986864153
ISBN 13: 9780986864155

For my loving parents,
My father, who never backed down from a fight, and my mother,
who taught me faith

TABLE OF CONTENTS

PROLOGUE

He had just turned ten when the world ended. At first it was fun, because some of the teachers stopped showing up at school. The principal, tall and angry, kept stuffing the students into the gym to watch movies, promising each day that the next would be normal. Instead, fewer and fewer of Tevy's friends came to school, and one day neither did the principal.

In the evenings, his parents spoke in anxious whispers, careful to ensure he didn't overhear, but one word often leaked out: *rippers*. He heard their neighbor, old Mr. Costa, say to his dad that there were rumors of murders happening all over Chicago, but for some reason it was never on the news. "They don't want us to know," Mr. Costa said, pointing his cane south in the general direction of city hall.

One morning his parents didn't go to work, and they kept him home, letting him play *Call of Duty* when the power was up. That was another big change: the power failing, the lights going dark, sometimes for hours on end.

One day he helped his dad board up the ground-floor windows.

"Is there a hurricane coming?" he asked, passing his dad another screw.

"Not the windy kind," his father replied.

Nights became very scary. Sometimes he heard screams and running feet on the sidewalk outside, and one night Mr. Costa's house burned down, with all kinds of people standing on his lawn but none helping. Tevy's mother pulled him from the window and covered his eyes. He wanted to scream because he was afraid, but his mother whispered in his ear, "Don't let them hear you. We have to pretend we're not here, baby. Please don't cry. We must be silent."

Silence. He had learned that lesson well.

The next night, the world did end. The rippers came for them.

The shouting frightened him beyond all reason, and he hugged his mother with all his strength. They called out rude suggestions with foul language and promised to hurt them all if they didn't come out. He wanted to obey their commands, believing their lies, but his father knew better.

"Stay in the closet," he whispered as he shoved Tevy back amongst the shoes and the coats. "It's like hide-and-seek, but you mustn't lose. Do you understand me?"

The intensity of his father's actions, the fear in his eyes, and the pleading of his words warned Tevy not to argue. He had always known that his parents loved him, but from that day forward, he understood that loving parents lay down their lives for their children. Like his parents.

The last time he saw them alive, his mother was loading a revolver and his father was holding a hunting rifle. His mother blew him a hurried kiss. The closet door closed. Then came the shouting and breaking glass, and a whoosh accompanied by a wave of hot air and the stench of gasoline. Guns fired and his mother screamed curses at someone, foul language he had never before heard her use.

He wanted to leave the closet, but he remembered his father's last words. He wanted to scream, but he remembered his mother telling him how silence could save his life. He clamped his hand over his mouth and wept, but he didn't scream. He didn't make a sound.

But the dull roar told him that fire, or the choking smoke, would soon kill him. He had to leave the closet. Suddenly, there was a lot more gunfire and a lot more screaming, but not from his parents. Then his mother spoke her last words. "My son!" she shouted. "In the closet! Please—" Her voice choked off wetly. It wasn't a normal sound.

The closet door yanked open, letting in a billowing cloud of gray that stung his eyes and made him choke. A strange man on his hands and knees reached for him. Had there been a halo around his head?

"Come on!" He grabbed Tevy's arm and yanked him from the closet. "I'm here to save you."

Tevy climbed onto the man's back as directed and hung on around his neck as the house cracked and groaned from the flames. They spilled out onto the front porch, and the man stood, scooping Tevy into his arms and running from the house. It was the first time Tevy had seen dead bodies—real dead bodies, not like his grandfather in the coffin at the funeral home. These bodies had chunks of their skulls missing or bloody holes in their chests. They were splayed at strange angles and had nightmare-inducing expressions on their faces—gaping mouths and bloody teeth.

"We've got to get him to St. Mike's," said a woman with a machine gun. "What about his parents?"

The man, his savior, shook his head.

The woman turned, stared off into the distance for a moment, then shot one of the corpses on the lawn in rage.

Tevy understood. The world as he knew it had ended forever. But he remembered to be silent, so he bit his tongue as he wept and buried his face in the man's shoulder, breathing in the stink of a sweating saint.

———

Kayla had worried about homesickness when she showed up at Atherley College, but by the second week she was more concerned about where she could buy a gun. Her roommate, Ashley, had gone missing, and there was talk of a serial killer hunting around the campus. The police said they shouldn't worry, that Ashley had probably just succumbed to the strain of college and headed down south to live on the streets of Toronto or maybe even Chicago.

Neither Kayla nor the other girls in their student residence believed that for a second, and they all found it disconcerting that the police were downplaying Ashley's disappearance.

"Frigging cops have no clue," Rachel said. She was in her third year and a lot older than Kayla, who wouldn't turn eighteen until December. "Last time a girl was assaulted was in my first year, and they practically locked us all down for a month until they caught the asshole. This time they tell us to go about our business as usual? I got this." She showed them all the Taser her dad had sent. "Get some protection girls, and I'm not talking about condoms."

But Kayla's parents were committed pacifists, even though Sioux Lookout, the little town where they lived, made a lot of money from tourist hunting and fishing. The town was so far north that the only way to go farther was by plane, and she already missed the sound of those little aircraft taking off early every morning to fly campers up to the high lakes. She considered dropping out and going home, but her mom suggested she stay at the college.

"Something's going on in town," she said on the phone. "There've been a lot of house fires. Your father and I are thinking of taking Kevin and heading down to a hotel in Thunder Bay for a few days."

That frightened Kayla. Why would they take her little brother and abandon the family home just because an arsonist was loose in town? What about their teaching jobs? The news reports didn't mention the problems in Sioux Lookout, but they didn't mention Ashley's disappearance either.

Kayla found Rachel in the common area reading a textbook, her dark hair tied back in a tight ponytail.

"I need to buy a gun," said Kayla.

Rachel looked up from the book, and her expression showed approval rather than surprise. "That's pretty much impossible to do legally now." She slapped the book closed.

"I don't care about legally. It's my body and no one's gonna take me without a fight."

"My dad knows a guy." Rachel stood and stretched. In another time—a month ago—Kayla might have thought Rachel needed to lose a few pounds, but that seemed so irrelevant and petty now. "Dad's decided I need an upgrade from the Taser. He's getting me a Glock. If you want, I can get you one too."

Kayla did want, but her weekly allowance from Mom and Dad hadn't been deposited into her bank account yet. "How much?"

Rachel smiled. "Don't worry. You can pay in installments. We're doing it for a few other girls too. Dad says we need to be our own police force here, watch out for each other."

And they did. No one went anywhere without an armed partner, but it turned out this serial killer wasn't just interested in women. Boys started to disappear, and even a few professors. The college president responded by going on a rant about absenteeism. By mid-October, rumors began to circulate about a cult of serial killers. Some guy down in Chicago was all over the Internet talking about rippers—blood drinkers. He said you couldn't believe what you see on the news, and Kayla fervently agreed. Her parents had found Thunder Bay just as dangerous as Sioux Lookout.

"It seems like a house burns down every night," said her mother in a quick phone call. "We've decided we're better off at home, and things seemed to have quieted down since the band council took over policing from the OPP."

When Kayla's physics professor didn't turn up one day, she decided to go home. Teaching assistants now taught half of her classes anyway, and they seemed as lost as everyone else as to why the campus was in a state of crisis unnoticed by the administration.

But she was too late.

She managed to hitch a ride in a rusting Jeep Cherokee that took her all the way to Sioux Lookout. The driver was young, Ojibwa, and cute. He told her his name was Ted, but she was pretty sure that was just the name he used with non–First Nations.

He was twenty and chatty, his jeans snug fitting and his muscles lean. He'd been out west working on the oil sands projects, but things had gotten weird and his grandmother had asked him to come home.

"The farmers," he said about his journey thus far. "They're burning the fields out in the Prairies instead of harvesting—some kind of protest, the newspapers say. Don't know much but it seems stupid to me."

He continued to say, "Don't know much," several times during the two-hour ride, but Kayla began to believe he knew quite a bit, and she was really glad he was there when they pulled up in front of the burnt shell of her childhood home.

He let her cry for a while on the front lawn, and his hand on her shoulder was a comfort. Her knees were getting wet in the fresh snow as she let the tension of the last few weeks pour out. She was detached, almost watching herself cry. She couldn't stop.

"Sorry," he said finally. "You should come to the rez with me. Gran said I had to be there before sunset. She said that was really important."

Kayla considered saying it was okay, that she just wanted to be a here a bit longer, that she'd stay at the Sunset Motel, but she was angry. Someone was going to pay for this, and she had to be alive to deliver that punishment.

She went with him to the little bungalow in the woods, and his grandmother had clucked and shouted at him and reached high to cuff his head, but she reluctantly let Kayla stay the night on the frayed couch.

The next morning, Kayla helped Gran with the dishes while Ted went off to a band-council meeting. If Gran spoke English, she didn't use it with Kayla. Ted came back with a grim expression.

"We got to go. Most are going."

"Where?"

"Most are heading up north, flying to the high lakes, away from... people."

Had he been going to say white people? He looked embarrassed, guilty.

"I can't go there."

He nodded his agreement. A long chat broke out in Ojibwa between Gran and Ted. It rose to shouting, but never aggressive, just both trying to be heard over the other, both used to talking this way.

"I can take you back to the college," he said finally. A four-hour round trip for him.

"I can't ask you to do that. If I could just get a ride into town, I'll get the bus tomorrow." Every Monday morning a bus headed down to Atherley with people who spent the week working there or at the pulp mill in Dryden.

"There won't be a bus." He turned and began zipping up her pack for her.

"Well, I'll hitch a ride then. Don't worry, I can take care of myself."

But she didn't feel that way. Had her parents gone back to Thunder Bay? She'd checked her phone about a hundred times during the night, calling her mother, texting her little brother, but there had been no replies. In her heart she knew there was only one reason that little brat hadn't texted her back with some amusing or snarky message, or a least an excited 140 character tweet about the house fire. He had always loved trying to fit his sentences into exactly 140 characters.

"It's not safe to hitch a ride." Ted opened the door, letting cold air into the little house. "There are people in the day who work for them—for the rippers."

And Kayla knew the world had changed forever. They were talking about them, the serial killers that slashed throats and drank blood, the ones that guy in Chicago, Bertrand Allan, kept talking about in his YouTube broadcasts. The rippers were humans that had changed, that had millions of strange cell-sized parasites in their blood and their organs, parasites that only allowed them to digest blood. No other food could sustain rippers.

"Thanks," she said to Ted. "Really, I don't know how I can thank you."

They rode in silence back to the college, the trees frosted with fresh snow, the road unplowed. Ted's Jeep had four-wheel drive, but he rarely used it because it sucked too much gas. "A lotta gas stations closed. It's hard to come by."

She tried to give him every bit of cash in her wallet even though he had refused and even seemed insulted.

"You'll need gas," she said. "Please, you probably saved my life."

He took it in the end, perhaps just to get her to stop. "It's probably worthless paper anyway," he said before he sped away, clearly anxious to get back to his grandmother before sunset.

Kayla found the dorm in a panic, girls crying and packing.

"What's going on?" she said to Rachel, who wasn't crying but was stuffing a pack with clothing.

"We're getting the hell out of here." Rachel suddenly stopped and looked up. "Hey, I thought you'd gone home."

Kayla didn't want to appear weak, but it was too much. She shook her head and bit her lip, unable to speak but successfully fighting back the tears—until Rachel swept her up in a hug.

"Oh, baby. It's okay. It's okay," Rachel said over and over as Kayla wept. "We've got a place to go, a safe place."

"Where?" Kayla pushed back from the hug and wiped her cheeks.

"It's a new student residence about a mile from here, but it's built like a fort. I don't know why but everybody already calls it 'The Keep.' The contractor who built it is sending a bus over for anyone who wants to join him—and they've got a lot of guns."

"Good." Kayla pulled out her Glock and looked at it for a moment, sensing the new life that was before her. "I'd like an upgrade to a machine gun."

1

CHICAGO

Silence. Tevy was the best at it, which is why he preferred to go on his raids alone. None of the other kids in the Brat Pack could move with his stealth, and in the Loop, an incautious step on broken glass, or kicking a piece of rubble down a staircase, could mean capture and gruesome death.

He ducked under the window so that no one down in the street would see him flit past, and he put his back to the moldering drywall, keeping a wary eye around the whole floor of the office building, searching above the cubicle dividers just in case someone else was up there. A few light fixtures, the fluorescent bulbs smashed, hung perpendicular to the ceiling, and of course the building had no power, but this floor wasn't as trashed as some Tevy had seen. No one had lived here, built a campfire for cooking, or even smashed the computers at the desks. He should tell the others about this place.

The Brat Pack the old folks called them, but Tevy knew that in this world, his world, he was an adult. He sometimes tried to imagine what it would have been like if the rippers hadn't come into being, if they hadn't killed his parents and left him an orphan to be raised in the basement of St. Mike's with the other kids who'd survived their parents' bloody murders. Adults just five years older told him stories about high school, which is where he would be now if the world hadn't ended. They said that they used to hang out, study books a bit, and get drunk and smoke weed and fornicate. Bishop Alvarez and Helen often warned them about the dangers of fornication, how a girl could get preggers and be a burden to everyone, her runt joining the Brat Pack as like as not. Some of the younger kids didn't think the Brat Pack was that bad, but Tevy was old enough to remember his parents, to remember living in a house where he had his own warm room and all the food and love and attention he desired. Not that Helen didn't love them all and feed them when there was food to go around, but she was getting pretty old and tired, and she couldn't spread her love that far.

Voices. Tevy slid down. He hated the cubicle dividers when he was scrounging because they could hide so many enemies, but he loved them when *he* was the hunted. He pulled out his Glock, which was already cocked and ready for action. Some kids had trouble getting enough ammunition, but Bobs liked him, liked the fact that he brought her back the information she craved, liked the fact the he would sneak deep into Chicago's old downtown just before dawn, when the ripper slaves were still in shelter and the rippers were just heading for their lairs to hide from the sun.

It was risky, sure, but it was a calculated risk. The hard part, really, was getting out before sunset. The humans, the ripper slaves, hunted during the day for offerings for their masters, knowing that each sacrifice of an entire human body meant many less blood donations from their own ranks. There were more and more ripper slaves every day, coming from all over, offering their servitude and donations in exchange for food and relative safety. They called people like Tevy rebels, but he called them bloody traitors.

Glass crunched under someone's foot. They were on his floor.

Quiet as a mouse. That was what Tevy was best at, although the few times he'd been on a raid, he'd loved to attack, too. He craved to throw himself straight into a fight, charging at the rippers, shooting and slashing and shouting. It was always such a relief. He hated tension. But today even he knew that attack made no sense, that it would result in useless death. He was right in the middle of the Loop, and there would be hundreds of ripper slaves watching the streets for a reb like him, asking him to repeat back today's code word, which he didn't know—yet. Besides, they were still human, even if they were traitors, and Bishop Alvarez had warned the congregation of St. Mike's many times that killing a human was a ticket straight to Hell. Only rippers could be killed without need of confession, absolution, and remorse. So unless there was no choice, Tevy would prefer to save his soul over his body.

He eased across the aisle, careful to stay low, careful not to crunch or kick glass, and slipped under a desk, his knees curled up, his buttocks pressing into the damp carpet, his Glock pointing out. Unless they had a dog with them, he was pretty safe. He listened.

"Oh for Christ's sake, there's nobody here." A man's voice, older. Tevy labeled him 'A' for his report to Bobs.

"I know, I know." Younger woman—'B.' "Have a smoke and a coke and we'll tell them we searched the whole floor. Who'll know?"

A lighter clicked and soon marijuana smoke teased Tevy's nostrils.

"What's got everybody so freaked out anyway?" A asked.

"An evolved got killed this morning, right in the Loop not a couple of blocks from here. One of those rebs has got huge balls to come down here at night." B's comment sounded genuine, and Tevy tried to picture what she looked like. Maybe she had raven black hair, a nice figure that fit that nice young voice. Would she really like to see his big balls? He pushed the thoughts from his mind, fighting to will the erection down. This was no time for that kind of thinking. He needed to focus.

He hadn't felt brave before dawn when the ripper had rounded the corner in front of him. It was too far from sunrise to use the gun—that would've drawn rippers from blocks around. Luckily, Tevy saw the ripper first, and this gave him a chance to close the gap between them quickly, drawing his long hunting knife as he charged. The ripper barely had a chance to get a word out when Tevy's knife went into his throat. As he expected, the ripper, a younger guy and probably new to being a blood drinker, grabbed at Tevy's right hand, trying to pull the knife out. The ripper never saw the small knife in Tevy's left hand, the knife that he drove under the sternum and up into the ripper's heart. It was over in seconds, Tevy's heart still pounding as he wiped the polluted blood off the knives with the ripper's sleeve.

"So what's with all the new rations?" said the woman with the young voice - 'B.' "I haven't eaten this well in over a year. Are we being fattened up for something?" She was trying to sound tough and flippant, but Tevy could sense the tension.

"Not for donating, if that's what you're worried about." A's gruff voice failed to hide his own doubts. "Word is we're finally going on the big push. Units coming from all over next month to hit all the rebel posts up north, especially that bitch at St. Mike's."

"Like you would know." But she sounded interested.

"I do know. I got a quarter-master buddy. He's says the warehouses have never been so full—food, ammunition, guns. Even you must'a noticed all these new troops around, the ones with the red shirts with the lightning bolt. They come up from as far away as California. Just talk to them and you'll see cause they all sound like surfer dudes. This ain't the mayor running things anymore, not even the governor, not even the president. They say he's back. Vlad himself."

Tevy had often wondered why Bobs kept sending him back into the Loop. Some of the Brat Pack said she was trying to get him killed, but he never believed that. She liked him, always said he reminded her of the man who had saved her life.

"Soldiers talk," Bobs had said. "Just keep listening and one day you'll hear something really valuable, something that'll change the world."

And she was right. Vlad is back. Could that really be true? Bertrand, the Savior of Chicago, had killed Vlad at the Battle of the Mountain. Could this ripper above all other rippers have survived that fire? Even if this was some imposter or some impossible rumor, the news of a big offensive sounded very true, and it fit with everything else Tevy had seen in the last few weeks. Now he just had to get back to St. Mike's with the news, without getting killed.

Boots clumped down the far stairwell and a door creaked, the debris that blocked it toppling with a metallic bang and a smash of breaking glass.

"Blood dawn! Blood dawn!" shouted A and B together.

"Red sunset," replied a man's deep voice. "Put your guns down. Have you searched this floor?"

Tevy decided that this guy was a commander. The tone of his voice was arrogant and sure.

"Yeah," said B, her tone deferential. "Nobody here."

"Then move on, Sergeant. Head down to the third floor and continue your sweep, and don't let me catch you smoking pot again and looking for somewhere to screw. They need full supply donors at the tower."

The boots clumped back into the stairwell, A and B's footsteps following close behind. But Tevy wasn't fooled. He waited, listening with great attention to every sound, interpreting, measuring. Outside, troops marched in a column, maybe a hundred. In the distance a tank engine revved for a minute and shut down. *Just running the engine to keep it from seizing up.* A bustle rose from the city, busier than he'd ever heard it. There were way more people in Chicago's old downtown compared to last week.

A crunch of broken glass underfoot. That always gave them away. Who had snuck back onto his floor? Tevy guessed the commander, who wisely knew the floor hadn't really been thoroughly searched and was hoping to catch him unawares. Paper rustled and soft footfalls on moldy carpet teased Tevy's ears. Were these sounds real or imagined? Tevy held his breath. He wasn't here. He wasn't here. That was his mantra, his way of quelling the hero that wanted to charge out shooting, to kill the traitor and then run for the river.

Suddenly the boots pounded across the room, stopping at the far stairwell. This commander was good, trying to frighten Tevy out into the open. More silence, probably as the commander listened himself.

"Aw, fuck this."

The boots clumped down the stairwell, but still Tevy stayed put and dozed through the afternoon until his stomach growled—dinnertime. He crept out from under the desk and very carefully holstered his Glock. He was going to pose as a traitor, and traitors didn't walk around their own territory expecting a fight. He headed down the stairs.

Now was not the time for stealth. Tevy strode out into the late after-noon sunlight as if he owned the city, heading right down the middle of the sidewalk, fearlessly walking out into the street if smashed bricks or other debris from a burnt out building blocked the way. He had to dodge a few cars, and cops on motorbikes that still patrolled, but no one spoke to him. Troops in red shirts, the Daylight Brigades, marched down the center of the street in four lines, looking far too tanned for early June in Chicago. Tevy counted as he walked past in the opposite direction. You could sense their urgency. All these humans had to be safely secured by sunset, because not all rippers obeyed the commands of their central authority, even one as powerful as Vlad—if it really was Vlad the Scourge.

After sunset, rippers would flood out into the city, many hungry, especially those that shunned the cold blood donations organized for them by their government. They would surge out of the Loop in all directions, looking for humans foolish enough to be out after dark. Sometimes the rippers would even group together to attack a rebel blockhouse if it looked weak. Tevy had found one that went down, far out in the suburbs where no help could reach, a McMansion converted to a fort, the houses nearby bulldozed to create clear fields of fire. He and Elliot had counted thirty-five corpses in the noonday sun, some burnt to skeletons with the house, most killed on the wide lawns as they tried to flee in the night. No one had been converted. They'd all been bled out.

Tevy headed for the river and escape. Now for the hard part, to get past the bridge guards and out into the ruins of no man's land between the ripper forces and the rebels that had rejected the authority of the city hall, the state, and the federal government after every level had become corrupted with rippers.

The rusting steel of the Wells Street Bridge promised the best chance, because the traitors rarely bothered to guard the second deck that had once carried the 'L' trains, probably because a lot of people were uncomfortable up there, walking on ties. One old timer had also put it this way: "It used to be death to go up there. The third rail could fry you with a touch. Bam! Kentucky Fried Chicken! And trains came very fast and very often. Even now I can't get that out of my head, and I'm always looking over my shoulder when I'm on the 'L'."

Tevy did vaguely remember the 'L' trains, had even ridden them with his mother and father before the rippers appeared, but to him the tracks had almost always been just a rusting network of paths above ground. Sure, they were exposed to view from the buildings around them, but it was a calculated risk.

He stopped long before Wacker St.—Bobs had insisted he learn all the street names so that his reports were accurate—and shinnied up one of the steel I-beams that support the 'L' line, his feet braced on one side of the beam and his hands gripping the other. He could climb like a monkey, and heights didn't scare him. The hard part was just under the tracks, because the builders hadn't left any way to get from under to above, but Tevy knew this area well, and he knew of a gap in some planks that had once supported a walkway for transit workers. He squeezed through and stood. He preferred these pathways at night, because in the dark no one from the tall buildings that surrounded him could see him. He set his sights on the hulking Merchandise Mart across the river, a gray building with its four towers anchoring each corner. The bottom three floors were all bricked in with new concrete block—a ripper fortress if ever there was one. In fact, it was the only ripper stronghold north of the river.

Tevy started his walk, again projecting confidence and authority. There would be humans in the upper floors of the Merchandise Mart, but how closely would they check out a lone man walking along the tracks? Their masters were downstairs, sleeping or eating. Did rippers fornicate? They would need attention either way.

But luck was not with Tevy that day. While his concern had been about eyes above, it was eyes below that caught him. The guards at the checkpoint just before the bridge rarely looked up, but Tevy's shadow on the pavement must have caught their attention.

"Hey!" came the shout from below the tracks. "Get down from there! No one crosses the river today without going through us first!"

Tevy squatted down and looked between the ties. "Blood Dawn! Blood Dawn!"

He could see the guards, four or five of them in the red shirts with the yellow lightning bolt. The Californian traitors.

"Red Sunset," said one tall man, his hair shaved to a short bristle, a captain by the strip on his shoulder. He had the paunch of middle age that had been starved away, the skin of his belly hanging loosely over his trouser belt. "That's all very nice that you know the password. Now get your ass down here so that I can see your papers and you can explain why you're trying to end run around us."

"I'm to report to the boss right away," shouted Tevy, trying to look hurried. He pointed toward the Merchandise Mart.

Several guns suddenly pointed up at him. Uh-oh. Wrong answer. The boss must be downtown.

"Then why are you heading across the river instead of for the tower?" asked the captain.

Tevy had one hand on his Glock, but he'd never killed a human before, only rippers and only at night. Somehow it just didn't seem right to murder under the sun, and besides, he couldn't kill them all and still have the element of surprise when he ran, for right now they thought they had him, they thought they were in control. But he could run.

He sprinted down the plank siding, eyes on the boards ahead in case any looked rotten or loose. Gunshots snapped out, but even though his path was perfectly predictable, their shots came too late to catch him, and that was while they could easily see his outline above. Now, as they pursued along the metal deck of the bridge below, they had to contend with beams and piers that blocked their view up to the walkway, and even that only provided information by way of his shadow on the spaces between the planks.

The raw stink of the river filled his nostrils, but to Tevy it was the scent of freedom. He glanced up at the Merchandise Mart with its gothic proportions, but no one appeared at the windows, drawn by the gunfire. Maybe humans didn't go there at all, which, if true, presented an opportunity for a daytime raid on the rippers. Tevy filed that away for his report. That and the fact that the boss was at the tower. The Willis Tower?

He easily outran the humans on the deck below, not just because he was younger, but because he had never been forced to donate blood to the rippers. It was no secret that they commonly drained far more from their traitor slaves than was medically safe.

Tevy glanced up at the glass and red-brick building across from the Merchandise Mart, which had many of the windows smashed out during the chaos that followed the death of Vlad the Scourge over eight years ago. A young man's form stood in an empty window just two floors above the level of the 'L.' He had a rifle shouldered, the sight to his eye, aiming. Tevy felt a moment of panic. This guy could kill him, had a clear bead on him, and it was too soon for Tevy to try and go below the deck and down to the ground. The station was still fifty feet away.

Tevy forced the fear from his brain, remembering Bobs' instructions about how panic impaired cool thought. The sun moved from behind a cloud and splashed light onto the teen's red hair. *Thank God.* Elliot, one of Tevy's fellow Brat Packers, the same age. They'd been friends since Elliot arrived in the basement of St. Mike's the night after Tevy.

Elliot had wanted to come with him into Loop that night but had been ordered not to by Bobs. She knew Tevy had a better chance alone. But Elliot had come almost as far as the river and had obviously ignored Tevy's instructions to return home. Now he was glad that Elliot had waited.

The rifle cracked out, Elliot having aimed at the traitors on the bridge deck, hopefully forcing them back, but he was also making himself a target at the same time. Tevy wondered for a second why Elliot was standing up rather than lying down, but the sharp down-angle of the M4 made it obvious that it was the only way he could get a shot.

"Good enough!" shouted Tevy. "Go! Go!" The crazy idiot was going to get himself killed, and Tevy now owed him big time. Elliot may have even saved his life. He turned and vanished into the darkness of the office building and not a moment too soon. Wild gunfire from below put bullet holes into the surviving windows around Elliot's position.

Tevy rushed onto the platform at the Merchandise Mart 'L' station, now able to run free on the concrete, just watching for obstacles like overturned benches and footing hazards like shattered glass from the office building above the station. He didn't look back as he charged down the stairs and hopped the turnstiles, slamming out of the station door at full tilt.

He could hear running feet behind him, but Elliot had made all the difference: he'd held the traitors up long enough that they were well behind, and Tevy had turned the corner on Hubbard before they could get a shot off.

Elliot came rushing out of the office building, his red hair flying back and a grin on his face, his long knife slapping at his side, looking like a sword on the short teen. "I think I hit one of the traitors!" he shouted as they joined up, turning at full tilt into an alley between two buildings.

"Good shooting," said Tevy between short breaths.

Shouts of confusion followed them, the traitors baffled as to where their prey had gone. Tevy and Elliot now giggled as they ran, confident of their escape because they were brats from the Brat Pack, and every part of Chicago north of the Loop was their warren. They would vanish like rats down a sewer.

2

RAID ON ATHERLEY COLLEGE

As Kayla carefully made her way up through the woods at the top of the ridge, she half expected to see Atherley College down in the bottom of the next valley, still surrounded by green lawns, still intact even though empty of students. In her heart she knew that eight violent years had passed since she and the others had abandoned their dorms for the safety of St. John's Keep. It was unlikely the centerpiece building of the college had been spared the bitter fighting that followed the fall of Vlad and the death of Bertrand Allan. Rachel had warned her that it was a wreck and was only still standing thanks to its 1970s-era concrete construction—Brutalist Architecture, she called it. Rachel had been back to the college many times, hunting for books and tools, but Kayla hadn't gone back. She had lost her family within three months of starting college, and the two events were inextricably linked for her.

But even though Kayla tried to prepare herself, when she reached edge of a rocky hill, almost a cliff, that allowed her to see over the pines below, she drew in her breath sharply. The lawns were now long grass and weeds, that was no surprise, but the college itself had changed radically. It once swept in a graceful curve back against a granite hillside, as if the concrete structure was an extension of the rock. On this side the main floor used to have high windows along its entire curve. They had provided plenty of natural light into the first and second floor corridors, a precious commodity in the cold Canadian winters.

Now, concrete blocks filled in the windows, the mortar oozing from between the bricks. This change had been added in haste, clearly by inexpert builders concerned only with blocking out the sun from the interior of the college.

Jeff moved up beside her, his bizarre short rifle, an FN F2000, pointing for the sky, his back to a large maple tree far from the edge. Kayla had to remind herself that the short barrel was an illusion, because most of the barrel was hidden inside the gun, which looked more like a weapon from a science fiction film. He had tied his long blond hair back in a tight ponytail. Kayla liked it better when he let it flow, but she understood his need to keep it out of his eyes today. "Not what you remember?" he asked.

Kayla shook her head, careful to hide the awe she felt when in the presence of one of the former Companions of Bertrand Allan. "The front used to be all windows," she said. For a moment she experienced a huge sense of loss, recalling frosh week and the fun and optimism, when she still expected to receive a great education, find a great career, and develop a great future. The rippers had ruined all hope of a normal life. Now she just existed day-to-day, hunting for food, milking cows, and spurning all potential lovers.

Joyce, their leader and another Companion, moved up beside Kayla, who sheltered behind a young spruce, staring down at her former college through the branches. Joyce had cut her hair short just last week, a style she only adopted in the spring when the summer fighting season approached. Kayla had considered that style but was reluctant to cut off her ponytail, although she had shortened it.

"How many entrances?" Joyce asked Kayla.

"Used to be dozens, but it looks like most of them were sealed off when they bricked in the windows." Kayla pointed to the south side of the building. "The main entrance is just around the corner there, and there's a service entrance under the college for deliveries—see that road there coming up from the south? It runs right down to the loading docks in the basement."

Others had quietly joined them along the top of the hill, keeping back in the trees just in case traitors were on sentry duty below. Martin Morley, who had the distinction of being the first black man that Kayla had ever met in person, had moved close to Joyce and Kayla and had overheard. He was the only other Companion on this raid.

"We don't want to go in by the main entrance," he said to Joyce. "My guys have C4 and hammers. Give us ten minutes along that wall, and we'll fracture some of those blocks and stuff it in. Another five and we'll blow nice big holes and let in God's light."

"The rippers will hear you and head for the basement," said Jeff.

Kayla was amazed at how clear-headed the man appeared. Last night when she went to the single women's dorm to get a good night's sleep before the raid, Jeff was singing off-key in the cafeteria, drunk and still drinking his harsh moonshine.

Joyce nodded. "That's the plan. I've got someone on it, and we're going to be down there, too. We'll make use of that basement."

Jeff raised an eyebrow. "Visitor recently?"

"Let's not talk about it here."

Joyce's glance in her direction was not lost on Kayla. They had secrets, Joyce's Raiders, and Kayla was reminded once again that she was the newbie, still not trusted.

Martin nodded and pointed to Kayla. "She can come with us and give us a hand clearing the upper floors. How much time do you need to get in place?"

"Give us half an hour and then head down. If you hear Jeff's horn, get the hell back to the keep and tell Barry to batten down the hatches for an attack." Joyce focused her attention on Kayla. "Martin is your commander now. You obey him as if he were me."

Kayla nodded, careful to hide her disappointment. Joyce had yet to accept her, and it was only because of Jeff that Kayla was here at all. She had overheard him the morning after the manor house had been lost. "She fights just like you—all angry but clearheaded," he'd said. "That's why she should join our ranks and that's exactly why she bugs you."

Joyce and Jeff backed away from the ridge and turned south, followed by twenty-five of the Raiders, leaving Kayla with Martin and his troops. He checked the angle of the sun, to ensure he wouldn't be flashing signals at the college, before putting a set of binoculars to his eyes. "How many could be in your college?" he asked Kayla.

"Could be lots. There were three big lecture halls that could hold maybe three hundred each. Profs had their offices on the floors from three up to six, but I doubt there are any up there since the windows are open to the sun. The big problem is the basement: there were labs on two floors below the ground. Then there's the gym, cafeteria, and meeting place at the bottom of the stairs on the way to R-wing."

"Where's that wing?"

Kayla pointed to a long, blackened heap beyond the college. "It was over there. It didn't have concrete walls."

Martin, still bulky and strong despite middle age and graying hair, looked over from his binoculars and frowned. "Hey sorry, must be hard for you—to see this, I mean. Must bring back some good and bad memories."

Kayla nodded, wishing she was able to get more sleep last night. Her lower lip came close to quivering, but she turned it to anger. "Bastards."

Martin looked back through the binoculars. "That's what I say about the rippers whenever I see the ruins of a McDonald's. I ran one, you know, back in Chicago. It was a good life."

Kayla did know but saw no need to comment. She couldn't imagine what he left behind and how he became such a legendary fighter from such normal, middle-class beginnings.

For the next half hour, they watched the dead college in silence. Nothing stirred but the occasional bird. Finally, Martin gave a low whistle and started working his way down the easiest part of the rocky slope, his thirty troops following. When they reached the valley floor and moved out of the woods, Martin broke into a run. Kayla marveled that such an old guy, at least fifty, could sustain a run for so long. A cramp tore at her side before they were even halfway across the field, but there was no way she'd let them show her up. She did vow, however, to start running the old highway to the Mattagami Bridge and back to get in better shape.

Martin's troops understood his hand signs, and Kayla struggled to follow along, watching the results more than comprehending the motions. Troops spread north and south along the curve of the college, some with packs beside those who just carried guns. A shaggy man beside Kayla, an older Newfoundlander who she didn't know well, slipped off his pack and pulled free a hammer and a chunk of C4.

"Stay back there, girlie," he said, his voice guttural but not unfriendly. He was so skinny he looked rather like a mop with all the hair and beard.

Basil—that was his name, Basil Macintyre or Macintosh or something. He drank with Jeff a lot. He wasn't treating her like an idiot for nothing, because now he raised the hammer, his eyes on Martin. Basil didn't want her in the way of his swing.

Martin's next hand signal was clear: a finger in the air sharply turned to point at the wall.

Basil slammed the hammer into the concrete block with all his might. It took him three swings to smash into the block, not breaking through, but making enough of a hole on the outside of the block that Kayla could see into the manufactured core of the block below. Other hammers rang out along the wall.

"Now quick, there." Basil waved her back to the wall, grabbing the C4 and shoving it into the hollow core of the cement block below the one he had broken. He and Martin moved along the wall, reeling out wire as they went and urging Kayla with impatient waves to join them.

"Now's the time for your Uzi." Martin put his back to the wall. Kayla and Basil took up similar positions on either side of him.

Kayla let the fear rise as she unslung her Uzi and checked the mag: full clip.

"You okay?" Martin's question was more of an accusation.

"I'm fucking great." She chambered a round. He should just fuck off and let her deal with her fear her way. Already she could feel it changing to anger. How dare the rippers murder her family and ruin her life? Now she would make them pay, as she did every time she encountered them in a fight. Like she did the night they lost the manor house, when she thought she would die, when she thought Joyce had miscalculated.

"Kill any ripper that moves in there, but don't kill our Raiders. Watch for armbands." Martin pointed to the white armband wrapped around his biceps. Kayla had dressed like the Raiders for this day: black shirt with a white armband.

Martin moved out from the wall so that he could look up and down, checking the status of his other troops. They must've been ready, because he raised his fist to shoulder height and pulled down as if yanking on a rope. He barely had enough time to turn and crouch beside Basil before the explosions ripped out along the wall, sending chucks of concrete block flying out.

The blast dazed Kayla for a moment, but Basil and Martin lunged up immediately and charged along the wall to the new hole, prompting her to run after them, more terrified of being thought useless than she was of any ripper that might be waiting in the college.

The C4 had knocked a hole about four feet in diameter, and Basil widened it as he went through, kicking out a loose block with his boot. Kayla followed close behind, plunging into a world of white dust kicked up by the explosions and now highlighted with the sunlight that streamed through new holes. Shouts and gunfire echoed up down the corridor, and in less than a second she lost Martin and Basil in the white cloud. She ran toward the gunfire.

As the fog thinned, she discovered it was not the light, airy college she remembered. Bones littered either side of the corridor, as if a great battle had taken place years before and no one had survived to bury the dead. Yellow paper drifted in the air, blown off the floor by the blast, perhaps term papers or the rough drafts of some graduate student's thesis. A stench mixed with the choking scent of concrete dust, a stench that promised that somewhere nearby there were fresher corpses.

A shadow emerged from the fog, a knife in one hand. Kayla aimed the Uzi and let the anger flow, but she was careful to search for a white armband.

"Let me by!" It was a ripper all right, his clothing ragged, his face gaunt.

Kayla fired into the ripper's chest, one shot straight through the heart. He made a last desperate rush at her, but she sidestepped and tripped him as he passed. She followed up quickly, putting a second shot through the back of his skull as his face struck the floor.

Another figure rushed her, but she recognized Martin and lowered her gun.

"Where are the stairs?" he shouted. Several others rushed to the sound of his voice, and Kayla abruptly found herself in the center of a circle of people.

Before she could shout that she couldn't see shit, her eyes fell on a small metal sign above a set of double doors: S-316. How long she had struggled to find that lecture hall on her first day, late for her psychology class? The years fell away and she remembered Atherley College before the rippers, the way she sometimes had happy memories of a dead friends. Now she understood why the ripper was trying to get past her.

"Two sets!" Kayla shouted in her excitement. "One is just to the left here, and the other is about two hundred feet that way on the same wall."

The gunfire had diminished significantly, the rippers running for the basements in order to escape the sunlight, and that meant that Joyce and her other Raiders were about to take the full brunt of an attack.

"We have to go after them!" she shouted. "Follow me!"

At first she thought she was running alone, but she heard a shout from Martin and found him beside her as she reached the metal doubledoors. They yanked them open together, the hinges creaking but wellused. The light spilling from the main floor illuminated more bones scattered to either side of the stairwell as they charged down, but when they turned the first corner, the darkness closed in and hid both stairs and the obstructions. Kayla slowed in order not to trip, doubting now the wisdom of rushing into the dark, but Martin switched on a Maglite, holding the little flashlight close to his shotgun as he aimed it down the stairs.

The flashlights of Basil and other members of Martin's troops snapped on. Kayla owned a flashlight but didn't have any working batteries, because they were way too expensive. Now she vowed to find a way to pay. Her eyes couldn't go where she wanted them to, but instead had to follow the beam of someone else's light. It was distracting and infuriating, because the spot of light might change direction without warning, forcing her to either chase it or latch onto someone else's spot of light.

The fire doors at the bottom of the stairs stood open, allowing them easy access into the first basement corridor. They spilled out, fanning to either side along the walls. Kayla got her back to the concrete and forced a deep breath. She had to remember, had to picture the day she had turned the wrong way down here when she was late for her chem lab. For a moment, she remembered the corridor in fluorescent glory.

"That way to the loading docks," she called to Martin, pointing to the right. "That way to the labs." She pointed left.

"Loading docks first." Martin stepped into the hall, waving to his troops. "Gabe, cover the rear. Andreas hold this stairwell. Everyone else, Go!"

Kayla wasn't sure where she fit into all this since Martin's troops seemed to already know who should be with Gabe and who with Andreas, so she went with Martin, running beside the big man toward the sound of screams and gunfire. At least down here there was little of the fog of dust that had been generated upstairs by the C4.

They turned a corner to find a crowd of rippers running in panic down the wide corridor, heading straight for them, practically fighting one another to get away from the loading dock area. Their clothes were often little more than rags hanging from sunlight-deprived skin, which sometimes hung loose where fat had melted away. Grime and filth coated many, as if they had at times been buried and dug up.

Kayla had no time for fear or anger. She slid to a halt and put a bullet through the chest of the one closest to her. There were enough flashlights now concentrated in this area that she could dimly see even if she wasn't focused on a single spot of light.

"No!" screamed one ripper just before the discharge of firearms, his hands forward as if he could shield himself from bullets. "The demon's coming. It'll—"

Kayla put a bullet through his head, wondering madly for a second if he had been her physics professor before the end.

The rippers in front skidded to a halt as waves of gunfire poured into them from Martin's troops. Rippers behind piled into those still standing in front, others tripping over the bloodied bodies of their comrades. Screams and shouts were buried by deafening discharges from their guns, the echoes of the concrete corridor multiplying the explosions. Eye-dazzling muzzle flashes lit the whole corridor as if bolts of lightning were striking underground.

The rippers began to fire back, forcing Kayla to rush to the wall. She never stopped shooting, still trying to aim in the chaos, still counting her shots. But her enemy, trapped between them and whatever terror had driven them from the loading dock, now scattered into the kitchens and boiler rooms on either side of this service corridor.

Kayla followed into one room, diving to the right as soon as she was through the door, so as not to be a target. Others followed, judging by the beams of their flashlights, but there were only shadowy forms holding them. Kayla had no idea whether Martin was among them.

A gunshot and muzzle flash stunned Kayla, for a second totally deafening her, dazzling her, and making the flashlights irrelevant. She had been looking the right way, so she remembered what the flash had shown her even after the room again fell dark: several rippers, men and women who probably had once worked at the university, were crouched on the far side of a metal cupboard/workbench. A bulky machine sat on the bench, possibly a lathe. They were in a machine shop.

Kayla fired from memory, and the flash, less dazzling now that her eyes had adjusted, showed her that she had hit her target, a woman who looked middle-aged with bad plastic surgery, her skin stretched too tight, giving her a skeletal look—a starving ripper. More gunfire and more screams and shouts and curses. Kayla crawled along the wall, forcing herself to not think about the hundreds of students that must've died in the college, as bones crunched under her hands and knees. She found the corner and turned to follow along, keeping an eye to the workbench behind which the rippers sheltered. She pulled into an enfilade position, lying on her side, just her head and shoulder sticking out from behind another cupboard that was perpendicular to the rippers' shelter. From her angle, perpendicular to the workbench, it provided no cover for the rippers. In the muzzle flashes, she could see the ripper closest to her as he rose, fired blindly, and ducked back down, thinking the workbench hid him.

Kayla frantically changed mags, let a few staccato flashes illuminate the rippers again so that she could memorize their positions, and started firing into them, confidant that if she missed one ripper her bullets would just carry on to the next.

She threw them into total confusion.

The rippers saw their comrades fall or scream and writhe, but they couldn't determine the source of the gunfire. Clearly, some thought it was punching through the metal cupboards of the workbench, for they stood in panic to shoot at the other troops, only to expose themselves to more bullets. Others crouched low, and Kayla finished them off.

When the last ripper fell, Kayla called out, "Clear! Clear!"

Martin rushed forward, his flashlight and shotgun aiming at the corpses just in case, the haze of gunpowder smoke defusing the flashlights of his troops and giving the room a pale gray light. He came around the corner and for a moment his flashlight was straight in Kayla's face where she lay.

"Don't shoot!" She held up one hand, palm out in her panic.

"You shout, *Not Vlad's Blood!*" His tone was scolding, but his expression was admiring.

"Not Vlad's Blood." Kayla had forgotten the identifier.

Martin's shotgun and flashlight turned away from her and back to the rippers. Two more shots were required to put down rippers that hadn't completely died and might heal. Martin turned back to offer her a hand up. Gunfire could still be heard from the other rooms and the loading dock, but in this room a calm had descended in the middle of a storm.

"Good work," he said. "You just saved a lotta lives—maybe mine."

Kayla was proud that she didn't shake as she took his hand and stood.

"Take this." Martin handed her a Maglite. There was blood on it from a trooper who had been shot. He sat near the door with his back to the wall while Basil tied a bandage around his thigh.

Martin raised his voice to all his troops, emphasizing with hand signals for gun-deafened ears. "We go out in a rush, me and you three to the far wall. Basil, take Kayla and Marcus right. Simon, take the others left. We clear room by room."

But even as they followed Martin in a charge back into the corridor, it was clear that the battle was ebbing. The gunfire was more sporadic, the screams and curses fewer. Kayla followed Basil into the next room, only to find several rippers already dead.

"What the hell happened here?" Basil pointed to the ripper bodies, splayed about at contortionist angles, hearts and entrails gutted out and strewn about the heavy pipes and pumps and electric motors that were once the lifeblood of the college. One ripper leaned headless against the wall, gravity only overcoming him after they entered the room, pulling him to the floor.

"They're dead, but like a monster just tore them apart and—" Basil stopped in mid sentence. "Let's move on."

He led the others into the corridor, but a shuffling sound behind caused Kayla to turn back into room alone. Was a ripper still alive? She made use of the flashlight, even though it made her vulnerable, made her an easy target for any ripper in the room. To minimize this she held the light far to her left in hopes that any shooting would be aimed there.

The nauseating stench of entrails assaulted her nostrils, and while she wanted to put a hand to cover her face, she didn't have one to spare, so she took short, shallow breaths through her mouth. The pipes ran along the floor and up to through the ceiling, while cooling fans in cages sat dust-covered and idle. Some of the pipes still had signs on the insulation: COLD WATER, HOT WATER, and GAS. All Kayla knew was that a ripper could be hiding anywhere. Her heart pounded, but she let the anger flow. Was the bastard who killed Ashley, her long-missing college roommate, in here? What about the ripper who killed her parents and brother? *Whatever*. This ripper would pay. Kayla focused on that anger to bury her fear.

Another sound that suggested a stealthy tread. Something was definitely in here. Should she go for help? But now she was so deep in the room that she didn't dare turn her back. Basil had said something about a monster, and the rippers had screamed something about a demon. Kayla didn't believe in the supernatural, but she did believe in rippers, and she had enough experience to know that not all rippers were of equal strength. Some were newer and quite weak; others were very strong and hard to kill.

The voice that spoke startled her, despite the fact that it was little more than a rasp. "You're not one of Joyce's Raiders."

It was impossible to determine the source of the voice. Kayla searched up and down with her flashlight and scurried to put her back to a wet concrete wall. The cool damp was welcome after the running and the fear.

"Yes I am." She needed to find the ripper and kill it.

"So am I."

"Who are you?"

"A friend that you should not shoot."

"Did you do this?"

"I did. I kill rippers. That's what I do."

Kayla peeked around a concrete column and through the maze of pipes and wires. A shadow near the back of the room caught her attention. She shifted along the wall, trying to get a clear line of fire.

"You still want to kill me, even though I assure you that I'm one of Joyce's Raiders."

"Then show yourself, asshole." She hated that the voice disarmed her, made her anger fade, so she fought to pump it back up.

"I will."

A man stepped forward into the beam of her flashlight, a bloody knife in one hand and a sawed-off shotgun in the other. His clothes would have been clean and neat but for the fresh blood stains. He had the gaunt look of a ripper, his pupils wide and dark—the pupils of a man who has not seen daylight for many years.

"You're a ripper." Kayla raised her gun but something about his expression, weariness, caused her to hesitate. And something about him was familiar.

"I don't drink human blood."

The door swung in as someone entered with a strong flashlight.

"Kayla?" It was Joyce's voice, and Kayla had to fight not to weep with relief.

"Here." Kayla kept her tone angry, fearing the appearance of weakness. "This ripper says he's one of your Raiders."

The beam of the light went from her to him, and the combined flashlights, while weak to human eyes, made him blink and squint.

"Put it down a bit please, Joyce."

Something about that voice and face made Kayla struggle to remember. Was it someone from the college? A lost professor or teaching assistant? Who was this ripper?

"He's one of mine, Kayla." There was an odd smirk on Joyce's face, as if she and the ripper shared a joke. "You can leave now."

"I can't leave you alone with...with...that." She pointed at the ripper.

Joyce didn't raise her voice, but an edge of steel crept into her tone. "You can and you will. Go help Martin clear the other rooms. And Kayla, you don't tell anyone that you saw this man. Do you understand me? Can I trust you?"

Kayla wanted Joyce's approval, wanted to do her bidding, but this was crazy. She prepared to argue, but ripper spoke first.

"Joyce is—and always has been—safe with me." He spoke so gently that it frightened Kayla more than if he'd shouted. It didn't make sense, gentleness from a ripper. "You're a brave trooper and you've fought well. Don't abandon your friends now."

"Fine." Even Kayla was surprised at how harsh she sounded. "Fuck you both."

She stormed out the door into the corridor, turning toward the sound of a single gunshot. Several troops were gathered around the door to another side room, Martin among them. She rushed to join them, planning to warn Martin about the strange ripper who seemed to have hypnotized Joyce. It was as if this ripper had some magic hold over her, as if they had known each other for years.

The gears in her head turned and Kayla stopped in her tracks, her heart pounding more furiously than even during the battle.

She *had* seen this ripper before. She had seen him many times, but back when he was still a human, when he had meat on his face, for his face was all she had ever seen of him. It was the man who warned the world about rippers, back when everyone thought he was crazy, until people began turning up dead. It was the man who was supposed to have died in the mountain, killing Vlad the Scourge.

She turned to run back to the room and shout questions, but Basil now stood guard before the door, his hand up to warn her to stop, his head shaking, *no*. Now she was sure. This was one of the secrets of Joyce's Raiders.

Kayla had just stood in the presence of Bertrand Allan, the Hero of the Mountain, the Savior of Chicago. A man long grieved as dead was clearly a ripper. Undead.

3

A NEW WAR

Tevy fought to focus on Bishop Alvarez and the altar, not on Amanda's cute bum. She stood in the next pew in front, her head bowed, apparently listening to the reading with an attention that Tevy did not possess. It didn't help that Elliot kept nudging him and gesturing in her direction with his eyes. Amanda's tight blue jeans, faded and old like Tevy's, had developed a new tear just where her thigh met her left buttock, and pale skin showed in a thin line, tantalizing and forbidden. Doubtless, Helen would notice in a day or so and add a new patch.

At last the congregation sat for the homily, and Tevy was spared the temptation to stare, but now his concentration centered on her dark hair and the way she had it pushed back over her ear. He knew it was weird that he wanted to reach out and stroke that ear as if it were erotic rather than functional. He averted his gaze to where it should be: on Bishop Alvarez and the homily.

"It is a sin to use in common speech any expression that references the evil blood of Vlad. He was the anti-Christ, and his demonic blood should not be mentioned except in condemnation, for it is the opposite of the holy blood of Christ, which was God's precious gift to mankind to enable us to receive a true life everlasting, not a ripper's false hope of prolonged existence."

But Tevy's attention was drawn back to Amanda's ear and the curve of her neck. He missed another few minutes of sermon, his thoughts on forbidden desires, but the word *rebel* claimed his attention.

"They call us rebels," said Alvarez, "but we are Loyalists—loyal to humans, loyal to God. They are the traitors and should be reviled."

Again, Tevy's attention was taken up by Amanda's neck, so much so that when they finally knelt for the Eucharist he had to close his eyes, listening for the bells and thinking about the summons. That was a total erection killer, and since he would soon have to stand in line to receive the host, he definitely wanted that gone.

Why did Bobs want to see him? Why had Helen presented him with an old backpack and ordered him to pack lightly? Why did her eyes glisten as she tossed his hair and patted his shoulder, turning away when he asked where he was going?

When they stood to line up for the host, his puzzled thoughts had done the job, and he could stand without fear that his jeans would bulge where they shouldn't. He was able to receive the host with a clear head, and Bishop Alvarez used his name as he placed it into his hands. "Body of Christ, Tevy."

The mass was over minutes later, but Tevy stayed in his seat as everyone else filed out. The Brat Pack would be heading to the basement for Sunday lunch, the best meal of the week.

"Coming?" asked Elliot, standing to leave in turn as the rest of the people in the pew rose to depart.

"I've been summoned."

"What, again? What did ya do?" Elliot was often summoned to stand before Bishop Alvarez and confess.

"Not by the bishop."

But Elliot was already grinning, clearly knowing that Tevy had been summoned for being good, not bad. "You mean General Roberts?" he said with mock horror. Everyone called her Bobs behind her back. Only the Companions of Bertrand and a few close friends called her Bobs to her face.

"Yes, Bobs." Tevy rolled his eyes, feigning impatience but smiling.

Elliot patted his slim stomach. "I'll try and save you some lunch, but don't let them keep you too long, because I'm a growing boy. Can't resist a snack in the middle of the afternoon and all."

Tevy, staring up, lost in the gold and blue of the ceiling, waited until the church was empty. He let his eyes fall to the elaborately carved structure behind the altar, a faux cathedral complete with statues and doors. Helen said that German immigrants had built the church and rebuilt it after the Great Chicago Fire, and Tevy marveled at the labor of their love, their faith. They would be dead long before their church became a true sanctuary, housing hundreds in the last days of Vlad, still housing the Brat Pack, still the center of power in Old Town Chicago.

He genuflected before the altar and headed for the sacristy, where the altar boys were still tidying up and getting out of their vestments. He passed through into the rectory and found his way to Bishop Alvarez's meeting room. He checked the pocket watch that Helen had given him for Christmas, though he never took it with him into the city because the ticking seemed very loud. It was early, so he did what he did best: he stayed silent and pressed his ear to the door.

It wasn't long before he was able to separate the voices: Bobs, Bishop Alvarez, Colonel Webb from the Illinois National Guard, and good old Emile, a Companion of Bertrand Allan and the man who had taught Tevy and the rest of the Brat Pack to shoot.

"I understand what you people need, but I can't spare anybody." That was Colonel Webb. Tevy had only met him once, when running messages for Bobs last year. He remembered the man as balding, his fringes graying but his physique lean and muscular—the kind of man who never stops fight training.

"My information is stellar," said Bobs. "The best. I had a guy right down in the Loop last night, and he's confirmed everything else we've found out. We'll be totally overrun in the next few weeks."

"But your information also says that Vlad has miraculously returned from the dead and is back and in charge, so really, how good are these rumors? I thought he was supposed to have been eliminated in the battle at Cave Mountain."

"He was. Bertrand Allan brought the whole frigging mountain down on them both and there were dozens of witnesses, many of them right here in this room. Fuck, *I* saw it happen. This freak's an imposter, but he can do almost as much damage, because the traitors and the rippers believe it is Vlad. I need some troops or we'll be crushed."

"I can get you some Bradley fighting vehicles, and I'll see about artillery, but I can't spare any troops. Malmstrom was almost overrun last month for Christ's sake, and Rock Island is critical to you too. Nobody's making bullets anymore, in case you hadn't noticed."

Bishop Alvarez interrupted the debate. "Please, please. We can agree that there is a problem, but instead of competing for resources we must think of solutions." Tevy noted that Alvarez's Hispanic accent became more apparent when he was upset.

The Colonel spoke first. "You need troops that I can't give you. There's a whole new war this season and we're all pressed. The rippers are throwing everything they've got at us. It's as simple as that. I'll send you as much ammo as I can, but you're going to have to get your troops elsewhere."

Tevy leapt back from the door just in time. He had forgotten that Bishop Alvarez's council room had a deep rich carpet that muffled the sound of a chair pushing back from the big oak table.

The colonel opened the door and strode out of the room, noticing Tevy, who now stood against the paneled wall, staring at portraits of the previous archbishops that lined the halls of this corridor. He projected boredom and patience, the perfect combination for innocence. Webb gave him a curt nod and headed down the corridor. Tevy wondered how many rippers he would have to kill before Webb would consider him military rather than civilian—someone worthy of an exchange of salutes.

Bobs stepped up to the doorway, looking after Webb with a frown. She was nineteen when Tevy's parents were killed, and he still idolized her as the coolest person he had ever met. But it had been over eight tumultuous years, and for the first time, Tevy noticed the wear and tear. Bobs was still thin, preferring to lead by example during the famines, but early worry lines now surrounded her eyes, the fresh complexion of youth already fading from too many long nights of fighting. She had cropped her blonde hair mannishly short over her ears, but she wore new blue jeans and a crisp white blouse, so she still must care about how she looked. Tevy wondered if the clothes had been Bobs' pick from last month's raid at the Glenview Town Center, a shopping mall up north. Rippers loved the malls, especially ones with underground parking.

Bobs noticed him. "Good, come in, Tevy."

Tevy turned into the room to discover it much more crowded than he expected. Besides Emile there were a half-dozen other elders, all leaders of one blockhouse or another, all sitting in silence and studying him with an interest that made his ears burn. He'd splashed his face and hair from one of the rain barrels before mass, cleaning off the worst of the grime from yesterday's adventures and smoothing down the fly-aways, but his jeans, like Amanda's, were old hand-me-downs, torn and stained. His shirt and black hoodie weren't much better.

"Over here." Emile patted the seat of an empty chair on his right. His black beard reached down to his belly, which had shrunk during the lean years but never disappeared. As Tevy sat, Emile leaned over to whisper in his ear—loudly enough that probably everyone at the table heard. "Good work yesterday, kid." Stale beer from Emile's breath turned Tevy's stomach. He tried his first shine just a month ago and spent the next day nauseated and useless. Since then, he had stayed far from alcohol.

Bobs took her seat at the head of the table, directly opposite Bishop Alvarez, who now wore his simple black cassock. Salt-and-pepper gray laced through the curling locks of his hair, but Alvarez always seemed the same age to Tevy as the day he had received his first communion, the month after his parents had been murdered. Alvarez, even before Bobs appointed him bishop, had baptized all of the Brat Pack as they arrived at St. Mike's, making them all part of the new Chicago Catholic Church. Since the pope was a ripper the last time anything had been heard from Italy, Bobs and Alvarez had remade the Chicago diocese into their new church.

"Tevy," began Bishop Alvarez as if instructing at Sunday school. "We have a challenge—"

But Bobs cut him off. "Let's save time. How much did you hear while you were listening in?"

There was a murmur of disapproval, and several of the elders cast suspicions glares in his direction.

"Relax, people," said Bobs. "This guy's eavesdropping fetish is why we have as much info as we do. So, Tevy, you get that we're in a spot, right?"

Tevy looked around at all the old timers, many of them as old as fifty, many of them veterans of battles with the rippers. "Gonna be a fight—big one," he said. "They got all these guys up from California. You can tell 'em by their red shirts and their skin, all tanned-like. Word is there may even be some from, like, the east, too. They're harder to pick out."

"Whose word?" asked Alvarez.

Tevy shrugged. "Soldiers, rippers, and I can count. Lots more troops, and they got Bradleys, too. I hear the engines every morning when they turn 'em on to keep them from seizing up."

"Jesus Christ," said one man, Simon Gonsalves, who reminded Tevy of his long-lost school principal, because he was tall. He was one of the Companions that had fought Vlad the Scourge. "It's time to reconsider an alliance with the Ericsians. They've got numbers and they're well organized."

"No." Bishop Alvarez shook his head and tapped one finger on the oak table for emphasis. "They are sinners who have turned their backs on Christ. They are only the last resort if all else fails. And I don't like you calling them Ericsians. It makes them sound like Christians, but they are a cult. They are the Erics cult, plain and simple."

Bobs spoke before anyone else. "There's plenty of alliances we can make before going down that road. That's why I called in Tevy here. We need Joyce's Raiders to come back to Chicago."

Several started talking at once, but Emile's booming voice cut through all of them. "Not frigging likely. They're settled up there. Barry and Martin got their families up there. Joyce and Jeff seem cozy, maybe even married by now. They're not gonna risk everything to come back on a chancy fight. I tried to talk 'em into coming down last fall by the radio, but no how. They got their own fights up there and they ain't budging from that fortress."

"I think they will if we send the right person. That's why I'm going to send Tevy."

Simon spoke up again. "Why not someone Joyce knows—like me or Julia or Emile?"

"I can't spare my top people. Besides that, you guys might get up there and see how cozy everything is and not come back." Bobs' smile didn't belie her words, but it softened them. Everyone could pretend it was a joke. "But Tevy, he's my city mouse. Besides, he knows Joyce too. She saved his life way back at the beginning and brought him to live here. She needs to be reminded that there are people down here who depend on her."

Tevy considered reminding Bobs that it was Bertrand Allan himself who opened that closet door and saved his life, but he had the sense that he was to speak only when called upon. This was a company of greatness, and he was an orphan from the Brat Pack.

Another woman spoke up, someone Tevy knew was also from Joyce's original Raiders, also a Companion, an Asian woman who had to be way older than him but still looked young and hot—Chen, that was her name. Julia Chen. "It'd be great to have them all back," she said, "but we're talking less than two hundred people, here. What's that going to get us?"

"I know, I know," said Bobs. "We need serious numbers and serious gear. I'm launching talks with all the other cantonments, all the churches, the mosques, the synagogues, everybody."

"Everyone who's not with the Erics," muttered Emile.

Alvarez waved his finger at him. "I will consent to working even with them, Emile. I simply advise that we gather all those who believe in God before we start appealing to apostates."

"All due respect, Padre," said Emile. "We got about a month or so before we start crawling in panic on our knees to apostates, let alone appealing."

"But if this is all true and not just crap," said Simon, "the boy here won't even be halfway to Barry's Keep before we're all ripper cocktails. What's the point in even sending him?"

"He'll be there before you know it." Bobs looked Tevy straight in the eye. "Ready for adventure? You're gonna fly."

4

FLIGHT NORTH

Tevy's parents took him to Disney World when he was nine, just a year before they died, and he'd loved flying. The jet was so space-age, the in-flight movie magical, and all the food was a luxury he only appreciated years later. When pressed into his seat by the acceleration at take-off, he whooped with delight and was shushed by his dad. Tevy just loved big jets.

The plane on the Kennedy Expressway was a disappointment.

"I didn't know they made them this small," he said to Helen and Emile.

"That's a fine plane." Emile placed a heavy hand on Tevy's shoulder while they waited for the pilot to finish fueling from the small tanker truck of aviation fuel that Bobs sent. Fuel was precious, so this largess demonstrated the importance of the mission. "That's a Cessna 172, a very reliable little plane."

"I'd forgotten about propeller planes. I mean, I thought they usually had two on the wings." Tevy pointed with some distrust at the one propeller on the nose of the plane. "What if the engine conks out?"

"Trust me," said Emile. "You're better off with this just for that very reason. Good pilot like Novak here can set this thing down anywhere, so you're safer in that than one with two engines that needs more runway."

The Kennedy was not designed to be a runway, but Midway and O'Hare airports had been pounded by Colonel Webb's bombers from Malmstrom years before to prevent the government rippers from flying in supplies or landing their own planes for refueling.

But Bobs needed an airport, so she hired a guy to spend months with a tow truck clearing abandoned cars off the highway, siphoning each for precious gas and draining them of oil first, of course. He wasted nothing, and even now the cars were neatly lined up on the shoulders on either side, perpendicular to the highway's direction, as if waiting to be sold, as if one day the inert rusting hulks would find new owners and new life. Of course, anyone who wanted a car could have one. Tevy had picked out three that he liked—it was fuel that was prohibitively expensive.

Helen reached up and seized him in a hug. "You watch your butt up there, my little man." She patted his back as if he were still ten and shaking with the memory of his parents' deaths. "Don't go charging straight into trouble shouting and shooting. Think first." She gave his shoulders a shake, as if that could drive sense into his head.

Tevy turned to Emile, unsure what to do: shake hands? Knock knuckles like he always did with Elliot and the gang? To his relief, Emile was holding out a shotgun.

"Glock's okay as back up, but I thought you should take something with more stopping power." He passed Tevy the gun, which had a pistol grip instead of a stock, and its barrel carefully sawed short. "This here is a Winchester 1200 Defender just like the one Bert took into the mountain on that last day. Takes only five regular rounds, but I think that's enough for you since you're always so effing close to them when you kill 'em."

"That's...that's fantastic. Thanks so much. I promise to put it to good use," Tevy said. He looked up to Helen and Emile, and for the first time he understood that he had adopted them. He had unthinkingly relied on them as if it were their duty to shelter and raise him, a presumption usually reserved for parents. "I didn't get you anything. I'm so sorry."

"You're going to get Joyce's Raiders for us," said Helen. "That's a fine gift."

"Show her the shotgun." Emile cleared his throat, and for a moment Tevy panicked, thinking the big man might cry. "It'll bring back memories for her, 'cause it's just like Bert's." Emile shook his head and looked up at the blue sky for a second, blinking rapidly and composing himself, much to Tevy's relief. "But you know what's totally weird? *You* are a lot like Bertrand. I think that's really why Bobs picked you to go. You're really gonna stir up some memories."

Helen scoffed and shoved Emile's shoulder, catching him at just the right moment so that, small and old as she was, Emile tipped off balance and had to stagger a step to steady himself. "Enough of your nonsense you drunken lout. You'll start talking about the 1000 Souls next and get the bishop all pissed off."

Emile was still chuckling when the pilot called to get their attention.

"Ready to go young man? We're burning our daylight here."

The tanker-truck driver had finished winding the fuel hose back into its reel, and the pilot was standing by the propeller, inspecting his plane before the flight.

"Ready!" Tevy shouldered his pack, still awkwardly holding the shotgun in one hand while he tried to figure out how to store it.

Helen passed him a leather pouch with straps. "You carry it in this—no, not on the plane. I mean when you're walking or hunting. It's like a holster, but for your back. That way if you need it, you can reach over your shoulder and draw it real fast. Now get the hell out of here and bring back my people."

Tevy hurried over to the little plane, ducking under the wing and handing his pack to the pilot, who stowed it on the back seat. The plane was crowded with packages and crates, deliveries for the city of Duluth, their first stop along the way.

Novak, the pilot, was old, maybe forty or even fifty. He had shaved his sharp jaw a few days ago, but now a grizzle of gray coated his chin. The hair that wasn't hidden by his cap was still black, though, so he couldn't be too old. For a moment Tevy saw himself in the man's sunglasses: a scrawny, underfed runt who had shaved once and was still waiting for the peach fuzz to grow back. Tevy also wondered if his short sleeves and ammo vest would be warm enough, because the pilot wore a heavy jacket with a collar of dense sheepskin, indicating that the jacket was well-insulated.

"Should I put on a coat?" said Tevy.

"This depends on whether you want to freeze. I'm having trouble with the heater." Tevy only knew that the accent was Czech because Emile had told him a bit about the pilot, a man who had started life in the air force of another country before immigrating to America to get away from all the weirdness that was going on in Europe, only to find that it eventually reached here, too. The rippers were worldwide. Novak spoke English with the precision of a second language well-learned.

Tevy looked after his pack in hopes of putting on all his warm clothes, but Novak smiled and said, "Here." He yanked a down jacket from the back seat and shoved it into Tevy's hands. It may have once been a light blue, but coffee stains, grease smudges, and years had aged it to a grimy brown. "I reasoned you would come dressed for summer."

Thankful, Tevy put it on and climbed in, but for a moment he thought he'd got in the wrong side, for there was a steering control in front of the passenger seat, although most of the dials and controls were clearly for the pilot on the left side of the plane. His seat must be for a copilot, or perhaps someone training. He did up the seat belt and prepared himself for that powerful acceleration he had experienced on the way to and from Disney World. The engine fired up, coughing and complaining before settling down to a steady drone. Tevy waved to Helen and Emile, wondering what things would be like tonight as the Brat Pack settled down for bed on the boys' side. Would Elliot tell one of his crazy ghost stories? Would he try sneaking over to the girls' side so that he and Amanda could have a grope game and some necking?

Suddenly it felt wrong. Elliot should be with him on this adventure. They'd always made a good team when it came to fighting rather than sneaking. There was nowhere in the cramped plane, of course, and there was no way Bobs would trade the food or ammunition required to purchase a seat for Elliot.

It was a full ten minutes before the pilot turned the plane to aim north down the highway. "Name is Milan Novak!" he shouted. "Just so that you know who to curse if we crash. Here we go!"

Tevy gave a last wave to Emile and Helen and braced himself for the thrill of acceleration, only to be disappointed. This wasn't like a jet at all. They simply rolled up to a speed not much faster than a car, but suddenly the plane lurched up, pressing his bum into the seat. He grabbed the sides of his seat to fight the vertigo. They were high in a way you didn't get a sense of in passenger jets, because they flew too high for the ground to be real. From this height, not much higher than a tall office building, the houses and streets looked like a little model city, albeit one that had been damaged by an angry child stomping with muddy feet.

"You can see everything up here." Tevy pointed to the highway and the abandoned suburbs. "I bet you could even track the rippers at night!"

"Back when there were street lights, maybe." Milan ignored Tevy and the ground and concentrated on his instruments and the horizon. "But I don't fly at night anymore, unless there is an emergency. You cannot see anything below in the dark, and unless someone on the ground helps, you cannot land. Unless it's a full moon, I could fly straight into the Hancock building and not know it until my asshole passed through my brain."

They flew in silence while the plane climbed until they were so high that Tevy relaxed. The ground, the houses and streets, the trees, and now even Lake Michigan on their right, were so far below that Tevy's vertigo, his sense of helplessness, faded. The earth wasn't real anymore and instead a distant toy.

Milan leveled the plane. "Okay my ladies and gentlemen. We've reached our cruising altitude of 13,000 feet, which we'll stay at unless the head gasket blows, in which case we will land very quickly, probably nose first. The in-flight movie today is called *Sky and Ground*, and will hopefully feature more sky than ground. The weather forecast is who the hell knows, but I do see some clouds off to our left that I'm not happy about, and I'll decide when we reach Duluth whether we park for the night or go on to our destination. Please be advised that there's an emergency exit on your right called a *door*. Don't open it unless you are planning to jump out and die. In the unlikely event of a water landing, you will definitely drown."

Milan reached behind Tevy's seat and hefted up a small pack, which he thrust into Tevy's lap. "Our in-flight meal today is chicken or beef sandwich, courtesy of Helen, and warm beer courtesy of Emile. Very nice of him. They must like you. Be sure to drink plenty of water, too, because it is very dry up here. You will dehydrate quickly. Did I mention that you are the flight attendant? Open one of those beers for me, please."

There were only four brown bottles in the bottom of the pack, underneath sandwiches wrapped in wax paper. Tevy pulled one out and tried to figure out how he could open it. He knew that bottles used to be twist tops, but he couldn't get this cap to turn.

"Wait just a moment." Milan rummaged in a pocket and pulled out a bottle opener. "They're too old to work like they used too. The caps are sticky."

Tevy opened it and passed the bottle to Milan.

"Ah that is very amazing. Chateau 2012 I bet, and not at all skunky. This must be from Emile's private reserve. What a guy." Milan looked over. "Come on, young man. Don't make me drink all these myself. It doesn't make me a better pilot."

Tevy reluctantly opened a bottle and sipped at it, discovering that it was nothing like the hooch that had made him so sick during his first experience with alcohol. The beer was even a little chill, which gave him a clue as to the location of Emile's cache. The basement of his blockhouse was cool and damp, and one spring it had flooded a foot deep, which would explain why the labels were missing.

"So, would you be willing to tell me exactly why Bobs is willing to rush you all the way to St. John's on short notice?"

How to handle this without offending his pilot? Bobs had sworn him to secrecy during his last briefing.

"I don't want everyone panicking and running for the hills," she had said. "So you keep your mouth shut about all these new traitors and this fricking asshole who says he's Vlad back from the dead."

Tevy understood better than Bobs knew. It wasn't just losing troops that was the danger, but if everyone scattered to the countryside, the rippers would be able to go after them one small farmhouse at a time. Humanity, at least in Illinois, would be wiped out or enslaved.

"Just supposed to go see how things are going up there," Tevy said. "What's up and stuff. The general is worried about them." Bobs was the general.

Milan looked over, and Tevy deliberately looked straight into the man's sunglasses, hopefully meeting his eyes. When lying, always look them straight in the eye. Elliot had taught him that. He was much better at it than Tevy.

Milan nodded and looked back to his controls, the horizon, and the clouds to the west. "She has no need of worry. They're one tough crowd up there. They had a very big fight just a couple of days ago and cleared out a ripper hole in Atherley, a big one. Some ripper believed himself a general, I guess, and had built some college into a fort, but they didn't have any daytime slaves, thanks God. Word is that they routed the place."

"Things should be peaceful for a while, then." Tevy couldn't decide whether his head was light from the beer or the flying.

"This I doubt. The place was a maze, my friend Jeff told me. Yes, the very Jeff who was one of Bertrand Allan's Companions through the end." Milan glanced over, his chest puffed out, but when Tevy didn't express his wonder that Milan knew someone so famous, he continued. "Anyhow, at least some of those rippers must have found places to hide until dark, and they surely will not spend another day in the college, so that means they're out in the woods. And they must be very hungry."

"But they'll die when the sun rises. It's all good."

"You are very much a city man. Rippers can bury themselves very easy, especially in the swamps, if they need to hide from the light."

In Tevy's experience rippers always went into basements for the day. That's why you never went into a house without a gun and some friends. It had never occurred to him that they could shelter anywhere else.

"But how would they breathe?"

"The bugs make them hibernate. They hardly breathe all night, maybe just a few tiny breaths, until the sun goes down. I don't believe they like this very much, but it works."

Tevy had to rethink everything he had known about fighting rippers. If they could hide anywhere for the day, it meant even the country side wasn't safe. It also explained why there were still so many rippers—why they couldn't seem to get to the end of them with the daytime neighborhood sweeps, clearing them out of the basements block by block. They weren't all hiding in basements. They could be in parks or backyards. Hell, they could be anywhere. Did Emile know this? Did Bobs?

After a few minutes of silence, Milan turned on some music—heavy, rocking pre-Vlad recorded music—and Tevy lost himself in the miraculous sound, so much better than the choir at St. Mike's. It passed the time until Duluth.

They landed at the airport, its runway still clear, small and large planes still neatly waiting in rows, but the appearance of normalcy was an illusion. No one met them, and Milan cursed the absence of a promised fuel truck. He got on his radio and started an angry conversation with someone in town, his accent getting thicker in his excitement, but it was obvious they would be delayed.

"Damn them to Hell and back!" Milan hammered the mic a couple of times on the dashboard in his frustration. "I don't want to be landing in the dark with all the rippers running toward the sound of my engine. This could be very bad."

"That's enough to just book outta here and refuel in St. John's, isn't it?" Tevy pointed to the fuel gauge, the only one he'd been able to understand. It looked halfway to him.

"They have no aviation fuel at St. John's, none they can spare for my little plane anyway." Milan opened his door and hauled himself out of the plane, pulling a pipe from his pocket as soon as he was standing on terra firma. "Besides, I have cargo coming that is helping pay for this flight. I shall go for a smoke. You may take a break, but if you hear a truck, come right back."

Tevy wandered into the little airport building while they waited, and it was like stepping back in time. The place hadn't been ransacked, and the ticket counters still sat as if just waiting for staff and travelers to arrive. The floor-to-ceiling windows of the terminal building were grimy, yes, but intact. Tevy walked through the security checkpoints just for fun, amusing himself as he remembered the full-body scan on the trip to Disney World. He hadn't wanted to walk through, because his friends said the staff would take pictures of his penis and put them on the Internet, but the guy running the scanner gently assured him that wouldn't happen.

Tevy snoozed on the seats for a while as if he were a passenger waiting for a connecting flight, but he finally rose to stare out the windows at a line of intact planes, trying to imagine the airport in better times. A question for Milan occurred to Tevy, and he hurried to rejoin him when he noticed a tanker truck was now parked beside their Cessna.

"Why don't you have a bigger plane?" Tevy said as the truck owner reeled in the hose.

"I have many planes—many, many planes, but I don't have much fuel, and we're a little short on aircraft mechanics." He walked around the Cessna, doing his pre-flight check, and Tevy followed him to hear more. "I had a bit of fun at first when everything went to bad," Milan said. "I started flying a Herc, even though I have no license for those big babies, but people cared little anymore as long as you could get them where they wanted to go. Some of my clients were even government, not that I knew at the time, or I'd never have given those traitorous bastards the time of day."

"But you ran out of fuel for it?"

Milan stopped in front of the single propeller and ran a hand along one blade. "No, but fuel is expensive and this little plane does not use much. Ran out of many other things, though. Patience for one and a mechanic for another—anything as big as a Herc is much more complicated to keep in the air. Then the airports became a problem." He waved at the clear runway. "We are very lucky here, but most airports got bombed by one side or another, depending on who was winning and who was losing. I chose a little Cargomaster until a couple of weeks ago, but it wouldn't start one morning. I have no idea why." Something near the terminal building caught his attention. "Ah, finally, here's the mail.

Grab the bag and let's go. We are just going to beat sunset to St. John's. I hate cutting it very close."

A man about Tevy's age bicycled up in a big hurry, sweating and out of breath.

"Thanks for waiting." He passed Tevy the heavy pack. "Good flying."

"I can't believe people will pay for mail," Tevy said after they were airborne and back at their cruising altitude.

Milan's head turned, the sunglasses hiding his expression. "You're old enough to remember the internet. You must have used a phone now and then—watched TV."

"Of course!" But Tevy knew he sounded defensive. He vaguely remembered talking to his Grandma once via Skype, and he had liked to play *Halo* with other kids online. His dad and mom had watched the news on their big flat screen, but he had usually just watched movies—a magic that was only available on Saturday night at St. Mike's, and only if Emile felt there was plenty of fuel for the generator.

"People still need to keep in touch. They are mad to know how their family members are doing, and crazier still to know what's going on in the world. Maybe you're too young to remember, but we used to know everything that happened everywhere in seconds."

"I'm not too young." But Tevy only remembered his dad talking about the economy, house prices, and politics in impossibly far away places like Washington. Tevy had followed basketball but never really thought about the cities the other teams were from. They were just names.

He hoped that would all come back. There was talk that they might start up a power station and light up the city, making it easier to hunt rippers at night. Then they could expand out, doing the same thing in other towns. If they killed enough rippers, maybe things could get back to normal again, and Tevy could live in a house with a wife and kids like his parents' generation. Maybe even Amanda would marry him, although he knew if she favored anyone it was Elliot. Tevy entertained himself with these happy thoughts until he dozed off, still exhausted from his night in the Loop.

The change in engine note, a stutter that wasn't right, woke him. Tevy sat up straight and looked over at Milan to see whether this was normal. The set of Milan's jaw said it wasn't, and Tevy's heart rate picked up. There was nothing he could do but watch. There was no ripper to fight, nowhere to hide or run. The sun hung so low on the horizon that it was obscured by low cloud.

"What's going on?" he asked.

Milan shook his head as he struggled with the yoke. "No. This is very bad. I cannot climb. We're losing power. This could be bad fuel, or maybe the timing chain is stretched. I really don't know, but you are about to be very glad we're in a small plane. Get on the radio and start calling Mayday."

Tevy picked up the microphone for the radio, remembering that he had to push the button before speaking. "Anyone out there? We're in trouble." He tried not to let the panic, the sense of helplessness, flow through his voice.

"Wrong. Give me that." Milan snatched the mic away. "Mayday, Mayday. This is Milan Novak. Mayday. Mayday. St. John's come back." He passed the microphone to Tevy. "Keep saying that, but let go of the key after every repeat and give them a chance to respond."

Tevy continued, trying not to exclaim in surprise every time the seat dropped out from under him only to press back up when the engine stabilized for a few moments. They passed through a gray cloud and dropped again, and now an evergreen forest stretched below them, only broken by rocky hills and narrow lakes.

"Look for the highway," shouted Milan. "It should be close. Look for any landmark."

Tevy turned to look east through his window, and the plane banked for a moment, giving him a good view down. Trees and unforgiving rock were spilt by a deep gorge with a foaming river, but otherwise it looked hopeless: there was nowhere to land.

A man's voice crackled over the radio. "Go for St. John's. Is that you Milan?"

"It's Tevy. I mean, yes, it's Milan. I'm just using the radio for him."

"Are you putting down on the highway? Where are you?"

"Tell them we should be close." Milan squinted north through the windshield and through his side window to the west, where the sun hung low and red on the horizon. "Where the hell are we?"

"You don't know?"

"We had some headwinds pushing us around, so I was planning to find the tower. It is not like I have a GPS anymore."

Tevy keyed the microphone. "We should be close. Can you see us?"

"Not that close!"

The plane dropped again and stabilized. Tevy, still desperately scanning the trees, caught his breath. "Look, over there. I think it's a bridge."

Now Milan banked the little plane sharply, and, sure enough, a gray curve of steel rose up above the trees. "Thanks God. Good eye. Give me this." He snatched the microphone back. "St. John's, we're just passing the Mattagami River Bridge. I must put down soon, so we will only make it to a couple of miles north. Come get us, ASAP. I have brought Jeff some NATO ammo."

The engine went dead, and the rushing wind under the wings emphasized the silence. Milan dropped the microphone and took the yoke firmly in both hands. "Oh, my little baby. Just a little farther. Come on, please, just a little farther."

Pine and spruce trees raced under them, and Tevy could have jumped to a rock hill that swept below if they weren't going so fast. He even thought about it, anything to take control, to be the master of his fate instead of sitting there, helplessly waiting for the end, his heart pounding to get out of his chest

The rocky hill dropped away to reveal the gray line of the highway. Milan banked left as gently as he could, but the maneuver cost them precious height. A bough from a particularly tall spruce slashed their underside, pitching the plane forward, but Milan managed to pull them to level.

They were too low and too far from the highway. The top of another tree slammed the wing strut on Milan's side, ripping it away, but the wing held in place, giving him a fighting chance.

"Time is now to pray!" shouted Milan.

They almost overshot the highway, but a sharp twist on the yoke banked them north. It proved too sudden a maneuver for the left wing, which tore away from the craft but not off. The plane rolled sharply to Milan's side as they lost lift, and the left wheel hit the ground first and hard.

Pink granite and green spruce spun by so fast that they meshed into a blur. Tevy fought to maintain some sense of direction, holding onto the side of the plane and the roof as if he could stop them from crushing in as the plane flipped and turned and smashed. Sky, asphalt, shattering glass, more sky and asphalt that didn't flip from view. The plane came to a stop with a screech of metal.

Tevy stopped screaming, and took several choking breaths of smoke and fumes, relishing in the fact that, even though he was upside down and hanging from his seat belt, he was alive. But the shadows warned that the sun hung low, and he had no idea how far it was to St. John's Keep.

They were down in the wilderness at sunset—a wilderness full of recently displaced and starving rippers.

5

WHAT COMES OUT AT NIGHT

Tevy succeeded in releasing his seat belt and dropping onto the crumpled ceiling, twisting so that he could kick out the remains of the windshield for an exit. It would be impossible to open the crushed passenger door.

"Good idea," Milan said, also hanging upside down. His sunglasses were gone and his face was bloody. "Quick! Please, help me out of here. I smell gas."

Tevy twisted around and fought to release Milan's seat belt, but the buckle was jammed. He got his switchblade from his back pocket and flicked it open, sawing through the tough material of the belt near the seat. Milan dropped heavily to the roof with a cry. "My ribs! Fuck! Let us get out of here."

Milan twisted around and crawled along the roof and through opening left after Tevy had kicked out the windshield. Tevy followed, smoke stinging his eyes and gas dripping on him from the engine housing. He wanted to lurch up and run once he was clear of the plane, but Milan was having trouble getting out, so Tevy repressed the desire to escape and turned to help. Milan crawled on his forearms, his left leg dragging, and for a moment Tevy thought it was caught in the wreckage until he realized that it was injured. He reached back under the engine housing and took Milan's hands, standing to drag him clear of the plane. Milan tried to get up, but when his left ankle took weight he gasped and would have fallen but for his left arm around Tevy's shoulders. Together, they staggered away from the plane, Milan hopping on his right foot.

When Tevy stopped and sat heavily on the asphalt, Milan turned to look back at the crumpled little plane. He held his side and looked pale with shock. "You feeling lucky, young man?"

"Dude, I'm still alive, ain't I."

"There are four boxes of fifty-cal ammunition in the back of that plane, and another of 5.56 NATO rounds. It's worth very much to me and the good people of St. John's. Would you wish to make some friends very fast?" He turned to look Tevy in the eye. "Climb back in there quick and get it out. It is in the cargo compartment."

Tevy had to guess whether Milan was joking or not. *Go back in the plane?* "Don't those things blow up?"

"Not like in the movies. It may catch fire any second now though. Go! Quick!"

Tevy went, crawling over the asphalt and broken glass, ignoring the pain from cuts to his hands and knees, holding his breath as he got close to the wreckage. With the plane upside down, it was actually easier to squeeze under the seats and get into the back, and sure enough, when he wrenched open the cargo compartment, he found five military-grade metal boxes with convenient handles. He grabbed two of them and hauled them along as he backed out of the plane. He dragged them over near Milan.

"Dude, these are heavy."

"Go! Go! Very quick!"

Tevy obeyed the imperative, crawling frantically back into the plane, snatching the handles of two more boxes and heaving them out of the mess, gasping and choking as he crawled back out of the plane. He set them just clear of the wreckage and went after the last box, holding his breath against more fumes as he pulled it free.

He found Milan had dragged himself through the ditch at the edge of the road so that he could sit up with his back to a tree, comfortably far from the wreck. Tevy stood and hurried to carry the ammunition boxes across the street, making three trips.

"Don't put them near me, young man. The rippers must not find them. Hide them back in the forest and then get back to here." Milan pulled a large revolver from under his jacket.

"My shotgun." Tevy ran for the plane but didn't need to crawl back in. The rear window on the Milan's side had popped out, and Tevy was able to reach in and grab the shotgun and his pack from the back, but the mailbag was out of reach. He considered crawling in when a *wump* and rush of heat pushed him away. Orange flames enveloped the engine housing. Tevy ran.

"I thought you said these things didn't blow up." Tevy said as he slumped down near Milan, resting his back on another tree and uncontrollably trembling. The plane burned, the fire accelerating with frightening speed. Before Milan could even answer, the entire plane was engulfed.

"I said they don't blow up like in the movies. But they burn very well." Milan opened the chamber on his revolver to check that it was loaded and slapped it closed. "I thought since the engine was already stopped that maybe it would not catch, but I guessed wrong."

Tevy nodded and let his breathing slow. He was safe. He was on the ground. "How long till the St. John's people get here?"

"Depends on whether the rippers have felled any trees across the road in the last few days."

"Why would they do that?"

Milan looked over in the gathering dusk, the flames lighting his weathered face and giving it a reddish hue. "Of course because they like to try and catch people driving up the highway close to sunset. This is most unfortunate." He took a deep breath. "Fuck. Listen, young man, my ankle is hurt somehow, not broken I think because I can move it, but I can't be sure. I can maybe limp but I can't get far and that is going to attract rippers like moths to the flame." He pointed with his revolver at the burning wreck. "Save yourself. Run up the road for St. John's, travel like a mouse, very quiet, and when you see headlights, drop your gun and put your hands on your head so that they know you're surrendering.

They will probably put you in a cell overnight till the sun can prove you, but I promise you will be okay."

Tevy thought of the Brat Pack, of promises they all made to one another. No one would be left to the rippers. No one would be left behind alive. That left two choices: shoot Milan now or stay, and Tevy had never before killed a human. "I'm not leaving you to die—or worse."

Milan sighed in relief. "I was hoping you would say this, but in my conscience I had to give you the chance to leave. I will owe you very big for this if we live. That shotgun, is it your only weapon?"

"My Glock is loaded, and I've a couple of extra clips ready to go." Tevy stripped off the old jacket, even though an evening chill was settling. He wanted freedom of movement. "And as a last resort I've got my knives.

They waited in silence, watching the orange flames burn low, but the column of smoke from plane was turned into a gray pillar by the light of a rising full moon, even though it was still low and huge on the horizon. The stars, dimmed by the moon, were occluded by a column of smoke, and Tevy could imagine just how significant a direction signal this was from every hill and valley for miles. "Here are humans," it stated. It might as well be an arrow pointing down to the burning plane. They spent most of the time waving away and slapping at tiny blood suckers—mosquitoes.

When it was full dark, Tevy decided to move. "I'm going off for a bit," he said to Milan. "Over that way. Don't shoot that way."

"You are leaving after all?" Milan looked glassy-eyed and vulnerable in the fading firelight, and Tevy suddenly wondered how much pain the man was in. They hadn't even checked his ankle or his ribs, which seemed to be giving him more pain than his ankle judging by the way he held his side.

"I'm using you as bait. Let them come. Let them get close. Let me start the shooting."

"This all supposes they don't see you first."

Tevy stood. "They won't. I'm very good at being quiet and still." He trembled again, but this time with excitement. He would get to kill rippers and avenge his parents. It was a madness, a relief from all the sneaking around. He hadn't really stayed for Milan's sake, but his own. Was he crazy? Suicidal? It didn't matter now.

But Tevy was a city boy, and he discovered that pushing through the undergrowth on the side of the road was noisy and painful work, generating many scrapes. He finally found a wide spruce that had killed its competition with a bed of needles, and its lower branches, starved of sunlight, had died off and were easy to snap away so that he could put his back to the tree and wait. The smells were so different from the city. Mold from the needles, sap from the spruce, some of it sticking to his hand. He held his hand close to his nose and took a deep breath, for a moment transported back to a Christmas long past with his parents—their living room, the tree, and his father in his housecoat as Tevy tore at the wrapping paper. He couldn't remember his father's or mother's faces, though, as much as he tried. But under that tree near St. John's, Tevy did remember a presence, a sense of father and mother, of his loving parents.

Milan's form, his right leg bent at the knee so that his gun could rest there, was silhouetted by the firelight less than three car-lengths away. The plane may have been their nemesis, but its cremation provided the light they needed to see and shoot.

Milan began to sing, a ballad about Bertrand in the mountain, about the end of the Vlad. It was a song best sung with guitar, a lament for a lost hero. He switched to an older song, one Tevy remembered from his iPod, one his father warned him not to play too loud, one with electric guitars and drums, with amplified voices and lots of other instruments and strings. Tevy missed that song, but Milan's voice evoked it hauntingly, even though he sat alone and injured in the woods and waiting to die.

A crack of a breaking branch sounded behind Tevy.

Quiet as a mouse. Tevy pressed himself back into the tree, willing himself to be part of the trunk. He had assumed that the rippers would approach from up and down the road, not from deeper in the woods. An unpleasant thought crossed his mind. He could just stay here, silent and still. Milan was probably done for anyway, even if Tevy managed to surprise and kill the first few rippers that came along. When the St.

John's people came down the road, they would understand, wouldn't they? There had been no hope for a man who couldn't run.

But Tevy remembered Bertrand Allan opening the door to the closet to find a terrified little boy. That man had run into a burning building even when the odds of saving Tevy's parents were very low. He was a saint. Tevy drew strength from that, from the lesson that the fight must be brought to the rippers, no matter how hopeless. Good might come from it—even if Tevy died. His heart started to beat faster, the anticipation of the fight growing. Tonight, he would not just hide.

Another crack, closer this time and off to the right. Something approached for sure. Brush rustled, and Tevy sensed rather than saw a dark form between his position and the highway. Whatever the creature, the undergrowth ahead that Tevy had fought through now proved a barrier in the dark, because the ripper diverted onto the highway, crushing through the brambles that guarded bottom of the ditch that bordered the road.

Milan must be aware of it now too, for the singing faltered a moment, and the gun twitched on his knee.

Tevy willed Milan not to shoot. Not yet. Please don't shoot yet. The woods were alive. There were other cracks and creaks and scuttles. Some might be natural, animals that come out at night like the dogs, cats, raccoons and squirrels that still roamed Chicago, but others were rippers, Tevy was sure. He leveled his shotgun to track the dark form that now walked down the highway.

Milan stopped singing. "No good feeding on me, my buddy. I have the AIDs."

The ripper chuckled. "The bugs will fix that. Why don't you put the gun down so that we can make this quick. I'm an early evolver, eight years old. Got a lot of bugs that can rebuild fast." His left arm rose into the air, as if to point at the sky. With his right hand he pointed to his ribs under the arm, where his torn and bloody shirt exposed pale skin. "See there? Shot last week by those assholes from that keep up the road. Healed in less than a day."

"What if I shoot you through the head?" Milan's gun didn't waver. "Will they rebuild your brain?"

Tevy willed himself to patience. He wanted to charge forward shooting, to relieve the tension of hiding and waiting, but others were now stepping out of the woods and onto the highway. Let them come and there'll be more targets, he assured himself. Let them come.

"You'd have to be a very good shot." The ripper's voice was calm, soothing. "And what would it get you? How many shots do you have? Six?"

"Five," said Milan. "The sixth shot I reserve for myself."

"We can still feed on you as you die, even after you die. You're blood's pretty good for a few minutes, especially if you're still breathing, and you might be."

"I am not some uneducated vermin!" shouted Milan, the fear finally showing. "I was an air ambulance pilot. I know where my cerebellum is located. I know how to eat my own goddamn gun and stop my breathing in one quick shot."

They were all around him in a semicircle now, seven by Tevy's count, all restless, like wolves waiting to see who will strike first, ready to fight one another for a chance at the kill. The speaker was clearly alpha dog, as the others glanced from him to Milan, preparing for the charge. They knew he couldn't shoot them all. He was a dead man.

Tevy took aim, thanking God that Bobs had allowed him extra time and ammunition on the practice range. He chose the speaker's heart rather than his head, knowing if he missed it would still put the ripper temporarily beyond consideration.

"We're not going to let that happen." The alpha ripper was clearly about to give signal.

Tevy pulled the trigger.

The alpha ripper simply dropped, his legs giving way so abruptly that he appeared to vanish from Tevy's perspective, the body hidden by brush from where Tevy stood. All the faces turned in his direction, except Milan's. He fired at another ripper while Tevy pumped his gun and took aim. Now the rippers fled, but Tevy followed his target as he ran across the road. His shot brought that one down too.

Now he charged, taking the easier path out onto the road, his body coursing with adrenaline, rage, and relief. The tension had been released. He was finally the avenger. Two of the rippers fled down the highway, their backs to Tevy and Milan.

"Right!" shouted Tevy, firing at the same time. The ripper on the right dropped to the ground just before Milan's gun roared out. The one on the left stumbled but kept going.

As quickly as it started, everything went quiet. Whether it was from gun deafened ears or not, it seemed to Tevy that even the woodland animals had fallen silent.

The alpha ripper flopped onto his back, gasping. "Oh that hurt." His bloody shirt hung in tatters, exposing the clear entry wound bubbling from the right side of its chest. "But I'll live. My students will be back with more and you'll both fucking die!"

The defiance was empty. Tevy didn't bother to reply, the rage still smoking. He simply drew his Glock and fired point blank into the ripper's skull. Tevy turned to each of the other ripper bodies and shot them through the head, what Bobs called "passing lead through the brain" to make sure they were dead.

Milan reloaded, his hands trembling just a little. "I almost gave up on you. I thought I was on my own for a minute."

"We should maneuver." Tevy looked up and down the road, but the fire from the plane had nearly burned out, and the moonlight wasn't high enough to dispel the shadows of the forest. He took deep breaths, trying to calm the rage, fighting the desire to shoot every round he had into the dead rippers, the way Joyce had fired into a corpse in rage when Bertrand told her of Tevy's parents' murder on that night so long ago. Would he meet her again tonight? Would she come down the highway for him, or would it be someone else?

"I can't move, young man." Milan slapped the chamber closed.

"I can carry you."

"I weigh double your weight. That won't happen."

Tevy crouched close and grabbed Milan's left arm, putting it over his shoulder. "You got one good leg. Come on. Stand! If we can even just get across the road they'll be thrown off for a second or two."

"Oh, this is going to hurt, but I guess I cannot argue with my savior." He heaved on Tevy's shoulder, pushing up with his good leg so that he didn't just pull Tevy down. Milan was heavy. The grunts and curses that accompanied their stumble across the road indicated just how painful it was to move, but he bravely kept quiet, although when he slumped down under a maple on the far side of the road, actually closer to the remains of their plane, Tevy feared the man had passed out.

"You okay?" he asked.

"It's not my ankle but my ribs that hurt so much. I think the ankle is just a bit sprained." Sweat coated Milan's forehead despite the evening cool.

Tevy wanted to clean the gash on the side of Milan's head that he had got from the crash, but this was no time to go stumbling around looking for water. "I'm sorry. I haven't done anything about your hurts." But Tevy didn't know what to do. Should he try splinting Milan's leg?

"You're still here. That's very good enough for me."

Tevy stood to stare down the highway in the darkness after the ones that got away. "I guess they'll come back shooting." The fear returned, but this time of lead flying out of the dark. His stomach muscles tightened at the thought, as if preparing to stop bullets.

"They may have a few guns, but not like Chicago. God, I wish I had some whiskey." Milan shifted his leg with a wince. "Canadians had strict gun laws up here before the apocalypse, and they made them even tougher when the government was taken over by rippers. They brought back a gun registry and then just started rounding them up, usually along with the gun owners." Milan tipped his head back against the tree to look at the stars, and the pain on his face was such that Tevy wondered if he were near to passing out.

"Stay with me." Tevy put a hand on Milan's shoulder. "It's gonna take us both to fight them, so stay with me."

Milan looked back down and met Tevy's eyes. "Crossing the road was a good idea." He took several deep breaths. "Listen, if there are too many of them, you run. You've been very good. I owe you my life."

"Not until morning, you don't." But the fear and pain in Milan's eyes went straight to Tevy's heart. They would die together tonight. There was no sign of the St. John's people, and the rippers would return.

The sound of running feet made them both look south down the highway.

"You really should go."

Again Tevy was tested, but again he found strength in the memory of Bertrand Allan. "I'm not going anywhere."

But as he stood and sighted his shotgun, he thought of Elliot and Amanda, of Emile and Helen. He longed for just one more Saturday movie night with the Brat Pack. He knew he would be missed, and that was even more distressing. Some of the littler ones looked up to him and would feel the loss deeply. It was all so damn unfair. He let the rage build to bury his fear of death.

But as he aimed at the nearest ripper—apparently a young man when he died, his jeans and shirt muddy—the sound of an engine distracted everyone. Tevy looked north to see headlights. He looked back quickly before he lost his night sight. The rippers halted in their rush and fled to each side of the road and into the forests.

"Saved!" shouted Milan.

But Tevy had let the anger rise too far. It had to be sated. He fired at a ripper before he reached the woods, dropping it to the ground. A different muzzle flash splashed through the woods like a bolt of lightning, giving away a ripper's position, one with a gun.

Tevy charged into the forest, heading straight for it. He heard Milan's call to stop. He heard the horn of the approaching truck, but the world was a red haze, and he wouldn't stop until every ripper in the forest paid for the death of his parents. Tevy was lost in his rage.

6

TWO SIDES OF A TRIANGLE

Kayla knew it was luck more than anything that they brought her along on this desperate sortie into the night. She had just come out of the cathedral and was on her way down the grand stairway when Jeff overtook her, running down the stairs followed by Martin and Basil. All the men carried guns and were in a frantic haste, but Basil, the Newfoundlander with all the hair, turned at the bottom of the stairs to look back up.

"Hey Jeff, she's already packing." He pointed at Kayla, who had frozen on the stairs, wondering where they were going in such a hurry at sunset.

Her Uzi. Rachel had already made fun of Kayla for carrying it everywhere, but since the night the manor house had fallen, when she had given herself up for dead until they escaped, she just couldn't part with it. The gun had been her salvation, her refuge, and now it was her talisman. She kept it slung over her shoulder, loaded and always ready for fighting.

"Kayla! Come with us," shouted Jeff, his hair undone and flying as he turned at the bottom of the stairs to run for the garage, closely followed by the other two men.

They were taking the Toyota? This must be important. Kayla ran down the stairs, grabbing the ornate knob at the bottom of the stair rail to aid in the 180-degree turn to run for the garage behind the grand stairway.

The 4x4 was a jacked-up, tough little nut with an extra bank of lights over the cabin and a fifty cal on a pintle in the back. Jeff ordered her into the shotgun seat while Martin and Basil jumped into the back. The garage door opened, and before she knew it they were on their way, speeding down the highway, the high beams illuminating the dotted yellow line in the center of the road and the residual pink of the sunset lighting the tops of the trees of the encroaching forest.

"What's going on?" Kayla rested the Uzi on her lap and rolled up the window, wishing she had a jacket for the cool night.

"Novak crashed just north of the Mattagami."

It took Kayla a moment to remember that he was the pilot, a surprisingly cultured man with an eastern European accent, but different from her friend Radu's. Milan Novak was one of the inner circle of Barry's friends. A room was kept ready for him, even though he was rarely at St. John's for more than a few nights a month.

"Is he still alive?" she asked.

"Who the hell knows. Uh-oh." Jeff slammed on the brakes, tossing Kayla into her seat belt and bringing the little truck to a screeching halt on the asphalt. "Keep an eye. This could be an ambush."

Evergreen branches rose perpendicular to the road. A tree had fallen—but not naturally from age or wind. Saw cuts and chips near its base indicated the work of rippers with a chain saw, for no human would block their lifeline with the world.

Martin and Basil jumped from the back, each carrying a large chainsaw. It was one of Kayla's jobs to ensure these were fueled and functioning at all times in the back of the Toyota, so she was relieved when both of them started after only a few pulls.

"Get on the fifty cal." Jeff didn't look back to see if she was obeying this order, instead hurrying around the stump of the tree with his rifle aimed and ready in case rippers were hiding behind the branches.

Kayla hurried into the back of the truck and took hold of the fifty cal, swinging the barrel to point over the heads of the men. She made sure the belt of cartridges could run free from the box on truck bed. Did she even remember how to use this thing? Rachel had showed her a couple of times, but they hadn't actually fired any of the precious rounds.

She checked the shadows for movement, vowing that she'd make the gun work if needed. It was just another gun after all, if bigger and hungrier for ammo. Short bursts. She needed to remember to fire short bursts.

By the time a path had been cut through the downed pine, it was full dark.

Jeff hurried back to the driver's side. "Stay up there and hang on tight," he said before he jumped into cab. Martin and Basil had just enough time to scramble over the tailgate before the truck lurched away and down the road.

Now Kayla was cold, the wind stealing every bit of heat, but the exhilaration of the ride made up for the discomfort. She aimed the gun ahead and clung to it for balance, her feet spread wide apart. If her safety conscious parents could see her now—her Uzi slung over her shoulder, hands holding a fifty cal, ponytail flapping in the wind, and she was standing in the back of an open truck. No seat belt. No seat. If Jeff slammed on the brakes, she'd be lucky if she went cleanly over the top of the cab and the hood to splatter on the pavement. If she were unlucky, she'd bounce off the fifty cal and die in the back of the truck. Even now, the truck hit pot holes so hard that her feet would come right off the floor.

But the cold began to outdo the adrenaline, and Kayla worried that she would have to admit she couldn't take it anymore, but before that humiliation, Martin stood, grabbing the gun. "Take a seat out of the wind. We're doing shifts, here."

She crouched shoulder to shoulder with Basil, her back to the cab and out of the worst of the wind. It wasn't warm because there was still wind, but it wasn't the fifty-mile-per-hour wind that streamed over the cab. After ten minutes Basil stood and took Martin's place.

"We should be there pretty soon," Martin said, shouting to be heard over the wind and the roaring engine of the truck. It was only a few minutes later that the truck slowed, the engine gearing down, which prompted Kayla and Martin to stand and look ahead over the cab.

Three wheels aimed at the sky and one wing still stretched across the highway, but otherwise it was hard to tell that this had once been a plane. Jeff blared the horn as they approached.

Martin's fist pounded the roof of the cab. "Shit."

But just as Kayla's heart sank, just as she gave up their mission as a failure, a muzzle flash exploded from the side of the highway, lighting everything for a dazzling moment. A young man—a teenager, really—with a shotgun stood over another man, one with a bloody face and a twisted leg. He sat with his back against the tree, a huge revolver, maybe a .44 Magnum, pointed for the sky. The young man screamed incoherent rage and charged into the forest, pursuing some unseen enemy.

"Milan!" called Martin.

Jeff swung the Toyota so that the headlights illuminated Milan, who waved and pointed frantically to the forest to the south with his gun.

"Was that the guy who was supposed to be with him?" Martin jumped the side of the truck. Basil swung around the fifty cal, preparing to shoot into the forest after the man, just in case he was a ripper.

"Don't shoot! Don't shoot! He's human!" shouted Milan.

Kayla jumped from the truck, her old sneakers and young knees absorbing the impact. "Where the fuck is he going then?"

Jeff ran around the front of the truck toward Milan. "Stay on the fifty cal! Martin give me a hand. Kayla—"

"I'll go get him," Kayla said.

"Wait, no."

"I can't lift him, so what the hell else makes sense?" Kayla pointed at Milan as Jeff crouched down to check the man's injuries.

"I owe the young man," said Milan. "Saved my life."

Jeff looked up, but Kayla had already made up her mind. This was right. Let the men look after Milan and cover the truck, their only way out of this mess. Let her go and get the other man, the reckless teenager who had obviously gotten carried away in his fight and fury. This was the best division of their resources. Kayla was absolutely sure.

Jeff nodded. "Okay, but when you hear the horn get your ass back here or I'll leave you to die."

Kayla rushed into the forest, following the path illuminated by the headlights of the truck, weaving between spruce bows and leaping underbrush. She unslung her Uzi as she ran, taking it in her hands and aiming ahead. The excitement buried the fear of the shadows. She was Kayla, a hunter and an avenger, and she had an Uzi with a full clip. The rippers would run from her, she was sure, but that human ahead wasn't thinking. Shit! She hadn't asked his name.

"Human! Milan's friend! Over here. Come over here!"

Muzzle flashes lit a clearing ahead and others responded. There was a firefight going on, but Kayla couldn't tell friend from foe. She'd hardly got a look at the guy before he charged off. A spruce branch caught her in the face, scratching deeply into her forehead and nearly knocking her from her feet.

"Shit." She was too far from the truck now, the headlights not providing enough light this deep into the forest. She slowed her pace, keeping one hand ahead in case of other unseen obstructions and fighting to keep the Uzi pointed up with one hand. It was heavy like this. She tasted blood that leaked down from her forehead. Great. The rippers would love the sight of that.

Taunting voices came from the clearing.

"We got you, you little shit. You should'a stayed with your friends."

A gun fired, the lightning of its muzzle flash for one moment showing where the shooter hid, low on one knee under the bows of a pine, a shotgun aimed. The flash also showed that a low hillock of fractured granite was what kept the trees at bay in this little circle.

If that was him, he'd just given away his position. Kayla stopped by a maple, thinking the man would die now and her rescue mission would be over. Sure enough, two guns across the clearing cracked out, answering his fire, but their light proved that he was gone.

At least he had some brains.

"Did I hit him?" A man ran into the clearing, his clothes muddy and torn, the style from before Vlad—no pocket vest for ammo, just a hoodie and blue jeans. He could have been in her physics class if he weren't such a mess.

Kayla had only a second to decide, because the man—possibly ripper—ran unknowingly straight for her, seeking the cover of the very tree she blended with as he tried to see where he'd just shot. *Is he the human or a ripper? The human must think he's alone, so why would he ask the rippers that?* And the clothes and the mud all spoke of someone who had been out of human society for quite some time. Kayla pulled the trigger, and a single shot from the Uzi tore into the man's chest. Dropping him to the ground.

She bolted away, using the dark for cover. Thank God she'd chosen a camouflage vest this afternoon. More gunfire cracked out, showing her trees and rocks, silhouetting spruce and pine boughs near the clearing edge, and giving her a good idea which direction to run. She saw another clear area ahead, and even though her night sight had been lessened by the muzzle flashes, the moon had risen high enough that she could discern more granite and a shrub nestling into a frost-fractured section. She was about to dare a sprint across this smaller clearing when another figure rushed in from the other side.

They were less than a couple of car lengths apart, and the rising shotgun indicated that he saw her at the same time as she burst into the clearing and saw him. She raised her Uzi to shoot first, but at the last moment knew she faced a human. He was slim, yes, but it was a teenager slim, not ripper gaunt, and his clothes were too well cared for to have been in the swamps or in the filth of the basement of Atherley College.

"Wait, wait, St. John's! Not Vlad's Blood!" Kayla raised her Uzi high above her head as she shouted, turning it perpendicular to her body to make the shape of a 'T.' For a moment she thought it was too late, and she braced in panic for the shot, turning sideways but not lowering the gun. At the last second, he froze with the shotgun aimed for her torso.

The shot would enter under her arm and travel through her chest, tearing holes in her heart and lungs. Kayla repressed the urge to dodge and lunge, to run or crouch. She had only seconds to gain his trust and get him out of here, assuming she was right and he was the man she had come to fetch. Instead she sized him up as much as the dim light of the full moon allowed. He wore a multi-pocketed vest not unlike hers, but gray. The pockets bulged with ammunition. He was about her height, and he was panting from his run. That was a good sign. The parasites gave rippers better oxygen uptake, so that they could run farther without rest.

"Ripper?" It was a question rather than an accusation, but his snarl betrayed the emotion, the loathing, the anger. He clearly wanted to shoot, and Kayla could guess that he was pumped full of adrenaline.

"No!" Kayla took two quick breaths, trying to calm her own pounding heart, suddenly aware of the sweat staining her armpits. "Come on, you stupid shit. We have to get back to the truck now. We're from St. John's."

Underbrush cracked near the edge of the larger clearing. Something human-sized ran their way. Worse, to the north and the south more running footsteps could be heard.

"Okay." He lowered the gun but still frowned in suspicion.

"Follow me." Kayla ran from the little clearing, heading straight for the headlights. She wished for a walkie now, because she'd tell Jeff they were coming and to shut off the headlights, for she and the teenager must be silhouettes, but there was no time. She would have to trust the trees to obscure their shadows and hope that the bank of lights over the cab would dazzle ripper eyes.

She trusted that he followed and kept up, but she didn't want the distraction of looking over her shoulder. All of her concentration now was on picking a path to the headlights, dodging to avoid trees and trying not to take too straight a line. It would suck to be shot this close to the truck and the protection of the fifty cal.

She leapt the raspberry brambles in the ditch and cleared the trees, running into the middle of the highway.

"Don't shoot it's me," she called to Jeff and the others.

She turned to face the forest. The young man, definitely a teenager, leapt the ditch and skidded to halt, turning to stand beside her and face the woods. Kayla fired three rounds back at the forest to force any pursuers to take cover, and he leveled his shotgun and also blasted off a round.

The horn blared.

"Get in! Get in!"

Basil still clung to the fifty cal, and Martin knelt in the back, presumably aiding Milan, but Kayla couldn't see the bed of the truck from the road. The passenger door stood open, and she pushed the man toward it. God, he better not be a ripper or she had just killed them all. He could shoot Jeff now and take over the truck, their only hope of escape. She pushed in right after him and slammed the door.

"Go! Go!" Kayla needn't have shouted. The door had hardly closed when Jeff geared reverse, stomping the accelerator and backing them at dangerous speed up the highway. He slowed even as figures emerged from the woods. The fifty cal roared out above the cab only for a second, but several forms dropped and the rest scrambled for the cover of the woods.

Jeff stopped and did a U-turn, accelerating north for St. John's.

In the dashboard lights, Kayla carefully studied the man. Man? Boy. Was he even shaving? She was now sure he was no ripper, though, for his complexion was fresh and red from the exertion, without a trace of anemia. It was the face of youth, and Kayla suddenly felt old and lined by comparison. He stank from his sweat, but strangely Kayla wanted to take deep breaths of it, almost as if the scent were a way of getting to know him, like small talk.

"So who's this?" Jeff didn't take his eyes off the road, but Kayla had no doubt that his peripheral vision was working overtime, and she noted that his Ruger was in his left hand in his lap, the barrel pointed at the new kid.

"I don't know." Kayla raised her eyebrows. "So, like, who are you?"

"Tevy Wexler." He held out his right hand, and it was somehow archaic, as if he were a pre-Vlad middle-aged businessman at a conference. But Kayla sensed that he wasn't mocking them, that he was serious, that someone had carefully taught him old-world manners. Or maybe he was just an old soul.

She shook his hand. "I'm Kayla Falco. Please to meet you. This is Jeffery Aubert, a Companion of the great Bertrand Allan, and a hero of the Battle of the Cave Mountain." Kayla waited to see Tevy draw in his breath, to express his awe at being in the presence of a legend.

Tevy nodded solemnly. "Nice to meet you too," he said to Kayla. He turned to Jeff. "Bobs says to say hi."

7

ST. JOHN'S KEEP

Tevy let the madness fade as the truck sped up the highway. Bobs would scold him if she found out about that momentary loss of all reason. His ears burned as he wondered what this woman from St. John's must think of him, for she was right: he was stupid to go charging into the forest after rippers in the night.

But he had killed one for sure, a lucky shot at close range between the eyes. They hadn't expected him to follow. They had turned only feet into the forest, intending to shoot back at the truck, and so he had come face to face with his enemy. She must have been a young woman when she had become a ripper, perhaps even pretty, but now she was a gaunt memory of herself, starved for too long of blood, her hair thin and straggly, her eyes bulging at the sight of him. She put up one hand to shield herself even as her other hand raised a rusting revolver. Lucky for Tevy it clicked and didn't fire, or they both would have died.

The tremble started, his knees shaking against Kayla's and Jeff's on either side in the cramped cab, his torso shuddering uncontrollably

"You okay, buddy?" asked Jeff, shouting over the sound of the engine.

"Yes, yes, I'm fine—just adrenaline and all." Tevy gripped his knees as if he could fight them to stillness. "Happens to me after a fight when I've been all pumped up." What must the woman—what was her name? Kayla, that was it. What must she think of him? A fool? A coward?

"Why'd you run into the woods?" she asked.

Tevy was tempted to say that it was to drive the rippers far from the truck, to give them time to load Milan into the back, but it wasn't true and he hated bullshit. "I lost my head. Things were pretty hopeless just before you guys got there, and I guess I... Like, I gave myself up for dead. Then you got there..." Tevy struggled for words and finally shrugged. "Just needed to kill some rippers and they were running away."

He looked over at Kayla, hoping for understanding, but her expression in the dashboard lights was angry. She was older than him, he was sure of that, way older, but there was something about her face, the curve of her chin and the set of her jaw that caught his attention. He resisted the urge to push an errant lock of hair back over her ear, to wipe the blood from a forehead scratch off her plump cheek. Sweat glistened from her skin, and a bead ran down her long neck into her collar despite the cool. She must've run pretty hard to catch him.

She met his gaze.

"Next time, control yourself," she said. "You can't go around thinking about getting back at the rippers. You have to think about beating them instead, and dying isn't beating them, no matter how many of them you take with you."

She was right, of course, so Tevy didn't respond, but he found himself more aware of her than ever—the touch of her knee on his, the scent of her sweat, the way she cradled her Uzi between her legs.

Suddenly, a new fear took hold. How could a woman so much older than him be causing that reaction? God, not here, not now. Bishop Alvarez would say that this was a time to pray, that you could cheat the body's lusts by immersing oneself in the rosary. Emile once gathered all the boys close to Tevy's age and warned them that their bodies would sometimes behave badly, that it wasn't their fault, and all they had to do to behave was think about cleaning guns and killing rippers.

Tevy reached into his vest pocket and pulled out the box of shotgun cartridges. He made sure the safety was on and began reloading. This not only calmed his lusts but calmed his trembling. By the time he was done, he could see the tower of St. John's and that took up his attention.

It was nowhere near as tall as the Willis Tower, a tiny fraction of the height really, but all twenty stories had lights. It was as if this building had appeared from his childhood, just the way condos and office towers used to be all lit up before Vlad, before the power plants died and before the darkness of their age.

"Whoa." It just escaped his lips, and as they got close he had to lean toward the dashboard so that he could look up through the windshield.

"What?" Kayla studied him with a frown.

"So many lights. It's like before—before Vlad."

"You don't have power in Chicago?"

Jeff answered. "No, they don't, not the humans anyway."

"We have some." Tevy knew he sounded defensive but didn't care. "Emile keeps a generator going at St. Mike's, and St. James and some of the others got some too. We just use 'em for the outside lights at night, though, so the rippers can't sneak up in the dark. Sometimes Emile runs a cable so we can turn on the TV and watch DVDs, but only on Saturdays."

"Welcome back to the twenty-first century, then." Jeff drove around the black tower to the back, and a large garage door rolled up magically as they approached, releasing the blinding light of fluorescents.

Jeff brought the truck to a stop in the middle of a garage crammed with trucks and cars and tool boxes and hoists. There was barely room to squeeze into a parking space, especially since several people with guns stood around it.

"We're good," called Jeff out his open window as soon as he'd cut the engine, but he re-holstered his gun and didn't get out. He and Kayla put their hands in the air instead. Tevy got the message and put his shotgun down on the floor of the truck and put his hands up.

A balding man, round and comfortable, with what little white hair he had hanging to his shoulders, approached with a stethoscope. "I'll start in the back with Milan. I'll get to you when I can."

Tevy watched in the rearview mirror as the doctor climbed into the back of the truck and listened in turn at Martin's and Basil's chests before finally crouching down over Milan. He also stuck a thermometer in each man's ear for a second or two.

"He can tell if they're infected?" asked Tevy.

Kayla turned to him in surprise. "Don't you people know down there? A ripper's temperature is about five degrees low, and their heart rate is like about forty."

"What's normal?"

"I don't know." Kayla looked back out the passenger window. "More than forty anyway."

"Anyone we're not sure about we just put in the lock-up until sunrise." Tevy avoided looking at her, because with her hands on her head, her breasts seemed more prominent, even through her vest. "Sun proves 'em one way or the other, but they usually confess before sunrise, 'cause they hate the burning so much. Then Bishop Alvarez decides whether we waste a bullet or let God's light do the work anyway."

Jeff snorted in surprise. "Bishop Alvarez. I forgot about that little promotion."

The doctor must've been satisfied, because he stepped out of the back and waved for a gurney for Milan. He came around to the front and checked Kayla and Jeff, and finally Tevy was allowed out of the truck for his inspection, his hands now on his head, fingers laced. The doctor paused over Tevy's heartbeat and frowned, checking his watch and listening a second time.

"What's wrong?" Tevy was certain that no ripper had fed him blood.

"Do you run a lot?" He checked Tevy's temperature a second time.

"Yeah. I'm a runner for Bobs to all the blockhouses when she doesn't want to use the radio. Been doing that since I was twelve."

The doctor nodded. "Okay, that would explain it." He turned to Jeff. "His temperature's normal, but his heart rate is low, like athlete low, but that's about ripper range too."

"Let's take him through the full-spectrum flos and see if he gets burned."

Kayla opened a door and flipped up a light switch, gesturing Tevy to walk ahead.

"What about my shotgun?"

Jeff was already reaching into the cab. "I got it. Let's go."

Tevy still had his hands on his head because he sensed that he wasn't yet allowed to put them down. He walked through a brilliantly lit white corridor—way brighter than necessary, complete overkill.

Kayla followed behind with her Uzi, and she seemed very tense until they were about halfway along the corridor. She exhaled in a sigh of relief. "You can put your hands down, now. I guess you pass."

"What was that all about?" Tevy was forced to stop at the far door because it was locked.

Jeff joined them and handed Tevy his shotgun before fishing a key from the pocket of his jeans and unlocking the door. "Full-spectrum light." Jeff turned to Kayla. "Take him up to see Barry and then show him the men's dorm." He looked over Tevy's head and back down the corridor toward the garage. "Basil, Martin. How's about a drink to celebrate our victory?"

The place was crowded, much like St. Mike's or any of the blockhouses in Chicago. Kayla led him into a large hall at the bottom of a great stairway. Huge concrete pillars supported the hall and the building above, and they had been poured to look like Romanesque or Greek columns. Two large chandeliers hung above, their lights dispelling the gloom, but smoke stained the white ceiling—smoke from cooking stoves. The whole hall almost to the bottom of the stair was crammed with the living, their humble homes consisting of plastic tarps or blankets for walls and cots for beds or couches. Children chased one another around the few corridors between the makeshift dwellings, while adults hung laundry or gossiped. In one corner an older man sat with his guitar, and many gathered around to join him in his song.

"This way. It's too hard to get to the elevators over there. We'll catch them from the second floor." Kayla led him up the stairs, an oasis of space that some of the children were putting to good use, bouncing a ball up and down in a complicated game that involved a bat and made Tevy think of a cross between basketball and baseball, with pillows for bases and plastic garbage cans at three levels for baskets.

"Is this the family dorm?" he asked.

Kayla didn't roll her eyes but looked like she wanted to. "This is the got-here-too-late dorm. People who didn't get Bertrand's warnings until this keep was already full. Mr. St. John doesn't turn anyone away, but we're going to have to start shoving people onto the roof if any more come along looking for shelter."

"Where are they coming from?"

"Prairies, mostly. Used to get some from out east, but that dropped off a couple of years ago. Ottawa and Toronto, they're all rippers now, always were, some say."

At the top of the stairs, she turned right and led him to a set of shining doors. They slid open to reveal a gleaming interior not much bigger than a walk-in closet. An elevator.

"Is this thing well-maintained?" Tevy didn't want to enter but didn't want to appear a coward.

"It's fine." Kayla entered. "What, you never been in an elevator before?"

God, she was infuriating. "I've been in lots before Vlad. My Gran lived way up in a condo, way higher than this building." Tevy stepped in and stood as far from Kayla as possible, one hand against the wall, as if he could find support there if necessary. "We just don't have any around Old Town that are powered up. Rippers got some down in the Loop."

He resisted the urge to grab the wall when the ground surged under his feet, and his knees buckled for an embarrassing second. He looked over to see if Kayla had noticed, and his ears burned because she was smiling. "I forgot they do that," he said.

The doors opened to reveal a place of wonder, and for a moment Tevy wished he lived at St. John's. The closest he could compare it to was the bridge of the Starship Enterprise from all those Star Trek movies and TV shows the Brat Pack loved—anything that took them away from this planet was very popular on movie night, even if they'd already seen it a dozen times. There were five control tables set in a circle, all with lights and buttons and dials. At one sat a woman with a headset, clearly speaking over a radio. At others technicians monitored...stuff. Tevy had no idea what. Beyond that circle, floor-to-ceiling windows provided a spectacular view of the stars and full moon over the forest.

"It's like a space ship," Tevy said, forgetting to step out of the elevator.

"It's the operations room. Come on." Kayla held the elevator door for him. "We control everything from up here—the power plant, the lights, door locks, everything."

A man, short and stocky with a large, bald head, looked out the window. A willowy woman nearby hung up a phone and stared across the room at Tevy, and emotions awoke for him, memories he couldn't place and didn't want, but she was connected with them. She nodded Tevy's way, and the man turned and waved them over.

Kayla made the introductions. "Tevy Wexler, this is Mr. Barry St. John and Ms. Joyce Skala."

St. John put his hands on his hips and frowned. "Jesus, Kayla. You should both have gone to the infirmary. Christ, he was in a plane crash, and you both look like you've been through a bloody fight."

For the first time since Tevy met her, Kayla looked rattled and uncertain. "Jeff told me to bring him straight up."

"It's okay." Mr. St. John stuck out his hand, and Tevy found his totally enveloped by the handshake. "Call me Barry, all right? Everyone does." The man may have been overweight, but there was a lot of muscle with that fat, and there was nothing soft about him.

"And I'm Joyce." She also held out her hand, and Tevy found himself frowning as he shook it in turn. She was slimmer than he remembered yet firm and strong, but Tevy sensed a different sort of tough than Barry, like a tree that could bend in a hurricane wind and then stand tall in the aftermath. But there was something so familiar about her. It was the same feeling he had when he met Kayla earlier in the evening, but more definite. Then he remembered. This was *the* Joyce.

"Wow," he said, forgetting to let go of her hand. "We met way back. I'm one of the Brat Pack."

She frowned. "Come again?" She pulled her hand free but held his eyes with hers.

"You saved me. I mean, Bertrand Allan saved me, but you were there that night, the night the rippers killed my mom and dad. You were really mad that they died, and then you gave me to Helen to join the Brat Pack, all the orphans at St. Mike's."

Joyce sighed and shook her head. "I'm sorry, I don't remember off the top of my head. There were a lot of orphans around that time."

Tevy fought the desire to detail that night for her, to somehow connect to a moment in time before his parents' murder, to find out what went on outside the house from her perspective, to find out if there would have been any way to save his parents if things went differently. But his nightmares from that night forbade asking too many questions.

Barry waved them toward a table off to one side from the operations center. "Grab a seat since you're here." He called out to a young man at one of the control tables. "Andreas, mind grabbing us a few beers?" He turned back to Tevy. "You're twenty-one, right?"

"I'm almost eighteen." Tevy took his seat, confused about the question, but the others shared a laugh.

"Just an old joke." Barry settled heavily into a cracked leather chair at the head of the table. "So what's so hush-hush that Bobs sent you instead of just using the radio. What's the big message?"

Tevy looked from Barry to Joyce to Kayla. "She told me to only tell you and Joyce and Jeff and Martin, the Companions."

The anger on Kayla's face made Tevy look quickly back to Barry, who had already raised one hand to forestall her protest. "Kayla, give us a minute okay? Go wash your face and come back in ten minutes."

Tevy waited until she was out of earshot.

"Chicago's in trouble. Vlad, or at least a ripper calling himself Vlad, has come back to Chicago, and he's brought a whole bunch of people up from California, human slaves and rippers. They're stockpiling weapons and they've got tanks. She believes that a major offensive is coming this summer."

Joyce answered first. "What the fuck does she want us to do about it?"

"Bring an army, like back at the Battle of the Mountain." Tevy had trouble keeping the surprise out of his voice. He had only thought to deliver a message, he hadn't expected to defend it. "I thought there were, like, too many people up here. She thought you'd be happy—"

"Wait," Barry said, while the young man, Andreas, passed around mugs of brown beer, each with an inch of foam on top. When Andreas returned to his post, Barry nodded to indicate Tevy could continue.

"She thought you'd be happy to send an army, to have some people move back to Chicago."

"Most of these people aren't from Chicago." Barry studied him for a moment, and Tevy knew to keep his mouth shut while the man considered. "You seem pretty deep in Bobs' confidence. Everybody still call her that?"

"Most people call her General Roberts." Tevy squared his shoulders with pride. "She told me to call her Bobs. Said she trusted me 'cause I'm such a good runner and snooper. Says I remind her of the man who saved her life."

Joyce sat up straight, leaning forward to stare at him with embarrassing ferocity. "She what? Did she tell you who that is?"

"No, she wouldn't, said that wasn't important."

Joyce slumped back in her chair, her expression puzzled, unsure, but her gaze still fixed on Tevy. "What made you charge into the woods?"

It was Tevy's turn to be confused. "How do you know?"

"Jeff told us, of course. You think he didn't phone up here when he got back? What made you charge into the woods?" She chopped out each word.

"I guess I was too pumped." Tevy shrugged. "I just wanted to get them, to kill some of them and scare the rest into running far away. I couldn't help myself."

Joyce and Barry exchanged a loaded look, and Barry shrugged. "Who knows? It's certainly possible." He turned to Tevy. "So Bobs wants us to come romping damn near eight-hundred miles with about a thousand people and do what?"

"Attack the Loop before they're ready to attack us. Take this Vlad out the way you took out Vlad the Scourge."

"Oh, come on." Joyce slammed her mug of beer down on the table, sloshing brown. "This is totally different. It's not like we can all just pile onto a few buses and drive across the continent anymore. Chicago might as well be the moon."

"She can fix stuff like that. If you can get buses. I mean, there must be some up here somewhere. If you can get to Duluth, the highway's good from there. We keep it clear."

"And how do we fuel these buses and feed our people when we get there." Joyce looked angrier by the second, and Tevy cringed under the onslaught.

"I don't know. I figured she'd sort that out with you when the time comes. Look, I'm just a runner and a scout, and all." He took a gulp of the beer, wondering why anyone liked this bitter taste, and wiped the foam from his lip. Disgusting drink. He'd prefer a nice glass of apple juice, but he didn't want to offend his hosts.

"But she sent you." Barry eyed him thoughtfully. "And you know a lot it seems. Where do you scout?"

"The Loop. I go in near dawn and come out after sun up. It gives me a chance to check out ripper numbers and traitor numbers. I hear things."

Joyce leaned forward, and there was an intensity to her stare that baffled Tevy.

"You hunt rippers at night, don't you. Why?"

Tevy shrugged. "Isn't it obvious? I don't want to just sit around while they kill or convert more people. Every ripper I kill saves hundreds."

She turned to Barry. "Sound like anyone you know? It's pretty eerie, isn't it?"

Barry shook his head. "I don't know. Sometimes, you know, we see what we want to see." He turned his attention to Tevy. "Why doesn't she just get help from closer to home, like from that National Guard colonel she's chummy with?"

"He can't help 'cause the rippers keep attacking his bases, too." For the first time, it occurred to Tevy that these people weren't all-seeing and powerful—that being so far up north they might not understand. "Do you how many people have died since you saved me?"

"Hundreds of thousands, we know," said Joyce. "We monitor every channel."

"Millions." Tevy couldn't keep the surprise from his voice because it was so obvious to him. Bishop Alvarez reminded them every Sunday and ordered them to pray for the dead. "Millions and millions. It's not just the rippers, there's the famines."

"Were not idiots." But Joyce frowned and exchanged a glance with Barry.

"We saw what happened in Thunder Bay and Atherley," Barry said. "So we know it's in the millions."

Tevy had been taught to respect his elders, but the beer had lightened his head.

"So you know a lotta people offed themselves the first couple of years? You know what it's like to smell the stink in some house you're foraging through, knowing you'll likely find a body hanging from the ceiling or lying on bed?"

"We've had some experience." Joyce didn't look angry now. In fact, she stared intently at Tevy and let him speak.

"I've seen thousands of bodies. It's worse if they had pets, cause then they get eaten and you find bits of them rotting all over the house. Fidos, we call them. Worse than what's left after the rats."

His frustration grew, perhaps because the presence of Joyce took him back to that first night, the night his parents died, the first night of the rest of his life. "We could all die down there while you sit up here in your tower, with your electricity and all the old-world softies. I got little kids from the Brat Pack who ask me at night to tell them it's gonna be all right, and I always tell them it will, that I'll kill the rippers and keep them away from St. Mike's." He was shaking again, his passion burying his control. "I mean it! I won't let them die. I won't let them rippers take them. We desperately need your help. A thousand fighters could make a huge difference, if you don't come too late."

Barry held up one hand to stop him. "Settle down, settle down. You've made your point."

Tevy hadn't realized that he had stood, that he was leaning over, that his fist had been pounding the laminated tabletop.

"You're tired and you've had a rough time." Joyce's voice was gentle this time, the voice you use with a crazy person. "You get some sleep and leave this to us."

But Tevy wasn't finished. If he could just make them understand. "There's maybe two thousand around St. Mike's, maybe twenty thousand souls living north of the Loop, but the rippers have probably got fifteen grand in traitors and way more in rippers. If we don't hit 'em soon and hit 'em hard, they'll kill or make slaves of every free human in Chicago. You have to come before it's too late. Bobs says if we can take the Loop and hole up there, we can survive the coming storm."

"What storm?" asked Barry.

"Rippers out of California. Don't you guys hear anything on the radio? There're millions of them out there. They're hungry and they're looking our way. Bobs says so. Says we're going to need drastic action. She said it just like that, 'drastic action.'"

Joyce turned to Barry. "What the hell would *she* consider drastic?"

"Damned if I know. What about you?" He pointed a finger at Tevy, who shrugged.

"She doesn't tell me everything."

Joyce nodded. "Don't worry, she doesn't tell anyone everything."

8

VAMPIRE ROAD

Kayla had never seen so many buses in one place. Twelve of them were lined up along the side of the highway, all grimy from disuse. On the bus nearest her, someone had used their finger to write WASH ME DUDE in the dust of one of the windows. People milled around, shoving luggage into the open compartments in the bellies of the buses, hugging loved ones goodbye or shaking hands with friends, and checking weapons.

"I saw one of these in a gas station last year," Kayla said to Rachel, who had come out to show off her baby and see Kayla on her journey. "I just assumed it was junk."

"That was the idea." Rachel seemed unaware that the baby was fussing in Kayla's arms, working itself up to tears. "Those buses were another one of those secrets that Barry and Joyce's Raiders kept. They had them stashed in garages all over Atherley, all over the county. I guess the idea was to have them ready in case we needed to evacuate if things went totally sideways." She looked along the line of buses. "But now you'll be gone, and we'll be stuck here."

Kayla rocked the baby, practically bouncing it in her arms, terrified that it would sense her fear and know that she was totally uncomfortable holding the little creature. What if she dropped it or something? At the first real cry, she shoved the bundle back into Rachel's arms.

"Don't worry." Kayla tried not to show her relief at handing back the baby. "We'll be back. I mean, Joyce's Raiders and me anyway. I heard Joyce and Jeff promise Barry that."

"I'm surprised you guys are going at all, but I guess we'll all be breathing a bit easier here for a while, have some space to raise our families. I hear there's like six hundred volunteers going, mostly single young men. Better pick a hubby while you're down there, because it'll be slim pickings up here after this."

Kayla checked the magazine on her Uzi for the hundredth time. "I don't know Rach. I'm not as brave as you, bringing a kid into this world with no guarantees it'll grow up."

"There never were guarantees. Kids got killed in car accidents, from falls, from cancer."

"Now we're lucky if we live long enough to get cancer." Kayla cursed the words before she'd even finished. "Oh Rach, I'm sorry. I'm sure Justin will grow up strong and healthy here at the Keep."

Rachel had lost none of her toughness over the years, but to Kayla's surprised it now cracked. "Just you be sure to come back for his first birthday, okay?" Her lip quivered. "It's been you and me since the end, until the baby that is. Now you're with Joyce's Raiders and going out into the world to do something, and I can't imagine life without you."

Kayla swept her up in a hug, careful of the baby between them and fighting to prevent the flow of her own tears. "I'll be all right and I'll come back. You'll see. It's going to be fine." She patted Rachel on the back and stepped away, again checking the magazine on her Uzi.

"It's full," said Rachel.

Barry's voice broke through the crowd. "Kayla." He waved from two buses down, where he stood near the open door with Joyce and Jeff, the latter looking hung over. "A word, please."

Kayla gave Rachel a peck on the cheek and trotted over, knowing that with the sun above the trees, Joyce must be anxious to get them on their road. Just as she reached them, Kayla saw the little hands of seven-year-old Margaret holding on to Joyce's thigh from behind. One blonde pigtail peeked out from the level of Joyce's hip, also giving away the child's hiding place. Kayla had forgotten about Joyce's daughter. Surely, the child wasn't coming along?

"Listen," said Barry. "This kid, Tevy, he's Bobs' man, no doubt." He crossed his beefy arms and studied Kayla to see if she understood. "I'm sure he's a good fighter and all, but I want you to stick with him, keep an eye on him. There are things he doesn't need to know."

"What things?"

"None of your business." Joyce picked up her daughter, an aggressive maneuver that the child interpreted as play.

"Turn me upside down!" she called.

"You're too big for that, Mags."

Jeff shook his head. "Be reasonable here, Joyce. She can't keep him from knowing shit if she doesn't know what the shit is." He turned to Kayla. "We don't want Bobs to know that Joyce has a daughter, okay? I know that's weird, but just don't mention Margaret, and if she does find out, tell her it's really Alison's daughter, okay, but Barry didn't want anyone knowing she was having a baby so young."

Margaret chose this moment to chase after another little girl, and they ran a weaving path through the piles of luggage lining the road adjacent to the buses.

Kayla fought to keep all the subterfuges straight. They weren't to talk about Margaret, but if she did come up, they were to say it was Barry's granddaughter, but that everyone was pretending it was Joyce's because Barry was embarrassed that his daughter had a teenage pregnancy—his daughter, who was now married and eight months pregnant.

"Okay," she said, her voice a tentative experiment. "Pretend, within pretend, within pretend."

Jeff gave one of his mischievous winning smiles that had melted so many hearts. "Told you she was smart."

But Kayla wasn't done being smart. She had always assumed Jeff was the father, but they weren't even the least bit like a couple or an ex-couple. Joyce and Jeff genuinely seemed to be just friends and comrades-in-arms.

"Who's Margaret's father?" Kayla asked.

The angry expression on Joyce's face didn't put Kayla off, and the sudden tension of everyone else in the little group told her she had hit a very important nerve.

"None of your fucking business," said Joyce.

But it was too late. Kayla did the math, thought about who else Joyce had been close to nearly eight years ago and the fact that, as far as she had heard, there was only one man in line for sainthood down in Chicago. One martyr.

"It's Bertrand Allan, isn't it?"

Jeff actually reached out and held down the barrel of Joyce's Uzi, as if he feared she would shoot Kayla.

"Keep your mouth shut," Joyce said. "You don't tell anyone."

"I still don't get why this is such a big deal. So you and Allan did it before he died."

Jeff held up one finger to quiet what was clearly going to be an angry retort from Joyce. Kayla decided that it was a true sign of the trust of their friendship that Joyce nodded and let Jeff speak.

"Bobs has made Bert out to be some super martyr. During the famines she constantly reminded people to be like him, to go out and kill rippers and sacrifice themselves if necessary. It was more than just her publicity stunt. It helped rally people around her, to point to the Savior of Chicago and say that thanks to him everything would be okay if they could just survive one more starving winter. It would be a disaster for her and Alvarez if Bert turned out to be less than perfect."

"Okay," Kayla said. "I can be very good at keeping my mouth shut."

Barry nodded. "Good, but Kayla, I don't want this Tevy kid knowing anything more about the Keep than necessary either. Don't tell him about the backdoor or the generator or the mine or anything else. You never know who's going to end up a ripper, whether they're the type or not."

"Got it. I ride by him and isolate him."

But Joyce wasn't satisfied. "Especially," she said, skewering Kayla with her glare, "don't tell him about the man you met in the bottom of Atherley College."

Now Kayla was confused, because she didn't recall meeting a man who wasn't from the Keep, but as she reviewed those crazy moments in the fight, she suddenly understood and she whispered his name. "You mean Bertrand Allan."

Jeff whistled, and Barry turned away for a moment to look up at his Keep and mutter, "Jesus Christ, she knows."

"At least she had enough sense to whisper." Jeff's own voice was so low that it was barely above a whisper.

Joyce looked like she wanted to rend her limb by limb, and Kayla involuntarily clutched her Uzi close to her stomach.

Joyce pointed a finger right between Kayla's eyes, less that an inch from her head. "That is our deepest secret. No one must know, ever, about him. Let Bobs have her fantasy hero. Let her have her martyr." Her voice rose into a strangled crescendo. "Do you understand?"

Jeff reached out and pulled down Joyce's hand. "Whoa, dude. I think she gets the point. Give her some credit."

"So much rides on this." Joyce still looked furious. "We can't control him and now this."

Suddenly, Kayla understood that she wasn't the main problem. "Look," she said. "My lips are sealed and the last bullet's for my brain, so you don't have to worry about me passing secrets to rippers." She held up the Uzi, aimed for the sky, and pointed to the full magazine for emphasis.

Joyce nodded. "Remember that promise."

She looked like she wanted to say more, but at that moment Alison St. John, her belly showing every month of her pregnancy, chased Margaret up to Joyce. Alison was there to take Margaret back into the Keep for breakfast, but she didn't want to go. More importantly, she wanted very much to go on the bus with her mother. Kayla used the resulting tears and screams as an excuse to withdraw, and she headed along the line of the buses looking for Tevy.

A little flutter of arousal surprised her when she saw him leaning one shoulder on a bus while he stuffed a sandwich into his mouth. Barry had given him a free card for the cafeteria, and Kayla had been surprised to find Tevy there on many occasions over the last five days, usually raving about how much more food there was up here. Rachel's husband also mentioned that Tevy had taken a long shower every evening, marveling about the hot running water. His hair looked spiky and damp, presumably because he'd just had a farewell shower and toweled quickly before running for the cafeteria.

His shotgun's pistol grip stuck up over his right shoulder, and Kayla walked past with other people while pretending she hadn't noticed him, wondering if he would call out, but he didn't see her go by, because he was staring up at the Keep, apparently in awe.

Kayla turned around and headed back to him in order to get a look from behind at how he had rigged the shotgun. Someone had sewed an unusual holster for it in heavy leather so that he could carry it on his back, ready to draw as fast as a handgun. Her glance went to the Glock at his hip and then his narrow hips and his cute behind in those patched blue jeans. No man had caught her attention this way in years, had made her wonder what it would be like to touch and maybe even hold him, to let her hands wander down to cup those firm buttocks while they embraced.

She shook off this image, for the last thing she needed now was clouded judgment, although the thought of stopping beside him and slipping her arm around his waist teased at the edges of her awareness, thoughts of what it would be like to be a couple, to be casually comfortable with touching.

"Hey," she said, stopping and crossing her arms under her breasts as if she too just wanted to take one last look up at the black steel and gleaming windows of the Keep. "Pretty amazing, isn't it?"

Tevy licked the last of his breakfast off his fingers. "It's a bit weird. It's like time travel or something, like someone took an old world office building and a chunk of 2015, then just dropped it here in the middle of nowhere."

"That's pretty much what happened. It was supposed to be a student residence and built less than a kilometer from campus, but St. John built it over here instead. The administration was all rippers and didn't really care what he was doing or said. Never came to site meetings, just accepted photos of progress. Never occurred to them that he wasn't building it where he was supposed to."

"Weird."

"Assholes were too busy snacking on my roommates at night to go looking at new construction."

Tevy picked up the pack at his feet. "You picked out a bus yet?"

Kayla prayed she wasn't blushing, didn't show that she was happy that he'd essentially asked to sit with her. It was what Barry wanted, of course, but suddenly she knew that she wanted it, too, wanted to get to know this strange teenager who chased rippers into the woods at night.

"Naw." Kayla made an effort to sound non-committal, as if this was all no big deal. "I was thinking maybe this heap." She tilted her head in the general direction of the bus beside them.

"Great, we can sit together." He tossed his pack into the belly of the bus on top of the pile of luggage that had already been loaded. "I'll save you a seat." He headed for the door without looking back.

It was a relaxed maneuver, so confidant, perhaps even arrogant, that Kayla wanted to go to another bus. She never said she'd sit with *him*, just that she'd be on the same bus. The cheek to assume. Yet, she had orders, but what made her angrier was that she did want to sit with him.

She went and got her backpack from where she'd left it lying on the road when Rachel had insisted she hold the baby. It was the same bag she'd packed to go to college, a pack she had hoped she would one day use for a long post-grad trip to Europe. That was never going to happen now. Who knew if it was even possible to get a boat to Europe, and it had been years since she'd seen jet contrails. As she tossed her luggage onto the pile beside Tevy's, it did occur to her that this was a much more exciting trip than wandering around Europe, photographing churches and drinking at youth hostels.

She gave one last look up at the black tower of the Keep, promising to herself that she would return, and she climbed onto the bus to find Tevy.

———

Tevy didn't seem to mind that Kayla didn't want to talk much about life at the Keep. Instead, as the bus rolled down the highway toward the Mattagami, he chatted about his life, telling her about growing up under St. Mike's, about the Brat Pack and Chicago. He described the Loop downtown and told her which areas had to be avoided because of flooding after the sewers clogged.

He described his adventures with a matter-of-factness that Kayla found refreshing. He didn't brag so much as he seemed unaware of how crazy it was that he liked to raid into ripper territory, that he liked to spy and listen to gain advantage. The first half hour to the Mattagami bridge passed quickly, with the only problem being that the usual suspects who tried to get into Kayla's pants every Saturday night stood in the aisle and hung over the seat. At first she thought they were hanging around for her, and she did sense that sexual tension, but soon it was obvious Tevy's stories of Chicago were a draw. How many of these guys had ever seen Chicago? Even if they were from there, they were desperate for information as to how it had changed.

It wasn't long after the river that they had their first halt.

"What is it?" asked Tevy, half standing in an effort to see up the bus, but everyone else stood as well, blocking his view.

Radu, a guy who'd asked Kayla out many times to no avail, stood tall in the aisle. "A truck. A very big truck." His very slight Romanian accent, somewhere between French and Eastern European, was a little more evident than usual. "It blocks the road, turned on its side." Kayla knew Radu's story, for he'd told her many times. He came over from Romania before the end, studying at Lakehead University and hoping to get landed immigrant status in Canada. He was visiting friends at Atherley College when the invitation to go take shelter from the rippers in the Keep had arrived. He accepted, but many times since, he expressed his desire to return to Romania. Some blamed him for Vlad the Scourge, since most believed he was connected somehow to Vlad Tepes, the prince of Wallachia in Romania and the inspiration for Bram Stoker's Dracula. Many had whispered about Radu's accent, the same as that of Vlad the Scourge. Kayla liked his thick hair and his sun-darkened complexion that spoke of Roma heritage, but something about his body didn't attract her, the sense that, while he was slim now, a chubby, lazy man would appear in middle age.

The bus driver's voice cut above the hubbub. "Taking a break folks. This is a good time to use the forest."

Tevy sat while they waited for the bus to empty. "Do you have a bulldozer or something?"

Kayla shook her head. "We've got a big tow truck, one that can move big rigs even if it means dragging them. We've done this before, you know. For a long time, we tried to keep the highway open but the rippers keep blocking it at night, trying to catch people driving up from away."

Tevy did know, for a favorite tactic of the rippers in the early days was to get their human slaves to stall cars on the highways, creating huge traffic jams that lasted until dark. The carnage after sunset taught people pretty quickly that it was better to abandon a car and go to ground in someone's house as far from the road as possible than to wait for the rippers.

The drive continued that way all day: the convoy pausing, the tow truck clearing—in one case a barricade of old-growth trees—and another half hour of driving until the next blockage. By mid-afternoon everyone knew they wouldn't reach the relative safety of International Falls. People began cleaning and loading guns.

"There can't be many rippers up here in the forest, can there?" Tevy asked.

Kayla had a hard time not frowning at him. "The forest isn't the problem. The highway is, and that's where we'll be spending the night. Look at the crap they block the road with. They've been catching people out here for years, even if it has slowed to a trickle lately. And they're not deaf. They make their hidey-holes close to the road, and believe me they've all heard our buses pass today. Every ripper for forty miles will be coming for us tonight."

As soon as the bus stopped in the late afternoon, Kayla headed for the luggage bay, deciding she wanted to carry a couple more spare clips for her Glock. The luggage had shifted a fair bit, and she had to toss first one bag and then another out of the way, digging deep to find her backpack. But just as she saw it, the big hockey bag to the right shifted of its own accord. Kayla startled and leapt back, a superstitious dread rising in her gut until the warm sunlight on her back convinced her that it couldn't be a ripper. But maybe an animal?

She raised her Uzi and leaned forward, intending to prod the bag with the barrel, but then the zipper began to descend, pulled by something or someone in the bag. Kayla stepped back now, ready to shoot. It had been years since she had seen a raccoon, but what other creature could perform this trick? A person could never fit in that hockey bag.

Not a grown person. A little hand appeared when the zipper stuck, and seven-year-old Margaret wiggled halfway out of the bag before she saw the Uzi and stopped to stare at it with a puzzled frown. Her pigtails had come free, perhaps while she was asleep in the bag, and her blonde hair hung in a tangled mess, framing her pale face. She rubbed her eyes and squinted at Kayla. "Are we there yet?" she said. "I have to pee."

Kayla tried to think. How could she keep Joyce's daughter a secret from Tevy when the little girl was a stowaway on the bus? How could he ever believe she was really Alison's daughter when she'd runaway from the Keep to go with Joyce? This was a disaster, but maybe it could be saved if she could rush the little girl to a different bus, keep her away from Tevy's inquiring mind, the one that liked to know secrets.

She lowered her Uzi and reached for the little girl's hand, putting a finger to her lips to indicate quiet. "We mustn't let anyone know you're here."

But it was too late. A shadow joined Kayla's shadow on the luggage, and Tevy said, "Hey, whose kid?"

Kayla panicked. How could she keep this girl a secret as she'd promised?

Suddenly, inspiration.

"She's mine."

9

MONSTER IN THE NIGHT

Tevy struggled to remember his mother, but the diesel fumes weren't quite right. It had been gasoline that last night, and thus that rare scent was what he sought when his memory failed. Sometimes he'd find a rusting car and pull off the gas cap to sniff, not just to scavenge, but to aid memory.

Radu stood high in the back of the pickup truck beside a forty-five-gallon drum, sweat dripping from his forehead as his arm worked the pump handle up and down. Tevy kept the hose, which barely reached, from slipping out of the bus's fuel supply pipe.

Did she have black hair? Tevy took a deep breath of fumes and closed his eyes, searching for that last moment when his mother blew him a kiss before continuing to load her revolver. He focused. He could sense her close, teasing at the edge of his memory, but her face would not conjure, and he had to settle for the memory of her presence rather than her visage. He savored it until Radu interrupted.

"It's not full yet?"

Tevy tried to see down the tube into the bus's fuel tank, but that was impossible. "I think you have to pump the whole barrel in."

But Radu had stopped to wipe his forehead. "But we only drove about six hours. How could it be empty? Is it leaking?"

Tevy let go of the hose and got down on hands and knees on the asphalt to look under the bus. Dark fluid did drip from under the engine, but it was a slow black drip, which Tevy decided must be oil. He stood up and climbed into the back of the truck, pulling his shirt over his head so that he could use it to swat at black flies with his free hand. "My turn." He took over on the pump.

It turned out Radu had almost finished, for after just a few minutes, he called out, "Stop, stop! It's full."

Joyce and Kayla approached, both looking grim and serious, both carrying slung Uzis.

Tevy had tried to get Kayla to talk about herself and the Keep while they were on the bus, but she had been a closed book, and he recognized the signs of painful memories. Some kids in the Brat Pack were okay talking about how their parents died, and Elliot made up endless stories of heroism and adventure, all with bloody endings in which his parents died while killing hundreds of rippers at once. His stories were a favorite on Friday nights. But other Brat Pack kids didn't want to go there, didn't even want to talk about how their lives were before the end. For them conversation was reserved for the present and for important things: food, weapons, and killing rippers. If they were post-pubescent like Tevy and Elliot, they might talk about sex.

So Tevy filled the empty air on the bus with chatter about Chicago while Kayla sat there looking grimmer and angrier with him by the mile. He would have stopped talking altogether, but he was sizing up the young men who stood in the bus aisle and in the row ahead to eagerly listen. Who would be useful and who would run at the first gunshot? Only Radu had Tevy's cautious vote of confidence so far, for he had seemed totally unimpressed with the stories, and he had expressed disbelief at the right places.

Kayla looked up at him now and turned her head away to look at the sunset over the forest, her cheeks blushing as if she'd caught him naked. While Helen and Bishop Alvarez had made it clear that men and women, and boys and girls, should not be unclothed in front of one another, casual glimpses of nudity were common in the basement of the church and often a source of amusement. Tevy wasn't used to feeling immodest or self-conscious about going topless, especially in summer, but suddenly he wanted to put on his shirt. He knew he was painfully underfed.

Joyce was already speaking before he got the shirt over his head. "You stick with Kayla tonight. Her daughter will be on my bus."

Tevy noticed a catch in her voice and sensed a lie. Where was Margaret really going to be? Why didn't they want him to know? He filed that away for future consideration.

Joyce was already walking away when Kayla spoke. "I'm in the shit house, okay, because of Margaret stowing away and all."

Tevy nodded but didn't think it was fair. Kids in the Brat Pack were always getting into trouble, but Bishop Alvarez didn't blame Helen or Emile, essentially the parents.

"Kids just do stuff." He jumped down from the truck. "Where you going to be, Rad?"

Radu looked up from capping the fuel tank on the bus. "I don't know. I have no assignment."

"Great." Tevy retrieved his multi-pocketed vest out of the cab of the pickup and slipped it on. "Why don't you hang with us? Where are we going to be anyway?" He looked to Kayla while he slung on the holster for his shotgun.

"Joyce's Raiders are going to patrol the perimeter. We won't hold fixed positions like everyone else."

"Joyce's Raiders." Radu raised his eyes, and his accent, that Vladian lilt, became more pronounced. "So I am to be trusted for a change. I fight beside the best."

"No." But Kayla looked uncertain. "I don't know actually. I just do what I'm told and I was told to patrol the forest with Tevy."

"Great," Tevy said. "And I think Rad should be with us."

Tevy knew that he was looking for a substitute for Elliot, his dependable comrade-in-arms when it came down to a fight with the rippers. It wasn't that he didn't trust Kayla, but something was missing. There should be three of them. Elliot had talked about that a lot, and they tried several different kids from the Brat Pack, but they never found one that could work with them very well, that was in sync with them.

Kayla gave a short nod and a suspicious glance at Radu before she turned away. "Whatever."

Radu looked to Tevy for guidance and he waved him along. "Come on, three's better than two."

The moon was over a quarter on the wane, but it was high by 11:00 p.m., and nearly three quarters was still bright enough for the trees to cast dark shadows. Tevy had a sense of why Barry St. John had chosen a location so far north: this late in June, the sun didn't set until nearly 10:00 p.m., and then it was a lingering sunset, giving lots of warning and lots of time to prepare. The winter nights must be long, but did rippers feel the cold? Tevy didn't know.

He did know that he didn't particularly like the woods. The undergrowth crawled near the edges of the highway, and the mosquitoes buzzed incessantly, worse than Chicago, but at least the black flies vanished as the chill settled. Those evil little creatures were new to Tevy, and he was amazed how much blood could be drawn so quickly by something so small. Already his ears and neck were inflamed with bites and smeared with the blood of those that didn't get away.

Tevy also didn't like the woods because of the sounds, not the crickets or hoots, but the snap of twigs and the mysterious distant rustles. Sometimes it must just be wind through the trees, but other times he wondered. Was that the sound of a ripper approaching in stealth?

Joyce had pulled the twelve buses up into four tight rows of three, a square fortification of sorts. Most of the troops now sat in a perimeter around the buses, but her Raiders, like Tevy and Kayla and Radu, patrolled in small groups through the woods to ensure no surprises. Basil, a man Kayla knew, had a couple of generators ready and big lights standing on tripods on the tops of the buses, but for now they were dark and the generators were off. If by some chance the rippers weren't anywhere near them, there was no need to advertise their location. When

Tevy looked back at the highway through the trees, all was dark and silent. He might have been alone in an empty world.

He stepped on a dead twig and it snapped.

"Sh-h-h," Kayla hissed from just a body length away. "God, you're noisy."

Tevy wanted to say that this wasn't the city, that he wasn't used to forest, and he didn't understand how she and Radu could step so quietly, but this was no time for excuses or instruction. He probed the ground with his foot before his next step, ensuring he wasn't stepping on another branch before he gave his foot his weight.

A distant gun fired and others joined, the forest and the buses muting the shots. Tevy turned to run toward the sound of fighting, but Kayla caught him as he turned, her hand pressed flat to his chest to stop him.

"Where do you think you're going?" Her whisper was strangled with anger. "They've got that. We're here."

Tevy took a breath to calm his heart, his desire to attack and find relief from the tension. She was right, of course. They were patrolling south and west of the buses. The gunfire was from the north and east. They could be attacking there as a feint, drawing fighters over that way so that other rippers could raid quietly from this direction, taking unwary people from the buses. Joyce had warned them that the rippers might think this was a convoy of refugees, not fighters, and so they might think they'd find lots of helpless children and seniors hiding on the buses. But there was only one child—Kayla's.

They continued their quiet patrol despite the growing ferocity of the gunfire echoing though the night. The muted roar of gas generators starting up gave warning that the big lights were coming online, but they pointed north away from them, their glow above the trees providing little light for Tevy's eyes. He craved to go to the fight, but Kayla kept him there, and once, when she caught him looking over his shoulder, she pointed to her own eyes with two fingers and pointed into the trees to the southwest. The command was clear: eyes front. Worry about our zone and trust Joyce's plan.

A dry branch snapped ahead. Kayla held her fist in the air, and Radu and Tevy froze. They all sank slowly, Tevy placing one knee in the dry pine needles on the ground, suddenly hyper-alert. The scent of mold and fungus were unfamiliar to him, the wind in the trees disturbing and distracting. A small cloud swept over the moon, for a moment plunging them into serious darkness, before it continued past and the moonlight again lit the forest.

Something moved toward them. A different crack sounded from over on the left, a rustle from the right. The woods had come alive with stealthy creatures—man-sized creatures. Many.

Kayla's hand signs were not unlike the ones they used in Chicago. Tevy shoot right. Radu left. Three shots, pull back ten yards, and then take up the same configuration. On her command.

She let the rippers approach. Tevy picked out three figures closest to him. The moon and the glow of the lights back at the convoy were enough to illuminate their pale faces, and, in one case, an entirely white figure—a ripper with little or no clothing. The rippers' cautious steps made it obvious they intended to attack the buses, but weren't so stupid as to ignore the possibility of human patrols, like Kayla's. The fact that they continued to move forward showed they didn't know a small ambush waited.

More and more pale shapes materialized in the brush, and it was soon obvious that Kayla's little patrol could be in very big trouble. Tevy feared she would change her mind, that they'd slink away to get help rather than engage, and he was desperate to pull the trigger, to attack. He sensed her arm rise and glanced over, praying it wasn't a command to retreat. He may not have been able to obey.

Her fingers were raised, counting down: three, two, one.

Tevy's first shot hit the naked ripper. He was certain because of the way it dropped, an uncontrolled slump to the ground, indicating that maybe Tevy had hit the spinal column. The parasites could fix that, but it would take days. The recoil shoved the barrel of the shotgun up, which made it easy for Tevy to pump the slide while bringing the gun back to level. The next target ran right, using a clearing for speed, but the lack of trees also gave Tevy moonlight to follow, and he fired again, bringing that one down too.

He never got a chance for his third target.

Shouts and screams erupted all through the woods, and even a few muzzle flashes exploded, throwing the forest into dazzling freeze frames of light.

Kayla was up and running, Tevy and Radu close behind. Bullets zipped through the branches, some thudding to a stop in tree trunks. They made use of those trees now. Tevy stopped ten yards back, putting his shoulder into the trunk of a pine, the scent of sap in his nostrils as he aimed at the nearest shadow bounding through some underbrush.

He fired and it dove, and Tevy had no time to guess whether he had hit the ripper.

They were everywhere, easily a hundred, all charging recklessly at them, trusting the parasites to repair them if hit by bullets or perhaps just so hungry that they were near madness. Tevy fired at one and another, counting his way down to the end of his shotgun shells and death.

"Covering!" shouted Kayla. "Go!"

Tevy and Radu ran another ten yards. Tevy hit the brakes, wondering if he'd judged correctly about Radu. A lot of people would just keep running for the buses now, would leave Kayla to die. Radu stopped.

It was brighter here because they were closer to the buses, but they were still desperately far away. Had anyone heard their gunfire over all the shooting at the north end? Tevy managed to frantically reload three shells before he had to fire, shot number five, which meant he only had the three he'd just loaded remaining. Kayla ran back under their covering fire, a ripper practically catching her ponytail before a shot from Radu brought it down.

There was no time to be afraid, no time to think, although there was a panicked boy in his soul begging Tevy to fight, to save him. Tevy fired again, and again. One, two, and last, his third shot. He dropped the gun and drew his Glock barely on time to shoot a ripper, a muddy creature barely recognizable as human, at point blank through the skull.

A scream erupted from behind the charging rippers to mark the location of a struggle, that and thrashing vegetation.

"A bear?" Tevy shouted the question.

The rippers were close enough that one of them answered. "Bears don't attack us," came the voice out of the dark. Tevy shot at that voice and was rewarded with a curse. "Fucking bastard!" Tevy fired again and this time was met with silence.

"We're coming!" shouted a man's voice from behind them. Dozens of people crashed through the trees from the direction of the buses.

"It's Kayla! Over here. We're way outnumbered."

But not outgunned. Whether the rippers had few firearms or simply were so hungry they didn't want to risk wasting human blood with bullets, there were not many bullets flying in their direction.

Friendly gunfire from behind might be fatal though, and Tevy crouched low, retrieving his shotgun to stuff it into its holster while debating which side of the tree he should be on. A shadow ran through the same clearing on Tevy's right as before, rushing up a hillock of bare granite, but not toward him. It was running to the side, pursued by another ripper. Tevy sighted, debating which one he had a better chance of bringing down. The first shot from the Glock missed both, but before he could aim again a hand closed over his gun and pushed it down, causing a discharge that sent the bullet into the rock.

"No!" Kayla had leapt across the space between them. "That's one of ours."

The second ripper tackled the first, the two shadows going down and now hidden by undergrowth at the edge of the clearing. More screams and more thrashing.

Tevy didn't have time to wonder who would chase and tackle a ripper barehanded in the woods. The fighters from the bus were arriving and might shoot him if he weren't careful, and for a moment he knew true terror.

"Human, human!" he called as gunfire discharged all around him with dazzling and disorienting muzzle flashes.

"Not Vlad's Blood. St. John's!" shouted Kayla and Radu together.

Tevy joined them. "St. John's, St. John's!"

By this time the rippers were crashing away through the forest as men and women Tevy recognized arrived, taking cover behind trees and shooting at the retreating forms. He didn't know their individual names, but he knew that Joyce's Raiders had come to their rescue. He knelt close to Kayla, her hand still holding his Glock down, the scent of her sweat in his nostrils, their breath mixing.

Her face was so close to his that when he turned his head his lips were inches from her cheek. She turned to look at him and they both breathed deeply, Tevy was suddenly drawn to her, curious to lean in just that little bit until their lips touched. It wasn't so much that he was trying to kiss her as just to commune with her on their success, celebrate that they were still alive. The spell, less than a second old, broke.

Someone had caught Kayla's attention, and she looked up sharply, her lips missing Tevy's—perhaps even unaware. "Joyce, over here," she called.

Tevy stood with Kayla as Joyce ran up through the forest like a deer, effortlessly identifying and jumping obstructions in the dark. Tevy was impressed that a woman so old, over thirty at least, could be so fit and energetic.

"How many?" she asked, her Uzi pointed to the sky, her eyes searching the forest.

"Over a hundred," Kayla said between deep breaths.

Joyce nodded. "Jeff," she called. "We should pull back out of the woods. They'll come back."

"Got it," came the reply from farther down the line in the darkness. Orders were shouted and gunfire ceased, and when it did, it was apparent that the fight to the north was over as well. The whole forest became eerily quiet as if even the crickets had been shocked to silence.

Joyce turned to head back with the others, when Kayla called out, "Joyce, he was here. I saw him again."

Joyce turned sharply, stalking back with an angry look that went from Kayla to Tevy. "You're sure?" It sounded more like an accusation.

Kayla nodded quickly. "Certain. He took out another ripper, maybe a few." She nodded in Tevy's direction. "He almost shot him."

"Who are we talking about here?" Tevy looked from one to the other, but neither woman looked at him or spoke for a full ten seconds.

"No one." Joyce fixed her gaze on Tevy. "No one, okay?" She turned and marched back toward the buses.

But Tevy didn't buy that for a second. He added it to the list of mysteries about Joyce's Raiders.

———

Tevy waited until near dawn and so did Joyce, but she didn't know that he was watching. He hadn't had his eyes on Joyce every minute because he'd gone on several more patrols with Kayla and Radu, but Tevy kept tabs on where she was hanging out, which was usually at a makeshift command post south of the buses.

Kayla's little team had completed their latest patrol and were grabbing a sandwich from a folding table set up as a lunch counter, the teenage volunteers making the sandwiches as fast as the troops could eat. Since evading the rippers was no longer an option, the generators ran full throttle, and lights on top of the buses illuminated the forest, casting deep shadows. The rippers had not come back.

"It's very close to dawn," said Radu in between mouthfuls, gesturing with his sandwich at the false dawn in the southeast. "This is good."

Kayla nodded as she finished hers. "Close, but I can't wait. I have to go on a little relief patrol by myself, so don't follow me this time, guys. I'll be back in a squirt."

She picked a dark area with no lights shining directly on it and walked into the forest.

That was when Tevy noticed Joyce, a bus length to the south, strolling casually toward the trees as if bent on a similar mission, but he wasn't fooled. There was a purpose here that had nothing to do with the call of nature.

"I gotta go too," he said to Radu.

He reached over his shoulder and drew his shotgun. "I'll head that way so I don't bump into her."

Now he practiced his quiet step, which he had gotten much better at as the night progressed. Check ground with foot, edge onto soft ground or rock, and step. Faster time could be made over the occasional hump of moss-covered granite. He'd learned to steer for pines and spruces, because even though their dead lower branches would snap if you pushed through them, the bed of needles below was soft and quiet as long as you were careful where you put your feet.

He might have lost her, for Joyce moved quickly, but near a clearing she halted and started calling in a strangled whisper, "Bert. Bert, are you out here?"

Tevy pressed close to the trunk of a large pine, his heart pounding as if he'd been running. That name! Surely she couldn't be conjuring a ghost. He watched Joyce's form, which was barely illuminated by the lights from the buses. After a few minutes more of her calling to no avail, Tevy gently released his breath. Nothing—no one—was going to answer.

A hoarse voice spoke from the darkness on the far side of the clearing. "I have to hurry. It's almost dawn."

Quiet as a mouse. Tevy froze, hardly daring to breath. She had conjured a ghost.

"How did you get down here?" Joyce asked as a figure strode into the clearing, stopping several feet from her in the moon shadow of a tree. Tevy could hardly make him out in that shadow and would not have known he was there if not for his arrival.

"I drove. You guys did all the work clearing the highway before sunset, and I never have trouble finding a car."

Was that laughter?

"You shouldn't come with us," Joyce said. "You know where we're going."

"Yes. I just don't know why. Everything is going well up here for you. Food, shelter." The voice had a rough quality, as if the vocal cords didn't get much use, or the use they did get involved a lot of shouting and screaming.

"Chicago's in trouble—big trouble," Joyce said. "If it falls what'll be left? We've lost the east coast and the west, and how long do you think St. John's can thrive? It can't get any bigger, and we can't repopulate the damn country if the rippers control everything."

"But Bobs, Joyce. You gotta be very careful of her. She has her own motives, her own plans."

"I've always known that, even before you, but she's right when she says that we can't last without Chicago. It'll just be a matter of time before the rippers sweep up through Duluth and International Falls, and then they'll swing down to take out Thunder Bay. When nothing else is left, they'll come for St. John's."

"Then you can't be angry at me for following. If it's that important."

"But what can you do down there against an army?" Joyce hefted her Uzi. "A bullet in the right place can kill even you, Mr. Demon of St. John's."

A low chuckle, just a shade manic, came from the ripper, the man, whatever. "I'd heard they called me the demon. I guess I don't look much like my former self." He stepped forward out of the moon shadow. Tevy tried to draw in his breath but discovered he had clamped one hand over his mouth and nose in his surprise. *Quiet as a mouse.* Even when shocked he knew how to stay silent. He relaxed and drew a slow careful breath through his nostrils.

Tevy knew the man, and while he was gaunter than Tevy recalled, it was definitely Bertrand Allan. His body was clothed, but it was far slimmer than any of the photos that Bobs had posted all over the basement of the church, photos designed to inspire the fight against the rippers.

"You look worse than ever, Bert." Joyce's voice cracked and Tevy frowned. That rugged leader, the one who always seemed angry at him, neared tears? She had seemed so emotionless.

"I starve. Ripper blood, it keeps me going, but it doesn't fill me. There's no bang. Joyce, I'm following you to Chicago. There are unfinished things there for me too. I haven't been back in a couple of years. You can't control me."

"I never wanted to." Joyce took a steadying breath—even Tevy heard that from his hiding place. "Just don't get messed up in the fight. Don't go charging in like you always do. That's what got you into this... this condition."

"I'll watch over you. It's dawn."

It didn't look like dawn to Tevy, but the creature fled before Joyce could even say goodbye. The sobs began slowly, building quietly only to be choked off. She turned and headed back for the highway, wiping at her cheeks as she marched within an arms length of Tevy. If she'd looked his way she'd have seen him, but he was still and quiet and thinking.

How was this possible? Everyone said that Bertrand Allan, the Savior of Chicago, had died in the fire that destroyed Vlad the Scourge in the mountain. But Tevy had no doubt that he had just seen him, had just seen the man who pulled him from the closet in a burning house. And he had no doubt that the man was now a ripper.

Bishop Alvarez had been planning to beatify Bertrand Allan, the first step to sainthood. But saints aren't supposed to still be alive, and they sure as hell weren't supposed to be rippers. Bobs would not be happy.

10

CHICAGO

Kayla had visited three big cities during her life before the end: Winnipeg, Toronto and Chicago. Of the three, Chicago was by far the biggest, densest and had the most to offer. It had also been the most terrifying to a small town girl, and that was before the rippers.

Kayla knew that it wouldn't be the same city she and her parents had toured when she was fourteen. Tevy had told them that the rippers took over the city government and the police department first so that the Loop was completely ripper territory. He said they even used to raise the drawbridges on the river during the day—those that still worked—to make it harder for loyalist humans to get in and raid, and difficult for the ripper's human slaves to escape or for Daylight Brigades to desert.

But she hadn't expected the emptiness as the buses rolled through miles and miles of abandoned suburbs. Rusting cars lined the highway, and the side streets were coated with mud, which Tevy explained was actually eight years of fall leaves, unraked and choking the sewers. The streets were remarkably litter-free.

"Rippers don't eat chocolate bars," Tevy said when she pointed this out. "There's a lot of garbage out there because the city stopped picking it up before the end, but it's mostly under the mud now."

There was less mud as they got closer to Chicago proper, simply because there were fewer mature trees than in the suburbs. But that was changing. Saplings pushed up everywhere: on front lawns, through cracks in the sidewalk, and even in the middle of streets. They surrounded houses, perhaps because the former flower gardens under windows and near front doors provided fertilized soil.

"How many died in the famines?" Kayla stared out the bus's window, wiped somewhat clean a few days ago while they were camped at International Falls. They rolled past street after empty street.

"They say millions," said Radu, who stood in the aisle and stared out the window, too. Although his seat was in the next row up, he often wandered the aisle, restless and bored with sitting. He shrugged before he continued speaking. "But who is there left to do the counting. It is a mystery, this number. How many are rippers? How many are traitors and how many are dead?"

Tevy seemed unusually silent, his eyes staring not out the window but at the back of the seat in front of him, as if a disturbing movie played on the blank screen.

"What do you think, Tevy?" Kayla had learned over the last two weeks of travel that when Tevy was silent he usually had the most useful information to share.

He looked startled at the mention of his name and glanced out the window before he slumped back into the seat. "I started out as a scrounger, me and the other Brat Pack kids. No food if we didn't bring it back to St. Mike's. The rippers cleaned out the grocery stores so they'd have food for their slaves and all." Tevy pulled up his shotgun from the floor and began wiping the spotless barrel with a rag. "We stayed away from the fridges, 'course. Mostly went into basements looking for canned food."

"Yah," said Kayla. "We used to do that through Atherley too."

Tevy looked to her in surprise. "So you saw lots of bodies too I guess."

It was Kayla's turn to be surprised. "No. The houses were just empty unless maybe there was a ripper in the basement."

"Guess that's why you got so many rippers up there in the middle of nowhere. Must have made too many. Down here it's different." He pointed at a long street of bungalows, houses with big lawns that would have been considered the home of the future in middle of the twentieth century. "Houses like that, at least one or two dead bodies in better than half of them. They were pretty fresh back then, back when we were starving. Wouldn't have gone in their houses otherwise."

"Holy crap." Kayla tried to absorb the numbers and then noted the dead look on Tevy's face, the look of someone with memories too horrible to contemplate, someone who just blocked them out.

She wondered if she ever wore that expression, like when she remembered the McMansion in Atherley with the sweeping circular staircase in the front hall. The second-floor corridor was open to the front hall, so a railing up there had provided the support for four ropes, one for each of the two children and one for each parent. Did the children willingly hang themselves? The flies coated the bodies so densely, the stink was so intense, that she promptly barfed on the shining wood floor before turning to flee out the door. That was what Tevy meant by fresh, she was sure. Five years later she dared to enter the same house through the back door and ventured a peek into the front hall. Skeletal remains had been scattered around the floors, and the ropes, still with nooses intact, hung empty.

"We were lucky at St. John's," she said. "We farmed the fields around the Keep, and when the rippers tried to burn them the first fall, they found out that a fifty cal can do a lot of damage, and that we don't just hide in the Keep at night."

"We didn't starve too badly at St. Mike's." Tevy now watched the dusty storefronts of the street flash past, some of the windows smashed but most not. "We scroungers made sure of that. We went anywhere. But others, the beggars, well, the bishop could only do so much back then."

Kayla nodded as if she understood, but she was only beginning to get an inkling of how desperate things had been down here during the famines. What had they done to survive at St. Mike's? Surely there must've been thousands coming to beg for food during the day and shelter at night. How had they kept the peace, kept St. Mike's from being overrun?

"How do you feed everyone now?" she asked.

"There are farmers out there, again." Tevy returned to cleaning his gun. "They get protection from us, and they pay in food."

"But how do you protect them?"

"We send patrols all through the countryside, sweeping basements and crypts for rippers all the time. We just keep it so clean that the rippers can't get to the farms to burn 'em. You saw the gate, right? We got those circling a bunch of land up north where all the horse farms and rich peoples' houses used to be. Rippers can't drive in, and they can't cross country in numbers."

Across the Kennedy Expressway, Kayla had seen the gate, a medieval-looking checkpoint with a stone tower on either side of the road and a double iron door that the bus could just get through when open. The rest of the highway was blocked by a thick stone wall, anchored by two more towers, one on each shoulder. At night, rippers would have to scale walls three stories high to get up to the garrison that defended the gate, and Tevy had pointed out the machineguns on the top of each tower. A wrecked transport truck, a shell burnt down to its axles, lay shoved aside just south of the gate. Everywhere there were signs of battle.

A ripper truck, Tevy had said. *Tried to ram the gate but didn't figure on the rocket.*

"But how much land for farms do you have?" asked Radu. "How many do you feed?"

Tevy shrugged. "Everybody in Chicago who does their part. Not so many of us at all anymore, not after the Third Great Famine."

Kayla tried to recall her economics classes and found herself fascinated by the market. "How does Bobs decide who gets food and who doesn't?"

Tevy looked up at her, apparently to see if she was serious, judging by his expression. Her cheeks warmed with embarrassment, but that only made her angry. It wasn't a stupid question.

"Soldier's rations for me, but there's the bounty on rippers too. Every confirmed kill gets you some extra pay. If you can't fight, you just have to do something useful."

"But what if you can't do something useful?"

Tevy looked genuinely puzzled. "Like if you're too old or too wounded?"

"Yeah, like that."

"If you got wounded fighting the rippers, we fighters take of our own, share our rations. If you're old you need your family."

Kayla wondered what her socialist parents would think of this harsh environment. "What if you don't have family?"

Tevy shrugged. "I guess you head out of the city and scrounge."

Radu also looked uncomfortable. "So you have no beggars."

"No beggars. Bobs says they'd drag us down. Bishop Alvarez wants to set up a monastery though, one that can take in the useless."

The words burst from her lips before she could stop them or moderate her tone. "Holy fuck, you people are shameless."

Tevy looked up, surprise showing in his eyes. "What? We'd all be dead if we didn't stay strong. And they kept all us orphans, didn't they? A lot of the other churches didn't, not unless their parents were in their church. I saw other kids scrounging in the early days, kids not from the Brat Pack at St. Mike's or any other stronghold, kids with nowhere to go. Ripper snacks. Some of them made it, most of them didn't. We were lucky to have the bishop take us in and watch over us."

Kayla decided not to fight about this ruthlessness. She craved to know more about how the city still worked. "So who owns that gate we passed. Does everyone take orders from Bobs?"

"We got the biggest following if that's what you mean." Tevy looked proud now. "Over a two hundred block houses follow Bobs, more than any other church in the city."

"But what do the other churches do for food?"

"They either got their own farms or they buy food from us when there's extra."

Kayla still couldn't understand the payment system. "How do you pay without money?"

"Ammo. Bobs will trade a lot of food for ammo. If a church has got no ammo, they can send troops to our army, and then they send their rations, what they don't eat, back to their families. Or a church can join. St. James joined with us last year."

"How do they join?" Kayla wanted to return to Barry St. John's benevolent dictatorship more than ever. This place was simply medieval, and Tevy didn't even see it. She had to remind herself that he was eight years younger when the world ended. Maybe this just didn't seem so strange to him.

"Join?" Tevy had finished cleaning the shotgun and put it back in the leather holster. "Simple. Just convert to the Chicago Catholic Church and agree to join Bobs' army. It's all good. About twenty churches joined us so far. We're all Christian, after all."

"What about Muslims or Jews or the Ericsians."

Tevy nodded and looked thoughtful for a bit. "Uhm, never thought about it. I just figured they wanted to stay on their own. I mean the Ericsians, they don't need to join. They're way organized, maybe even better than us. They got block houses and their own farm country out on the Prairies. I think there's a lot of them, but they don't come to Chicago much, only one fort that I know of over at Wright. Used to be a college."

The bus changed gears, idling down as it pulled onto an off ramp, and suddenly Kayla could see all of Chicago's downtown, and for just a moment in the bright sun, she could pretend that it was twelve years ago, the first time she'd seen those immensely high office buildings shining in the distance. She wanted to believe they were still full of people pushing paper, making phone calls, and tapping away at their keyboards.

But even from this distance, she could tell that the windows were dull with grime, that some were missing, and several buildings had holes with blackened edges from artillery or rockets. Some buildings had the office windows bricked in: ripper strongholds. The Willis Tower rose above all, so high that it looked immune from the destruction, but Kayla knew from Tevy that this was the center of ripper control, deep in the no-go zone. Except that he went. What was that like?

Margaret marched down the aisle of the bus, not like a child running to play, but one sent on a mission. She climbed into Kayla's lap and gave her a perfunctory kiss on the cheek. "Hi, Mommy," she said very loudly while looking at Tevy to judge his reaction. She leaned in close to Kayla's ear and whispered, "Mommy told me to say that."

Kayla could see Joyce and Jeff standing near the front of the bus looking back their way. She wanted to raise her eyebrows and shake her head to indicate that this wasn't a good idea, but the last thing she needed to do was draw more attention from Tevy. She looked over but he was staring out the window, apparently oblivious to the charade put on for his benefit.

Margaret slipped off Kayla's lap and headed back up the bus to Joyce, leaving Radu and Kayla to exchange a glance, Radu's eyes raised high in disbelief. Kayla could tell he knew this wouldn't fool anyone who could remember their mother, but what about an orphan raised in a pack of kids? The other problem was that too many people were in on the secret. How long before someone from St. John's made an incautious comment?

"Must've been tough." Tevy's gaze stayed with the city streets as they rolled by, a retail area before the end, now a lot of smashed windows, the sidewalks liberally sprinkled with crystalline shards.

Kayla wished she understood this strange young man. Sometimes he spoke as if completing a conversation in his own head, one that she was somehow supposed to have been party too. "What?" she asked.

"Being pregnant at the end. Having to fight the rippers with a big belly." Tevy looked away from the window and met Kayla's eyes, and she fought to keep the panic from her face. She wasn't good at lying.

"Oh, my friend Rachel took good care of me." Kayla rewrote history as best she good, taking Rachel's experiences from last year and trying to imagine them as her own from eight years ago. "I hated it, though, hated having to stay behind the walls as if I was some fragile princess while everyone else went on ripper raids. That really bummed me out, especially 'cause I was sick just all the time."

Tevy studied her so closely that Kayla had trouble not blushing. This made her angry and that could help.

"Who was the father?"

Kayla let the anger surface, and it came naturally. "None of your fucking business." But she thought of Ted, the young Ojibwa man who had saved her life, first by giving her a ride to Sioux Lookout in his battered Jeep, and a second time by insisting on giving her another lift back to Atherley. She often wondered what became of him after he flew with his tribe to the high lakes, and she often caught herself looking across the fields in the early morning as if he might come wandering in to join her at St. John's. She would take him to be the father of her child if she were ever to have one. In this imaginary world she was building for Tevy, she pretended that she and Ted made the mistake of having a passionate encounter on the couch at his gran's before they parted forever.

Tevy still frowned at Kayla, but her blush was gone, to be replaced with an angry frown. Surely that would carry the lie? Kayla was spared further scrutiny when the bus pulled up to another medieval-like gate, except that it was constructed with poured concrete rather than stone and anchored at each end by older buildings that might have once been retail stores or early twentieth-century apartments. Now their windows on the ground floor were bricked in, and circular razor wire hung between the first and second floors to make it difficult for rippers to scale the walls.

Radu leaned down so that he could look up through the window as they passed under the wall. "Does this go all the way around?"

Tevy shook his head. "We wish. We just got the main roads like this covered, but everything else on the perimeter is just row houses and whatever got bulldozed. They cleared some good fields of fire around the St. Mike's cantonment just after I joined the Brat Pack. Rippers can get into Old Town all right, just not with cars. Tanks, though, that's what I worry about. Some of the streets are just blocked with piles of stuff from the bulldozing. Tanks can climb piles."

The bus stopped in a large square in front of a gothic church, it's bell tower rising high. Kayla stepped into the afternoon sunlight, stretching in relief and staring up at the church. It was old world, for sure, but given that it was the center of humans in Chicago, given its huge reputation, she had been expecting something more like St. Peter's in Rome. This brick edifice, while grand in a regular urban neighborhood, was not as large or imposing. She knew the history from Joyce, that it had been built by German immigrants before the Great Chicago Fire and then rebuilt even better after the fire. Their passion showed in the ornate flourishes, yet the brown brick was local and practical.

Joyce had said that before Vlad it was a twelve-hour drive to St. John's. They had taken nearly two weeks, although most of that was clearing the highway of ripper roadblocks down to International Falls. There were only a few between there and Duluth, and the closer they came to Chicago, the faster the trip. General Roberts, the leader Tevy called Bobs, had been clearing the way for them.

Kayla looked up in awe at the church, not so much because of the architecture, but because of what St. Mike's represented. This was the center of resistance to the rippers in the early days of Vlad. This was where Bertrand Allan had planned the Battle of the Mountain. In this square, one of the first riots against ripper police took place, and she recognized it even now from the grainy YouTube videos that she had seen so many years before, back when people were just discovering that the rippers existed, let alone that they had infiltrated the governments first.

On the far side of the square stood the white statue of St. Michael, but near where the buses stopped was a new and larger monument: a tall pillar of stone on top of which sat a stone triangle, the symbol of the mountain and the memorial to Bertrand Allan for his sacrifice for humanity. Kayla stared up at it now, thinking of the man she met in the basement of Atherley College. What did he think of this monument to his passing?

"Better watch your daughter." Tevy had come to stand beside Kayla and look at the monument, but now he pointed to where Margaret ran ahead of Joyce toward the statue of St. Michael.

"Oh, she's okay with her aunt Joyce." But Kayla felt the blush returning to her cheeks. How could she end up having to fake the role of mother? She wasn't one and wasn't the least interested in being one.

"You're very trusting," Tevy said. "My mother wouldn't have let me out of her sight for a second in a strange new place."

"Well, I'm not your mother."

Tevy shrugged and turned to their bus, which now had its luggage bays open, to retrieve his small pack from the pile before others could start crowding around on the same mission. He had already put his back holster on and stowed his shotgun so that the pistol grip was handy by his shoulder. He turned and stood awkwardly in front of Kayla, as if suffering some internal debate.

"They'll clear a blockhouse for you guys, maybe Emile's." He pointed to a three-story brick building that faced St. Mike's head on across the square. "I guess I'll be seeing you around."

"Wait." Kayla suddenly didn't want him to go, and it bothered her. Sure he was cute and all, but he was just a teenager. Why should she be disappointed at no longer having to watch over him, even spy on him.

"Listen," she said, awkwardly sticking out her hand to shake. "Thanks for your help and all on the way down. You're a frigging good fighter."

It was Tevy's turn to blush, and seeing him look vulnerable somehow pleased Kayla. So he did have emotions, this strange, serious, and underfed man.

"So are you—a damn good fighter." He started to turn away but then stopped, his eyes up on the monument and his top teeth coming out to bit at his lower lip while he thought.

Kayla held her breath, for she sensed that he had something very important to tell her, something she should hear, and that he needed a moment to find the words.

"You're a really great fighter," he said again, turning his blue eyes to meet her gaze. "But you're a lousy liar."

11

AMONG BELIEVERS

Tevy ran down the stairs to the church basement, desperately hoping to find some of the Brat Pack around. He wasn't disappointed. He'd hardly rounded the corner into the common area when a shout went up from Elliot.

"There he is!"

A bunch of the smaller children, the five- to ten-year-olds, had been sitting in a circle on the gray carpet, one he and Elliot had proudly liberated from a Home Depot several years before and lugged back to cover the concrete floor in the common area. Subsequent raids carpeted the whole basement, even the dorms. Tevy hardly had time to take in the room, the heavy wood shutters open to let in the light, with the bars throwing shadows across the floor. The gray office dividers that separated the dorms from the common area had new art on them, indicating that Helen must have found someone to scrounge an art store or a school for fresh paper and paints. Talented children had been busy.

The younger children now charged Tevy, and he swung several into the air to squeals of delight. Some of the older kids, the ten plus, came over to knock knuckles and admire the new shotgun and holster. Elliot came over last, and Tevy had to resist the urge to give him an undignified, back-pounding hug. The unruly red hair, the freckles, and the big grin with the crooked teeth were all such a welcome sight. Tevy settled for a high five and a knuckle knock.

"Dude," Tevy said as he waded through children, heading for the boys' dorm and his cot. "Good to see you."

Elliot grinned and shook his head, putting out a hand to stop him from passing the curtain into the dorm. "You sinner. Didn't you know we're not allowed to say 'dude' anymore?" Some of the smaller children giggled as if Elliot had made a fart joke.

"What?"

Elliot nodded and couldn't contain himself. "Should I?"

Several of the older boys nodded, and the children all huddle into a circle around him.

"These are the words we must never say, for fear of angering God." His smile belied the seriousness of this statement. Elliot began a string of profanity, the usual like the f-word coming first, followed by body parts and combinations—these Bishop Alvarez had punished them for since the formation of the Brat Pack. But then Elliot launched into ones that were new to Tevy: blood, stinking blood, Vald's blood, Bertrand's blood, and finally yo and dude.

Elliot finished this litany of profanity with a devilish wave, his hands rising as if he were a ripper with claws, ready to pounce. The kids broke into laughter and scattered to run screaming in circles around the common room, except for one small girl, Mia, who fell out of the crowd, weeping, curling in the fetal position to bawl.

Tevy pick her up and sat in a cracked La-Z-Boy, cradling her on his lap. He remembered when her parents died on a raid, how the other families in their blockhouse brought her to the church, saying they had no food to spare for orphans. Tevy had rocked her many times in that same chair then, too. It had been two years ago, and she had just turned four.

"Make him stop," she said. "The bishop says saying those words is like calling Vlad to send rippers up from hell."

Tevy almost said, "Dude," in accusation to Elliot, but he caught himself just in time.

"It's hard, isn't it," said Elliot with a grin.

"But why that word? It's totally harmless."

Elliot sat on a stool next to the La-Z-Boy. "Little ears might not want to hear." He nodded down at Mia. The other children had settled down from the screaming and gathered around and the questions started to fly.

"Did you kill any rippers, Tev?"

"I heard you flew a plane."

"Why do they live up there? Are they sinners?"

"How many rippers did you kill?"

"Did any get close? Did you see anyone die?"

Tevy gave Mia a hug and he whispered in her ear, "I'll never let the rippers anywhere near you. I swear I'll keep you safe."

He was about to respond to the questions when Helen's voice called over the hubbub. "Let the man speak!"

The kids parted way for her, and she arrived smelling of stale tobacco and looking smaller and more bent than even two weeks ago. Tevy deposited Mia on Elliot's lap and gave Helen a warm hug.

"Good boy," she said as if he were still ten. "You brought yourself back and you brought my friends, too. Very good work."

"But did you kill any rippers, Tev?" persisted one boy's voice from the back of the crowd.

"Yes. I killed eight for certain, maybe more."

The room erupted in cheers, and some of the younger ones again started running in circles screaming.

"That's quite enough!" shouted Helen, her arms out like Moses preparing to part the waves. "Time to wash up for dinner."

It took the help of several of the teenage children to quiet the younger ones, but when they were all upstairs and outside to use the latrines, Tevy sat with Amanda and Elliot and several other teenage members of the Brat Pack in the common room to get caught up. Elliot passed around a flask of strong hooch.

"It's all about the traitors," Elliot said. "They caught a bunch of them on a scouting patrol one day over in the west end and they were all 'dude' this and 'yo' that. It's how they talk in California I guess."

Tevy shook his head to clear it from the fumes of the hooch. "But that's how we talk."

"Sort of, but different. There was more of it and more slang that I didn't even know." Elliot took his hooch flask back from Amanda. "Anyway, the bishop added those words to the list. I think it's really because if we don't use them and the traitors do, they'll be easier to catch. Just have to listen to them to know they're traitors and not Loyalists. That's what we're supposed to call ourselves now, Loyalists to humanity and God."

Helen hurried back into the common room and stormed right up to Elliot, snatching the metal flask from his hand. "Jesus boy. Don't be passing around Emile's hooch so late in the afternoon. You should be saving this for dawn." She took a long drink and passed the flask back to him. "You," she pointed a finger at Tevy. "I hope your head is still clear, because Bobs and the bishop want to see you right away."

Tevy left his pack of dirty laundry on the floor and headed for the staircase with Helen, who despite her age was able to climb at a careful pace. Tevy matched her slow progress so they could chat.

"It's not just me that's glad you're back, boy," she said when she paused for breath at the landing. "A lot of the younger kids have ears, and the rumors are frightening. They took you being gone as a bad sign, because you're their fighting hero, their protector. The one who stands between them and the rippers."

Tevy felt the weight of being one of the oldest members of the Brat Pack. There had been few orphans older than him in the last days of Vlad, because any teenagers simply joined a blockhouse. There had been a few eleven and twelve-year-olds, but some died while scrounging for food, making the mistake of going into a basement without the backup of someone like Elliot or Amanda. Others married into a blockhouse by sixteen as a way of getting out of the confined dorms of the church basement, some even being forced out by the bishop if a new influx of orphans required space.

Tevy had been allowed to stay because he was Bobs' scout, but that could only last so long. He and Elliot had been conspiring with some of the other teens to start their own blockhouse, but the only way the bishop would allow them to share it with the girls would be if marriages took place. That meant choosing a mate. Courting and competition was complicated in the confines of the dorms.

Helen renewed her assault on the stairs, shoving away Tevy's hand when he reached out to take her arm. "I'm not dead yet." But her smile proved that she wasn't angry. "You need to watch out for yourself. If you died it would strike terror into the hearts of some of the little ones. Knowing you're out their killing rippers makes them feel safe."

Tevy knew she was right and it pricked a nerve. "Believe me, I want to live, too."

They reached the top of the stairs and Helen caught his arm, not for support, but to get his attention. "Then don't always charge straight at the rippers when you see them." She poked a finger at his forehead. "Think." She looked into his eyes to see if her point had sunk in, but she shook her head. "You're so like him. It's freaky."

"Like who?" But Helen pushed through the heavy wooden door into the church.

The late afternoon sun streamed through the upper stained glass windows, the lower ones having been bricked up during the days of Vlad the Scourge. Tevy thought he noted a few new bullet holes high up, which could only mean that rippers were sending a message of intimidation and invitation, since those shots couldn't have hit people. They were meant to lure out a patrol to ambush.

Tevy looked above the windows and struggled to remember the blue and gold ceiling of the church, so intricate and so brilliant the first night he was here, when the church was packed with refugees. A gray film of soot from years of candles now coated the ceiling, dulling the colors and the paintings, although the sacred heart with the sword through it, Tevy's favorite, was still clearly visible.

Helen genuflected in front of the altar, and Tevy did as well, crossing himself automatically as he rose, but a gesture of Helen's reminded him that he had nearly forgotten the new motion he was supposed to do after crossing himself: the Sign of the Mountain. Touch three fingers to one's left shoulder, forehead, and right shoulder. This was the bishop's decree last fall on the seventh anniversary of the Battle of the Mountain, that everyone should thank God for the victory over the anti-Christ, Vlad.

They crossed the altar and passed the tabernacle, genuflecting again, on their way into the rectory, heading up for the bishops' council chamber, but they never reached their destination. Shouts stopped them in the paneled corridor, dulled at first by the deep carpet until a door halfway along opened and Joyce burst out of a room closely followed by Jeff and Kayla.

Bobs' voice chased her. "You can't just turn those buses around and leave."

She rushed out of the room, her hair cropped even shorter and her Beretta 92 in a holster on her hip. It suddenly occurred to Tevy that Kayla and Bobs were close in age, and he had to rethink what he thought about both women. Did this make Kayla seem older or Bobs seem younger?

Joyce turned in fury. "Just watch me. I didn't come down here to stay anyway. We came down to fight just for the summer season because that little shit convinced me it was the right thing to do." She was now extending a finger to point her accusation at Tevy. "Before winter me and my Raiders will be going back to St. John's come hell or high water, but while we're here we fight together and we live together or we're on the way right now."

Jeff stepped between the two women before Bobs could retort, his FN slung over his shoulder, his camouflage vest open in the Chicago heat.

"Listen, Bobs," he said. "There's plenty of houses we can convert to a blockhouse for the Raiders. The rest of the St. John's people, the immigrants, they're going to want to mingle anyway. A lot of them are looking for wives, so you can billet them wherever you want. But the Raiders, we've fought together and lived together since the end. You don't split us up."

Bobs put her hands on her hips and turned her attention on Jeff. "You won't have time to do that before sunset, so where do you suggest I put you?"

The bishop, in a simple black cassock, strode out of the conference room and stopped in the middle of the corridor. "They can sleep in the church tonight, of course. That way they'll all be together."

Bobs looked ready to fight, but the bishop shook his head in a way that Tevy recognized: no argument. She shrugged instead. "Whatever. Thanks for coming out."

Joyce and Jeff left without further word, and Helen hurried after them. Kayla followed them too, but Joyce stopped her, whispering something in her ear and looking back at Tevy before she turned away. Kayla looked after her, tapping her foot a few times before she made up her mind and walked in Tevy's direction, clearly wanting to talk to him, perhaps about his liar comment, but before she could, Bobs turned her attention on him.

"Good work," she said. "I want to hear all about it. Everything. But right now I need you to load up and go out fast before sunset."

Bad news and worse. He glanced at Kayla, wishing she weren't hanging so close. Somehow he didn't want to tell Bobs that Bertrand Allan was undead and a ripper with Kayla listening. He debated pushing for a private meeting, but he knew that look in Bobs' eyes: she was in a big hurry and had no time for him.

The worse news was that he had hoped for an evening with the older Brat Pack kids, but after days on and off a bus, perhaps a chance to move and maybe have some adventure would be a good thing. "Where am I going?"

"The Erics." Bobs glared at Bishop Alvarez, and Tevy interpreted the look as warning to the cleric that on this point she would accept no argument.

The bishop heaved a sigh and crossed his arms in judgment. "I don't like aligning ourselves with these heretics."

"I don't have a fucking choice, and I'm sure as hell not going to talk about it now. This is tactical. This is my decision." She turned back to Tevy. "I want you to head over to the Erics. Don't worry, I told them by radio that you'd be coming, so they won't shoot from their walls if you get there after dark. Your job is to do the same thing you did at St. John's: convince Mabruke that it's in his best interest to join us."

Tevy fought to keep the amazement off his face. "They'll never convert to Catholicism. They're heretics."

"This isn't about converting anymore." She shot a withering look at Bishop Alvarez, who sighed again and turned his back to swish off to his study at the end of the corridor. Bobs turned back to Tevy. "Like I said, they don't have to frigging convert, but when the offensive comes, we've all gotta be working as one army. The rippers will be, believe me."

"Should I set up a meeting between you and Mabruke?"

"I'm not going over there and he's not coming over here, so no." Bobs crossed her arms under her small breasts. "You haven't been back long enough to hear the rumors, I guess. Tevy, the rippers could be coming tonight. There's been a lot of movement down there, and some bastard traitors have been raiding up north of the Loop yesterday and today, grabbing people and taking them as sacrifices back to the rippers. I don't have time now, but you need to move hard and fast before sunset to the Wright Sanctuary and get Mabruke onside and handing out the ammo to his people. By midnight."

"What if he won't listen to me?"

"Just be yourself, Tevy." She leaned in close, dropping her voice to make it difficult for Kayla to hear. "You're my secret weapon. You remind people of the man who saved my life."

Tevy knew not to ask who that was, because while they had learned in Sunday School in detail about all the other heroes of the Battle of the Mountain, Bobs had kept her own history out of the lesson plan.

"Okay. I'm on it," he said.

Bobs nodded. "I knew you would be. Don't travel alone this time though. Take a couple of the Brat Pack with you. You pick 'em, but only the fast ones, the ones who can run or ride. Emile's got word to give you all the ammo you want." She held up one finger. "Don't let me down."

"I never do."

12

NINE MILES

The carpeting of the corridor didn't hide the hurried footfalls behind Tevy. Kayla spoke before he could ask why she was following him.

"I want to go with you," she said as she drew alongside, matching his hurried pace.

Tevy looked over to see if she was kidding. With her vest open to reveal her sweat-stained tank-top, she looked younger, closer to his age. Could he really be so attracted to an older woman, one in her mid-twenties?

"Why the hell?" He led the way into the church, stopping to genuflect at the tabernacle, an action she mimicked in a hurried fashion. She got the Sign of the Mountain backwards, and her attempts to fix the gesture made it look more like a circle.

"Because I've just spent a week on a bus and I need to get out," Kayla said, continuing to chase him as he rose and hurried off the altar.

There was something else, some other reason. Tevy couldn't put his finger on it, but he was sure she hadn't told him the whole truth. And she looked very excited, ecstatic. Maybe she had a thing for him? Maybe she wanted to be around him. But Tevy quashed that hope by remembering Joyce whispering in Kayla's ear. And there was that lie about the girl, Margaret. Whose daughter was that really?

Tevy glanced up at the angle of the sun through the stained-glass windows before he headed for the stairs to the basement. "We've got nine miles to go in about an hour and a half. It'll be running the whole time. You any good at running?"

"I'm good."

He led her down to the common room and was delighted to find Elliot and Amanda chatting on the couch. They looked cozy, and Tevy had to repress a surge of jealousy, reminding himself that it was a sin.

"Perfect," he said. "I'm going on a run for Bobs. Looking for two volunteers."

Elliot practically leapt off the couch. "Finally, some action. I don't think the general likes me very much, because she's given me shit all to do since you left. Whoops!" he covered his mouth and feigned horror. "I used one of the words."

"I'm fast." Amanda stood and met Tevy's eyes with her own, a challenge. "But why don't we take the bikes? Elliot and I've got a new shortcut out of the cantonment."

Tevy wondered what else she and Elliot had been up to while he'd been up north. He pushed that thought down as unproductive. Stay with mission. "Let's go load up, then. Emile's supposed to give us whatever we want."

"Wow!" said Elliot. "We are fucked." Again he held his hand over his mouth in mock horror. "Dear, dear me," he said in a good imitation of Helen. "Who is that foul-mouthed boy?"

"Don't mind him," Tevy said to Kayla. "He always jokes before a raid. Let's go."

He led them through the opening in the office dividers and into the boys' dorm, almost every square foot of space taken up by cots or beds, all crammed together to allow for the maximum number of children. Beyond that a set of stairs ran down to the boiler room, now useless since the natural-gas-fired boiler had no source of fuel. Emile still talked about converting it to coal and rigging the boiler to generate electricity, too, so that the pump motors for the heating system could work. It took Tevy a few years of listening to Emile's drunken dreams before he understood that it was never going to happen. Emile didn't have the knowledge or a supply of coal.

But the old boiler room did make a great armory and gun shop, one Elliot vowed to take over when Emile got too old to keep it going. Tevy whistled as he hurried down the metal-grate stairs into the bowels of the boiler room. One barred window, high up on the wall even though it was below grade outside, filtered light into the room. Down at a desk in the corner, Emile sat cleaning a handgun with a dark rag. But that wasn't what had caught Tevy by surprise.

"When did all this get here?' he asked Elliot. Stacks of wooden and metal boxes filled every available space around the boiler until the furnace itself was lost to sight. Tevy only knew it was there from memory. Guns lined the wall above Emile's desk and more ran along the stone wall under the stairs.

"Just in time." Emile looked up from his work and gave a rosy-cheeked smile, one that would have fit Santa if he had a black beard and you caught him drunk in his basement off-season. "I heard you was back."

Tevy stood in the only open space in the basement, near Emile's old desk, and turned in a circle with his arms out, waving at the ammunition. "So the colonel finally came through."

Emile stood and gave Tevy a back-pounding drunken hug, almost unbalancing them both before he pulled back to study him, one hand still on Tevy's shoulder, Emile's hooch breath soaking the air around them. "I think you've grown. In just a couple of weeks, I think you've grown."

"Sorry to rush," Tevy said. "But we're on a run and Bobs said we could load up."

Emile waved an expansive arm at the shelving near his desk. "For once I can say take whatever you want. I got word this afternoon." The shelves held row after row of plastic bins, all neatly labeled with black marker on white tape: 9mm, .38, etc. Tevy hurried to the 9mm bin and started stuffing boxes of cartridges into the pockets of his vest. The others crowded around too, grabbing and clutching as if they were a pack of wolves fighting over a corpse. Tevy switched to the 12-gauge bin to load up for his Winchester.

"You kids want a drink before you head out?" Emile held up an old wine bottle, but the fumes were his hooch.

Elliot looked to Tevy hopefully. "It might steady our shot," he said.

"Maybe," said Tevy, "but we're not going to the target range. I need you clear-headed."

Elliot started reaching for the bottle anyway, but Emile pulled it back. "Tevy's right and he's your captain."

"And he's no fun."

"Thanks, Emile. I got lots to tell you when I get back." Tevy led the way up the stairs and out the side door to the street. They had only just started for the field when a dark-haired man walking along the wall of the church caught Tevy's attention. It was Radu, the Romanian who ended up stuck at St. John's at the end, the guy who fought so well beside he and Kayla that first night on the road.

"Hey, Rad!" Tevy called. "Up for some fun?"

Radu didn't take a second to decide. "Yes," he said. "This would be very good. It's already quite boring here, and I'm very tired of the sitting."

Elliot cast a suspicious glare. "He sounds like Vlad."

"Well he's not," Tevy said, before Elliot could put Radu on trial. "And you're just going to have to trust me that he's good."

"Okay, if you say so." Elliot pointed to Radu's sidearm and the M4 slung over his shoulder. "At least he's packing big time. Come on, this way."

Elliot led the way across the field, the remains of some of the bull-dozed houses still evident amongst the weeds: concrete blocks, cement floors, and occasionally gaping basements only half-filled with bricks and smashed two-by-fours. Just after Tevy's arrival at the church after his parents' murder, he watched the destruction of the houses on the closest streets, creating a clear field of fire for defenders of St. Mike's and putting a dangerous obstacle course with little cover as a barrier to rippers.

The Brat Pack, of course, knew a hundred safe routes through this mess of wonton destruction, and on the far side, dozens of bikes—many rusting but some cleaned and greased—waited in a line.

"Which one should I take?" asked Kayla.

Tevy looked up from picking his own ride to make sure she wasn't joking. "Take any bike. We got hundreds all round the hood. Just make sure it's a good one, not rusty and all." He stood up his favorite, a mountain bike with shocks, still gleaming red with only the chrome rusted. It reminded him of the bike he had asked of his parents for his tenth birthday, the last year of normal life for him, the bike they had promised to get him when he was a bit older and taller.

He let Elliot and Amanda lead the way, chasing after them, fighting to focus on the ground and not Amanda's buttocks. Tevy suddenly wondered if Kayla was looking at his backside, a disquieting sensation. Did she like what she saw? Did she care? Why should it matter, since she was so much older? But it did.

Elliot led them to a pile of debris that had been shoved up against the houses of the Meyer Court. The doors, bricks, couches, and wood frames were all that was left of the houses between Cleveland and Meyer, the first block west of St. Mike's. The bulldozed homes now filled Meyer, effectively blocking any wheeled approach or exit—unless you were riding a mountain bike and really knew your way.

A pair of boards, heavy two-by-eights, formed a ramp going ten feet up the side of the pile. Tevy wondered why he hadn't known about this route, until he noticed the cross boards underneath holding the pair of boards together. Elliot and Amanda must've recently constructed this ramp. From a distance it just looked like one more chunk of detritus.

Tevy had to work hard to peddle the bike up the ramp, and it wasn't until Amanda plunged sharply out of view that he had any idea what to expect. The far side of the pile had a metal garage door on the downhill side, leaning onto the roof of a house that once fronted on Meyer before the pile took up the street. Tevy's bike slipped sideways on the slick metal before the tires caught purchase on the asphalt shingles. These roofs were long slopes, and Elliot and Amanda had already rushed down, turning onto a garage roof. Tevy turned just in time to see Elliot bounce down onto the roof of a van and from there to the roof of a car parked against it as if it had just been t-boned. From the hood of the car to the ground was an easy jump.

"Look out! Look out!" Kayla's shout from behind prompted Tevy to let go of the brake. She had crested the top of barrier and was on her way down the garage door, and Tevy was stopped at the bottom. Radu was right behind her, looking wide-eyed and sweating.

Tevy surged down the roof, banking sharply on the garage and taking the impact as he hit first the roof of the van, with the satisfying sound of crunching steel, and then the roof of the car. His heart pounded and he grinned at his fear. One bad turn now and he'd splatter on the pavement. Instead he hit the ground and skidded to a stop by Elliot and Amanda, giving them each high fives.

"That was fantastic," Tevy shouted, turning to watch first Kayla and then Radu complete the descent with a little less style and a lot more hesitation.

Kayla looked furious. "You people are crazy. One mistake and the mission would have to be scrubbed while we scraped someone's brains off the pavement."

Elliot shrugged at Tevy, his meaning clear: *you invited them, you explain.*

Tevy nodded. "Let's roll."

A metal gate hung open, and the laneway it provided between the townhouses was their route to the next street over, where Elliot turned right to peddle fast for Eugene Street. It was at the intersection that Tevy pointed east and shouted over his shoulder to Kayla, "That's why."

Hundreds of people pushed through the narrow opening in the stone wall that blocked Eugene, a flow of humanity that was going in one direction: into the cantonment of St. Mike's, where the high school and the block houses would be refuges against the night and the rippers. Tevy hoped it would be obvious to Kayla that trying to push out through the gate against that mob would have resulted in bruises and lost time, assuming they got out at all before dark.

"What are they doing?" Kayla rode with Tevy now that they had a clear street with only a few humans hurrying in the opposite direction, many of them on their own bikes.

"They're going home." Tevy pointed at the sun, which hung low on the horizon. "Isn't it like that at St. John's? Out to forage in the morning and rush the hell back before dark?"

"I don't know," said Kayla. "We don't have so many people, I guess. I've never seen a crush at the gate anyway."

"Welcome to the big city."

They had no breath for talking now, though, as they peddled hard to keep up with Elliot, who seemed to feel he was a tour guide as well as the point man. He shouted things like, "It's down that way to Bertrand Allan's old house," and later, "I lived up there." When they went under a rusting metal bridge he pointed up and called, his voice echoing, "That was the 'L' train line. The brown line."

Tevy wondered what the city looked like to Kayla. The cars rusting on either side, many parked as if their owners might return one day. The Old Town storefronts increasingly gave way to late-twentieth-century plazas with parking lots fronting the street instead of stores. The windows had years of grime to prove that not enough people were left even to smash them, although a few were missing. He and Elliot had taken out their share with rocks until Bobs caught them and told them to stop. "Glass might be valuable one day," she had said. "The rippers sure don't like it."

Under the Kennedy Expressway, they all whooped and hollered, the echoes off the concrete far better than under the 'L.' Now they were on a four-lane road, again cutting northwest at a sharp angle through the rest of the city's organized east-west roads.

Elliot loved to yell things like, "Hey, someone's parking in the bike lane," pointing to an SUV on flat tires at the side of the road. Tevy had forgotten that those white lines and painted symbols of a cyclist ever meant something. They always rode right down the center of any street, keeping a wary eye to each side in case some ripper trap was set up near a building to snare them or damage their bikes to make them easier prey after dark.

They neared the Harrison High School, one of Tevy's favorite buildings along the way because he would have been a student there if the rippers hadn't destroyed his world. The building consisted of three large wings surrounding a grassy quadrangle. A low metal fence bordering the street made up the forth side of the quad. The wing closest to them looked more like a church than a school, with tall windows and a peaked roof of red tile. The orange brick of the school had stayed remarkably pristine, perhaps because there was little car exhaust to dull it. Tevy sometimes came over to walk the dim halls or through the quad, imagining what it would have been like to attend this school. This would be his graduation year, and he'd heard that it would've been three seasons of school festivities and drunken parties, culminating in a summer of debauchery at lake houses and campsites.

But just as they neared the first wing, Elliot turned back to shout again, but not as a tour guide. "Tev, someone's been clearing for gunfire. Uh-oh."

Now he pointed to the ground floor windows of the high school, newly bricked in and sealed from the sun. The quad that Tevy sometimes walked had sprouted a lot of young saplings over the last eight years, but they had all been slashed down and left to wither and die, their new spring leaves already brown, proving that this change happened recently.

They were looking at a new ripper fortress, the first that Tevy had seen north of the Merchandise Mart, and far into Loyalist territory.

Elliot veered away, riding on the opposite sidewalk and close to an older building, a two-story brick affair from early twentieth-century Chicago, the shops clearly abandoned long before the rippers, overtaken by economic depression rather than the ripper apocalypse. Amanda and Tevy followed, even though keeping distance from this new fortress didn't really matter. The rippers couldn't look outside, not yet, because it was still half an hour from sunset.

Something dropped from the roof of the building and draped over Elliot, catching up his bike and tossing him off. Amanda ran into him, and the two crashed to the ground. Tevy braked hard, but the back brake on the bike failed while the front brake pulled the bike up short, tossing

Tevy far over the handles and onto the tangled pile that was Amanda, Elliot, their bikes and the heavy net. Something, perhaps a handle bar, punched hard into his back, knocking the wind from him and sending waves of pain through his body. Had he broken a rib? Shouts and screams brought him back to the present. The net over Elliot warned Tevy that this was no accident. Someone threw it. Not a ripper, because it was before sunset. A human. A traitor.

A boot kicked Tevy in the ribs on his left side. He rolled frantically to get away.

"Stay down, Reb." It was an older man's voice, a rough man with a drawl that wasn't from Chicago. "If I bash your brains in, an evolved can still have you for dinner before you die. We don't need you to be thinking."

But they did need him alive. The traitors couldn't shoot him for fear of losing the very blood they were trying to get for their masters. That meant he didn't have to do what they said. When the boot appeared close, the man standing over him with the club, Tevy moved, turning his Glock and firing straight through the bottom of the holster and into the boot.

The man screamed and Tevy rolled farther, turning his roll into a crouch and standing while on the move, the pain from his ribs minor compared to the panic of the moment. Elliot, still tangled in a net, fought and screamed, and his M4 was yanked from him by one of the traitors. There were easily half a dozen of them. Amanda wrestled with one now, a big brute of a man with a gray beard and a mean laugh, as he fought to pin her to the ground. Radu was also caught in a net and surrounded by several, but Kayla was free, a bloody knife in one hand while she kicked the shreds of a net off her right foot. On the ground beside her a man held his stomach, gasping and struggling to hold in the blood.

"Shoot!" Kayla shouted at Tevy.

He drew the Glock and pulled the trigger, but his aim was high, going over the heads of several of the men, but it had the desired effect: except for the ones fighting with Radu, they all turned on Tevy, weapons aimed.

"Don't shoot him!" shouted one man.

Tevy ran up the street, cutting an arc toward the sidewalk so that he would be moving but not going farther away. Kayla yanked her Uzi free of the net and fired at the men with single shots. The brute over Amanda gasped and fell on her. Elliot's knife slashed at his net. Several men shot at Tevy, and his muscles stiffened, expecting the impacts that didn't come, because he was too fast. But being a moving target cuts both ways. He shot wildly in their direction as he ran, but he fired high, not wanting to hit Kayla by accident.

She was the real threat to the traitors. Three men died from her bullets before the others realized that Tevy was not the one killing them. They turned on her now, but it was too late. Elliot was free, retrieving his massive Ruger from the sidewalk near his bike and firing with deafening explosions, his feet planted far apart to help him keep his balance from the recoil of the heavy revolver. Amanda lunged from under the dead brute, her vest coated in his blood. She had drawn her sidearm in the process and shot the man closest to her through the head.

Tevy stopped and leaned against the brick of the building, breathing deeply, as if he'd just finished a hundred-yard dash rather than three car lengths. He took aim at the only traitors still standing, the ones behind Kayla, who now ran across the road carrying a netted and limp Radu. But it was too late. Tevy couldn't shoot without fear of hitting Radu.

"Shoot, for fuck's sakes!" Kayla dropped the clip out of her Uzi and pulled a fresh clip from a vest pocket. "Shoot, Goddamn it!"

Now Tevy understood the danger. The nearest door to the high school stood wide open, and other humans waited in the entrance, guns drawn but not firing. Elliot and Amanda opened fire, and Tevy fired another high shot, trying to scare them into stopping by hitting the brick above the door. But they weren't cowed into surrendering. He should shoot one of them to make them drop Radu, but Bishop Alvarez had always stressed that "Thou Shalt not Kill" meant that you must never kill humans or you would go to Hell. Tevy feared hell. He had killed rippers who were down there, had sent them to their eternal hell. If he committed a mortal sin, if he killed uninfected humans, even if they were traitors, he would meet his victims in hell, and he feared the welcoming committee.

He had to find another way to save Radu. But before Tevy could run after them, before he could think, the door to the school slammed shut, locking out the sunlight and locking Radu in with the traitors and their ripper masters. Tevy suddenly knew he had made the wrong decision, knew he should have murdered humans and risked hell to save Radu. He ran for the school, promising to himself that he wouldn't hold back this time, that he would murder every human and ripper between himself and Radu.

13

THE ERICSIANS

Kayla wanted to scream and shout and shoot, but she knew immediately that it was to no avail. Radu was lost, maybe dying this very moment. Hopefully dying this very moment, because he knew too many of the secrets of St. John's, but hopefully not about the back door. That was information she didn't want to rippers to use to assault her home.

Tevy charged across the street, firing wildly at the metal doors, obviously bent on a frontal assault on a fortified position. Joyce warned her about this last week, apparently having assessed Tevy during their few engagements with the rippers: "I know his type. He's brave as all get out, but he'll charge without thinking. You have to think for both of you."

"Stop!" Kayla shouted it over and over, chasing after him across the street, trying to check for movement among the traitor bodies at the same time.

Tevy was at the door, pounding and shouting, but thankfully the red-headed kid helped her pull him to the side before return fire punched outbound holes in the doors. The three of them tumbled into the long grass of the quad, and Kayla sat up quickly, her Uzi aiming for the door in case the traitors sortied out to try to capture them.

"We have to go get him before they bleed him out!" Tevy shouted while the redheaded kid held him down.

Kayla let her anger rise because she needed it now to make him understand.

"Stop it, you stupid moron! If we could have brought the traitors down before they reached the doors maybe we could have saved him, but it's way too frigging late now. They're bleeding him to death as I speak, and going in there will be our own useless deaths."

Tevy stopped struggling, and Kayla almost regretted the harshness of her tone.

"But he was your friend," Tevy said.

Kayla fired a bullet into the grass near him in her fury. "You're fucking right." She would grieve later. She would weep later. "He was *my* friend, but use your thick head. It's about fifteen minutes to sunset. Why do you think all those traitors are hiding in there right now and not coming for us again? Because the rippers will be pouring out of this place in minutes. We've got to get the hell out of here."

Across the street a man screamed, a horrible cry that cut wetly off. Amanda stood over him, a bloody knife in one hand, holding up his head by the hair. She had just slashed his throat and blood pumped onto the pavement. Amanda looked up at them, her face impassive as if she were simply taking out the garbage.

Kayla nodded. "Quick, Tevy, and you, dude," she pointed to redhead. "We've got to bleed these guys out and get on our bikes. Move before they get the idea to try and wing us."

She ran across the street hoping the others would have the sense to follow. Amanda had already moved on to the next body, pulling back the head and slashing the throat, but very little blood spilled, this one obviously already dead.

Kayla grabbed a handful of long gray hair of a skinny man lying face down and yanked back his head. He groaned as she pulled her knife from her belt, but she reminded herself that this man would have handed her to the rippers to have her throat slashed for feeding. She hauled the blade across his throat, pulling up strongly to ensure it bit deep. Blood sprayed onto the pavement. The man never regained consciousness enough to scream.

"That's all of them," said Amanda. "Guaranteed nothing left for the rippers."

"Good idea." Kayla didn't have time to determine if Amanda was in shock, but the emotionless expression was worth noting. Either she was as cool as a cucumber or she had totally lost it.

Amanda looked past Kayla, and thankfully a tremble of her lip proved that she there were emotions fighting inside her. "You okay, Elliot?"

That was the redheaded kid's name. Kayla now remembered Tevy shouting introductions as they rode away from St. Mike's, but while navigating that crazy pile of crap she had missed the name. She wouldn't forget again. Elliot had been helpful with Tevy, had taken her side and kept his head. He was dependable.

Elliot had just finished freeing his bike from the net, and he took a second to give her a quick thumbs up. He had already retrieved his M4 and slung it back over his shoulder. His Ruger was again holstered.

Kayla caught Tevy looking back at the high school, the last rays of the sun reflecting orange from the second floor windows. "Tevy!" Her shout made him start. "You with me? I heard you tell Bobs that you never let her down. Is that true?" She had to get him focused on the mission and not a suicidal attempt at rescue.

He nodded, giving her one angry glance before yanking his bike from the ground.

Kayla didn't take it personally. He could be angry at the rippers, or himself, and even if he was angry with her, well, you need to accept that you can't make everyone happy when you're a leader. The mission was more important.

She hadn't intended to take over this little group, but Joyce was right: Tevy was a good fighter, but you wouldn't want him leading you into battle. By sunset Kayla knew she was in command.

The campus of Wright College looked so normal at first that Kayla could almost believe she could walk through the doors and find students at night classes and profs in their offices. It was a modern campus like Atherley, with the buildings constructed in the late twentieth century, built to receive design awards. She could imagine them filming Star Trek here when they needed an exterior Star Fleet Academy set.

But closer inspection revealed that this was not the old world. The expansive lawns weren't mowed, they were sowed with rows of crops, perhaps new corn, although it was hard to tell in the dark. The lights shining from the lower floors came in neat rows—gun slots. In the dark she couldn't tell for sure, but Kayla guessed that all the ground-floor windows had been bricked-in back in the days of Vlad the Scourge.

Even the second floor windows looked smaller than the architecture would suggest, and they reminded Kayla more of the shape of windows on a subway train frozen in place. The light looked dim compared to what the college must've once boasted. The occupiers either had only a few bulbs connected to a small generator or they relied on oil lamps and candles. The yellow suggested kerosene lamplight.

"How do we get in without getting shot?" she asked of Tevy.

The four of them had dumped their bikes in the backyard of a bungalow. They now stood close to the vinyl siding of the little house across the street, although it was so dark they could probably have stood in the open and been invisible. The moon had waned to a crescent, and in couple of more nights there would be no moon. A good time for rippers.

Tevy stepped forward to look up and down the street, a four-lane road that had been kept clear of weeds and saplings. "That's mined." He pointed to the long grass on the strip between the street and the sidewalk, the only uncultivated space on the campus. "Leaves us no choice but one of the entrances, but I think we might be better off to wait for a patrol. Just jogging up with all our weapons could get us shot pretty damn fast."

Suddenly, Tevy pushed them back against the house, pulling his shotgun off his back and handing it to Elliot, followed by his sidearm his vest and shirt, and, to Kayla's horror, the rest of his clothes. Apparently he didn't wear underwear and lacked any modesty. Her cheeks burned

MICHAEL ANDRE MCPHERSON

in the dark and she briefly looked away, but she had to know what he was doing, so she fixed her eyes on his face.

"What the hell are you doing?" she asked in a whisper.

"There's a patrol coming." Tevy pointed down the street. "Can you hear it?"

Kayla listened carefully and picked up on the patter of feet in running shoes, trotting up the center of the street from the south.

"I'm going to meet them. If it turns out they're rippers or traitors, then cover me and I'll get my butt back here."

Kayla considered stopping him, but that would mean looking at him, and even with this weak moonlight she might find herself glancing down and worse, get caught checking him out. Amanda and Elliot seemed oblivious to his nudity, and that made Kayla wonder what it was like to grow up in a church basement.

Tevy walked out into the street with his hands on his head, a slim figure of white in the moonlight, practically an ethereal spirit. Kayla watched as he knelt in the middle of the street facing the sound of the patter of shoes, now occasionally pausing as someone whispered commands.

"How do we know they're Ericsians?" Kayla asked of Elliot, but Amanda beat him to the answer.

"The first thing they'll say is 'The 1000 Live On.' It's a heretic thing."

"Heretic?"

Amanda shrugged, but her concentration stayed on the road, focusing down her gun sight in the direction of Tevy, waiting for targets to arrive. "They aren't Catholic or Muslim or Jewish, so they're heretics from some religion."

An internal shiver unsettled Kayla. Did Joyce and Jeff know that this is how the Ericsians were perceived in Chicago? Did anyone from St. John's know? She would go to Joyce first thing tomorrow and warn her that people should keep their mouths shut, shouldn't talk about the 1000 Souls. Even she would have to pretend she knew nothing of the Ericsians.

Kayla aimed her Uzi into the darkness near Tevy, his pale form distracting her. How could she be attracted to such a young kid? He was more than five years younger than her and barely shaving. Yet she had to push away the thought of kneeling face to face with him, her just as naked, her breasts against his chest, her hands around his back and reaching up to his shoulders.

The sound of hurrying feet stopped.

"The 1000 Live On," called Tevy in a quiet voice, but in the stillness of the evening, with everyone straining to hear, it sounded like a shout.

Dark figures with aimed weapons converged on Tevy. They were visible more because they occluded the light from the gun slits of the college as they ran in, because their black clothes made them nearly invisible in the dark.

"The 1000 Live On," said a man's voice. "Are you from St. Mike's? We were told they were three of you."

"We were five. Three are waiting nearby. One didn't make it. Traitors ambushed us at sunset. There's a new ripper stronghold north of the Loop, and it's not a mile from here."

"Call your people. Let's get inside."

Clearly it had been a lecture hall, but now Kayla thought it looked more like a church, and yet unlike any church she had ever visited either before or after the apocalypse. They entered from the top of stadium-style seating, walking down the stairs between rows of congregation seated at long tables, as if they were students here for a lecture, although no one had laptops or notepads. Seen from above, the hall was a semi-circle, designed to concentrate everyone's attention on the lecturer and the glass board, a dead smart board, at the focus. Kerosene lamps that would have once been for camping sat here and there on the tables to provide yellow light.

The walls on one side of the lecture platform had a huge mural of Erics and the twelve on fire in the square of Billings, Montana. Their eyes, miraculously pain-free, were all focused on three figures: rough caricatures of Bertrand, Jeff and Joyce. Did any of those three know they were honored here? For the painting also showed smoke-like souls shooting from Erics and his followers toward the trinity.

On the other wall was a mural of Bertrand in a death struggle with an evil shadow: Vlad the Scourge. Flames, but little smoke, filled the sparse room around them. Bertrand was light and Vlad, darkness. Underneath the first mural in beautiful calligraphy was the phrase THE 1000 LIVE ON. Underneath the other in the same gold-leafed calligraphy: HE IS STILL WITH US.

A table occupied the lecture platform with twelve men and women seated behind it, some very old and others very young, all from different ethnic backgrounds, some Asian and some African, several Caucasians, and one man who looked to be of Indian extraction. In the center sat a middle-aged man, his skin a light shade of black and his long hair tied up in a tight bun on the back of his head. He stood and spread his arms.

"Welcome fellow souls. I'm Edward Mabruke, host to the Captain Soul." He wore an immaculate if tight-fitting suit, but the style was odd with its vest and pocket-watch chain, almost as if he'd stepped out of the late nineteenth century, yet it was a shade toward purple with gray pinstripes. Kayla remembered that Erics dressed in a similarly unusual get up. He had an accent that Kayla couldn't place—maybe South African?

Mabruke studied each of them in turn as they marched down the stairs between the crowd, and Kayla had to shake the sense that she and her companions were prisoners being escorted to trial. At least they were allowed to keep their weapons.

Since there was nowhere to sit, the four spread out to stand facing the table.

Mabruke pointed to Tevy, Elliot, and Amanda in turn. "I've met you and you and you." His finger stopped on Kayla. "I've never met you."

"I'm not from Chicago. I'm from St. John's."

Mabruke met her eyes and smiled. "I'm so happy to see one of our soul hosts from up north."

Tevy spoke up, sparing Kayla from finding some way to prevent Mabruke from spilling the beans that so many at St. John's were Ericsians. She didn't want that information tossed about Chicago until she had a chance to talk to Joyce.

"I've come with a message from General Roberts that she didn't trust to radio," Tevy said.

Mabruke sat, a frown creasing his forehead. "What does the host of the Ruthless General have to say?"

"That we need one another, that we have to fight as one army. The rippers may be coming even tonight, or maybe their traitor armies tomorrow. She suggests I could be your contact for organizing combined operations, attacking or defending at the same time."

Mabruke tapped at the table with one finger, studying it as if it were an amazing clockwork. Everyone else in the room held their breath.

"I need to know who we're dealing with," he finally said.

Kayla had wondered if this would happen. Several of the Ericsians in St. John's tried to persuade her to take the test, and she had been considering it, but she worried about the outcome. What if she were host to an evil soul?

But it was Tevy they were after, judging by Mabruke's concentration, and he figured that out pretty quickly. "I'm not taking your test." Tevy crossed his arms in his defiance. "Why are you guys always after me for that anyway? I'm just one guy. Why you gotta be sticking your noses into my religion."

Mabruke pulled on a gold chain around his neck until he retrieved a gold circle with the circumference of a coaster from under his shirt. "Do you know what this is?"

"It's your circle," Tevy said.

"It's our circle." Mabruke swept his hand in a gesture that encompassed the whole room, including the guests. "But while twelve stood in the circle, only three soul portions were present. Those are three special souls. They come together only in times of great need, and somehow they find one another. We're always on the lookout for this combination, for it is always essential to support the three."

Kayla suddenly had a sense of where this was going, and she found herself studying Tevy and Elliot and Amanda in a new perspective. Was it possible that they were the three? Kayla's heart rate quickened. Tevy reminded Kayla vaguely of someone, but she couldn't say whom. Was Amanda the same soul as Jeff or Joyce? Somehow, she didn't seem like the Angry Captain, but she surely had been quietly dependable, but not at all like Jeff, who was dependable but always drunk or fornicating.

Mabruke continued. "Before we can agree to any alliance with General Roberts, you must all take the determination, starting with you." Mabruke pointed straight at Tevy.

"No bleeding way." Tevy looked shocked himself that he had used one of Bishop Alvarez's forbidden words.

Kayla had to fight the anger that welled up. "Oh for fuck's sake, what's the big deal? Five multiple-choice questions and your done. It'll take you less than a minute."

That got Mabruke's attention. "So you've taken the determination?"

Kayla straightened under the attention of the crowd and decided the truth was the best. "No. I haven't yet, because I'm afraid."

Tevy and the others looked over in surprise, but Mabruke nodded his understanding. "You host the soul that you host," he said. "Knowing or not knowing changes nothing, my daughter. Take the determination. It may be a relief."

Tevy looked ready to argue, and that's when Kayla really lost it. "You want to come through for Bobs or not? Take the damn test before the rippers start pouring over the walls."

Tevy looked ready to argue more, but he shrugged instead. "All right. If it'll make everybody so amazingly happy."

They led them off to a side room, a lab next door to the lecture hall, judging by equipment--outlets for gas and sinks. They took their places in a row and sat on the lab stools while Mabruke himself placed a single sheet of paper in front of each of them. "Wait," he said, when Kayla started to turn it over. "It's best if you all begin at once. Answer with your first instinct and don't try to think about what is the right answer. There is no right answer. There is simply your answer."

He stood back, sitting on a stool so that he could watch them all.

"Okay, now begin," he said.

Kayla flipped her page and read the first question about a smoke alarm. Would they have to update this test, since younger people wouldn't even know what it was? The questions about the flower dated well, but the questions about taxes and investments might challenge even Tevy. He would never have paid taxes in his life. She glanced at him for a second and found herself wanting to touch his neck at the base, where his short dark hair came to such an abrupt end. His skin was so pure.

Mabruke cleared his throat and she got back to her determination, ticking off her answers with the bit of pencil as quickly as she read them. As she had promised Tevy, it was over in a minute and Mabruke collected their papers. "Just wait here," he said.

They still had their weapons, Kayla reminded herself, adjusting the strap of the Uzi on her shoulder while two guards with holstered handguns stood at the door to the lecture hall.

"I could sure use a drink," said Elliot, running a hand through his hair.

One of the guards, a woman in her forties, Kayla guessed, pulled a metal bottle from the back of her belt and handed it to Elliot, who took a quick drink and gave her a winning smile. "I was thinking about something a little stronger."

Suddenly, Kayla thought about Jeff and his hangovers, the ones he fought through when he was needed. Could it be? Could Elliot be the Dependable Rogue? He was flirting with the guard even though he was sixteen and she was forty. Amanda had certainly noticed and was pissed, her arms crossed under her breasts.

Mabruke's voice carried back to them from the lecture hall, and when Kayla heard him say, "...and her answer to question two is..." but she missed the rest, exchanging a glance with Amanda, whose red face probably reflected her own. He was reading out their answers to the whole room!

A cheer went up from the crowd, and judging by Mabruke's shouts, it took a while to quiet them. He read out more answers and now they all strained to listen, but Kayla always seemed to miss the answer.

"What'd you say about the smoke detector?" asked Elliot. "I wanted to write in an extra answer that said thank God there's a smoke detector. Maybe this was all a bad dream and I'm nine."

"Quiet," said Tevy. Of all of them he looked the most anxious.

"I thought you didn't believe in this," Kayla said.

Tevy lifted his chin and looked defiant. "I don't. But what if they read something bad in that test like you were worried about? What if they think I have the same soul as Vlad or something like that? They're not going to give us any effing help then, will they?"

More cheering caught their attention.

"There you go," said Elliot. "That's two good souls anyway. Maybe they'll help me get a drink."

The female guard studied Elliot intensely for a moment before she turned to Kayla and asked, "Is he dependable?"

She was still shaking her head and about to explain that she'd just met him when Tevy answered, "He's always there when I need him, and he's never run unless we're bailing together." He and Elliot knocked knuckles and high-fived.

For a moment Kayla felt a wave of jealousy, like she should be part of that camaraderie even though she hardly knew them. Amanda didn't seem interested in the boyish bonding ritual.

The crowd spoke again, a polite clapping with a few "woots" thrown in for good measure. Mabruke began to read answers again, but this time Kayla was sure he cut short. The door opened so fast that, for a moment, Kayla thought they were going to be attacked, and she reflexively raised her Uzi, but Mabruke stood in the doorway, his hand frozen on the handle and his eyes wide. He was trembling! He was in some weird kind of religious ecstasy.

"Bring them," he finally said, and it came out as a gasp. "Praise the 1000, bring them."

Kayla wanted to fight, to shout, anything rather than be pulled in front of the crowd, but there was no denying Mabruke or the guards short of a firefight. No one threatened them with weapons or gestures, they were just beside themselves excited. Yet she now wondered: who was she?

The twelve people who sat at the large table had changed sides so that their backs were to the crowd. This allowed Mabruke to line the four of them up, still standing and facing the crowd, between the table and the smart board. Mabruke stood behind Amanda first.

"You are the first portion of your soul we have met, and so we have no name for you. Until we have learned more your soul number will be assigned your name: Amanda."

The crowd cheered, but clearly this was the warm up, for they knew something big was up. They all knew the results of at least two other determinations. Mabruke moved behind Elliot, but the crowd was already cheering.

"The Dependable Rogue!" shouted Mabruke.

Kayla caught her breath and looked over in shock. Elliot was jumping up and down with his fists in the air like a prizefighter before the fight who loves the crowd. He smiled at her in between jumps. "So who the fuck is that?"

"Jeff. Jeff Aubert is the Dependable Rogue according to Erics." But Elliot didn't hear her reply and didn't seem to care, still hamming it up for the crowd.

Mabruke moved behind her, and the cheering only got more intense.

It couldn't be. She couldn't be. Maybe this was all bullshit. What were the odds that they would all answer their determinations in that configuration?"

"The Angry Captain," shouted Mabruke, but the crowd already knew and some of them were chanting, "Joyce! Joyce! Joyce! Joyce!"

Kayla wanted to tell them all to fuck off. She wanted to storm out of the room or shoot a few rounds into the ceiling to shut them all up, but she was afraid that would only convince them of this madness. She had fought alongside Joyce and they were completely different people. How could anyone say that they were both host to the same soul?

Finally, Mabruke moved behind Tevy, who glanced over his shoulder with a suspicious frown before turning to Kayla. "They think you're Joyce Skala?" he asked just as the room went silent, his voice carrying to the back of the hall.

Mabruke, still trembling, hardly able to contain himself answered for her. "She hosts a portion of the Angry Captain. The same soul is hosted by Joyce ."

Now a dropped pin could be heard, and Kayla knew by the intensity of Mabruke's stance what was coming. So did the crowd. She couldn't believe it. This was simply fantastical.

Mabruke put one hand on Tevy's shoulder. "And this, my fellow hosts, is the Dormant Hero. The trinity has come to us tonight."

The crowd went crazy, weeping and screaming and applauding. Mabruke went down on one knee and kissed Tevy's hand. Kayla stepped back, afraid the crowd would charge, her Uzi coming up just as Elliot leveled his M4 and Tevy drew is shotgun.

This only seemed to make the crowd more ecstatic, but at least they stayed back.

"What the hell?" asked Tevy of her.

Kayla had to re-evaluate every interaction she experienced with Tevy. Could this teenager really host a portion of the same soul as the ripper she met in the basement of Atherley College?

"You're the Dormant Hero," she shouted to him. "You answered the determination the same way Bertrand Allan and Erics answered it."

He shook his head, now pointing the shotgun to the ceiling with one hand since it was clear that the crowd would keep their distance.

Kayla wondered if he'd heard and just didn't believe. She could hardly believe it herself. "You host a portion of the same soul as their prophet Erics, and Bertrand Allan. How can you be so thick? You're Erics!"

Mabruke stood and kissed each of Tevy's cheeks.

"Thank you for coming back to us, master."

14

FIRST DAY OF HIGH SCHOOL

Tevy pushed away from the Mabruke's kisses in horror, but it was the shining in Kayla's eyes that really stunned him. She believed it. Did that mean she was a heretic? An Ericsian?

"No way," he said. "No effing way."

But the crowd couldn't hear him, and apparently Mabruke didn't care, but Kayla just kept shaking her head in wonder and saying, "What are the odds? What are the odds?"

Tevy couldn't get his head around it, so he turned to Elliot, who was grinning like an idiot and blowing kisses to the girls as if he were the star of a boy-band. Tevy resisted the urge to punch Elliot's shoulder to get his attention.

"Dude!" he shouted instead.

Elliot turned his grin on him. "You're not supposed to use that word. You'll get in trouble with the bishop."

"Whatever. Surely you don't believe this crap."

Elliot shrugged and continued his waves. "What does it matter? Bobs wanted their cooperation and you've done it, dude. Oops!" He held his hand over his mouth as if he'd just burped. "If their believing this 1000 souls thing means they'll do what you tell 'em to, isn't that a good thing?"

Suddenly, Tevy had an idea, saw a chance to right a wrong. He turned to Mabruke. "How many troops can you put in the field tonight? Now."

Mabruke thought for a moment. "We could get two hundred together in half an hour."

"Will you do it?"

Mabruke didn't hesitate. "If that's what you believe we should do."

"Yes, I do."

But to Tevy's surprise, Mabruke turned to Kayla. "Once they're ready I assume you will lead them?"

Kayla seemed to know way too much about the Ericsians—and Tevy made a note to ask her about that later—because she knew exactly what to say to Mabruke. "Of course. I'm the Angry Captain."

Mabruke ushered them away from the crowd and back into the lab so he could muster his troops, and that's when Kayla turned her eyes on Tevy, and she did look angry. "What are we supposed to be doing with these two hundred troops?

Tevy had never been so sure of anything in his life.

"We're going back to get Radu."

Tevy fought to contain his frustration. They stood around one of the lab tables, a yellowed map of Chicago spread wide and held down at the corners with beakers that Mabruke had pulled from a cupboard under the table.

"Every second is precious," Tevy said, looking around the table in the weak light of the kerosene lamp. "Radu could still be alive." He usually found the scent of kerosene soothing, reminding him of Helen's storybook readings to the Brat Pack. But tonight nothing calmed him, especially with Kayla glaring at him across the table as if he were the stupidest person alive.

"By now, he's either dead or a ripper," she said. "There's no chance he's alive and I'd shoot him on sight just in case."

Why was she always angry with him? Tevy could remember several instances of this long before she'd been declared the Angry Captain, so it wasn't that she was putting on a show. But now he thought of a weakness in her argument.

"So why did you agree to lead this raid if Radu's dead?"

Kayla put a finger over the location of the high school on the map. "Because they obviously fortified the school to prevent exactly what Bobs wants: coordination between the Ericsians here at Wright and you guys at St. Mike's. As long as that's there, they might as well have built the Great Wall of China between the two strongest human fortresses in Chicago."

Mabruke nodded but didn't say anything and couldn't seem to stop smiling every time one of the three spoke, as if everything they said confirmed his belief. Tevy wanted to punch him, but more than anything he wanted to fight the rippers. Ever since he'd aimed high, fearing to kill humans and go to Hell, he regretted it. Radu stayed with them in the forest. He proved himself a worthy companion, and Tevy let him down.

"So, like I said," continued Kayla. "We go in at dawn."

"Six hours! For eff's sake." Tevy was tempted to rush out and try to shoot his way in right now.

"Come on, Tev," said Elliot. "You can say it. Fuck."

Kayla didn't even glance at Elliot, let alone acknowledge his joke. "You want to catch this place full of rippers or not? If they've got as many as you say from all those trips downtown, plus all those traitors from California, we want to take as many of them out tonight as possible, or we'll be fighting them tomorrow or next week."

Several of Mabruke's captains were with them, and they all muttered in agreement. They might treat Tevy with the honor due their prophet, but they all knew their history very well: it was Bobs and Joyce and Barry who commanded the armies that fought into Cave Mountain, not Erics and not Bertrand.

Tevy knew she was right, which didn't make it any easier. Sure, it was unlikely Radu was alive, but maybe, just maybe, there was a tiny chance.

"You guys got any C-4 to blow the doors with?" Kayla asked of Mabruke.

Tevy found himself fascinated with Kayla's expression, the intensity, the focus, the way her brow creased as she studied the map. One day maybe there would be lines, but she was younger than he thought, her skin still fresh.

Mabruke shook his head. "Nothing as subtle as C-4. We've got some good dynamite, but best of all, we have some M-72 LAWs."

"What are those?" she asked.

Tevy suddenly remembered playing *Call of Duty* in the living room and his dad asking the same question. "They're light anti-tank weapons. One and done. How many you got?"

Mabruke looked at the map for a few moments before he looked up and met Tevy's eye. "I think we could spare two tonight. We have others, but we should save those for the next battle. These were very hard to come by, but I guarantee they'll blow the doors off this place."

Kayla's eyebrows rose even higher, and Tevy could practically see the calculations going on in her head.

"This changes everything," she said.

"This is just great." Tevy could hardly contain his excitement. "We blow big holes in the side of the building, it doesn't even have to be at the doors, and we charge in and get Radu."

Kayla fixed him with a cool gaze. "Part right. We blow holes in the doors and go in through the second floor." She turned back to Mabruke. "You must have some ladders around here?"

"We're going to kill their human slaves?" Tevy still couldn't break free of Bishop Alvarez's warning.

Kayla looked up from the map in surprise. "We're going to kill traitors. We killed a few today just in case...." That frown deepened. "Is that why you were such a lousy shot? You didn't want to kill human traitors? What the hell's that all about?"

"It's about hell." For once Elliot wasn't in joking. "I got this," he added to Kayla before taking Tevy by the elbow and turning him farther down the lab and away from the pool of light and humanity.

"I know they deserve it," Tevy said. "I just get the heebee jeebies and all. There are a lot of rippers in hell waiting for me."

"Remember how the bishop said that rippers weren't human?" Elliot looked older than his seventeen years now, all the youth and mischief leaving his face.

"Of course."

"We're going into a ripper fortress, dude, and for all we know there are no traitors. Everyone you come across will be a ripper, and God's okay with killing them. We just shoot everybody and let God sort them out."

"But we saw humans go into there." Tevy leaned back against a wall.

Elliot tapped a finger into Tevy's chest. "Last evening. They've been in there with hungry rippers all night. It's fair to say that anyone we come across is a ripper, and if you do shoot a human, well, you thought you were killing a ripper. No intent to murder. No harm, no foul. You don't burn in hell."

Tevy took a deep breath. "I sure hope you're right."

"If I'm wrong, I promise we'll at least be together in hell."

***

The cold produced a steady tremble in Tevy, rising and falling depending on when they were moving and when they were waiting—like now. Dawn had yet to blush the horizon, and the moon set made it difficult to travel without using flashlights, a tool only a few possessed and even then were forbidden from using for fear of warning the rippers. The stars shone in a brilliant display above, now fading in the east, but they didn't provide enough light to see the ground, which was littered with lumps of brick from burned and smashed buildings. Tevy had one aching knee from an encounter with these.

Now they all waited on the sidewalk opposite the high school, which sprawled around three sides of the quad, with its peaked roofs making it look more like an alpine hotel than an education center. Tevy decided it was a shame they were going to blow holes in the building, for it had survived relatively unscathed by the apocalypse until now. It would be harder tomorrow to imagine what high school would have been like without this huge piece of architecture frozen in time as if the teachers and students were off for the summer.

Two wings of the school protruded at right angles from the main building and ended close to the street. It was the street side of those two wings that they would assault. One group here with Kayla, the other at the far wing with Mabruke.

Dim light glowed from the upper-floor windows, proving that power of some kind must be in use. Tevy strained to listen for the drone of a generator and crossed his arms close to his chest in an effort to stop trembling.

"Don't be scared," whispered Kayla, standing close while studying the school and the sky.

"Just freezing." Tevy tried to sound relaxed to prove his point and not seem defensive. He'd done stuff that would turn her white as a ghost. How dare she suggest he was afraid? But he had to admit that the source of the tremble did seem beyond the cold. It also came from excitement, the exhilaration that he would get to fight rather than hide.

The high-tech weapons that Mabruke provided also excited Tevy. One of the Ericsians, an older man with a trimmed gray beard and black skin, stood nearby with the tube of the LAW now aimed at the front door of the building. Tevy had watched with interest when the man had extended the tube and set up his position, ensuring that no one stood behind him.

"This would fry you good," he'd said, his accent suggesting Jamaican origin before the apocalypse. Tevy remembered that Erics himself had been from that country before becoming an American.

Elliot had nodded when he moved to stand clear. "Back blast from the rocket. I should've thought of that. This is going to be great."

"Will it blow through the doors?" asked Kayla.

The rocket man nodded. "Through the doors and down the hall and out the ass end. Made for tanks, this was. Not piddly little high school doors. We'll make a fine mess as soon as you give the word."

Tevy was desperate for her to order the attack, too, and he really wanted to just charge in right after the rocket, but Kayla had the plan and he would follow it. Surely, she would call soon. The rippers all had to be back by now, and any that weren't would likely trip into the little army that waited in the pre-dawn. But it was another ten minutes—when the school began to resolve in the early light, looking more like a building and less like a hulk occluding the stars—that Kayla tapped the man with the rocket launcher on the shoulder and hurried to join Tevy and Elliot.

"Hide your eyes, children," said the rocket man.

Tevy clamped one hand over his eyes, his other hand already holding the pistol grip of his Winchester, but even then the light dazzled him through the cracks of his fingers, and the scream of the rocket deafened him, prompting an involuntary switch of his hand from eyes to left ear. The explosion sent a concussion of air back at them, as if a giant had exhaled.

Tevy yanked up his end of the aluminum ladder and rushed ahead, Elliot barely having a chance to pick up the back end before the charge across the street. Small fires inside the school now provided light, and that saved Tevy from stumbling over errant bricks from the blast.

The open door beckoned, undefended now because of the explosion, but Kayla had been insistent, and Tevy turned onto the lawn, dropping his end of the ladder. He holstered his shotgun, cursing himself for getting it out too soon, and helped Elliot raise the ladder to the second-floor window.

This was it. A chance save Radu or at least avenge him. Tevy again drew his shotgun and rushed up the ladder, keeping a wary eye on the window in case a defender appeared. None did, and Tevy smashed the window with the barrel of his gun, the glass raining around him and slicing at his hands as he dumped his body over the sill and onto the floor.

There was dim light from the hall, enough to show student desks shoved and tossed to either side of the room. Tevy scrambled up, ignoring the pain and the sound of falling glass as others smashed into the classroom. He headed straight for the door, gun leveled and ready to fire, but now a figure rushed through the hall. Tevy peeked left and right out the door, not seeing the figure but discovering that the dim light came from a single bulb hanging from an electrical cord strung like a lazy clothes line down the hall. Farther down the hall another single bulb also hung.

Elliot moved up to the other side of the door. "They must have a generator going somewhere," he said louder than necessary. "Where the hell are they all?"

"Let's go!" Tevy charged into the hall, aware of his heartbeat but ignoring it as he searched for that first target. He found him at the staircase, rushing down from above and headed for the first floor, unaware of the intruders already on the second floor.

The Winchester kicked up when it fired, the shot unusually quiet to Tevy's rocket-deafened ears, and the man stumbled, turning in surprise as the shot punched through the glass by the fire doors and into his side. He fell down the stairs, his own gun clattering across the tiles of the floor.

"He was a ripper," shouted Elliot, reading Tevy's mind. *Was he going to Hell?*

Shots came from the landing above now, from other rippers needing to get downstairs to join the fight at the main doors, where they assumed the Ericsians would all be attacking. They may have even wanted just to get to the basements, for the upper-floor windows weren't bricked in against the pale light that would soon wash into the classrooms.

Muzzle flashes dazzled the combatants, and Tevy and Elliot hit the floor, going to either side of the fire doors where glass provided a view to shoot, although the wire embedded in the glass kept it from shattering, recording the incoming and outgoing shots with relatively neat bullet holes. Tevy's shots punched big holes.

He fired at the dark forms as they ran down the stairs, turning at the landing where they were lit from above by a distant bulb that was not visible from this floor. *They were rippers*, Tevy promised himself as two and now three tumbled down the stairs, prompting a pump from his shotgun between each death.

In all, a dozen had fallen from their fire, others from the Ericsians joining to stand above Tevy and shoot. Finally, the flow of rippers stopped. Elliot leapt up and shoved at the fire door against a body, Tevy standing to join him while others shoved at the other fire door until they both stood wide.

"Let's go!" shouted Tevy, but a woman's hand caught him, the white bandana around her head showing that she was an Ericsian. Mabruke had made them all wear these bandanas, which had a circle with the number 1000 written in black marker in the center of each above the eyes. Elliot had complained about the fashion with a grin.

"Wait!" From her belt the woman pulled a grenade, a weapon both Tevy and Elliot earlier noted with envy that several of the Ericsians carried. She pulled the pin and tossed it down the staircase, the sound of its tumble distant and innocuous as it turned at the landing and disappeared.

The flash was brilliant, and for a moment every detail of the stairwell was sharp as nails, only to seem darker afterwards, but the moment was enough to show Tevy that one of the corpses was far from dead, sitting with its back to the wall, its handgun rising to point at Elliot. Tevy shot from the hip with no time to aim or think, but he was only a body-length from the ripper, and the blast took it in the chest.

"Whoa, shit!" Elliot had noticed too late. "I owe you."

He charged for the stairs and Tevy rushed after him, leaping a splayed body near the landing and turning to find more corpses farther down. Gunfire from the main-floor hallway indicated that Kayla's assault with her people was well under way. Tevy feared for her. What if she were shot, or worse, made a ripper? He charged into the main-floor hallway to find rippers behind banks of tumbled lockers or improvised defenses of broken doors turned sideways and supported with desks. The rippers were turning their way now, alerted by the grenade if not the gunfire that there were Loyalist humans in the building behind them, blocking any retreat to the basements.

Elliot grabbed Tevy by the collar and yanked him back into the stairwell before a dozen shots whizzed by them. It was such a mighty heave that Elliot tripped and they both went down, Tevy sprawling on his back on top of Elliot.

"We don't go into the hall, remember," shouted Elliot as they scrambled up.

Kayla had been specific. *Don't go into that main floor hallway because we'll be there and we'll be as likely to shoot you as them. Hold the stairwells and don't let them into the basement. You'll have plenty of targets, don't you worry about that.*

And she was right, and now Tevy and Elliot retreated, backing down the stairs toward the basement, firing at rippers as they surged recklessly from the main floor into the stairwell. It was as close to a crossfire as the stairway could provide, with Ericsians on the first landing above the main floor shooting down, and Tevy and Elliot on the first landing below the main floor shooting up. The fire door to the main floor was the kill zone, and the rippers continued to pour into it, desperate to get to the basement now that true dawn had arrived. Some were clearly rippers, their figures gauntly nonhuman, their clothes little more than rags, their eyes mad with hunger. Others looked suspiciously normal, except that they were willing to risk everything to get to the basement, and some took more shots to kill than any human could withstand.

Tevy counted five from his shotgun and dropped it to draw his Glock. It didn't have the stopping power of the Winchester at close range, but it was better than his knife. One ripper made it right to him, taking three hits in the chest before falling, draping his bleeding body into Tevy's arms. Tevy shoved him away and put a bullet through the skull for good measure.

"Tell me that wasn't a ripper!" Elliot's call was a challenge. He dropped a clip from his M4 and shoved in a new one, but no more rippers charged the doorway, which was now partially blocked with a pile of bodies, at least a dozen.

"Hold here!" shouted Tevy to the Ericsians still up one landing. But the woman with the grenades was already with them, slipping over the pile of ruined humanity.

"Allow me," she said, obviously guessing that Tevy intended to assault the basement. She pulled a grenade from her belt but waited for agreement. Tevy waved her to the landing but put up one finger to indicate she wait. He retrieved his shotgun, pulled a fist full of shells from his vest pocket, and reloaded the gun as quickly as he could. Sporadic gunfire continued out in the corridor—Kayla's troops polishing off the main floor.

Tevy gave the nod to the Ericsian trooper, the woman looking old, like forty, her dark hair tied up in a tight bun. She pulled the pin on the grenade and lobbed it around the next landing. This time Tevy closed his eyes and covered his ears. The flash still showed through the eyelids and the explosion was still deafening through his hands. He charged down the stairs, his shotgun ready. They were below the ground level now, and any windows high up were bricked in, but the Ericsian trooper had a small flashlight, and she turned it on now, guiding them into the hall. Lockers ran down the wall on each side.

"Seems like a weird place for lockers." Elliot kept his voice low. "The basement?"

"No locks on them like upstairs. Maybe these were extras or something," said the woman with the flashlight. "What does it matter, anyway?"

Farther down the hall, a light bulb had survived, and it provided enough white light for the flashlight batteries to be spared. They had almost reached this illumination when a dozen dark figures rushed from a doorway into the light, turning to flee. Tevy and company opened fire, chasing the rippers down the hall, shooting them in the back as they tried to escape the school. Some did make the far stairwell, but shooting from above stopped them in their tracks. They turned to face Tevy's little squad, but it was too late for them to properly aim and shoot, because the humans already were firing, a steady and calm aim as opposed to the panicked shots from the trapped rippers. In a moment it was over, and Tevy drew his Glock and walked over to shoot each one in the head to ensure they stayed down.

"Repair that!" he shouted to the parasites in their bodies.

"Tev." Elliot had returned to the doorway, and now he waved Tevy over.

Elliot's wide-eyed expression of horror was enough to warn Tevy that the room held a gruesome sight, but he was still appalled when he turned the corner and found a gymnasium full of bodies hung upside down from the ceiling, tied by their ankles, their hands stretching toward the floor. The high windows were bricked in, the only light provided by bulbs strung from the ceiling on white electrical line.

The lights dimmed, and the sound of a generator outside puttering to a halt warned that the room would go dark, either because the generator was out of gas or someone had shut it down. But before the room went black, Tevy counted twelve people hung upside down with their throats slashed and buckets underneath them to catch every last drop of blood.

"I guess that's why he calls himself Vlad Who Bleeds," said Elliot.

A voice in the room disturbed them, a tortured plea with a familiar accent. The woman turned on her flashlight, and they entered the room ready to shoot, but the only conscious being sat naked and tied to a chair at the far end, his chest hair matted with blood.

"Rad!" Tevy hurried forward, elated to find him alive, and if he was tied to a chair that must mean he was still human. They had done it! They had saved Radu against all odds even if he was a bit bloodied. But as Tevy knelt down to untie him, the man shook his head.

"No." His voice was a desperate wail. "I said, 'please shoot me.'"

"What?" But as Tevy looked up he could see a lot of the blood around Radu's lips and teeth.

"Get back." Elliot aimed the M4 at Radu's chest. "It's not his blood. They made him drink. They converted him. He's a ripper."

15

RIPPER ON THE INSIDE

Kayla was never in love with Radu, but she did like him. When she spurned his attempts to get her in the sack, he wasn't the least put off, like Canadian men, many of whom seemed to think they were God's gift to women. She never had to suggest that they "just be friends," because after she said no to his shameless advance, he became a friend as naturally as if they were kids or seniors, and sex wasn't an issue.

Sure, he always made it obvious that if she changed her mind he was willing, and he never failed to miss an opportunity to let her know how attracted he was to her, but somehow there was no pressure, no sense that he was expecting her to cave. He talked about other women freely, asked her advice, and even followed it, like when she said he should stay away from Rachel because she had her eye on a different man, the man she would later marry.

Now, Kayla stood before Radu's bound and naked body and had to judge his fate. The room stank of blood and excrement, and a subtle scent of rot promised a lot more to come if they didn't bury the corpses today.

"We've got to kill him," she said. "What choice have we got? You can't let a ripper live."

Mabruke had come when summoned, and Tevy and Elliot and some other woman were there, but the rest of the troops were using the dynamite to blow out the concrete blocks sealing the ground-floor windows. Occasionally, the ground under Kayla's feet trembled, but the school was old and built on strong foundations during the beginning of the twentieth century. There was no fear that it would collapse as long as only the ripper fortifications were destroyed.

Tevy stared at one of the swinging corpses. He reached up and tore off the victim's shirt, then carried it over to drape Radu's lap, hiding his genitals and giving him a modicum of privacy.

"Can't we let him go if he promises not to feed on humans?" asked Tevy.

Kayla wished it could be so, and she understood Tevy's need. He must feel responsible for not shooting the human traitors and saving Radu when he had a chance. But this was no time to be soft.

"And what the hell would he feed on then?" she asked, trying not to sound angry and failing.

Tevy met her eyes and she read an accusation in his expression. "Maybe you should ask Joyce," he said. "Maybe she or her friend up at St. John's knows the answer to that."

Kayla swore that her heart skipped a beat. Did he know about Bertrand Allan? Had he seen him that night in the woods?

"Stop," she said, before he could reveal the secret in front of everyone. She pleaded with her eyes, and Tevy gave a short nod. He would keep it secret, but Kayla sensed that he would be expecting explanations later.

"She's right." Radu's voice had strengthened, and that wasn't a good sign. The parasites were repairing his body.

"What happened?" she asked.

"They wanted information more than blood. They kept asking stupid questions like, 'how many troops can the bitch call on?' as if I would fucking know. They asked about tanks a lot, too. They beat me. They flogged me, but I tell them only that we came from St. John's. I know I shouldn't, but it hurt so very much." His accent thickened as he spoke, his eyes roving around the corpses as if that was a better sight than his memories.

Kayla feared even that was too much. "What exactly did you tell them?"

Radu gave a slow and understanding smile. "Nothing important. I tell them we come by the buses. That we will fight under the general's command. I tell them more buses are coming, many more and they are getting here today, now."

It took Kayla a second. "That's a lie."

Radu nodded and smiled again, looking stronger by the minute. "Yes. Is a very good lie. They want information and I give it too them. I make them work for it, but I am hoping my death is good. I am hoping they are too scared to attack until they know about new troops."

"That's it." Tevy turned to Kayla, and she could see that he could hardly suppress his excitement. "That's why we let him go. He can be our spy, feed them disinformation and feed us information."

Elliot let out a slow whistle. "You gotta know what the bishop would say about this. Aiding the devil if you let a ripper feed." Elliot had slung his M4 and stood behind Radu, his Ruger drawn and aimed in the general direction of Radu's left temple.

"We don't tell him." Tevy turned to Kayla now. "He's your friend. It's your call, but wouldn't it be totally awesome to have a spy right down in Chicago?"

"But he'd have to murder to feed." She wanted a way out but didn't see that there was any loophole she could honestly use.

"No he wouldn't." Tevy turned to Radu. "Look, if you go down there tonight, just tell the bridge guards you want to join up. Better yet, go to the Merchandise Mart. We could really use a spy in there. I tell you, they'll take you once they see you're a ripper, I'll lay bullets on it. Just keep making stuff up about us and about how you became a ripper. Hey, even tell them that you, like, joined the rippers here voluntarily, that you figured St. Mike's was going to tank and you wanted to be on the winning side."

Kayla resisted the urge to jump in between them. "Whoa, whoa, whoa! Come again about how he wouldn't have to murder to feed?"

"They've got all those traitor troops up here from California donating blood. I know the rippers don't like it so much, but it keeps them alive." Tevy turned from Kayla to Radu. "Have you fed on a live human?"

Radu shook his head. "They murder them." He nodded up at the inverted corpses. "They murder them and tell me I'm next, but then one says he has better idea, that he can make me sweat bugs. He gets a cup..." Now Radu looked to the ground as if ashamed. "He gets a cup of blood and puts it to my lips and plugs my nose. I promise myself that I will suffocate first, but my body breaths and I swallow blood."

"I'm so very sorry," Tevy said in the silence that followed.

Radu looked up. "Why? This is not your fault. You even come to rescue me when it is clearly hopeless. I am very grateful."

A metallic bang and a scream from the corridor followed by panicked gunfire stole their attention. Kayla ran for the corridor, the others in close pursuit, except Mabruke, who had enough sense to tell his trooper to stay with Radu.

It was all over before Kayla got there.

A dozen fresh corpses lay on the floor, and several people stood over them with guns aimed. Amanda already had her knife out.

"What happened?" asked Kayla.

"Bastards were hiding in the lockers." Amanda pulled a head back and slit a throat. "Luckily, I got curious and opened one up. It was empty, but I spooked the ripper in the next one and he made a break for it, then a bunch more. It was a crazy turkey shoot for a second. We're fucking lucky we didn't shoot each other."

Kayla cursed herself for not thinking of this. It could have been a disaster.

Mabruke took control before she could put her thoughts into words. "I want these all aired out and I want those bricks blown out of those windows." He pointed at the fresh concrete block high in the wall above the lockers. He turned to Kayla. "I'm going to put together search parties to raid through the basement. You decide what to do about your friend, the ripper."

Elliot stood close to Amanda and took her left hand before she could move on to the next body. "Hey, clean the knife and come with us. Someone else can make sure they're dead."

Amanda dropped her knife and hugged Elliot tightly, her head buried in his shoulder even though she had to crouch because she was taller. Judging by the shudder, she was quietly weeping.

"It's okay. It's okay," he said, patting her back with his free hand, the other carefully pointing the Ruger at the ceiling. He caught Kayla's eye. "I'm gonna be a minute." To Amanda he said, "Come on. Let's go get some sunshine."

Kayla and Tevy headed back to stand in front of Radu, Tevy looking at her expectantly, Radu uncertainly. Mabruke called his trooper away, leaving just the three of them.

Kayla knew the quick solution, the obvious solution to all this, was to put a bullet through Radu's brain before Tevy could offer up any other arguments. That would be the easy way out.

"How would he get information to you?" she asked instead.

"We'd pick a place to meet just north of the Loop near the Mart. I go down there all the time anyway."

"Wait." Radu looked panicked more than anything else. "They make me a ripper as torture, you see? They plan to starve me and say that I will tell everything when I get hungry for blood. It makes men mad."

"But no one will be starving you," said Tevy. "You'll get a ration of dead blood, and that'll keep you from going crazy. The good thing is that you've never had living blood, 'cause that would be a mortal sin."

Kayla didn't like it, but she could see the value. "This will only postpone the inevitable. He's a ripper! Sorry, Rad, it's not your fault and it's killing me, but if we win the day in Chicago, there won't be anymore blood donations, and then what?"

Tevy looked uncertain but Radu was not.

"Then you put a bullet through my brain and save me. The 1000 Live On."

Kayla looked up sharply at Tevy, but he was nodding as if not surprised.

"You guys already are with the Ericsians, aren't you?" he said. "That's why you wanted to come along to meet them."

Kayla ignored him and turned her attention to Radu. "Promise me you won't give away any secrets, especially about St. John's."

Radu looked at Tevy and nodded. "He knows them all anyway. But the rippers, I only tell them lies."

Kayla took a deep breath and cursed the circumstances. Joyce would probably kill someone when she found out. Kayla knew that because even she would be furious if someone came to her and said they'd let go a ripper. And she and Joyce were the same soul.

"Fine. Cut him loose and get him some clothes and find somewhere to hide him until sunset. But you," she said, pointing at Radu, "don't let me down. And you," she said, pointing to Tevy, "you better be right. We're taking a huge risk here."

Tevy nodded and didn't look that certain himself. "He stayed with us in the woods. He didn't bail. He won't now."

"You better be fucking right."

———

Mabruke accepted Kayla's decision without argument, and this produced her first doubt in the 1000 Souls. She was young and untested. Was it wise to have such faith in her just because she completed a multiple-choice test with the same combination of answers as Joyce? What if Radu told Vlad about any weaknesses at St. John's? Did he know the secret of Bertrand Allan, that he was alive and a ripper? One thing she was now sure of was that Tevy knew, and Radu had said that Tevy knew all the secrets. What did he mean? It was time to ask.

They walked together back toward St. Mike's, because it was too far to go back to Wright Sanctuary and retrieve their bikes. Amanda and Elliot followed at a distance, holding hands and debriefing each other about the battle. Kayla put them in different groups, intentionally, before the attack, not wanting either to be distracted by the other's safety. Amanda was with her in the frontal assault through the blown doors. Kayla chose to be in a different group from Tevy for the same reason, because even before she found out he was the Bertrand soul, the Dormant Hero, she was aware of an attraction, one that began that first night when she had to rescue him from the woods. It flamed when he stripped and stepped out to meet the Ericsian patrol, not because she was aroused by his nudity, but his selflessness, his bravery, both of which he seemed totally unaware of.

The sun warmed them as it climbed through the morning. When they walked into the shade of the underpass at the Kennedy expressway, no one shouted to hear the echo as they had less than twenty-four hours before, when outbound on adventure. How long had it been since any of them had slept? Weariness overcame her, a desire to bust into the nearest house and find a couch or clean carpet where she could sleep. The thought of Tevy curled up next to her crossed her mind, but she forced the image away so that she could concentrate on the real issues. They would be at St. Mike's soon, and she would be out of time to interrogate Tevy. She took the plunge.

"Tevy, Rad said you knew all the secrets of St. John's. What did he mean?"

It was hard to tell what he was thinking, because he never stopped looking around, checking each side of the street, over his shoulder, and up at the higher buildings. Kayla made a note that she should learn to do the same. This was how one survived in the urban jungle with traitors as well as rippers as enemies. If only they'd seen the traitors with the nets on that building last evening, Radu might still be human. If only they'd traveled quietly as they did now, maybe the traitors wouldn't have heard them coming and been prepared with nets.

"Don't know much," he finally said. "Anything I should know?"

Kayla forced down a surge of anger, but some of it slipped out just the same. "Don't bullshit me."

Tevy nodded. "Fair enough. You don't bullshit me, and I won't bullshit you." He met her eye in challenge.

"Okay." Kayla feared what he might ask, but it was a reasonable request. "We fought the same battle last night. Let's just promise to always be on the same side."

"As long as you're fighting rippers, I'm on the same side."

But he hadn't answered her question. "So what was Radu talking about?"

"I know that Bertrand Allan is a ripper and fights for St. John's."

Kayla kept all her curses to herself. No need to let him know what power he had with this knowledge. "What else?"

"I know that at least some of you are Ericsians." He spared her a glance before he returned to his ceaseless vigilance of their surroundings. Kayla became more aware of their surroundings because of it. They crossed the river, the scent of algae rising over the bridge. Ahead lay big box stores and the River Point Shopping Center. Cars sat on flat tires, still parked as if the owners might return from Starbucks or the sports store. Kayla remembered when she loved sports: hockey, lacrosse, volleyball, all a part of her life that seemed so childish and futile now. She should have been learning shooting, hunting, and combat. On her right a McDonald's, the windows dirty but intact, reminded her of her empty stomach. How many times had she been this hungry since the apocalypse, a sensation totally outside her experience before her eighteenth birthday?

He let her silence hang, and she was grateful for that. How to respond? She had promised no bullshit. "Yes, not everyone at St. John's are Ericsians, believes in the 1000 Souls, but I am."

"Why?"

Since Kayla struggled with that faith herself, now was not the best time to answer, but she made an effort. "Haven't you ever met someone, and they were just like someone else you know or knew? And I don't mean that they look the same, or they're the same age or race or anything. They're just the same."

Tevy shook his head. "Nobody comes to mind. I mean until I met you and Joyce." He frowned and glanced at her before returning to his scrutiny of their surroundings. "That is weird, cause that's what the Ericsians said, that you're the same soul. Totally weird actually, 'cause I thought that after the battle that night just south of St. John's, the way you both get angry when going into battle, like everyone around you are effing morons."

Kayla suppressed an angry retort. "I just like to make myself emphatically clear so that fewer people die."

"Fair enough. So now it's your turn. I know that Margaret's not your daughter, and you're trying to keep her parents a secret from me. Who are they?"

Kayla was still debating an answer when Tevy suddenly let his breath out in a rush. "My God, it's Joyce isn't it? Crap, I'm thick sometimes. That kid spends way more time with her than you, always holding onto her leg and playing at the front of the bus."

"Please." Kayla forced the panic down, trying not to let Tevy guess how important this was to her. "Just keep it our secret, okay?"

Tevy shrugged. "Sure. Like it's not like anyone would care that Joyce has a daughter, anyway."

Kayla didn't look in his direction, didn't give any indication that he'd missed the mark, but it wasn't enough. He suddenly stopped and grabbed her arm, turning to face her and look into her eyes.

"Sweet Jesus." His eyes were wide with disbelief. "Sweet effing hell. Who's the father?"

Amanda and Elliot would catch up to them soon and Kayla didn't want this spreading farther than necessary. Maybe Tevy would keep the secret.

"If I tell you, will you promise to keep the secret?"

But it was too late for bargains. Kayla could practically see the light bulb over Tevy's head.

"Holy, holy frig," he said, his eyes very wide. He at least had the sense to whisper so that Elliot and Amanda wouldn't hear. "She's seven. It's Bertrand Allan, isn't it? The Savior of Chicago himself."

Kayla shook free and hurried down the center of the road, Tevy having to trot to keep up. She had to convince him to keep the secret or she had to kill him, kill all three of these Chicagoans, her new friends, her comrades-in-arms, her troops.

"Look, Tevy, Joyce is convinced that Bobs would kill her daughter, okay? You've got to keep this secret."

"Why ever would she do that?"

"Because Bertrand Allan is practically a saint now, and saints don't have children, especially out of wedlock. It makes them too mortal."

Tevy digested this for a full minute. "But Margaret's not a ripper, right, so I mean, when did they do it?"

Kayla double-checked his expression to make sure he wasn't kidding. He looked genuinely puzzled. "Before the Battle of the Mountain, of course. You can't have a baby with a ripper. They're infertile."

Tevy's brow still furled with confusion. "So the baby was born after..." He stopped speaking and his cheeks blushed.

"You didn't get any sex education at that church, did you? Babies are born nine months after the sex."

"Right, right, they did tell us that."

They walked in silence for a long time, turning onto a street that, Kayla noted from a dangling sign, had been called Clybourn Ave. She remembered this street from their ride out, but she viewed it differently. The century retail stores that she thought so quaint last night seemed far too close for comfort, rising three stories with the apartments on the second and third floor providing an excellent street vantage. They walked along the dotted yellow line, and she and Tevy agreed to watch the opposite side of the street for traps. Kayla now preferred the ugly modern plazas, single-story aluminum-sided buildings with parking lots in front, meaning the buildings were set far back from the street.

They moved into a trendy neighborhood, passing the entrance to a parking lot with a sign proclaiming MARKET SQUARE. Kayla remembered when stores like Pier 1 Imports and Pottery Barn were shopping opportunities that a kid from a small town considered exotic. The office buildings of downtown rose in the far distance, and the black hulk of the Willis Tower, a marvel to visit when she was fourteen, dwarfed all rivals.

"That's where he is." Tevy must have noted that it grabbed her attention. She nodded and returned to her scrutiny of closer threats. "Vlad Who Bleeds."

"We'll have to go get him, won't we?" Kayla said, and for a moment a desire to flee came upon her, to just run back to St. John's and the safety of the woods and the river and the Mattagami Bridge. Barry should just blow it down and they should shut out the rest of the world.

"Like the Battle of the Mountain." Tevy's voice held a strange awe now. What did he see in that tower? "We have to go and get the Vlads. They never come out to fight."

They heard the engine before they saw the truck, a 4x4 with a machinegun in the back, racing toward them, very much like the truck at St. John's with the fifty cal.

"That's Emile's!" shouted Elliot as Kayla unslung her Uzi. "Don't shoot."

They had less than a minute and she wasn't finished her interview with Tevy. There was no time left for subtly. "We got a deal. You going to keep this a secret from Bobs?"

Tevy didn't answer right away, but as Amanda and Elliot rushed to join them, he leaned in and whispered, "Okay. I don't see how it could help Bobs. But no more secrets between us."

Even as Kayla nodded and watched the truck rush up, she knew she was already breaking the promise, for she would never tell him that as he had leaned close, the scent of his sweat erotic rather than repugnant, she had an overwhelming desire to embrace him, to touch his body, to meld. He was eight years younger, an eighteen-year-old teenager who wouldn't be old enough to drink in pre-apocalypse Canada let alone America. He hadn't shaved at least since yesterday and still the stubble was soft, not demanding attention. Yet she sensed something in him that she craved, that meshed with her complicated persona. That was when she knew the Ericsian faith was true. He was the Dormant Hero, and she was destined to love him.

Luckily, he seemed oblivious.

16

END OF THE WORLD

Tevy watched Kayla go with Joyce to Emile's blockhouse, the first and strongest one north of the church, one of the few buildings within a hundred yards that hadn't been bulldozed during the days of Vlad the Scourge. It surprised him how much he wanted to go with her, to be near her—not like sex or anything weird. She was twenty-five, after all, and yet the idea of sleeping beside her, knowing that they had each others' back, that would be a sound sleep.

But despite his exhaustion, the summons was urgent. Emile, delighted to see them, had sped them back to St. Mike's, laughing and proud that Tevy had been sent as a messenger and not only formed an alliance but provoked and won a battle against a ripper fortress. They'd heard all about it by radio from the Ericsians right after dawn.

"You're just like Bert," Emile said, waving a fat finger. "You won't give them time to settle down and build up, you go right after them right away."

Kayla had given him a very significant look at that point, but Tevy shook his head, begging her to keep quiet about the Ericsians and their newfound belief that he hosted a portion of the same soul as Bertrand

Allan. Kayla nodded in response to Tevy's unspoken plea, and the tit for tat wasn't lost on him. He now had a secret he didn't want Bobs hearing, just like Kayla and Joyce.

He headed into the rectory through the back door, avoiding the church and morning mass, something he was usually required to attend. Elliot knuckle knocked and yawned before splitting away to go the basement and their dorms. Tevy hoped he could soon follow, for the exhaustion was heavy, and the chicken sandwiches, sent by Helen, that Emile had handed them in the truck had only started to fill the hole.

A knock at the bishop's conference room door brought an immediate invitation to enter. Tevy found Bobs standing at one end of the table, maps spread out, and Colonel Webb, dressed in gray camouflage, standing beside her, one finger on the map as they talked. Tevy wondered if the man would ever age, for he looked just as Tevy remembered him when he was ten: his gray hair brush-cut short, and his body as trim as any athlete, even though the sun and worry had weathered his face.

Bobs looked delighted. "That's my man! I knew I could count on you."

They were only using a fraction of the polished table, and for a moment Tevy had the crazy idea that he might lie down on the unused portion and get some sleep.

"We took a high school," Tevy said. He cursed the stupidity of the statement, for it hadn't been a high school in well over eight years.

Colonel Webb moved around the table, one hand extended. "You did excellent work, young man. We didn't know about that ripper fortress yet, and it could've been a real problem, especially if they hit us by surprise."

Tevy shook the man's hand, wondering if this is what it was like to meet a rock star, for to him Webb was a star, the man who had kept the country's nukes out of ripper hands, who still defended the last operational air force base in America. He'd seen Webb on many occasions, of course, but the man had barely acknowledged Tevy's existence.

Bobs poured red wine into three crystal glasses, handing one to each. "To taking the initiative," she said, raising hers in toast.

Tevy sipped the liquid, tasting mustiness and sour grapes. He didn't understand why everyone liked alcohol so much. After tasting beer, hooch, and wine, he still preferred milk, or better yet, that rare treat: apple juice. Orange and grape juice were distant memories, although cans of flavored soda helped keep the memory alive, despite getting harder to find every year.

"Sit and tell us about the battle." Webb took a seat himself and gestured to the chair at the head of the table.

Bobs slid a map of Chicago over the map of America that she and Webb were looking at when Tevy arrived. She took a seat on his left and pointed to a grid on the map. "Hairy High, right? Funny, I graduated from there just before the end. Tell us what happened."

Tevy told them of Radu's capture, of meeting the Ericsians, and of convincing Mabruke that an immediate attack would take the rippers by surprise. He left out the soul determination test and its results. He left out finding Radu in the school. He considered a lie, but just made no mention of him. Neither the Colonel nor Bobs asked, perhaps because Radu was from St. John's and meant nothing to them.

"And the St. John's people." Bobs sat back with her wine glass, studying Tevy in a way that made his ears burn, as if she bored holes into his brain with her eyes. "Can they be trusted to hold a line?"

"They fight damn well." He told them about his rescue and the fight in the woods. For a moment he almost slipped, nearly telling them about the part where a ripper started killing rippers, but he caught himself in time, focusing on how brave Kayla and Radu had been holding the line.

"Yeah, she sounds like she could be useful. Too bad he bought it."

Webb looked more thoughtful, as if he sensed something was missing from Tevy's account, but more important things must've have been on his mind. "Good work," he said. "I think we should send this young soldier to bed before he falls asleep in that good wine."

But something about the way he looked at Bobs caught Tevy's attention. Did he want to talk about Tevy after he was gone? Tevy stood up and gave handshakes again. Webb showed him how to salute and promised to put him through basic training, and in moments the heavy oak door shut him in the corridor.

Tevy didn't leave. Bobs always sent him into the city to listen, and it had become a habit, and he was very good at being quiet. After walking as loudly down the carpeted corridor as he could, and slamming the door to the stairwell for good measure, he crept back to the conference room and placed an ear near the door jam. Their voices were raised—a civil debate but a tense discussion.

"We have to use them sometime. Who knows if they even work?" That was Bobs.

"There are a lot of innocent Americans in those cities. I simply can't accept killing them in all good conscience."

"Then you can accept a country run by the rippers?"

"No!"

"Colonel, you know you're really the top ranking military officer left in America. You know this is up to us. You've been polite and very political to keep your rank and all, but there's no one to promote you or give you orders except me. You're the frigging general of the army, navy, and air force, and I'm the closest thing you've got to a commander in chief. The president is a fucking ripper, and if you'd listened to him eight years ago, you would be too."

"But to strike our own people. It's evil."

"They're not our people." Bobs shouted this, and Tevy could picture her angry eyes, imagine her fist striking the table. "They don't just feed the rippers, they're up here now to fight. Even with the Bradleys and all the outliers I've called up, we might not be able to hold them off. But let's say we do, best-case scenario, keep them from overrunning all the Loyalist strongholds north of the Loop. They'll just come back again with even more numbers, and this Vlad, this Vlad Who Bleeds, he won't be taken like Vlad the Scourge. Fuck, how many Vlads are out there anyway? And don't think they won't take Malmstrom eventually. They'll be coming for you again."

"Malmstrom will hold for a time." But now the Colonel did sound old and weary to Tevy, the years catching up with his soul if not his body.

"You're running out of parts and you're holding on to that base out of nostalgia. Soon nothing will fly out of there no matter what. It's time to use what we have and abandon it. You bring every soldier you've got and come and join us here in Chicago. Together we'll be strong, but we have to eliminate the ripper's source of supply."

"By killing millions of innocent civilians?"

Bobs' shout was loud enough that Tevy drew back from the door. "They are not innocent! They're feeding the rippers and they're working as slaves. Those are still organized countries out east and west, but organized around Vlad's new world order. They still have food, and they starve anyone not with them. They've starved the whole Midwest and most of the south into non-existence. Millions dead. What's so fucking innocent about that?"

There was a long pause, and Tevy prepared to hurry away. What if they were coming to the door, finished their debate? But then Webb spoke, his voice low, again indicating the weariness that seemed to have overtaken him. "I see your point. It really is over. I'd always hoped that maybe something could be salvaged, that maybe people would rise up against the rippers as we did, but there's certainly no sign that's ever going to happen."

"Three nukes," said Bobs. "Los Angeles, New York, and Washington. It'll gut all of the rippers' supplies in one shot, and it'll destroy all command and control. Then the remaining people can rise up like you hoped. Then we can complete the revolution."

Tevy's hand covered his mouth to prevent a gasp.

There was silence.

Finally Webb answered. "Three nukes."

Tevy fled.

17

BELL TOWER TO BOILER ROOM

Tevy had never been to Los Angles, New York or Washington, but as he sat on the rafters of the bell tower above the clock, he tried to recall every movie he had seen that featured those cities. Los Angeles was sprawling and huge, New York dense and high. Of Washington he only remembered shots of the White House and secret agents. In movies the president was sometimes a hero and sometimes a villain, but since Tevy's parents' murder, he had always considered the man evil. He was a ripper. He had demanded that the people of Chicago submit to his will and the new world order of Vlad the Scourge. He had sent riot police, many of them rippers themselves. Later, an army came to "pacify Chicago and restore good government." That army had retreated in panic in the face of the first alliance of Chicago Loyalists.

A pigeon fluttered up against the screen over the steeple vent, trying to find a way into the tower, but Bishop Alvarez made sure that his church was well-maintained, even though they had only rudimentary plumbing and rare electricity from the generator. The screen frustrated the bird and off it flew. Despite the bishop's best efforts, the clock below

Tevy no longer worked, but the bell below it still marked the hours of the day.

Tevy often came here when he was troubled, and he'd learned to wedge himself against the steep peak while sitting on a loose board over two rafters. He actually spent most of the day asleep. He woke each hour for the bell, of course, but his gun-deafened ears didn't find it nearly as loud as when he first found his way up here as a child. So each hour, Tevy spent a few minutes before drifting back to sleep, thinking about the murder of millions of people and trying to decide whether it was justified. They'd murdered millions of Loyalists humans after all, because intentionally burning crops and withholding food was slow murder—the worst kind.

He had always assumed that the killing would end. When Bertrand Allan killed Vlad the Scourge, there were wild celebrations in Old Town Chicago. Surely, people thought, with the head cut off the snake, things would get back to normal, even if it took a while to drag out the last of the rippers into the sun's cleansing light.

But it was too late, the parasites having spread too far. If the famines hadn't come, maybe the humans would have been able to kill all the rippers, maybe they could have purged Vlad's disease and stopped the forced conversions. But Vlad laid the groundwork to ensure that his new world order would survive his death. There were simply too many rippers and too few humans left to fight them. The president made broadcast after broadcast telling the resistance to lay down their arms, to surrender to the inevitable, and for all Tevy knew, he still did, not that there were many in the Midwest with the electricity available to turn on a TV and watch.

Yet Tevy had still believed that one day the rippers would starve without enough humans to feed them, that they would starve in vast numbers just as the humans had through the first three winters. He had clung to the belief that one day they would march into Washington and reclaim the government, that all the cities controlled by the rippers would fall and things would get back to normal.

Normal. Factories producing goods, farmers plowing fields, and Hollywood making ripper war movies and people answering phones. Tevy had even fantasized about staring in an action film, perhaps even landing the role of Bertrand Allan. He could picture the last scene, setting off the bomb that would destroy both he and Vlad the Scourge.

How would they make the movie now, though? Bertrand wasn't dead. He was a ripper watching over his secret daughter. Vlad the Scourge may be dead, or perhaps he too survived that last conflagration and renamed himself Vlad Who Bleeds.

And now Bobs wanted to save the world by ending it. Three crucial cities to America were to be wiped from the face of the earth. For the first time in his life, Tevy had to face the reality that the world would never go back to what it was before the rippers. The apocalypse could not be healed or undone. He wept.

Elliot was privy to this illegal hiding place. He was one of the few who knew how to pick the lock on the trap door, and he had first proved that it was possible to squeeze past the clock. So Tevy wasn't surprised when, sometime after three bells, Elliot's red-haired head poked above the rafters, and a smile spilt his freckled face.

"What the hell are you doing up here? The Brats want to throw their heroes a party. Helen even promised some cans of orange soda and fresh bread."

Tevy hurriedly wiped his cheeks and sat up on the board to make room for Elliot. It was hot up here today, the dust and old wood creating a musty smell, but it was comforting one. As a child it had meant safety, security, and precious time alone.

"Have you ever been to Los Angeles or New York or Washington?" asked Tevy.

Elliot sat, but unlike Tevy he restlessly swung his legs in space, like a child in a chair that was too big for him. "My family went to New York when I was like six or so, but I really don't remember much except tall buildings and the subway pretty much always underground. Why?"

Tevy and Elliot never kept secrets from each other.

"I heard something," whispered Tevy.

Elliot leaned closer and whispered with a conspiratorial smile, "What?"

"We're going to nuke L.A., New York, and Washington. Wipe them off the map."

"Vlad's stinking blood!" Elliot had been amusing himself since Tevy's return by finding interesting combinations of Bishop Alvarez's forbidden words to create new strings of profanity. But this time it wasn't enough. He looked at Tevy with wide eyes. "Holy fuck! I mean Jesus Christ, you're full of shit, right?"

"Wish I was, but I heard it from Bobs herself."

"She told you?" Elliot had stopped kicking his legs and studied Tevy with an expression of disbelief.

Tevy shook his head. "I was, like, eavesdropping on her and Webb. I don't know why, but I just gotta sometimes, just need to find out what's going on before the news hits us like one of them LAW rockets. Webb wasn't too keen on using his nukes, but she talked him into it. Three nukes. Three cities."

Elliot was nodding even before Tevy finished.

"Should've seen it coming," Elliot said. "I mean, what choice have we got?"

"So you're okay with this? 'Cause it's like ending the world. We can never get back the old America if you blow those cities off the map."

Elliot resumed his kicking. "I don't know that we ever could. After Vlad got toasted, I thought for a bit that things would go back to normal even with my folks and sister gone, but after the first winter, I knew that wasn't going to happen. Didn't have to be a genius to count the bodies and know that this was major."

"I guess I'm no genius."

Elliot smiled and shook his head. "Endlessly optimistic, maybe even a little new, but not stupid. The nuke thing though, it is a bit harsh. Problem is the collateral. Must be a lotta people who don't want to serve the rippers, who are slaves, not traitors, but it's not like we can save them. If they haven't freed themselves, we sure as hell can't do it, except by killing them."

Tevy slid off the board and hung down to the next set of rafters. This used to be a difficult maneuver when he was ten and his feet could barely reach, but now it was effortless, and Elliot followed his lead as he headed for the narrow space by the clock.

"Hey, where're you going?" Elliot asked.

"Gotta talk to Emile. He'll know what to do."

"You'll have to wait until later or tomorrow," Elliot said as he slipped down past the clockwork. "All the Companions of Bertrand are having a reunion. Come on and join the Brat Pack. The kids want to hear some bedtime stories about killing rippers. Little Mia says they gotta be true stories, so I'll leave that to you."

Despite his worry, Tevy told many stories that night. He fell asleep in the La-Z-Boy with Mia curled on his lap and Collin, nearly a teenager himself, asleep on the carpet at his feet. It was good to be home and Tevy slept well.

—————

The next afternoon they found Emile in his boiler room/gun shop.

"The man of the hour!" Emile's cheeks were a brighter red than the damp boiler room could account for, so Tevy guessed he was already drunk on his moonshine.

Elliot was more observant. "Hey, where did you get the beer?"

Four empty brown bottles were lined up on the bench like soldiers, and the scent of hops mixed in the air with stale farts and wet foundation. The afternoon sun streamed through the bars of the basement windows, highlighting dust motes that would usually be invisible.

"Boys, boys, or should I say men." Emile reached into an old plastic cooler beside him and pulled out two dripping bottles. "All I had to chill 'em with was cold water from the well, no ice a course."

Elliot twisted the cap and took a pull. "Hey, these aren't skunky at all!"

"From my private stash, kept cool down here and never frozen. I decided it was as good a time to open them as any, what with us moving soon. Want to travel light."

"Moving?" Tevy twisted open his beer and took a sip. He would have sworn it was bad himself, but he had no experience with fresh beer. "Where are we moving?"

Emile smiled and sat back on his stool, leaning one chubby elbow against his bench for support. "I'm thinking downtown. Thanks to you we got a real chance now." He gestured at Tevy with his bottle before taking a sip.

Tevy looked at Elliot to see if he understood, but when he shook his head, Tevy turned back to Emile. "What are you talking about?"

"We got an army now, don't we?" Emile said. "We got Joyce's Raiders back, and they're like the old days only on steroids. I mean, how many did you bring back from St. John's? Six hundred, and all trained and fighting veterans? That's an army. We were amateurs back in the day compared to this new crew. And now you got us the Ericsians, too, and that's gotta be at least another two thousand. With all of us working together, the rippers'll never know what hit them."

"They've got more, Emile," Tevy said. "Way more. I've counted them."

"Yeah." Emile frowned and met Tevy's gaze. "But none of the traitors are used to fighting, and the rippers can only fight at night, so we'll do okay."

Elliot reached into the cooler for another bottle. "But this is all defense, right? They're all here to stop the rippers from crossing the river and pushing up north."

Emile shook his head, one hand scratching under his long beard, now flecked with more gray than Tevy remembered, as if Emile had aged in just a few weeks. "When did Bobs ever win a battle by sitting and waiting for an enemy come after her? She's got Webb on side this time. I mean, look at this place." He waved around at the stuffed shelves and piles of ammunition boxes. "They opened the doors of Rock Island for us, and even heavier stuffs coming our way. Strikers and Bradleys. Stuff that can drive right into the Loop and blow holes in all those ripper lairs. This is gonna be great."

Tevy wanted to bring up the nukes but found he couldn't. Emile was in such a good mood. How could he ruin that? He decided that instead he would find a chance to talk to Helen or maybe even the bishop during confession. He could start by confessing to the sin of eavesdropping and then tell him what he heard. Surely, the bishop wouldn't condone murdering millions of humans.

"So what about the nukes, though." Elliot, probably because he was already into his second beer and drinking fast, slurred his words.

Emile squinted at him. "We can't use the nukes, boy. They'd blow us apart."

"No, I mean on New York and L.A. and..." He turned to Tevy. "Where else?"

Emile turned on Tevy. "What the hell's he talking about?"

Tevy explained, relieved to be able to unload this burden on someone of authority. Emile listened silently, his eyes going wider until he had to put his beer down to look around the room, as if an answer might be among the boxes or the pipes up near the ceiling.

"So that's what's really going on. That's why she says we just have to take them on now and there'll be no ripper reinforcements, that we'll have them on the ropes." He drummed his fingers on the bench. "Well, if this don't beat all."

"Can we stop it?" asked Tevy.

"Question is should we stop it," Emile said. "Crap. This is a biggie."

Tevy had wondered himself. "But the bishop says that if you murder a human, like intentionally shoot a human, you'll go to Hell. Won't we all go to Hell?"

"You won't." Elliot weaved a bit on his stool. "I bet you didn't even shoot any humans last night. Don't you worry, dude." He put a hand over his mouth. "Damn, said it again. I just can't stop." He reached for the cooler for a third beer, but Emile's foot got to the lid first and pinned it closed.

"Take a breather there, kid. This isn't water." Emile turned back to Tevy. "You won't go to Hell for the nukes, 'cause you told me. Now it's up to me to see what to do about it. Joyce and Jeff and Martin are here now, and with Simon and Julia and Helen that means we've got almost all of the original Companions of Bertrand except Barry. The bishop may have a thing or two to say about this before all's said and done. Now drink up, you've earned it." Elliot reached for the cooler, but Emile kept his foot planted firmly on top. "Not you. You've chugged your share. You got to learn to sip, boy. Savor it."

Tevy continued to force himself to take swallows to be polite, but he never got to the end of the whole beer. Amanda burst through the door of the boiler room, stopping on the metal grate landing above the stairs and leaning on the railing to call down.

"Hey guys, you gotta come now! There's tanks rolling up through the Loop and headed our way."

Tevy wondered if the alcohol had already affected his brain because for a moment he thought she was talking about the promised Bradley's and Strikers. "Our tanks?"

Amanda looked furious. "No! We don't have any tanks. They're ripper tanks and they're buttoned up and heading for all the bridges. The rippers are coming."

18

KAYLA'S FIRST COMMAND

Kayla tried to see it from Joyce's perspective: the newest member of her Raiders goes on a mission to keep an eye on a guy who could be trouble, and instead she ends up leading him and about two hundred others into battle against a seriously fortified position. Despite her attempts at understanding, Kayla still didn't like being interrogated.

At least the food, a sandwich of chicken with butter and fresh bread, was good. Even at St. John's, fresh meat was rare and had to be hunted and widely shared. Jeff reclined on an old couch in the corner of the cramped third-floor room having a bottle of beer that was a gift from Emile. Above Jeff was a gun rack, the temporary home of his FN F2000 and Joyce's Uzi and three other rifles.

Martin also had a beer in hand. He stood by the window with his back to Kayla as he looked out at the view from this blockhouse to the bell tower of St. Mike's and the distant Chicago skyline, menacing because of the ripper strongholds. Joyce sat across the table from Kayla, a yellowed map of Chicago under her fingers as she extracted the story.

"So the high school," said Joyce. "You took it out with a two-pronged assault and LAWs?"

"Four pronged." Kayla paused to swallow so that she wouldn't be speaking through a mouthful. "Second floor and first floor at the same time, simultaneous assaults at opposite wings of the school."

"Did you find Radu's body?"

"No." Kayla had been offered a beer, and she took a cautious sip now. "We found Radu."

Jeff sat up on the couch, and Martin turned from the window.

Joyce's eyes looked knives. "What do you mean, you found Radu? Was he a ripper?"

"Yes, and we let him go." Kayla braced for the storm.

"What? Are you crazy? He knows about Margaret. He knows all kinds of stuff about St. John's."

Kayla stood her ground. "He doesn't know about the secret exit, and he doesn't know about Bertrand Allan, and he wants to work for us."

"He's a ripper!" Joyce stood, leaning over the table in her fury.

"So's your boyfriend, and he works for you."

Jeff stood quickly and put a hand on Joyce's shoulder. "Wait, wait, wait." He looked to Kayla. "What's the plan?"

"He's to go and join the rippers at the Merchandise Mart and live off the dead blood, the blood donations. He's promised he won't murder humans for blood." Kayla was tempted to stand and meet Joyce eye-to-eye, but that would only inflame the situation. "He wanted us to shoot him at first. Tevy talked him into it, made him promise to be our spy, to bring us information. Apparently Tevy gets down around this Merchandise Mart a lot after dark."

"And why did you listen to that little brat?"

"Because he's right." Now Kayla did stand to meet Joyce's wrath head on.

Jeff pulled Joyce back to face him. "If he is the Dormant Hero, if he didn't just fluke out on the test, you're going to have to learn to trust his gut the way you trust Bert."

Martin came over to the table, looking from Joyce to Kayla and back. "I don't think it's an accident that she answered as the Angry Captain. I've suspected this for months, and when she took command in the college, I was ready to insist on the determination, but everything else changed before we could meet." He put the empty bottle down and met Joyce's blue eyes with his brown ones. "Joyce," he said gently. "You're arguing with yourself."

"I'm not arguing with myself." But Joyce sat and stared across the table as Kayla did the same.

Martin sat heavily in the third chair. "She takes command just like you did after the riots at my restaurant. Nobody voted for you and nobody opposed you because it worked. You saved hundreds of lives because you just knew what to do." Martin nodded in Kayla's direction. "She saved dozens of lives last night with her plan. Bert would've just headed straight at the front door, bravely leading the way in a stupid charge. Sounds like this Tevy kid would've done the same. You heard what he did at the crash site, charging the rippers when help had arrived and it wasn't necessary. He just couldn't help himself. He had to go get them."

Jeff reclaimed his seat on the couch. "I want to meet Elliot. I don't really remember me as a teenager, but I think I was a constant party."

Kayla couldn't help a smile. "He's reckless and fun, but when you need him he's like a rock."

Jeff raised his beer in a toast. "Dependable Rogue, that's me." He reclined back on the couch, raising a puff of dust that tickled Kayla's nostrils.

Joyce studied her map for a moment. "I bet Bert's in the bunker." She looked up to Martin. "I should tell him about this. He could maybe find Radu one night, make sure he doesn't turn."

"Allan's here?" Kayla asked.

Joyce looked up with a frown. "None of your business."

Jeff shook his head. "How's he going to do that, Joyce? He's probably the most famous man in America. His YouTube broadcasts had millions of hits. You think the rippers wouldn't recognize him and decapitate him ASAP?"

"He's changed."

Suddenly Kayla understood some of Joyce's anger. Her lover wasn't dead and he wasn't alive. She couldn't be free of him and move on with her life, and she had to watch him become less human with each passing year. What if that happened to Tevy? Kayla tried to think of something to say, something comforting, but all she could think of was the hope that Bertrand Allan would die soon, and that was unlikely to lift Joyce's spirits.

Pounding feet on the stairs warned them that someone was coming in a hurry, and Kayla reflexively snatched her Uzi off the table and pointed it at the door. Basil burst through, and the normally implacable man looked more excited than Kayla had ever known him.

"Ripper tanks are moving up the Loop with their traitor troops following. We barely got here on time, I guess. It's tonight. They're coming for St. Mike's tonight."

Joyce hurried to grab her Uzi from the gun rack above Jeff, and they all pounded down the stairs, following Joyce's lead, even though Kayla didn't know where they were going. Apparently she wasn't the only one.

"Where the hell are we going?" asked Jeff as they sprinted across the square to the church.

"To see Bobs. We need to coordinate this carefully." Joyce didn't look excited or alarmed, and Kayla was impressed.

Joyce led them through the church and into a side door to the rectory, taking them deep into the building until they found a crowd in the hall outside the bishop's conference room. Bishop Alvarez pushed out of the room, dressed in a simple black cassock, and even though Kayla didn't know him, she guessed he was angry by the thundercloud expression. But he saw Joyce and broke into a smile.

"My Joyce. I'm so glad you have come to our rescue." He hurried to make the Sign of the Cross and started to make the Sign of the Mountain but stopped halfway through the motion, perhaps catching the glare. She had been a leader at the Battle of the Mountain.

"Father, it's so good to see you."

"I wish we had time for a proper visit, but you are needed immediately." He waved her into the busy conference room.

General Roberts, Bobs, stood at the head of a long oak table, maps and little flags and even toy tanks and trucks marking positions. The room stank of too many bodies in an era of no deodorant. It took Kayla a moment the recall that Bobs was only a year older, and yet there were already worry lines around her eyes. Her blonde hair was cropped very short, as if to warn men to stay away. She looked up when they entered.

"Joyce, perfect. You and your Raiders can take and hold the Wells Street Bridge. I'll send several detachments of St. Mike's regulars to support you."

Kayla suddenly saw an opportunity. She leaned close to Joyce and whispered, "Demand the Ericsians. Say you want to keep an eye on them."

"What was that?" Bobs hadn't missed that exchange and her attention fell on Kayla.

Joyce looked over with her own frown, studying Kayla, who nodded emphatically. "The Ericsians," said Joyce to Bobs. "Kayla just reminded me that they've already followed her into a fight, and she's one of my trusted captains. Send the Ericsians with us so that I can put them under her command."

"Her command?"

"She can keep an eye on them for us. They trust her."

Bishop Alvarez shook his head in frustration. "I don't like allying ourselves with these unbelievers. They could end up spreading their false God among our good people."

Kayla spoke up. "All the more reason to put them with us, then. They won't be with your flock and at least some of the St. John's people will be going home after this."

But Alvarez wasn't placated. "I don't want them infecting St. John's either. This cult is like a disease. It's catching."

Bobs shook her head. "There are at least five hundred of them right here in Chicago right now and lots more out west. I need them until Webb gets those Bradleys and Strikers here." She turned her attention on Kayla. "Okay, you command the Ericsians. If they fuck up it's on your head."

Tevy and his friends pushed into the room, and Kayla had to hide a thrill at seeing him, had to push down the desire to touch. Luckily, Tevy took up a position across the table from her before he even noticed that she was there. But before he could speak or be spoken to, a stir outside announced the arrival of Mabruke and a half-dozen captains of the Ericsians. People had to push back into the corners to make room for all the new arrivals.

Mabruke was dressed so like Erics in a tight-fitting pin-striped suit that it might have been a statement to Bobs. *I am like Erics.*

Bishop Alvarez left with a swish of his cassock, pushing past Mabruke without a glance.

"Mabruke," said Bobs. "Good of you to come."

Mabruke stopped at the opposite end of the table, flanked by his captains, and clasped his hands. "The trinity has come together. It is clearly the time of great and terrible events."

Bobs eyes narrowed with suspicion. "What trinity?"

"Why the Dormant Hero, the Angry Captain, and the Dependable Rogue, of course."

"I thought Bert was the Dormant Hero. How the fuck could he be here?"

Kayla experienced a moment of panic. What if Tevy told her about Bertrand Allan? Even if he didn't mean harm, even if he just thought he was clearing things up this would be a disaster. She caught his eye across the width of the table and tried to beg his silence without words or expression. Tevy met her eye and gave her a subtle nod.

"He means me," he said to Bobs. "I had to take their determination. They wouldn't trust me otherwise. I guess I answered the same way Bertrand Allan answered, so I'm supposed to be a portion of the same soul."

"And I'm the Dependable Rogue." Elliot slurred his words, and Jeff had to restrain a laugh.

"You?" Bobs' outrage was focused on Tevy, but before she could say more, Mabruke interrupted.

"We have anti-tank weapons and a howitzer," he said. "We only have illumination rounds for that, but perhaps Webb can find explosive rounds for us now that we're allies."

"A howitzer?" Bobs' anger was diffused by the opportunity. "What, like a 777?"

"An older M198 but still quite functional, I can assure you."

"Where the hell did you get that, and why didn't you tell us about this before?"

"The Trinity has come together for the first time since the Battle of the Mountain. It is a time of great consequence, and we will put all of our efforts and weapons at their disposal. The Angry Captain has already used the LAWs to great effect." He waved at Kayla with an open palm face up.

Kayla now found herself under Bobs' withering attention, but she stood firm.

"So that's why the Ericsians follow you." Bobs looked down at her map. "Fine. I can make this work. You guys will cover the Franklin and Wells Street bridges. Take these two with you," she nodded in the direction of Tevy and Elliot. "Gonsalves and Chen will cover everything east of Clark."

"What about LaSalle?" asked Joyce.

"Right, you haven't been here. The rippers pulled that bridge up one night about five years ago, just before dawn. We fought our way in there and jammed all the gears and stuff with bags of cement. It's not ever coming down. Okay, we gotta move people. The Brat Pack will be my runners. Tevy and Elliot know them all."

But Joyce wasn't satisfied. "What about all the westbound bridges."

Bobs shook her head. "Too many of them and too far away. Let them cross those if they want. They'll have to come north and back across the river close to us, and there are a lot fewer bridges up here and those bridges are a lot closer to Old Town. Be ready to swing around to defend Kinzie and Grand, but that's later. Right now you just don't let them across Wells and Franklin. Those are your babies. Don't blow them up unless you absolutely have to. We're gonna need them when we go on the offensive."

Kayla hurried out with the general flood of people, rushing out to the courtyard in front of St. Mike's where Joyce pulled them all to a stop near the statue of St. Michael. Mabruke and his Ericsian captains had come with them, and everyone formed a circle around Joyce. The sun indicated about four o'clock. Jeff didn't stop with them, heading for the blockhouse across the square, presumably to get the St. John's people armed and moving.

Joyce addressed Mabruke. "Do you have transport?"

"I have several trucks fueled and ready to go just outside of the cantonment."

"Okay, then get your people down to the river, as close as you can get. Kayla, you go with them and take the rest of your...trinity...and hold the Wells Street Bridge. Do you know where that is?"

Kayla made an effort not to look too relieved to be given some responsibility. "I don't, but he does." She pointed to Tevy.

"The Merchandise Mart's a problem," he said. "The rippers have fortified the bottom two floors."

Joyce gave him an irritated shake of her head. "Then unfortify it. I don't care how, you just hold that bridge." She may have been answering Tevy, but the order was to Kayla. But Joyce wasn't finished. She took Kayla by the arm and led her away from the circle so that she could speak to her alone.

"If Tevy really does host a portion of the same soul as Bert, then think of him as a bullet: you point him in the right direction at the right time and you pull the trigger. Keep the Dependable Rogue, what was his name?"

"Elliot."

"Keep Elliot close to Tevy. He'll have a balancing influence that'll keep him from doing anything crazy. Bert only got into trouble when he was left alone in a battle. Now go and go quickly."

Kayla led them toward the Eugenie Street gate, Tevy on one side and Elliot on the other, the Ericsians close behind. She was glad that she had no warning of this battle, no sleepless day worrying about tonight. She was well-rested and she had been trusted with a command that had a clear objective.

She was terrified only of failure.

19

WELLS STREET BRIDGE

Kayla hardly had time to think or plan, because once they reached the trucks of the Ericsians, it was only a ten minute drive down to where Tevy convinced her to stop. Many of the trucks were pickups with machine guns mounted in the backs, others were five-tons, the rear doors open in the heat to show troops sitting on benches.

For the last mile they traveled on Wells, they passed mostly older buildings, three and four-story affairs of red or light-brown brick. Those didn't worry her, because they couldn't provide much cover for rippers, especially since a few of the structures were little more than burned-out husks, but ahead the rusting steel of the 'L' train curved in from the west and ran overtop of the street, blocking out the afternoon light. At night it would be a very dark tunnel. Tevy identified the hulking building on the right as her target, the Merchandise Mart, and it wasn't hard to see why the rippers chose it. The building rose around twenty stories as far as she could tell. The lower floors were faced with permanent-looking gray stone, the rest of it was strong concrete. The large windows on the lowest two floors were completely sealed with concrete block, something done after the apocalypse. Like the windows at Atherley College, the bricklayers were amateurs, and for centuries the mortar that dripped down the sides of these newer walls would testify to the haste and incompetence of the workers. A domed turret on the corner gave it the appearance of a giant medieval castle.

"What about those?" she asked Tevy, pointing across the street at a high glass condo, only a few of the windows smashed. Behind it, rising far higher, towered a glass-and-steel office building. The upper ten floors looked to have burned out of control at some point, as evidenced by the exploded windows and smears of black covering the structure. The lower floors, however, looked untouched by the conflagration.

"Not held by the rippers as far as I know. There's a smaller building fronting the street in front of the tall one back there." Tevy pointed to the rusting overpass. "That's the Merchandise Mart 'L' station. Up there we can shoot at the traitors in the Mart, but they can shoot us, too. Hey, do you think Radu made it down here last night?"

Before Kayla could speculate, Mabruke joined them, hurrying up the line of trucks from one of the five-tons. She spoke even as he arrived, again flanked by several of his captains. "Can we use the LAWS on that concrete block?" she asked.

Mabruke shook his head. "We only have twelve left. We should save them for the tanks and make sure every one counts. We've got dynamite that would be better for that."

The sound of a heavy engine and the squeal of treads from south of the river warned that they had little time.

Kayla studied the buildings, creating fields of fire in her mind, watching assaults and retreats and checking for possible surprises. Her concentration was fierce, and no one spoke to her for a full minute.

"Why the hell did they keep their tanks so far away anyway?" she asked. "I'd have kept them hidden and close and brought them across the bridge before we knew what hit us."

Elliot grinned proudly. "That was us. They used to keep them up here, but Tevy and me snuck in a few weeks ago just before dawn. Caught all the traitors still napping and the rippers just closing down. We got two by dropping grenades down the open hatches and then ran for it."

Kayla liked that the rippers had miscalculated. What other mistakes could they make?

"Okay, I want two teams of five each sweeping that condo. Make sure there's no traitors in there. Then take two of these machine guns," she said, pointing to one mounted in the back of a pick up truck, "and place them on the fifth floor at either end of the building, so that you can rake any traitors in the upper floors of the Mart. You see someone and you kill them until I say otherwise."

Mabruke nodded. "What about the tanks?"

Kayla debated, but decided she couldn't protect Tevy or keep him safe. He would never allow it and he would wonder why. "Tevy and Elliot know this hood best. You guys go straight through there," she said, pointing south on the street where it went under the station. "Send a couple of your rocket men with them," she said to Mabruke before turning back to Tevy. "Block the street. Hit one tank and back away. Wait for another tank to try and go around the wreck, then destroy it, too. I want two tanks blown to hell burning side by side in the middle of that bridge." Kayla checked to make sure Elliot understood. "Then come back to us, because we're going into the basement of the Mart before sunset." She turned to Tevy. "Then we'll see if Radu's there."

Watching Tevy and Elliot run off caused a surge of jealousy, but she couldn't be part of their little team and run straight for the action. She had a bigger job. "Mabruke, get your dynamite. We're going in along the back here. But meanwhile ..." She pointed to the stairs that led from the sidewalk to the station. "Let's send a couple of teams up there to make sure that station is empty. If they take fire from the Mart, make sure they know what floor, so that your machine gunners can return fire."

Mabruke was relaying orders as fast as she delivered them, but now she had a moment when there was little she could do but check her own weapons. She felt all the pockets on her vest, a nervous habit before battle, to ensure she had lots of spare clips.

Gunfire erupted from the Mart over the station, and she couldn't help herself, running up the steps to find men and women retreating quickly but efficiently, some stopping to shoot up at the Mart. Fifth floor, just where she would put them—not too high, because then they'd have to lean out from the building to cover the tracks. The platform had a roof that provided some cover, so Kayla used it to run to the far end of the station. She wanted to see the tanks, but the tracks of the 'L' hid the street. She could hear the engines clearly now.

Gunfire echoed back across the river, the distinctive blast of a shotgun like Tevy's and perhaps an M4, possibly Elliot's. She tried not to fear for Tevy, not to imagine bullets burying themselves in his young flesh. A flash of a rocket and an explosion followed by several more informed her that the rocket man was at work. Black smoke rose through the 'L' tracks at the far side of the river, rising skyward to mark the death of a tank.

Kayla headed back through the station. Her machine gunners in the condo now opened up, dueling with the guns of the Mart. This was just a distraction, a feint to get the traitors drawn to this side of the building, to keep them from targeting Tevy and his anti-tank crew out on the bridge. She hurried down the stairs to find Mabruke's troops jumping from their trucks and heading for the intersection, all of them with the white headbands on. She pulled hers from her pocket and put it on.

An explosion rolled through the street from a block west.

"That must be Joyce's Raiders. We need a runner to go down there and let her know that we're going into the building. If she can attack it at the same time at the other side, it'll divide the rippers in the basement. Send a bag of dynamite with your guy."

Mabruke waved a young teenager forward, his face smooth and his eyes blue. "This boy comes from Bobs," said Mabruke. "He is to be our runner."

"Go down this street. Keep as close to the Mart as you can so they can't shoot down at you. Tell Joyce or Jeff that we're going through the walls in half an hour. If she could go in at the same time, that would be good."

Good. It would be essential. As the kid ran west with an energy only a pubescent teen can possess, Kayla wished she had stressed this urgency, but Joyce would understand. Joyce would totally get it.

A five-ton pulled out of line at Mabruke's waved instructions and drove past the other trucks and into the intersection, where he stopped it. The back rolled up and Mabruke's demolition men and women, many of them with small backpacks, all piled out. Kayla directed them to the concrete block walls, some on the north side of the building, some on the east under the 'L' station. The walls had been built inside the windows, some of which were still intact. Those they smashed in with rifle butts so that they could get the dynamite right against the block.

Hundreds of other troops now hurried her way, their captains encouraging them to all group near Kayla in the intersection of Kinzie and Wells.

"No, no, no!" she shouted. "Don't you guys have ranks? I thought you had captains or something?"

Several with white armbands as well as bandanas pushed closer, many looking too reverent for Kayla's liking. She wasn't a saint or something just because she knew what to do.

"Break them up into platoons and spread them out so that each one can take a different window. Keep them back so that they don't get hit when we blow the walls, and for fuck's sake, don't clump up. A single rocket or a fifty cal could mow half of you down in a second, for fuck's sake!"

They only looked more reverent. She had been shouting like an angry captain, but if it worked, all the better. One captain looked uncertain and ventured a question.

"How many is a platoon?" he asked.

"Forty or fifty will do. It doesn't have to be exact. Just make sure they know which platoon they're in. Mark them with armbands or something." But if Kayla had time, she would have instructed them to form three or four squads within the platoon, the way Joyce had done with her Raiders at St. John's.

Mabruke oversaw his demolitions teams, each placing three of four sticks of dynamite and shoving in detonators while others hurried up with sand bags on their shoulders to place against the dynamite. Kayla made a note to learn about demolitions, for she wouldn't have known to do this, but it made sense right away: force the explosion into the wall. Halfway down, three broad steps led to a new block wall—a sealed door that once led into the Mart.

Kayla waited there for Mabruke, who caught up in just a few minutes.

"Put a charge here, but no one goes in this way," she said, pitching her voice to be heard over the staccato of the machine guns. "Same with that doorway up at the intersection. They'll have all kinds of prepared defenses here and a narrow corridor to funnel us through. It'll be a kill zone. Got that! We don't go in this way."

"Blow it to make them think we will. Got it." Mabruke received some dynamite from his crew and placed it on the ground at the block.

The engine of another tank caught her attention, so she risked going up onto the 'L' platform again and running toward the river. The station seemed vaguely familiar, and the Merchandise Mart had been enough of a tourist attraction that she wondered if she had stood on that platform in happier times with her parents on their only trip to Chicago.

The column of black smoke from the dead tank bent to the east, although enough washed her way to carry the scent of burning oil. But the engine noise of another tank seemed close to the dead tank. Was Tevy alive? Were they going to get the second tank and what if they didn't? What if it crossed the bridge just as she was forming up her troops to assault the Mart? Perhaps a truck sideways across the road could slow it down if Tevy failed. She was about to go and order Mabruke to pull one of the five-tons under the station to block the road, when the scream of another rocket slammed her ears. This time she saw flashes of sympathetic detonations as rounds inside the tank exploded, but she couldn't see the tank itself because of the 'L' tracks. A new column of black smoke rose beside the first, the two blending together and twisting away to the east. Tevy had done it, Kayla was sure. The bridge was blocked for now to tanks. But not troops.

Kayla hurried down the station platform, the machine gunners still battling between the buildings above her head, each using short bursts. Did Mabruke's guys know to keep relocating to up their chances of catching the traitor gunners exposed? She hurried down the stairs to find Mabruke about to run up.

"We're just about ready," he said.

"Get two of those platoons to either side of the bridge on this side. If you can, get some of those sand bags and build nests for machine gunners. Don't let the traitor soldiers across the bridge. Keep your guys under the station for cover." He started to turn away to issue these orders, but she caught his arm. "And get a machine gun crew into that other building on the east side, the one Tevy said is in front of the office building. They can fire down on anyone crossing the bridge."

Until they ran out of ammunition. If only she'd had a chance to get to know Mabruke's army, understand on whom she could depend, take stock of their ammunition. Train with them.

The runner she sent to Joyce came flying down the street without his backpack. From the excited grin on his face, you'd think he'd hit a triple and was racing for home plate.

"I got through," he said breathlessly, giving the hasty fist at shoulder height salute that the Ericsians preferred. "I talked to Jeff himself! It was amazing. He totally got it right away, and he brought me to Joyce herself. Joyce! She said I did great and to tell you they'd attack the Mart at 6:30."

Kayla looked at her watch: 6:15. Thank God she remembered to wind it this morning. Thank God she had been able to salvage a winding watch. The batteries in her old watch died years ago, which was why she started searching dresser drawers in abandoned houses until she found this one, obviously designed as a man's watch.

"Mabruke," she called. "We've got to go through the walls in fifteen minutes. I want to speak to your platoon leaders. What do you call them anyway? Captains, Lieutenants?"

Mabruke turned from shouting instructions. "They're all hosts of a portion of the Captain Soul, like me."

Why did she outrank them because she hosted a portion of the Angry Captain? She filed that question away for later. "Whatever, get your captains assembled back behind that truck." She pointed to a battered white five-ton that said EXPRESS DELIVERY on the side. "But not the captains from the platoons defending the bridge. I'm going to check on them right now."

She ran down the side of the street under the rusting steel gird-ers of the station, the 'L' tracks filtering the afternoon sunlight where not in shadow from the Mart, the smoke from the burning tanks more pungent, drying her nostrils but not thick enough to prompt coughing. A 4x4 raced past her, stacked dangerously high with sand bags. These Ericsians thought of everything. What was their history? They fought a lot of rippers, Kayla was sure of that, but where and when? This obvi-ously wasn't their first canoe trip.

She reached the steel of the bridge, rising up out of the sidewalks on either side to support the 'L' train tracks above. She found many men and women taking shelter behind the girders. Four figures ran along the east sidewalk toward them. Tevy's form was unmistakable, and Elliot's thick red hair was just as obvious.

"Hold your fire," she yelled to Mabruke's troops. "Friendlies, Friendlies!" Kayla pushed down the panic that she was about to see Tevy shot and ran out to meet them.

"The 1000 Live On, but they sure as hell won't," shouted Elliot. "It was great!"

Kayla could see the burning tanks sitting on the metal-grate deck of the drawbridge. But as she turned she also caught a muzzle flash from the fifth story of the Mart, reminding her that this was no time for heartfelt congratulations or warm reunions.

"Let's go! Let's go!" Kayla aimed her Uzi down the sidewalk in case any traitors were in hot pursuit, but too much smoke obscured the far side of the bridge. She hurried after Tevy even as others unloaded the 4x4 of sandbags, building positions for guns on each sidewalk.

She had to sprint to keep up with Tevy and Elliot and the two rocket men, who still carried the M72 LAWS, even though they had been fired and were now useless. Tevy slowed as they approached the intersec-tion at Kinzie and looked to Kayla for direction. She led him behind the EXPRESS DELIVERY truck, where a dozen men and women, the Captain Souls, waited with Mabruke.

Kayla checked her watch: five minutes. Not enough time for a real briefing, not enough time for much planning.

"After we blow the holes, you'll need to go in right away while they're still dazed. This is the ripper part of the building, so make sure you tap the brain of any ripper you bring down. The torso should be your first target, sure, but don't assume it's dead if it takes a shot to the chest."

"We know." Mabruke wasn't arguing, just stating a fact.

"Great. They'll be heading for the basement like crazy to get away from the light. It'll be dusty at first, like yesterday. Just watch for the friendly fire. Remember the St. John's people will be in there too, coming from the other side. Okay, let's go."

Mabruke stopped her even as his captains hurried to their platoons. "Here." He opened a small pack and tossed her a grenade, then another when she was ready. He tossed two at Tevy and Elliot as well. "The 1000 Live On!" He gave the should-high fist salute.

Kayla returned it. "See you in the morning." She turned to Tevy and Elliot. "We three stick together. Let's go in over there."

They sheltered across the street behind one of the rusting girders that supported the station. A demolitions man crouched there, wiring up to a small box.

"How do you set them off?" asked Kayla.

"Electricity to the detonator." He finished tightening the terminals and flipped up the red protective cover over a toggle switch. "We got rechargeable batteries and juiced them last night. They mostly work." He gave a wry smile and made a circle with one finger, the Ericsian equivalent of the Sign of the Cross.

Kayla checked her watch. The second hand still had thirty seconds to go until 6:30, but an explosion from the direction of Joyce's Raiders forced Kayla to move. No one had synchronized watches.

"Do it!" she shouted, not just for their man but for all the others. She covered her ears just in time.

The girder shook and shards of glass and stinging sand flew across the street. Even though they were crouched in a line behind the girder, Kayla's cheek stung as a something sliced a deep cut. That was going to leave a mark.

"Go! Go! Go!" Kayla charged across the street, Tevy and Elliot close behind. She reached the far side and discovered that some of the sand bags were piled on the sidewalk to give an attacker a hill up to the window, saving her from having to pull herself up. She should've thought of that! Thank God Mabruke's troops did. She charged up the sandbags and through a rough hole in the blocks, crouching to fit under the blocks above that still held.

It was a gray and choking world, the concrete powder clogging her nostrils and stinging her eyes. Before the apocalypse she would have worried about lung cancer. Now all she cared about was surviving the next hour. She dodged right to make room for others and moved deeper into the room, turned sideways and expecting gunfire at any second.

A dark form rushed away and Kayla fired after it.

"They're heading for the basements!" she yelled.

She sprinted after the ripper but had to slow, because so much debris, mostly fractured concrete block, littered the floor. Tevy caught up on her left and Elliot on her right. The figure led them through the remains of a store, complete with manikins dressed in what would forever be the latest fashions.

They almost missed the door to the stairwell, but Elliot saw the sign and pointed. They pushed in and discovered that here, too, the rippers had electric light for their lairs. The three of them rushed down the stairs, and Kayla expected the resistance to begin at any moment, but all she could see ahead was that running figure. Others from the Ericsians had followed, so they had a squad-sized unit when they bottomed out in a service hallway lit by bare bulbs. Here, as in the high school, the rippers had shunned the existing electrical system and strung their own line outside the finished walls.

A muzzle flash lit the hall far from them. The building was so impossibly big that it was hard to tell if the gun was even aimed at them or some closer target. Several male forms, most likely rippers judging by their gaunt forms, emerged from side rooms and ran away from them down the corridor. Kayla was about to charge toward them shooting, but one of the rippers turned toward them, running the opposite direction of all the others, his hands on his head in surrender.

"Don't shoot! Do not shoot!" That Romanian accent was distinctive, but with all the adrenaline it was impossible to stop everyone. A gun went off and the ripper clutched his stomach as he fell.

"Kayla!" There was panic in that call.

She rushed up, flanked by Tevy, who was now also shouting, "Don't shoot. Stop shooting."

Kayla bent over Radu, who had flipped to face up and still held his stomach.

"Kayla! Don't shoot! It's me, Radu! Thanks God I find you."

Radu looked paler than yesterday morning, and his eyes had a strange sparkle, just a little crazy.

"Radu." She stopped above of him, heaving for breath and wondering what to say. *Good to see you? How's death?*

"It's a trap. You have to get out."

Tevy knelt beside him, but the Ericsians continued in pursuit down the hall. "What do you mean?" he asked. "We've got them on the run. Their tanks are burning on the bridge."

Radu shook his head. "No, no! The tanks are just to distract. They do not need these tanks. The whole city has tunnels. Deep, old tunnels. They have train lines but no trains, but they are big and easy to travel."

"Subways?" asked Kayla.

"Those are close to the surface. Those are there, too, but these are much older tunnels. Much deeper and much older. Who builds these tunnels, I don't know. And they're full of rippers. Many, many rippers. One ends right in the basement of this building. There are many others. They go under the river. That is why they don't need bridges."

"What the hell?" Kayla struggled to understand, the adrenaline inhibiting clear thought.

"The tanks lure you here, all along the river, all your armies. But tonight the rippers leave these tunnels and get behind you, trap you against the river and kill you all. You must get out before sunset. You must run. Forget tanks. Forget everything. Go to secure forts."

Kayla understood. That's why the rippers didn't oppose them as they poured into the Mart. Somewhere down here in this maze waited hundreds, maybe thousands of rippers, and they weren't trapped or surprised. They could bring in reserves and fresh ammo. They would be well dug in around the tunnel entrance, maybe a whole floor of the basement. Perhaps Radu could show them the entrance to this tunnel, but what of the others? What other buildings were they in? It was nearly seven o'clock.

Radu reached up and took her by the shoulders, and Tevy placed his shotgun to Radu's chest just in case he was about to sit up and rip into her neck. But he was only trying to make her understand. His breath reeked of blood and his desperation was catching.

"They are coming for you."

20

FALLING BACK

Tevy had never run so much in his life. A few of the St. Mike's troops had working walkie-talkies, but the only way to get word of the ambush to everyone else had been with runners, and when Kayla looked up from Radu and said, "go," he knew exactly what she meant.

He ran back up the stairs to find thirteen-year-old Collin, the blue-eyed boy from the Brat Pack that had fallen asleep at Tevy's feet last night, waiting just outside the Mart, a gun in one hand as he looked desperately into the building. Clearly, he wanted to join the attack.

Tevy sent Collin east to warn Simon Gonzales and Julia Chen, two of Bertrand's former Companions who always led St. Mike's troops. Tevy ran back through the haze of dust in the Mart to find Joyce. He got to the far side and was nearly shot by one of the Raiders before several others recognized him and shouted for a ceasefire.

Jeff received the message with disbelief. "But the traitors up stairs have laid down arms," he said. "We've won the Mart."

"We've won the day," Tevy had shouted. "But we'll be massacred tonight."

The rest of the evening, as the sun dipped into the west, Tevy spent running. He went up and down the whole line from Lake Michigan to the river, ensuring that Collin was believed, that the message had gotten through. He never even paused to wonder if Bobs would be angry that Kayla had given the order to withdraw on the basis of one ripper.

Later, when they had withdrawn into the St. Mike's cantonment, he was pulled off the barricade for an interview. Bobs had grilled him at length and then looked at her map.

"I thought this was too damned convenient. Starting up their Bradleys and moving so fucking slow up to the river, just giving me lots of time to get everybody there to fight."

In fury she swept all of the toy soldiers and trucks that represented her forces off the table. But her anger stopped there, and after one deep breath, she was as composed as if in church.

"This Kayla, she's smart and she saved our collective ass. Stay close to her and the Ericsians. But I don't want them acting independently this way again. It worked last night, but it might have backfired. Keep me posted on what they're up to. I'll see if I can get you a walkie, but in the meantime keep Collin or some of the other Brat Pack kids as runners."

But that wasn't the end of Tevy's running for the night. He and Elliot and the older Brat Pack kids fanned out south of the cantonment after dark, probing down toward the Loop. It was a new moon night, a moonless night, and it would have been impossible to navigate but for flashlights that Emile had loaned. Even then they used them sparingly. It wasn't long before Radu's warning proved correct. Thousands of rippers flooded into the streets well north of the river, and even Tevy might have been trapped, except that this was his territory. He was the rat that knew every nook and cranny, every burned-out building and hidden alley or connecting rooftop—the latter were the best, giving the safest vantage.

The dark forms mustered in the streets and began to march north, only to stop and turn south again in confusion, shouting commands and questions at one another, pushing and shoving in the streets in their disappointment. Tevy heard them more often than he saw them, but even the rippers needed a bit of light, and the few torches and flashlights gave them away. Tevy decided that they were starving for blood, that Vlad Who Bleeds may have withheld donations so that they would fight more recklessly, crazed by their hunger.

Bobs was in conference in her war room in the rectory when Tevy returned with the news that the rippers were flooding back into the Loop, but he had to wait for Helen to finish with her story. She sat relaxed at the conference table, a place Tevy rarely saw her, and her easy way with Bobs reminded him that Helen was one of the first Companions of Bertrand.

"You kids are too young to remember the flood," she said, lighting a cigarette. Rippers didn't smoke, and the corner stores were overstocked right until the apocalypse. "That's no ripper work down there, although I imagine they might have dug a few new exits up into basements."

She looked old and tired, her white hair under a kerchief tonight, her fingers yellow from the tobacco. Every year she seemed to shrink, and at first Tevy just thought it was because he was growing. Now he had to admit that it might not be long before the Brat Pack needed a new mother. It had never occurred to him before that Helen could grow old.

"Well who the hell built these tunnels?" asked Bobs.

"Oh, way back. They were built to bring goods into downtown underground back in early Chicago, before prohibition even. Trains ran through those tunnels. The bridges used to go up a lot for shipping in the early days, and that made getting into the Loop a traffic nightmare, so this really helped. But times changed, and they stopped using them in the fifties, and everybody pretty much forgot about them. Then came the flood."

Joyce sat up in her chair. "Wait a minute. I remember my dad talking about this. It was in the eighties, wasn't it, some accident?"

Helen nodded. "Part right. I remember it was in the early nineties because I had my flower shop just new and open for business. Someone with a drill or something punched a hole through the river into one of the tunnels and it flooded basements all over the Loop. The Merchandise Mart was one of the first to have its basement flood. Even city hall got it. All kinds of buildings saw their basements turn into swimming pools, because their owners didn't even know they were still connected to the tunnels. They might have walled them off and stuff, but bricks and mortar aren't waterproof, and drywall makes a lousy dam. Had to shut the Loop down for weeks."

Bobs was already shaking her head. "But if they flooded, how can the rippers—"

Emile interrupted her. "I remember now. They drained them through a deeper tunnel, a newer one they were building for sewage. I remember the drawings in the newspaper. They had to see? You can't run a building 'cause all the electrical, everything like that, is in the basement."

"Right." Helen exhaled smoke. "And they were still using the tunnels for cables and stuff. It was a cable guy who first warned them it was flooding. Cost billions of dollars to fix. Lawsuits left and right. The city ended up taking them over and maintaining them until the end."

"Right," said Jeff, who had one of Emile's beers clasped in his hands like it was a hot drink that warmed his hands. "Now I get why the rippers always controlled the Loop. I thought it was just because they converted city hall first, but it was the center of their hidey-holes. No wonder you guys could never cleanse the north, even with all those basements sweeps. The rippers didn't need the basements. They could just go back into the tunnels.

Bobs noticed Tevy standing by the door. "What do you want?"

Tevy delivered his report about the rippers turning back.

"Good," said Bobs. "That means Vlad doesn't have unlimited troops, or he'd just throw them all at us now. The bad news is it means this Vlad is as smart as Vlad the Scourge." She looked up at Tevy. "You can go. Good work."

Tevy hoped to get some sleep, but the littler kids in the Brat Pack needed his attention, his reassurance that all was safe and good, that their heroes were alive and defending them, despite the rumors they'd heard of thousands of rippers heading for St. Mike's to bleed them all to death.

It was a relief when it was time for morning mass, and Tevy had never been so happy to sit for one of Bishop Alvarez's sermons. A moment of respite after the battle. He tried to concentrate on the homily, but the exhaustion won.

The bishop was well into his sermon when Elliot nudged Tevy awake.

"You were snoring," he whispered. "I think I know where his holiness is going with this, and if I'm right you should hear it."

Tevy shook his head to clear it and focused on Bishop Alvarez in his pulpit.

"So while 'Thou Shalt not Kill' is a most holy commandment, it did not refer to rippers. Rippers are not human, so no one need fear going to eternal damnation for killing a ripper anymore than they would need fear it for killing a mad dog."

Tevy found himself nodding in agreement. Nothing new there.

"The servants of rippers are also feeding the rippers with blood. This is a sin above all others. This is a sin punishable by death." Bishop Alvarez looked slowly from left to right over the whole congregation to ensure he had their attention. "And most of those in the service of the rippers are waiting only for permission to become rippers themselves. They seek to turn their backs on the eternal life in heaven offered by Jesus Christ in favor of an extended mortal life down here. Mark this: our planet is not forever. Our sun is not forever. Only heaven is forever. The ripper promise of eternal life is a false one, and the human traitors who serve the rippers are servants of the devil. Hell will be their reward. It is not a sin to kill them, for they have abandoned their humanity in favor of the rippers. Whether they are rippers already or traitors only waiting for their turn to be rippers matters not. Once they agreed to serve the rippers, they are no longer human."

Alvarez drew a deep breath and again cast his glare slowly over the whole congregation to ensure they understood, a full ten seconds of pause.

"When God passed down the commandment 'Thou Shalt not Kill,' he meant that you shall not kill one of your fellow humans. This was not referring to dumb animals like dogs, and it certainly wasn't referring to humans who serve the devil. Killing a traitor is God's work. No one need fear going to Hell for this. In fact, they will be rewarded in heaven for preventing another human from absorbing the ripper evil, from turning into a monster."

Tevy sat up straight. He could shoot human traitors as if they were already rippers and he wouldn't go to Hell? He thought back to other sermons, trying to remember where exactly he had gotten the opposite idea, that you couldn't shoot humans no matter what. Was it from his parents? He remembered his mom telling him that capital punishment was wrong. But he somehow thought Bishop Alvarez had always stressed not killing humans. Yet he couldn't think of a moment when the bishop had clarified this one way or the other. Surely, he wasn't changing church doctrine just for convenience? Tevy wanted this freedom, this knowledge that if he had shot any humans in the high school he wouldn't go to Hell, but he worried about how this fit so nicely with Bobs' plan to nuke three cities full of humans serving the rippers. A suspicious man would think the bishop was laying the groundwork to excuse mass murder.

The name *Erics* caught Tevy's attention.

"What'd he just say?" he whispered to Elliot.

"He said don't you dare join the Erics. They're an evil cult and they're going to Hell. And he said we shouldn't call them Ericsians because it makes them sound like Christians. He says just call them the Erics cult."

Tevy paid attention now.

"They will lead you down a false path," Alvarez was saying. "They too promise a false eternal life, again one that says you don't leave the earth, but I tell you that your soul is your own. God granted unto each man one soul. He granted onto each woman one soul. Your soul is your own, and you are responsible for its redemption. No one, mark this." He waved a finger at the congregation. "No one shares your soul. You will be tested in the next few weeks, because the evil that is Vlad must force us to work with these unbelievers. I have faith in all of you. Do not be tempted by this false cult, this false god of one thousand souls. Better yet, educate them in the miracle of Jesus Christ. Educate them about the Savior."

Tevy's mind wandered until the name of Bertrand Allan caught his attention.

"Know this," said Alvarez, if anything in angrier than before, totally on a rant today. "Know that Bertrand, the Savior of Chicago and the Chicago Catholic Church, destroyed Vlad the Scourge. Bertrand's selfless martyrdom gave us the moment we needed to rise up against the rippers. Cities like Los Angles and New York and Washington fell under their sway because no man rose up to lead the fight, to spread the word of God about the evil rippers.

"The new Vlad we fight today, Vlad Who Bleeds as he calls himself, is not the same ripper, is not the same devil. He is not the anti-Christ. Vlad the Scourge was the anti-Christ and our beloved Bertrand cast him into the fire, even though it meant his own excruciating death. Word of miracles performed by Bertrand since his passing from our earthly torment have been reported to me. I believe that he may be a saint, and certainly he is worthy of beatification. Once Vlad Who Bleeds has been cast into Hell, we will hold a festival on the anniversary of Bertrand's martyrdom and begin the first holy steps to sainthood. If you experience any miracle that you can attribute to our beloved Bertrand, be sure to relate them to me so that they can be entered into the church record."

Tevy remembered the ripper in the woods, soon to be saint. His first instinct was to run to the bishop after mass and warn him that maybe this wasn't such a good idea, but he had promised Kayla he would keep it a secret.

Kayla. What was it about her that attracted him? When he stopped and thought about it, she wasn't really that old, so maybe it was because she was almost as old as Bobs that it seemed weird. Kayla was really quite attractive. He worried about her last night, had kept trying to get in front of her so that she wouldn't be shot, but she led from the front. When she shouted, *"go, go, go,"* before charging into the Mart, she had thrilled him, inspired him, and made him want to know her.

Bishop Alvarez finished his sermon and they knelt for the Eucharist, the ringing bells as he offered the host up to God helping to keep Tevy awake, but he found carnal thoughts polluted his mind and distracted his attention—thoughts of his lips against Kayla's, his hand around her back and sliding up under her shirt.

He would have to stand soon. Why did this always happen in church, right under God's eyes? He focused on the gold, on the paintings, on the stations of the cross. Mercifully, exhaustion helped, and when he stood to go for communion he no longer feared he would humiliate himself with a most unreligious bulge in his jeans. But he vowed to find Kayla right after mass to warn her about what the bishop had to say of her religion. He promised her no secrets, and he was desperate to see her even if he couldn't touch her.

Finding her turned out to be easy. The St. John's people were housed in several blockhouses north of the church, but the core of Joyce's Raiders, the people Tevy knew best, were in Emile's blockhouse right across the street from the church. The building was a solid century-old three-story building, originally built for the church but granted to Emile by Alvarez. During the apocalypse, Emile bricked in the basement and ground-floor windows, except for gun slots, and he placed bars on the second floor windows. He and his friends also dug a well through the basement floor until they found water. Later, they dug a side tunnel into the basement of the church so that they could support one another when besieged by rippers. On the top floor of the blockhouse, in a front room facing the church, he found Joyce standing over a yellowed map on a table with Kayla at her side. Jeff relaxed on a couch and smoked while he listened.

Joyce's welcome was less than warm. "What do you want?"

Tevy decided on the bald truth. "Just thought you guys might want to know that the bishop is promising to canonize Bertrand Allan."

"What?" Joyce's expression was not one of confusion but disbelief.

"They're going to beatify him in November, and that's the first step to becoming a saint. The bishop said a lot about the Ericsians too." Tevy waited to see if they wanted to hear all this news, but for a moment no one said anything.

Jeff stood and reached into a cooler, pulling out one of Emile's bottles of beer, the label long since dissolved by the cold water. He popped it open with a bottle opener and handed it to Tevy. "Tell us everything."

Tevy sat on a wooden chair by the table and related the details of the sermon.

"Bert's to be a saint, and Alvarez practically declares a jihad against the Ericsians." Jeff stood and walked over to the window to look across at the church. "Is he here?"

Joyce shook her head. "I was over at his house, but he wasn't there, and no sign that he was."

"What about the bunker?" asked Jeff.

Joyce's eyes went briefly to Tevy and back to Jeff with a subtle shake of her head. She wanted something kept secret from Tevy. He nearly protested, intending to point out that he had been forthright with them and kept their secrets, but the word *bunker* caught his attention. He kept his mouth shut and allowed Kayla to usher him out of the room and down the stairs.

They stood in the morning light on the front steps of the blockhouse, the church still inspiring awe in Tevy as much because of what it had survived as because of its ornate exterior.

"Thanks for coming to tell us," said Kayla. "I know Joyce isn't the warmest and all, but you do remind her of Bertrand Allan, and when I told her the Ericsians said you hosted a portion of the same soul, well, she seemed a little freaked out."

"No worries." Tevy put down the crazy desire to embrace her and kiss her good morning. That would be totally inappropriate, since she had been his captain last night, not his friend or his lover. Besides, he stank from the running and really needed to get Elliot to pour a bucket of water over his head behind the church in the little wood cubicles they called showers, even though they had no plumbing.

"So I guess I'll see you around." Kayla seemed just as uncomfortable with this tired small talk.

"Yeah. I don't know where I'll be fighting tonight, but I'll ask if it can be with you guys again. I've kind of, like, gotten used to all of you and all." He covered how lame that was by putting up his fist for a knuckle-knock.

Kayla's brow furrowed in confusion for a moment before she broke into a smile and knocked knuckles with him. "Okay. Keep out of trouble, and I'll see you on the line tonight."

But once she had gone back inside the blockhouse, Tevy changed course, starting out slow so as not to attract attention, but breaking into a run once he was past the cantonment gate.

He knew every basement within ten miles of St. Mike's, having searched all of them several times over the years for canned food and rippers. There was only one house with a "bunker." It was risky, but Tevy intended to go and visit that house now, because if Joyce was right, that's where he would find Bertrand Allan hiding from the sun.

Tevy desperately wanted to meet this man, this ripper, that was supposed host a portion of the same soul as Tevy, if you believed the Ericsians. He also wanted to know why Bertrand Allan was still alive, if it really was him, and what he thought about his pending sainthood.

21

THE SAINT

Nothing on the exterior of the house suggested there was anything special about it. It was fully detached, clapboard-sided, and its windows had survived, but Tevy knew that it had one totally weird feature: there was a concrete bunker hidden in the basement. It had a door like a bank vault, and it was hidden behind a fridge so that there was no chance of stumbling across it.

Tevy and Elliot discovered it when Elliot leaned against the fridge one day a few years ago. When the fridge easily rolled to the side, both boys thought they might have found a secret store of food or guns, but they were disappointed: the gun racks were empty and only two couches took up space in the room. It stank of mold and mildew. They left the door open in hopes that it would dry up and they could use it as their own special hiding place if they got stuck too far away from St. Mike's before dark some night, but they'd never needed it.

Today, the door was closed, and someone had slid the fridge back into place.

How do you knock on a ripper's door and live? Tevy drew his shotgun and debated going back to find Elliot, but somehow he wanted to meet this ripper alone. Would it be like meeting himself?

Tevy set the candle down on the counter of a small wet bar. There were other candles there from his last visit, but fewer than he expected. Had Bertrand Allan borrowed some? Was he reading a paperback in the bunker now? The basement windows were bricked in, so a ripper could have sat in the small seventies-era armchair out here and been safe from the sun. But the bunker provided protection from hunters like Tevy.

He pushed the fridge aside. Was that movement inside the bunker? Had he awakened a sleeping ripper? Tevy rapped with his knuckles on the vault door, heavy metal that bespoke of amateur welding. There was no handle or latch on the outside. Tevy remembered a simple iron rod that slid in place on the inside to seal the door. It was designed to lock people out.

Nothing happened, so he pushed on it, but it didn't budge. Someone was in there all right. His heart beat faster, and again he considered running back to the church to get Elliot, but his curiosity wouldn't allow him to leave.

He used the barrel of his shotgun this time, tapping the door with more confidence. This time he definitely heard movement, a shuffle, the sound carrying through a narrow plastic pipe above the door, possibly installed there for ventilation.

"Who's there?"

"A friend of Emile's. You saved me way back at the beginning, and Emile and Helen raised me. My name's Tevy."

Silence. Finally, "I don't remember you. I saved lots of people. Anyone could say that just to get me to open the door and shoot."

"I don't want to kill you. I saw you in the woods that night, talking to Joyce. I've kept it a secret from Bobs that you're still alive."

The grate of metal on metal warned Tevy that the bolt was sliding back and the door was about to open. He stepped away even though he knew the door swung inwards, wanting space between himself and the ripper. He kept his shotgun aimed and tried to convince himself that this was not a very bad idea.

The door swung in and the ripper, the man, Bertrand Allan, stepped out into the room, his own shotgun aimed at Tevy. He was taller than Tevy remembered, and the blue jeans and t-shirt were new and fresh, the shirt proclaiming CHICAGO IS GREEN in bold letters over a marijuana leaf—a shirt more for hippy-chick tourists. Allan must have stopped by a store that hadn't been looted or burned. His face held the gaunt look of a starved ripper, and his eyes reflected the candlelight with the glitter of very dilated pupils. His facial hair clung thinly to his chin, not so much shaved as if it had just stopped growing, as if the hair follicles were starving or dead. It occurred to Tevy that he'd never seen a ripper with facial hair and that a lot of them were thin on top or even bald, although Allan still had dark hair. Did the parasites starve facial hair?

"Who are you?" asked Allan.

"I'm Tevy Wexler. You rescued me on September fourteenth of the year of the apocalypse. I've been in the orphanage at St. Mike's since then."

"You're too old to be an orphan." Did Allan smile when he said that?

"I just haven't been kicked out yet, because the little kids like to know I'm there. I mean me and Elliot and Amanda. It helps them sleep, knowing we're there with guns to protect them."

"Same gun as mine. Why did you choose that Winchester?"

"Emile picked it out for me. Said you always used the 1200 real good and I should too."

Allan moved to his left, circling around until he could back up and sit down on the couch, placing his own shotgun across his knees. "How is Emile?"

"Alive. Good." Tevy sat in the little armchair. "But we've got some troubles. There's this ripper named Vlad who says he was Vlad the Scourge, but now he's renamed himself Vlad Who Bleeds. He says he survived the Battle of the Mountain."

"He's lying."

"But you survived when everybody said you were dead."

Allan sighed, a weariness that radiated out like the concentric waves in a disturbed pond. "I escaped by an exit that I denied to him. He took a grenade to the face, the same grenade that set off the propane explosion. His flesh would've burned from his bones. There was nothing for the parasites to rebuild, and they would be dead, too, anyway."

"You're sure?"

"I'm sure. You aren't facing Vlad the Scourge, but there were many Vlads sent all over the world for this apocalypse. I hunt them. I've killed two since the end of everything. Vlad the Scourge at Cave Mountain, the Chicago Vlad, and Vlad the Angry in Seattle just last year. As far as I can tell, there were five in America, so this Vlad Who Bleeds would have to be from L.A. or New York or Washington, either that or some ripper has just poached the name. Anyone can call themselves Vlad."

"There are other troubles. The rippers look to be attacking soon, and they've got all these old tunnels that go under the river."

"You came to tell me that? Joyce knows what she was getting herself into. Really, I'm just one guy. I don't know what you think I can do about this that an army can't."

"I was thinking you could fight your way in and get this Vlad, like you did in the Battle of the Mountain. Cut the head off the snake." Tevy could picture it. Bertrand charging in to avenge with his hair waving back and a righteous look on his face, just like that biblical mural that Amanda painted on the wall of the basement when they were young teens.

"He'll be too heavily guarded. I'm not invincible, you know. I may be a ripper, but I can die. Maybe...maybe I can try to get a look at him, see if he looks anything like Vlad the Scourge. I need a rest first though, need to find some ripper blood to feed. It dulls the pain. I'm always so goddamn hungry."

Tevy suddenly wondered if he was being fair, if it was right to burden this ruined and weary man with all of Chicago's troubles, but he'd been educated for so long about Allan's superpowers that, even though Tevy knew the stories were blown out of proportion, he couldn't shake the feeling that Bertrand Allan could do anything—that he was worthy of sainthood.

"The bishop wants to make you a saint."

Allan stood so abruptly that Tevy raised his shotgun and pushed back in his chair.

"A saint? That's completely nuts. That's completely fucking nuts."

"It's not my idea. It's Bishop Alvarez's idea."

"Oh, so he's a bishop now."

Tevy nodded, relieved that Allan again sat. "I think he'll be elected pope. They're going to have a convention or something of all the Christian priests and ministers in Chicago in September. I'm betting the bishop will get the nod, 'cause Bobs wants him to be pope."

"Yes, it always comes back to what Bobs wants, doesn't it? Are you her man, Mr. Wexler. Did she send you?"

"I told you I kept you a secret, just like Kayla asked. Bobs doesn't know you're alive and she doesn't know Margaret's your daughter. She thinks she's Kayla's daughter."

"You know about my daughter?"

"Yeah. They did a lousy job keeping it a secret on the bus, trying to pretend it was Kayla's daughter when it was obvious she didn't know the first thing about taking care of kids. Like, I saw through that damn fast."

Something about the sudden rigidity of Allan's stance warned Tevy of a dangerous storm. He braced himself.

"My daughter is here. Now. In Chicago?"

Tevy was seriously afraid for the first time since Allan came out of the vault.

"She stowed away on the bus. Nobody knew she was there until the first night out, and it was way too late for anyone to go back. The rippers close the road a lot through there I hear, and Joyce wouldn't send her back with anything less than an army."

Allan trembled on the couch, and Tevy feared the rage would burst on him.

"My daughter! Bobs! Vlad Who Bleeds. My God, do you have any other bad news before I totally loose it."

"Please don't," said Tevy. "I know how you feel, really, but I just thought you ought to know. I mean, the Ericsians, they made me take their test and they say you and I have the same soul, or at least I've got part of it and you've got another part, or something like that."

"I thought you were Catholic."

"I am, but we're dealing with them even though the Bobs and the bishop hate them. Their religion, it's weird but it's kinda interesting. I guess I sort of wish it was true. It'd be cool being the same soul as Bertrand Allan."

Allan settled back in the couch, the rage replaced with weariness. "If you're hosting a portion of the same soul, God help you. We're a tortured soul in peace and in war."

"I just thought you should know everything."

Allan suddenly studied Tevy closely, a frown creasing his forehead. "You were brave to come here, brave to tell me all the bad news. Messengers have been killed for bad news many times in history."

Tevy let the silence hang as he debated whether to deliver the worst news, but Allan noticed the silence. "You haven't told me all the really bad news yet, have you?"

Tevy shook his head. "The bishop. This morning in mass, during his sermon, the bishop told us it's okay to kill human traitors who serve the rippers, that we won't go to Hell, that it's like killing a ripper."

"That doesn't surprise me. You're going to have to kill a few humans if the rippers throw them at St. Mike's."

"I think it's about the nukes." Tevy couldn't decide why he was whispering, perhaps because he hoped that the soft tone wouldn't inflame Allan's anger.

"What. Nukes." Allan chopped the words out through clenched teeth.

"Malmstrom's in trouble. I think they're gonna evacuate to Chicago, but before they do, they're going to nuke L.A., New York, and Washington. Use 'em or lose 'em and all. I just thought you should know."

Allan stood and looked down at Tevy, but he looked distraught rather than dangerous. "Jesus Christ," he said. "It is the end of the world." He walked into the bunker and slammed the door. When Tevy heard the grate of the bolt shooting home, he knew the interview was over. He headed for home to get some sleep.

22

THE OFFENSIVE

Kayla didn't want everyone else in the room to know how awed she was to be in their presence, so her answers to their questions may have come out shorter and angrier than she intended.

"Of course I ordered the pull back and I was frigging right. We'd have been massacred."

Emile put his hands up in surrender, a smile on his face as he looked from Kayla to Joyce with raised eyebrows. "I was just asking," he said.

They were all there, all the living Companions of Bertrand except Barry St. John. Kayla already knew Joyce and Jeff of course, and she had met Emile and Helen at the last meeting in the bishop's conference room, now undoubtedly Bobs' war room. Simon Gonsalves, the man at the end of the table with the thick black locks of hair, was older than he was in the YouTube videos, of course, and so was Julia Chen, the very serious Asian woman and former cop. Even Bishop Alvarez, who sat opposite Bobs dressed in a black cassock with a red cap, looked as if the gray would soon outnumber the black in his close-cropped hair. In fact, all of them had aged so much in the seven—nearly eight—years since the apocalypse that it made Kayla wonder what she would look like if she lived another decade. The sleepless nights had aged her more than would have happened had she lived a normal life, of that she was sure.

"You were right," said Bobs from the head of the table, where she stood over her maps, even though Bertrand's Companions were seated. The rest of the room was crowded with standing people who trickled in during the last hour, like Kayla, who stood to Bobs' right.

Bobs wasn't finished with her. "But don't you dare go ordering my armies around again without getting my approval first. I'm going to get you a walkie, but you'll have to learn our code. The rippers have better tech than we do, and they listen in for sure."

The others at the meeting were representatives from many of the churches, mosques, and synagogues from around Chicago that had become the center of resistance to the rippers and their government. Kayla knew that the gathering of Loyalist humans at St. John's was unusual, because it was secular; everywhere else, the resistance had centered on religious establishments. People who had turned their back on religion in the twenty-first century had quickly sought help from their gods when destruction and death rose to the level of a medieval plague.

Bobs removed her focus from Kayla and addressed the whole crowded room.

"Our objectives haven't changed. They're getting more supplies by the day, more traitors and more rippers. We need to go on the offensive before they're ready for us. Vlad thought his feint with the tanks would give him a quick victory but that backfired, so now he's taking his frigging time. We can't wait for him to come after us."

She turned the map on the table so that everyone could crowd around.

"My Brat Pack has identified fifteen exits from the tunnels north of the Loop. There may be more, because a lot of these are freshly dug exits as far as we can tell. We have squat on the entrances in the Loop, but you can bet there's at least one at city hall.

"So here's what we're going to do." Bobs looked up to make sure she had everyone's attention. "We're going to take or block these entrances and we're going to secure this side of the river."

"What good is that?" asked someone from the back of the room.

"I've got some plans for the rippers that I'm sure as hell not going to talk about now. But the river is the natural border. We take our side of the river and I guarantee we'll take the whole city."

"What's going on with Webb?" asked Emile.

Bobs tensed. Kayla could tell because she was standing so close to her, but she doubted anyone else in the room noticed that Emile had struck a nerve.

"What do you mean?" Bobs asked.

Emile lost all the smile from earlier, and his stare was an accusation. "You know exactly what I mean."

"That," said Bobs, looking down at her map as if there were some very important piece of information she needed to check immediately. "That is definitely a conversation for later. Safe to say that Webb is giving us every support for this operation." She looked up. "I'm going to meet with each of you throughout today to give your more details about your assignment. We need to move as quickly as possible."

Kayla got her meeting sooner than many, waiting out in the corridor for only twenty minutes while the Companions met privately with Bobs and the bishop. Kayla was surprised to hear quite a bit of shouting, but when she tried to drift closer to the door to hear, several kids from the Brat Pack, some of them as young as three, formed up in rows in front of the door and began singing a song about the Battle of the Mountain that sounded like a cross between a Christmas carol and "The Battle Hymn of the Republic." It wasn't lost on anyone that their purpose was to prevent eavesdropping.

When the Companions did emerge, several looked furious, especially Joyce, who looked like she was going to say something to Kayla but changed her mind. Jeff simply raised his eyebrows as he passed.

"Come on in," said Bobs to Kayla. "And close the door." Bobs waved her over to the map as the caroling began outside again.

"I don't want you sharing this with others. I think we've got a spy, maybe more than one, feeding the rippers with info. As things stand, you're my liaison with the Ericsians. I need them, but I don't trust their stupid cult. For all I know, their supreme leader might one day decide that they should all off themselves or join the rippers or attack Loyalists. Who knows?" Bobs pointed to the map, and Kayla recognized Wells Street and the Merchandise Mart.

"You want me there again?" Kayla asked.

"I want you to crush it. I want the Wells Street Bridge, and I want that ripper tunnel sealed up tight. The traitors who surrendered from there have given us a detailed map of where it is, and you can trust me that it's accurate." Bobs handed her two sheets of paper with a pencil sketch of corridors and doorways. "These are the lower two levels that the rippers control. You go in right after dawn tomorrow and you close up that tunnel entrance. Keep this in mind: I don't care about the building. Blow the thing to Hell, set it on fire, whatever those Ericsians can do to destroy that tunnel, you do it."

Kayla reentered the Merchandise Mart the same way she had left, through one of the holes they'd blown in the concrete block. Again Tevy and Elliot were with her, and this time Amanda was there too. Mabruke stayed close as they made their way down the same stairs as last time.

They stopped at the first landing, guns ready, and Amanda did the honors, pulling the pin from a grenade and dropping it over the railing after a nod from Kayla. The explosion provoked a scream, and Kayla led the rush down stairs, practically having to elbow Tevy out of the way so that she could lead.

She could hear several explosions from other stairwells, indicating that the other assault teams were on the move, too. At the bottom of the stairwell they found one ripper, bleeding but not dead. Kayla's heart pounded as she fired a single shot through his forehead to keep him down.

A quick peek into the basement corridor proved that there were a lot of rippers waiting for them. Some of them behind a sandbagged machine-gun emplacement, probably even the Ericsian's sandbags from yesterday.

Apparently they didn't wonder what the jackhammers had been doing upstairs all morning. Kayla had no intention of a frontal assault that would kill many of her troops, so when Mabruke had told her that he had a working air compressor and enough diesel fuel to run it, she'd decided it was worth the wait. But the Mart was built of poured concrete, and it took two hours to jackhammer in holes for the dynamite, and even then there was no guarantee they had enough to blow a hole in the floor.

There were a lot of risks, but Mabruke had assured them that one thing they needn't fear was the whole building coming down from their charges. *"This place was built for heavy goods and forklifts, not manikins and dresses. We could only wish the whole place would collapse."*

If he was wrong, they were about to die.

Kayla pulled up her particle mask and pulled down her goggles. What would they do when the Home Depots ran out of stuff like this, she wondered, allowing this distraction to supplant the fear for just a moment. She also wondered how long the yellow hard hat would last on her head once the real shooting started.

Mabruke looked in askance, putting his own mask up, and she nodded. He used a hand signal, as if pulling a down on an invisible handle, and it was echoed by others up the stairs. They all plugged their ears and looked at the ground. A few moments later, the floor shifted under their feet and several giant explosions ripped through the Mart.

Tevy charged through the door before she could, rushing into the gray haze of concrete dust. Insulation from piping floated in the air, too, probably asbestos given how old the building was, but Kayla hardly cared. She could die at any moment. Tevy could die at any moment. Ripper bodies, males and females, had been tossed away from the machine gun emplacement. They shifted, some groaned, and Tevy was already busy shooting the strongest-looking with his Winchester.

A ripper lay near Kayla, his back to the wall and his eyes pleading for help as blood dripped from his mouth. Kayla put a single shot into his forehead at point-blank range. The weak light from the ragged hole they'd blown in the ceiling didn't let down much sunlight, and all of it was indirect and diffused by the concrete dust, but it had the desired effect: those rippers that could run were fleeing. Kayla didn't know if this was enough light to kill parasites in their hosts and cause the inevitable stroke and heart attack that came with a massive die-off of parasites, but the rippers weren't taking any chances.

"Go! Go! Go!" she shouted. "Leave the clean up." That was for Tevy, who was still carefully giving the double tap to any ripper wounded. There were others who could do that behind them, people just as capable.

They followed the floor plan, not having to search for the stair into the deepest part of the Mart. This Kayla expected to find well defended, but the grenades didn't produce any screams. They ran down into the heart of the building, where pipes and wires and ductwork all came together to find boilers and electrical panels and phone boxes. The rippers had another machine-gun emplacement, but Elliot had a good arm. Kayla took a deep breath to prepare herself. She would live. She wouldn't be shot. Luck would be with her. This ran like a mantra in the back of her head.

Kayla made sure Elliot was ready, gave Tevy the one, two, three with her fingers, and they charged into the hall, he going high and straight across to the far wall while she stayed low, firing three round bursts to push the machine gunners down before they could fire with aim. Elliot stepped into the hall and flung the grenade. It landed perfectly behind the gunners, and Kayla and Tevy barely cleared the hall and back into the stairwell before it exploded.

They turned and rushed back into the corridor to find utter and complete black. The explosion had shattered every bulb, forcing Kayla to make a heart-stopping pause to fish the flashlight Mabruke gave her out of her pocket. There were no holes to let in the sunlight this deep. She made a note that she should have foreseen this problem. She turned the little Maglite on, holding it away from her body.

Muzzle flashes exploded in the corridor, and for a freeze-frame second she could see Tevy charging forward with his shotgun aimed. She rushed after him, but the rippers ran after discharging wild shots, and the next danger was from friendly fire, for other teams had made it down different stairwells.

"The 1000 Live On!" She shouted the Erics proclamation. Others around her echoed her cry, and so did voices up the corridor. She kept an eye on them because the rippers could shout this just as easily, but she was relying on surprise. The rippers didn't know one group of Loyalists from the others. By the time they did figure this group was from the Ericsians, or even what the Ericsians stood for, hopefully the battle would be over.

"This is it!" Tevy pointed with his light. Its batteries already looked weak, so far past their best-before date as to hardly hold any charge. These had come fresh out of the packaging this morning.

The ceiling was high for a basement, but the room was pretty empty, a warehousing room that had been partitioned off with modern drywall. Once it might have been much larger. At the far side was another machine gun. It opened fire, throwing the room into more freeze frames of light, a pulsing image that made movements look strobed. The three of them rushed for the cover of a descending pipe and its machinery, but Elliot stopped and flung another grenade.

Kayla closed her eyes so that the flash wouldn't totally destroy what little night sight she had obtained. A second later she rushed the gun, Tevy and Elliot with her, but this time Amanda was in the lead, having caught up with them from the stairwell. The first shot prompted a cry and she turned and fell. Tevy and Kayla fired, discovering that two rippers still manned the gun, but they were aiming for Elliot as he stooped over Amanda, missing the real threat. Kayla shot one in the chest and Tevy hit the other in the head, splattering blood onto his comrade. Kayla jumped over the sandbags, shouting to vent her fear, relying on Tevy to cover her while she put a second shot into her target, this time between the eyes. The parasites couldn't rebuild brains.

Behind the gun emplacement was a block wall that had been broken open to reveal an ancient tunnel. She knew from Helen it was from the turn of the twentieth century, but if someone told her it was from several centuries ago, she would've believed them. It was lined with brick, in places patched with concrete, arched on the top to hold the weight. Train tracks still ran along the floor, but relatively modern cables and pipes ran along the walls. This must've been fantastic for companies wanting to run everything from gas to fiber optic.

Kayla stayed to the side of the tunnel, and it was a good thing she did, because a muzzle flash from farther down warned her that the rippers hadn't gone far. She backed out and took up a position with her back to the wall beside the mouth of the tunnel. Mabruke came running up, sweat staining his armpits and chest, gray dust clinging to his damp skin. He had pulled his mask down to speak, and his goggles were up on his forehead. Where were her goggles? She didn't remember taking them off, but she did remember that they had fogged up.

"We shouldn't go into the tunnel," Mabruke said. "It'll be an endless fight."

"No shit?" Kayla couldn't keep the contempt from her voice. She would feel better later, but right now she had to let the stress out somehow. "Tevy!"

He nodded acknowledgement from the other side of the tunnel mouth, looking hot in a way that had nothing to do with the temperature. Kayla pointed to a grenade hanging from her belt and again counted with her fingers to three. She turned the corner, going high while Mabruke went low, both of them keeping as much out of the tunnel as possible while still able to aim and fire. She emptied her mag, a bit reckless with the ammo, but there were only about ten cartridges left anyway, and she wanted to be damn sure Tevy didn't get shot. He threw the grenade, proving his arm was nearly as good as Elliot's. They all ducked back, and the flash and explosion indicated that the grenade wasn't a dud.

Kayla crouched down by Mabruke. "We'll keep them back. Can you get your air lines down here so that we can jackhammer up the ceiling."

Mabruke leaned out just enough to look up at the tunnel ceiling. "It's hard to use a jackhammer above your head," he called over the shooting from outside the room. "But we'll give it a try. Doesn't look like we'll have too much to take out. It might bring the river in, though."

"That would work."

Mabruke nodded and rushed off. Elliot joined her, putting his back to the wall and heaving for breath. His red hair was totally gray with the dust, and rivers of sweat on his neck were etched in the filth.

"She okay?" Kayla feared the answer.

"Flesh wound in her arm." Elliot pitched his voice loud so that Tevy could hear from the other side of the tunnel mouth. "As long as it doesn't get infected, she'll be fine. I got her as far as the stairs. She told me she could get out on her own and sent me back with this." He held up a static road flare, the kind truckers would have used back before the apocalypse. "Shall we give it a try?"

Elliot lit the flare and they covered him while he threw it down the tunnel. It landed near a machinegun behind some sandbags about four or five car lengths down the tunnel. Two bodies lay near it.

"They sure have a lot of hardware," Elliot said. "Tevy and I should go get it. We could use that."

Kayla nodded in spite of her fear for Tevy. "Go," she added, aiming down the tunnel and ready to provide covering fire.

The two ran down the tunnel and came back, the heavy gun slung over Tevy's shoulder while Elliot carried two metal ammunition boxes. Kayla hurried to meet them. "Wait. Set it up here. Can you work it?"

Tevy opened the bipod by way of answer and placed the gun between the tracks while Elliot set up the ammunition to feed.

Kayla hurried back up the tunnel to find Mabruke.

"Look," she said. "I need Tevy and Elliot to go out to the bridge. Get a squad to move these sandbags down there and operate that gun. It'll give you cover while you're setting the charges."

"The 1000 Live On." Mabruke gave their fist at the shoulder salute and hurried to shout to his troops.

It seemed forever to her before they had a fresh squad set up on Tevy's gun. The rippers tried twice to come back up the tunnel, but Tevy and Elliot sent them running with just a few bursts from the gun. Finally, she could have them relieved.

"Guys," Kayla said as they came out of the tunnel. "Let's go check the bridge."

"I wonder what happened to Rad?" asked Tevy as they ran across the warehouse sized room for the exit.

"Don't you know?" said Kayla. She had forgotten to tell him. "Before we bailed from here he was already healing, so I told him to get out after dark and try to infiltrate the Willis Tower, get info right from their command center."

Mabruke hurried out of the hallway, directing a squad with air hoses and the jackhammer and dynamite.

"No kidding. Do you think he can do that?" asked Tevy while they waited for Mabruke's men to pass through the doorway.

"He thinks he can. They're actually really interested that he's from St. John's. He's feeding them bullshit, I hope."

Now they hurried up through the stairwells they had fought down, Tevy rushing ahead of her. For a ridiculous moment it occurred to her that he had a nice bum before she pushed such distracting thoughts away. She'd been given another command. She had to prove it was a good choice, that she was worthy and not just because some multiple-choice questionnaire linked her with Joyce.

The sun outside dazzled, already mid-afternoon. Kayla checked her watch. Three p.m. How long had they been fighting their way through to the tunnel? She remembered it as minutes, yet her watch said that it had taken two hours.

The platoon she'd tasked with taking the bridge owned it, and Kayla walked right down the middle over the metal grate of the deck and under the 'L' tracks, the shade they provided a relief from a very hot day. On the far side, the two dead tanks still blocked the road, and the Ericsian troops had set up machineguns behind piles of sandbags on each sidewalk.

They stopped in front of the squat tower that must have been for the bridge operators and looked south, but a wall of office buildings blocked any view of the towers farther south in the Loop, like the Willis Tower, where Vlad was rumored to have his command.

Kayla liked big cities even less. The corridors of buildings would provide cover for ambushes every foot of the way. They could never fight their way into the Loop, day or night. Bobs was crazy. Far better to let the rippers throw themselves at fortified positions than the other way around.

"The rippers will attack right after sunset," she said to Tevy. "I want to make sure that this bridge is tight, and these gunners aren't going to do it." She pointed up at the office buildings across Wacker Street. "A single sniper will kill them, let alone some asshole with a rocket."

She buried the frustration that this was a hopeless effort and walked to the nearest machinegun nest. The two men looked up expectantly. "You guys, take your gun and get into that tower." Kayla pointed to the little bridge tower. "Stay on the ground floor so that they can't shoot through the roof at you so easy." She hurried over to the other nest and ordered them to pull back fifty feet so that their position was obscured by the overhead train tracks.

"Tevy, Elliot." Kayla pointed north across the river at the Merchandise Mart and the office tower. "Can you guys each pick a building and organize some guns up about six floors in those buildings. The gunners should be watching these office towers," she said, here waving back to the south side of Wacker, "for traitors or rippers. This is going to be a hot wall."

Kayla turned back to Wacker after they left and walked across the street under the 'L' tracks. Her intention was to check the ground-level windows of the stores to see if she could set up a crossfire for troops coming down Wells Street. The decision saved her life.

The scream of the artillery shell and the explosion of its impact came together and continued to echo down the street. Kayla found herself on the pavement, but whether she was thrown there by the explosion or dived for cover she couldn't remember. The second round came a full minute later, just as she was trying to get her muscles to move and pick her up. This explosion was oddly muffled, as if someone had stuffed cotton balls into her ears.

The shell hit the far side of the bridge, and the whole structure sagged toward the river, like a giant turning in its sleep and settling lower. Kayla's brain now worked faster than her muscles. They were targeting the bridge. The traitors were going to destroy the bridge, and Kayla was on the wrong side of the river.

She forced herself to run for the bridge tower, the gunners inside it wide-eyed but still manning their gun. "Get back across the bridge," she yelled. "Get the hell out of here!"

They didn't need to be told twice. The men in the other nest were dead, tossed about like unwanted dolls, their bodies riddled with shrapnel and a hole in the metal deck only a few car lengths from them showing where the shell had struck.

Kayla was about to run across the bridge with her gunners when she remembered the timing. "Wait! Wait! Wait!" she yelled, pulling one man to a stop. Sure enough, another shot hit the far side of the bridge. They needed a full minute to reload. This was definitely their target, and some of the 'L' line collapsed through to the deck.

"Now, run!"

They ran but they didn't make it. Whether there was a second gun or the traitors were getting faster at reloading, another shot hit the bridge abutment on the northeast side. The whole bridge tipped to Kayla's right, twisting and bending steel, because the south side still held while the north side collapsed. Kayla lost her footing on the deck and slammed her head into an I beam. She tumbled down to the sidewalk and against the handrail, for a moment nearly going over it into the river. The bridge had twisted over so far that the rail was canted at a sharp angle.

She hung on for a moment, blood in her eyes and her skull pounding from the impact. Another shell struck the bridge, and it gave a metallic groan and sank closer to the river.

Suddenly, a hand caught hers and someone heaved her to her feet, one foot braced on the handrail and another on the sidewalk. Tevy's face filled her field of vision, blood smearing his cheeks and forehead, and his eyes wild.

"Come on!" The cotton in Kayla's ears muffled his shout.

"What are you doing here, you fucking moron?" She tried to shout, but her vocal cords didn't seem to work because it sounded more like a whisper. "Saving me makes no tactical sense. We'll both die now."

"I won't live without you," shouted Tevy.

What the hell did that mean?

Another shell slammed into the bridge and they both fell into the river.

As the water closed over her head, cold and refreshing for a second, Kayla discovered that her arms and legs weren't responding to commands, and she sank toward the muck.

23

TRUTH

Kayla remembered the hands grabbing hers, feet kicking, bodies on either side of her pulling her up to the surface. Elliot's hair was red again, washed clean of the concrete dust by the river, plastered against his head, his particle mask hanging forgotten around his neck. Tevy's cuts were washed clean of their masking blood, and livid gashes on his forehead and cheeks looked likely to form permanent scars.

Her arms and legs began to respond to commands, and she kicked and splashed to the shore as far from the bridge as she could manage. Several times she sank, but Tevy and Elliot always pulled her back to the surface. Others helped drag them out of the water, even though the artillery rounds kept plowing into the bridge. She never lost consciousness, although her head throbbed.

No one would hear of her going back into the Merchandise Mart, and Tevy rode with her in the back of a pickup truck to Emile's blockhouse, where a doctor visited her in a top floor room. He was a little man who clicked his tongue as if it were dry or he disapproved—she couldn't tell which—while he took her pulse, her blood pressure, and her temperature. He declared she had a mild concussion and proscribed

bed rest. She asked for news of the battle, but instead he gave her a glass of water and shut the door.

Tevy visited at dawn. The doctor had stitched the gashes in his forehead and cheek. He spoke of the situation, of how Joyce had taken command of the Mart and the Ericsians, how she had ordered the blocked windows on the south side to stay that way to protect against gunfire from across the river. The artillery had stopped not long after the bridge collapsed, but the water in the river was low and most of the 'L' train deck was still above water—certainly nothing anyone could drive a vehicle across, but something Tevy was sure troops could cross.

Kayla listened clinically, detached and professional, but her emotions were a mess. She wanted to touch him. She wanted him to hold her while she wept. She wanted to ask him what he meant when he had shouted that he wouldn't live without her. Was that just some excited utterance, some lame thing he'd heard in a movie? Some excuse not to leave her to drown?

Instead, she asked military questions. Were any of the other bridges destroyed by the rippers? Yes, four besides the Wells Street Bridge. With LaSalle stuck open, that left four crossings to the north. Bobs took that as proof that the rippers were still planning an offensive and Gonsalves and Chen were setting up kill zones. Control of the open bridges had been ceded to the rippers, although their human troops did little to protect them during the daylight hours.

Tevy had to get some sleep, because he would go on a patrol tonight, and Kayla was left to debate what was going on in her head. She cleaned her Uzi, which had stayed with her thanks to the strap. In fact, it and the ammo in her vest pockets had nearly been her death, weighing her down toward the riverbed. But for Tevy and Elliot, she would be dead and rotting in the muck.

She had lunch with Margaret, who had her blonde hair in pigtails again and warmed up to Kayla, chatting contentedly about some of the friends she'd made at St. Mike's. She had joined Helen's reading and writing classes. Others from St. John's not based in the Mart were also at lunch, and several smiled at Margaret's cuteness, and others winked at Kayla as she pretended to be Mom whenever someone from St. Mike's was around.

Later, Emile stopped by to see Kayla, and she offered to give up her closet of a room to someone else, but he wouldn't hear of it. Besides, with so many of Joyce's Raiders now based in the Mart, there was room to spare for once. Dinner was served early in what was the little dining room of the blockhouse, with people eating chicken and last year's potatoes in shifts. Kayla helped some women from St. Mike's wash the dishes in an old bathtub out behind the house. The stink of the outhouse not far away spoke of the serious summer heat that now descended on the city.

One of the dishwashers, a much older woman, wore the lightest summer dress, but she gave Kayla a bikini. "These are great in the heat if you stay out of the sun."

Kayla had loved wearing a bikini in the summer in high school. She had loved the way boys' eyes tracked her lithe body when she walked along the beach or the poolside, but these days it just seemed obscene. The doctor condemned her to one more night of bed rest, however, so she retired to her stifling room and put on the bottoms but not the top. She now guessed that Emile wasn't just being nice: no one wanted the top-floor room on a sweaty day.

She was standing near the window when there was a knock at the door. The window was high enough and she stayed back enough that she knew no one could see her from the ground. All she had been trying to do was get a sense of where the gunfire she could hear came from, the sort of lazy back and forth that indicated sniping but not battle.

A light cotton blouse, nearly transparent, hung over the back of a chair and she snatched it and tossed it on lest someone walk in without waiting for her reply. There was no time for a bra.

"Who is it?" she called as she did up the buttons. She stopped two from the top, leaving her cleavage a little exposed in the heat.

"Tevy."

She debated making him wait so that she could get more appropriately dressed, and yet part of her wanted to know more about him. Would his eyes track her? Did he have any physical desire for her? The

227

room was gloomy enough in the sunset that she wouldn't to feel too naked.

"Come in." A spilt second after she said that she regretted it. How was she supposed to stand here, like some model or manikin displaying summer fashions? She turned back to the window to hide the awkwardness, the feeling of being on display.

"Hey," he said.

Kayla turned from the window trying to look like it was natural to be so scantily dressed. She had to fight to keep her expression neutral. He wasn't wearing his pocket vest with the ammo, just a light cotton t-shirt that showed off young muscles, the kind a man gets not from the gym but from real work, like carrying water or ammo, less defined and yet stronger.

He stopped in the doorway, hooking his fingers into the belt of his jeans, looking carefully at her face. "It's hot." His eyes flicked briefly down her mid-section and back up and he shifted his stance.

So he did like her body. He was too polite to stare, but Kayla was sure he wanted another look, and it gave her confidence. Instead of seeking some way to be more discreet, she found herself turning to look out the window again, one hand rising between her breasts to secretly undo another button. It wasn't that she was going to sleep with him or anything, but for the first time since the apocalypse she wanted a man to want her, to crave to touch her.

But when he stepped up beside her to look out the window, the touch of his elbow on hers gave her a thrill, and the scent of soap and his fresh sweat was oddly arousing. He had washed before coming to see her, and now that she thought about it, he had also made a rough attempt at combing his hair.

"You're feeling better," he said.

"I was fine yesterday. I just needed a bit of sleep, you know. Aren't you on the line tonight?" She looked out over the city but couldn't determine anything that was going on down south. It was too far away, and the church blocked most of her view.

"Joyce told me to take the night off, to check on you." Tevy shifted feet. "Do you want to sit down?"

Kayla looked over, surprised at how panicked he sounded. He glanced at her and even in the gloom she could see his blush. For a second he looked down at his own body and back up to the window. That was a mistake, because it prompted Kayla to look down at him, to see what had drawn his attention and caused him so much embarrassment. She almost missed it, because she rarely looked at a man's groin. A distinctive bulge explained the panic. He had a hard-on for her.

In any other man, this would have pissed her off or repelled her, but today she just wanted to know more about his lust. Was this just a teenage-boy reaction? How often did he see a woman this scantily clad? Perhaps this arousal wasn't just for her body.

At least he was trying to hide it. No wonder he kept shifting his feet, trying to find some pose that would minimize his erection. Kayla decided to spare him further embarrassment and sat on the bed. He sat beside her, not too close, and folded his hands in his lap, obviously unaware that they drew her attention back to the source of his embarrassment.

"How old are you anyway?" she asked. A sudden breeze from the window cooled the sweat between her breasts. Her top was open more than she thought, and she must be showing a lot of cleavage, but his eyes were fixed on a painting that hung on the opposite wall, a Norman Rockwell style of a light house and a small boat with two children, a boy and a girl, fishing.

"I turned eighteen while we were on the way down from St John's," said Tevy in answer to her question.

"Why didn't you tell us? We should have done a birthday party or something."

"Cake on the bus?" he looked over, met her eyes for a second, noticed her breasts and looked back at the painting.

The fact that he wouldn't look at her, that he was too polite, only made her want to draw his eyes. If he had sat there staring at her breasts, she would have either tossed him from the room or put on her ammo vest.

"I guess not," she said. "But we could have at least shared a drink with you. It's weird that you wouldn't be allowed to drink on your eighteenth birthday back in the old days."

"Don't like it much anyway. Elliot and I got into Emile's hooch one night, but it just made me sick. I can't even stand the smell now. God, it's hot up here."

"Why don't you take off your shirt?" The words were out before Kayla could stop them. What would he think she was suggesting? "I mean, if you're going to visit, you might as well be comfortable." Kayla hated the word *visit*, because it sounded like something her mother would have said.

Tevy looked at her again and swallowed. "That would be great if it's really okay?"

"Oh sure. We're at the beach after all." She pointed to the painting.

His grin was shy and pleased. "Yeah. We should go to the beach someday. I hear it's not very crowded anymore."

He took off his shirt and held it in his lap—more cover. Kayla wanted to pull it away, to say it was fine and healthy and normal that he was aroused, but she was dealing with a strange sensation herself. She wanted him. She had almost died so many times in the last month, and she was alive and she wanted to touch and be touched, to love and be loved. She was the one staring at his chest. There was a very thin patch of hair centered between his nipples, and she wanted to stroke it, caresses it. What was going on with her? She was aroused as he was, even though he didn't know.

He was a mystery she wanted to solve.

"Tevy, what did you mean, back at the river, when you said you wouldn't live without me?" There. She had asked.

"Oh, yeah." He stared at the painting again. "About that. I mean, I know I've no right. I know I shouldn't be thinking about you that way. I just—"

He turned to meet her eyes. He was trembling! Was he afraid? Aroused? What the hell was going on?

"Thinking about me what way?"

"I know I'm young." He looked back at the painting. "But we're so good together. It almost makes me think those Ericsians know what they're talking about. Like we were meant to be together."

He wanted to be together? That could mean anything from a quickie to marriage.

"Tevy." She placed a hand on his leg, thinking it would be comforting and then remembered that it was more likely to further arouse. She should pull her hand away, shouldn't she? Instead she held firm. "We are good together."

He gave a shy smile and returned to staring at the painting.

"I was thinking," he said, the tremble so obvious now he had given up trying to hide it. "Maybe after this is over, after Vlad's dead and the city is safe, I was thinking maybe you and I could get married."

Kayla had been proposed to a few times at St. John's, usually by men who had figured out they would never get into her pants any other way. With them it had been easy to say no. Today was different. It was sincere, awkward, and totally cute. It made sense to say no. They hardly knew each other. She was eight years older. They were at war.

"That's a bit of a jump, isn't it?" Her mouth was dry. "Maybe if we get to know one another. Maybe if we live and everything is good and safe for children."

But suddenly she knew the truth. She didn't want to talk about marriage or children or the future. She wanted him now. It was the opposite of the fear of battle, or maybe the same emotion turned sideways. She had to have him before either of them died.

Her hand slide up his leg, not too far, because she didn't want to frighten him, and she could sense that he was remarkably inexperienced. She leaned in with her lips parted slightly, terrified that he wouldn't understand, would leave her hanging in the air. But he must have sensed her movement, because he turned and met her kiss with passion and fury, an amateur mashing of lips, his arms going behind her back sliding up under her blouse.

She let go of his leg and wrapped her arm behind his back, loving the touch, loving the bare skin. Her other hand slide up to explore his chest hair and then down to feel his flat stomach. She couldn't help herself. She should be safe. It was the right time. She wouldn't get pregnant. She didn't care. Her hand slipped down over that bulge in his jeans, prompting a gasp from him, a tremendous shudder. For a moment she feared he'd lost it already, but he was still as passionate as ever. There was no sense that he'd found release.

She undid his belt and unbuttoned his jeans. He pulled back from her lips as her fingers found his zipper. He met her eyes, searching, questioning. "Are you sure?" he whispered.

She loved that he could hardly contain himself. She knew he wanted to yank her clothes off and thrust madly, yet he held himself in check, trying to be a voice of reason. But Kayla didn't want reason.

"I'm very sure." She leaned in to kiss him and pulled down the zipper, discovering no underwear and finding what she sought, causing another delightful shudder from him.

He broke the kiss again. "I've never done this before. I don't know what to do."

Kayla remembered her only experience with sex, drunk after a pool party in Atherley during frosh week. It was painful and she didn't enjoy it, but the girls in her dorm assured her that she would like it better next time. She never imagined that was years away.

"I've done it once before, a long time ago, but I think I know what to do."

There. She had told him she was no virgin.

"Okay, good." He was totally breathless now, as if at the end of a sprint. His hand slipped into her shirt and their lips met again, even more urgently.

She got him the stand so that she could peel off his jeans. He tore a button on her blouse in his haste and apologized. She pulled off the bikini bottoms and pulled him on top of her. She invited him to join, giving him the guidance he needed. He lost it right away, but not his erection. Thankfully, he was young and strong. He just kept going. It was hot and sweaty and desperate and innocent. By the time they settled, spent and exhausted, Kayla knew it was the best sex she would ever have in her life.

Now she was afraid. Very afraid. What if he died? Now she understood his panic at the bridge. She would not live without him the way Joyce lived without Bertrand. Despite the heat, she pinned Tevy close to her and kept her legs wrapped around him as if she would never let him go. Forever they would be one.

24

CONFESSION

Tevy had to decide whether to tell the whole truth to his confessor. When he reached the bishop's office door in the rectory, however, he had still to make up his mind about what was sin.

An advantage of having been one of the first of the Brat Pack was that Tevy knew Bishop Alvarez back when he was still Father Alvarez. In the early days of the apocalypse, Alvarez spent as much time educating the Brat Pack as Helen or Emile, and the priest hadn't limited his teachings to just catechism, often taking them out to shoot targets. If the weather was bad, he still found an hour for a lesson on the disassembly and cleaning of firearms.

So when Tevy had asked one of the deacons for an appointment with the bishop, he knew the request would be granted. Now he stood in front of the door, waiting for his knock to be answered and waiting for inspiration.

"Come in."

Tevy opened the door to find Bishop Alvarez seated behind his desk, an ornately carved and dark masterpiece that reflected the craftsmanship of the German immigrants that had built St. Mike's. Daylight flooded the room through two large windows, both open to allow a breeze. A green lamp still sat on the desk, although a Coleman lantern beside it indicated that even the bishop didn't often have electricity from the generators.

"Tevy, good to see you." Alvarez dressed today in a black cassock with a red lining and a red sash at the waist—more formal than usual, especially with the red cap on his head and the large crucifix hanging over his heart. He stood immediately and came around his desk to give Tevy a blessing, the Sign of the Cross. Tevy knelt and kissed the ring when offered, as he had learned to do just last year. Alvarez waved him to the leather chair across from his own and retook his seat.

"You've done God's work, my son. Your bravery is unmatched."

"Thank you, Father. I mean, Your Excellency."

"Please," Alvarez waved a dismissive hand. "I am and always will be your father in spirit. You are one of my children, and you may address me in this way. Now, what can I do for you?"

Tevy decided that the whole truth was essential. "Father. I have sinned and I want to put it right in the eyes of God."

Alvarez, who had been looking down at a document on his desk, looked up sharply. "This perhaps is a discussion for the confessional, not for my office."

"I want to get married." To Tevy's surprise, Alvarez looked relieved.

"Oh," he said, nodding. "You have had carnal relations with someone. Is she Catholic?"

Tevy doubted this himself. She seemed very in with the Ericsians, and yet she never said much about it one way or the other. "She's from St. John's," he said. "She never talks about the Ericsians, but she was forced to take their determination at the same time they insisted I take it."

Alvarez's eyes narrowed. "This is the first I've heard that they attempted to induct you into their cult. What did they tell you?"

Suddenly, Tevy sensed that it was time for a sin of omission, not an outright lie, but to state that he was supposed to host a portion of Bertrand's soul would inflame the bishop, would make him furious and dangerous. But had Bobs already told him about the results of the determination? Tevy decided to take a chance and go with a half-truth.

"Pagan nonsense, Father. Stuff about this soul and that soul as if I didn't have a soul of my own. It was all very confusing and silly. I know my soul is my own, but I went along with their shtick so that we could get their help."

Alvarez nodded. "I'm glad we sent you if we had to send someone. I worry about people of weaker faith interacting with this cult. What of your fiancé, what did she think of their determination?"

"I don't know, Father, but she never speaks of their cult."

Alvarez leaned forward, holding his crucifix by the bottom below the feet so that it rested just above the desk, not obscured by the oak. "Perhaps if you could bring her to mass and introduce us, I can arrange for a wedding in a month. But we need to ensure she is a good Catholic and not susceptible to a pagan cult. I must speak with her and hear her confession. What is her name?"

"Kayla Falco."

Alvarez sat back and let the crucifix drop onto his chest. "But she is our liaison to the Erics cult now. She even leads them in battle, I'm told. Surely, this is a dangerous woman to be involved with. Surely, she is susceptible to their ways."

"But Father, she hasn't succumbed to them, and perhaps meeting me is God's way of saving her soul."

But Alvarez didn't look convinced. "Who initiated these carnal relations?"

"We both did." But did they? He went to her room. She was nearly naked. He tried to prevent his erection, tried to think about cleaning guns and dead rippers, but his body was so alive, so attuned to her every movement, her every breath. He took his shirt off at her invitation. She touched him. He touched her. It was all a jumble, a memory he could not sort out without causing yet another erection.

Alvarez stood, leaning over his desk to meet Tevy's eyes.

"First," he said. "You must go to confession and seek absolution for this sin. Second, she must confirm that she is a good Catholic. If she has never participated in a confirmation, then she must, as well as communion. All this will take time."

Tevy stood. "But Father, with the offensive coming, who knows how much time we have left."

"God will protect you. Just ensure that you sin no more. You should not be alone with this woman again until you are joined in holy matrimony."

Tevy wanted to beg, to plead. He had hoped for a marriage this afternoon. He had hoped that by tomorrow he and Kayla would be sharing a marital bed. But he knew that look in Alvarez's eye, knew that there was no arguing. He stood, and when Alvarez came around the desk and held out the ring, Tevy knelt and kissed it.

Alvarez put his hand on Tevy's head for a moment. "Go with the blessings of Christ and the strength of Bertrand."

After the door closed behind him, Tevy stood in the corridor for a moment, resting his forehead against the wood paneling. Another thought had just occurred to him. *What if she was already pregnant?*

———

Tevy wanted to find Kayla immediately, wanted to tell her that they may have a problem getting married, but there was short line in front of Father William's confessional. He decided to immediately get through the proper confession. Father William didn't seem shocked at all, was happy to hear that Tevy wanted to make an honest woman out of Kayla and was disappointed that the bishop hadn't granted an immediate wedding.

"Far be it for me to question his Excellency," he said. "Ten Hail Mary's and ten Our Father's and an Act of Contrition. And my son, keep the zipper up until you're married."

The relief Tevy felt of having been absolved from his sins vanished as soon as he stepped out of the confessional to find Bobs leaning against the nearest pew and waiting for him. She wore a belt today with her favorite gun, her Beretta 92, in a holster on her hip. Her white blouse was not transparent like Kayla's and only the top button was undone.

"We need to talk. Follow me."

She led him at a brisk pace up to her war room and slammed the door.

"Take a seat," she said even though she stood at the head of the table. Her map was back in place and so were all the toy tanks and trucks and flags that marked the diverse units of her armies.

"Now," she said. "Are you with me? Are you still my go-to guy around here?"

"Yes. Of course." Tevy wasn't even convinced himself but this was no time to out internal debates. "You know I'll do anything to bring down Vlad and the rippers."

"But you listened at my door and you told Emile about the plan to nuke the rippers." That she contained her fury worried Tevy more than if she were to again scatter the toy army.

Tevy decided that offense was the best defense. "It's the only way I can find out what's going on, isn't it? And that's what you trained me for all these years, to go and listen." He stood, letting his own fury out. "And I'm damn good at it, but you know what I'm better at? Fighting. That's what I've been doing since you sent me to St. John's and then to the Ericsians. I've been fighting where you tell me to."

Bobs studied him for a long minute, Tevy not breaking eye contact: challenging.

"Okay, sit down," she said at last, taking her own seat. "It's just that I don't need to argue with everyone of the fucking Companions about whether we go for broke or not. A good thing this is way out of our hands by now."

Tevy sat heavily, remembering movies where they had shown what nuclear explosions would be like using stunning special effects. "They're gone?"

Bobs looked at her watch. "Not yet, and don't worry your pretty little head about it." She looked down at her map. "We have to be ready when it does happen though, because the rippers will be desperate to attack once they realize I've cut off their supplies. I need those bridges back. I need them tonight." She looked up at him, her turn to challenge. "You say you like to fight? Fine. I'm going to get you some boats. I want you to pick a platoon of the Ericsians and cross the river. They seem pretty cozy with you these days."

"What do I do on the far side?"

"Take the Franklin Street Bridge back from the ripper side. Joyce and the Raiders gave it up to hold the Mart when Wells Street ended up in the river. We thought the rippers would blow the crap out of all the bridges, but now it's obvious they want to keep some of them as much as we do."

Tevy shook his head. "Boats are targets. I don't need them. I've got a much better way across."

"Shoot."

Tevy stood and pointed to the map. "The Wells Bridge. Most of the 'L' train tracks are still above water because the river's weirdly low this year. A couple of long boards at either end and I cross at night there without anyone seeing."

"At night?"

"Just before sunset is the best time next to dawn, better even for surprise. The human traitors are getting ready to stand down and the rippers are not quite ready to risk the last of the sun. If we're attacking from behind like you say, I think we could mop up the traitors quickly and be dug in by the time the rippers were up and about."

"Good. You brief Joyce on what you're doing so that the Raiders can support you on our side."

Tevy suddenly sensed how close Bobs stood to him and he was reminded that she was only a year older than Kayla. Yet he had no interest in Bobs that way because she had always been larger than life. A commander. Military. Matriarchal. He headed for the door but she called after him.

"Tevy. I don't want you fucking this Kayla bitch again. She's too thick with the Ericsians. We can't trust her."

Tevy turned back in outrage. How dare Alvarez break the sanctity of his confession? Then he remembered that they had been in his office, not the confessional. Perhaps that meant he wasn't covered, although it still felt like betrayal.

"The bishop has ordered me not to anyway until we're married."

"Whatever. If you desperately need to get your rocks off just find someone else, someone from St. Mike's that we can trust. I bet there are lots of women who wouldn't mind bedding you. Now go get this done for me."

Tevy left. As he genuflected at the altar on his way back through the church, he had to shake the sudden concern that Bobs may be angrier with him than he knew, that she had just intentionally sent him to his death as revenge for his transgressions. It was the first time she had ever put him in charge of troops.

25

TEVY'S FIRST COMMAND

M agic hour. Last human hour of the day. The sun was half an orange on the horizon, its waning light already shaded from the river. Tevy stood inside the Merchandise Mart, wishing he could see Kayla just one more time, but she wasn't in her room when he checked. She wasn't with the Ericsian troops yet, but perhaps she might be with Joyce's Raiders. While they were in the same building, the Mart was too large for Tevy to go searching. Tomorrow, after they had taken the bridge, maybe there would be time.

He and Mabruke had gone to look at the tunnel work. Even before the Wells Bridge had fallen, the jackhammer and explosives had done their work, sealing the tunnel with a fall of bricks and earth.

"We're still hoping that the river will break through and flood the whole system," said Mabruke as they surveyed the jumbled mess. "That would flush all the rippers out pretty quick. Bobs found a drill, one of those truck-mounted jobs, the big ones. It's coming to us and we're going to see if we can drill through the river and into the tunnel on the other side of the blockage. Problem is they'll snipe the hell out of the guys as they drill."

Tevy saw the drill later on the street. It rode on a big truck and looked like a crane waiting to rise to vertical. In spite of the rust, the driver swore it was functional, but now he waited behind them, hoping to drill after dark when the rippers couldn't see across the river. The moon was waxing from new moon, but it was still a crescent that didn't provide much light. It didn't mean the rippers wouldn't shoot, but it did mean they would have to shoot by ear rather than eye. And they might not shoot at first, given that their muzzle flashes would bring return fire. Perhaps they'd just think the engine was a generator and not realize their danger.

Tevy checked the sun one last time, waiting till it was a sliver on the horizon, the thin clouds above turned pink and red. It was time to go.

Elliot munched a sandwich, his rifle slung over his shoulder with the barrel pointing to the sky. When Tevy walked over to him, he stood and gave one of the Ericsian fist salutes with a grin.

"Ready for action, sir," he said through a full mouth.

Tevy considered telling Elliot to stop with the jokes, but he knew that was Elliot's way of dealing with fear. Tevy had yet to figure out what to do with his own fear, except that he knew it always abated when he could attack. Somehow, that brought relief from the tension.

"Okay, let's get the boards and let's get across the river."

Mabruke had given him command of a crack platoon that was already organized into four squads. While they had trained together and fought as a unit several times, Tevy was a stranger to them. It was only their deep belief that Tevy hosted a portion of the same soul as Bertrand that subdued any discontent about this stranger from St. Mike's suddenly becoming their lieutenant.

Tevy had been introduced to the squad leaders but had forgotten all their names right away, save the first sergeant's name: Jemal. He was proud of his heritage, coming from a poor neighborhood in south Chicago.

"I learned to use a gun before I was ten," he bragged. "And that was before the rippers." He laughed a lot and Tevy liked that. So did the rest of the platoon.

The boards were easy to angle down from the blasted concrete abutment to the deck of the 'L' train bridge. The road bridge was deep in the river, but the 'L' was a good three feet above the water, even though it rested more than the height of a tall man below the abutment. Tevy slid down the plank, landing beside the fractured and bent rail of the train line. He didn't wait for the others, instead rushing across the bridge. This was the most dangerous part. If the traitors saw, they would open fire to pin them down until the rippers came out after sunset.

But Tevy's bet paid off. No one opened fire. It was an uphill run, though, because the south side of the bridge still clung to the shore, the tracks bending over but holding. It was so steep that Tevy had to use the rails and ties to pull himself up above shore level. From there he abandoned the 'L' deck in favor of monkeying through the girders that were once perpendicular to the road but were now angled like playground slides to the lower deck. Tevy was able to step onto the asphalt easily, and he hurried across the six lanes of Wacker Drive and put his back to the wall of an office building, one of those mid–twentieth century constructions faced with stone to emphasize stability and permanence, a couple of Romanesque concrete columns with high windows in between on the west side to break up the monotony.

Down the street two tanks waited, their guns aimed across the Franklin Street Bridge, the last rays of sun creating a halo effect around them. The office building's first-floor windows littered the sidewalk with crystal shards. Tevy waved to Jemal and Elliot and pointed into a bank and sports bar, letting Jemal organize the squads.

Tevy drew his shotgun and moved into the sports bar, running past the counter, the brass taps, and the overturned chairs and tables. He had to return to the sidewalk through a broken window in order to run a couple of car lengths to the next building, this one right at the corner of Wacker and Franklin. The ground-floor restaurant and offices of this building were set back, allowing a patio in front under the building. Large square columns held up the edifice close to the street, reaching up to the third floor. They provided enough cover in the dusk that Tevy's troops didn't have to go into the building proper.

Tevy peeked around a column at the tanks and saw that the tops were open in the heat. Elliot came up beside him and took his own quick look before smiling at Tevy.

"Confidant bastards, aren't they?" Elliot said.

Machine guns were set up behind concrete park benches dragged onto the road, one on each lane, again pointing north to defend the bridge from a frontal assault. Tevy had studied all this with binoculars from the Merchandise Mart earlier in the day. Even though he couldn't see them from here, he knew there were two more guns behind sandbags at the far side of the bridge. Unlike the Wells Street Bridge, there was no second deck above, only steel beams rising in a graceful curve on either side to twice the height of a very tall man. On the east side another squat tower—one the bridge operators once used—was surrounded by milling humans. Traitors.

Tevy hurried to the last column, the one closest to the tanks, and used it as cover so that he could lean out and look south. The street was empty, other than the usual collection of abandoned cars and trucks, one skewed across three lanes. In the distance, so close and yet so far, the Willis Tower rose to the heavens above lesser office towers, black and menacing even though its upper floors were still bathed in the orange light of the sunset. Most of the windows were still intact, but they absorbed the sun rather than reflecting it, due to years of grime and weather.

Jemal hurried to stand with his back to the same column. "So that's where the fucker hides out?" He nodded in the direction of the tower. "We'll get him one day, maybe sooner than he thinks."

"Two squads," said Tevy. "One goes across the street fast to that building." He pointed to the glass-and-steel office building that curved gracefully with Wacker Drive and the river. "The other goes along the side of this building. They're to cover our backside against counter attack. Their targets will come as ripper reinforcements from the south."

"What about those?" Jemal pointed to the tanks. "They can turn those gun turrets pretty fast."

"Elliot and I will take out the tanks. The other two squads should go straight for the gunners on the bridge. Take the guns on this side and use them to take out the gunners on the north side."

While Jemal rushed back to organize the squads, Tevy waved Elliot up and told him the plan. Tevy had hoped that Elliot would have comments or a critique, but instead he hung his M4 from his shoulder by the strap and pulled a grenade from his vest pocket. He looked at the tanks as a starving man looks at a rare steak.

Is this what Bobs would do? Tevy had been in a lot of battles, but always as a runner carrying orders and information. He could hardly wait for a chance to strike back, but he didn't want to make a mistake that would get his people killed. He debated his plan until Jemal returned and told him they were ready. Two squads were with Tevy, and now they were a pretty obvious and dangerously clumped bunch, all trying to hide behind the four large columns of the building and relying on the darkness in the recess of the first two floors.

The other squads moved through the inside offices. They would go out through the side windows on Franklin Street once Tevy gave the signal. He holstered his shotgun and leaned in close to Jemal, who smelled of cigars. "Everybody goes as soon as Elliot and I reach the tanks. Go quietly."

He turned to Elliot, who nodded and held up his grenade to show he was ready. Tevy pulled one from his many vest pockets. He took several deep, slow breaths to calm the beating of his heart. This was what he wanted. To attack. A charge. To strike a blow against the rippers, even if it meant killing human traitors. Bishop Alvarez said it was still God's work. He wouldn't go to Hell for this murder. He drew his Glock too. He ran for the far tank.

Just before he reached the tank, a man's head, the hair shorn bristle short, rose up from it, his back to Tevy as the man looked at the sunset.

"Hey, guys," the man yelled down into the tank. "It's almost Miller time."

He must have heard Tevy's shoes slapping the pavement, because he turned in a rush. Tevy fired the Glock, a wild shot that missed but had the desired effect. The soldier dropped into the tank, his hand reaching up to grab the hatch. Tevy fumbled and dropped his gun in his haste, but he got the pin out of the grenade and dropped it into the tank just before the hatch slammed shut. The tank's engine roared to life even as Tevy leapt away.

A muffled thump ended the lives of everyone in the metal monster, and the engine idled, waiting for instructions that wouldn't come. Before Tevy could retrieve his Glock from the pavement, another thump rocked the other tank and smoke poured out the hatch. Elliot ran around the back of the tank to join Tevy. By now the gun crews on the near side of the bridge knew exactly what was going on, but gunfire from the Merchandise Mart raked the bridge—the distracting fire that Joyce had promised Tevy would come when he attacked.

The two squads that had charged right behind Tevy reached the near guns, a complete surprise, firing at the gun crews before they could swing their machine guns. The men around the bridge tower had taken cover inside and behind it, but a squad had already enveloped it. For less than a minute, a fierce point-blank gun battle raged around the tower.

Tevy joined it. Elliot used his M4 and fired at the second-floor windows, shattering the glass and providing an opening for Tevy's next grenade. The explosion finished the windows and flung shards out to rain down. Men inside stumbled out with raised hands, only to be shot.

The other squad now manned the two machine guns and fired across the bridge at the other emplacements. Those crews didn't even try to turn their guns, running from them to jump in the river and try to swim. Tevy considered letting them live, but the squad around the tower had lost men and the fighting rage was on them. They fired into the river on the swimmers. It was a massacre of the helpless.

Their deaths saved Tevy's life, for they swam west, downstream, and that turned Tevy's attention just on time to see two more tanks rolling toward them around the curve of Wacker, buttoned up and ready for battle.

"Cover!" shouted Tevy. He ran behind the dead tank just as a deafening explosion slammed the bridge tower. Shards of metal and stone flew in all directions, and several men who weren't fast enough in seeking cover died.

Elliot joined Tevy where he crouched beside the tread of the tank.

"Damn it all to Hell." Tevy risked a peek around at the approaching tanks. "I told Bobs we should have at least one LAW with us."

"Time to book?" asked Elliot.

Tevy nodded. "Absolutely. This is a total disaster."

Jemal waved from where he crouched by the little tower. Tevy made a cut signal by pretending to slash his throat with a straight hand. He pointed to the office building and back at the Wells Street Bridge. It was almost full night, and their only hope was that they could get back across the river in the dark.

The report of a distant artillery gun came from far south, and Tevy crouched expecting a ferocious impact, but instead a pop sounded high above. Suddenly, a stark white light bathed the ground, throwing strong shadows.

Elliot's upturned face was abnormally pale. "Vlad's Blood, a flare! Fuck! A flare, Tev! It's on a parachute. We're butt naked for at least a dime."

"Get back to that building! We use it like a fort! Get up to like the tenth floor and block the stairways until morning. Go tell Jemal! Forget about crossing the river. I'm going to get word to those guys." He ran for the two squads that had moved south on the street to cover the rear against counter attack. They hadn't figured out that the source of the explosion was another tank, let alone that two were coming.

Tevy ran straight down the middle of the road, trusting his white headband to spare him being shot by his own squads. He turned the corner of the truck that blocked three lanes. An army ran toward him, some in uniforms but most dressed in the rags of rippers. Only creatures that no longer cared about weather or their appearance would dress in such ruined clothing when better could be had at any store for the taking. He skidded to a halt and turned to dive back behind the truck

The squads were well hidden in the office buildings on either side of the street, and they opened fire now. But the rippers came on, and they attacked any human traitors in their own army if they tried to stop for cover. They used the humans as shields or drained them for blood. If they were wounded, the rippers sliced their throats and drank.

Tevy rushed to the west side of the street and found the squad leader, identifiable by the red armband. "Get your people back across the street while the other squad can still cover," Tevy shouted over the gunfire. "We're going up the stairs in that building there."

He led the way back across street, using the skewed truck for cover, and had just reached the columns of the patio when one of the tanks arrived in the intersection. Fortunately, the operator suffered from battle confusion, for he swung his turret south, pointing his barrel at all the action down the street and his fellow troops.

It became a rout—everyone for themselves, all running through the concourse past the security desk and the elevators and into a dark stairwell. Tevy stopped behind the security desk, his shotgun out as he watched his platoon flee. A man entered the concourse not wearing a white headband. Tevy shot and killed.

"Go, go, go!" he shouted at the stragglers of his platoon.

Now rippers poured in through the broken windows, hideously silhouetted by the harsh light of the flare. Tevy turned for the stairwell, but just after he slammed through the doorway, he tripped over a body. He tried to stand and sprint up, but a hand closed around his ankle and tripped him to the stairs. He had to fling out his hands to prevent a face plant, and he lost his shotgun in the process. He struggled to reach for it as a ripper rushed up his body to pin him down. Breath that stank of blood washed into Tevy's face, and a guttural voice spoke in his ear. "Fresh meat."

The ripper grabbed a fistful of Tevy's hair to pull back his head, but Tevy's hand had found the Glock, turning it in the holster and firing backwards and up. The ripper screamed and fell back holding a bloody stomach. Tevy tried to rise but now it was a pile on, a half dozen rippers charging in to pin him down.

Others sprinted past him, pursuing his troops up the stairs.

Tevy prayed and struggled. Now he would die. He wouldn't get to see Kayla again, and that was the greatest loss. The only comfort was that he wouldn't die a virgin and maybe, just maybe, he had left offspring.

A loud voice shouted even as a ripper placed a knife to Tevy's throat.

"Wait, wait, wait! We're supposed to get a prisoner."

The knife withdrew and Tevy was flipped onto his back.

"Hey, I know this guy. This is the fucking sneak who ran across the 'L' way back."

It was the officer who ordered Tevy to stop at the Wells Street Bridge the day he discovered that Vlad Who Bleeds was now in charge of Chicago. Except the man was human then. Now he had clearly converted, his skin pale and stretched, his eyes slightly bulging.

"Captain." *What else to say?* "How's it hanging?"

The captain had no sense of humor. "Take him to Vlad. No drinking his blood, on pain of impaling. He gets there in one piece."

Tevy struggled to reach the knife at his belt.

Someone shoved his head from behind, slamming it into the concrete stairs. Pain. Massive pain and disorientation. His arms and legs wouldn't respond to commands. Then he was on his feet, dragged vertical by the rippers because he had lost the ability to stand without help. His hands were yanked behind his back and a plastic cable tie encircled his wrists. They marched him south, dazed and bloody, through a city completely controlled by rippers.

26

IT ALL COMES TOGETHER

Kayla heard the tanks first, and she knew they could mean the death of her lover. When she heard that Tevy was to lead an assault on the Franklin/Orleans Bridge, she begged Joyce to let her join him, but it was too late. They were already across the river. She had run up the stairs of the Merchandise Mart several floors until she found an open window facing south. The running figures were difficult to see as dusk descended, but she approved when Tevy led them into the office building and back out again, keeping in the best cover possible. When his assault began, it was too dark, only muzzle flashes and explosions told the story.

He had taken out the tanks first, that was good, and Joyce's fifty cal was now raking the traitor positions on the north side of the bridge, but the rumble of tank treads told Kayla this was all about to fall apart. The first shot from the barrel of a Bradley proved her correct. Tevy would have no choice but the fall back in panic.

When the flare exploded high above the city, the whole battle suddenly became tiny live soldiers on a board game. She could use her binoculars. The troops made for the office building. Good. Tevy must know that the bridge would be a slaughter in this bright light. Kayla's heart leapt when she saw Tevy crossing Franklin, leading a squad to the office building, their only hope, their refuge. The rippers, and it was rippers now, charged into the building close on their heels. Muzzle flashes pulsed out of the building, illuminating the lobby for seconds and telling Kayla that someone provided cover fire for that last squad.

All went silent, and Kayla prayed that Tevy had succeeded in blocking the routes to the upper floors. She imagined a frantic rush to throw desks, chairs and filing cabinets down the stairwells. Perhaps barricading doors. Tevy could last until morning, when a thin screen of less than enthusiastic humans traitors would be left as a holding force. Kayla would launch her attack at dawn. She would free Tevy and bring him back across the river.

The rippers brought a prisoner out of the building, his hands secured behind his back, his face bloody. Even in the last of the light of the flare, Kayla recognized Tevy's skinny figure. They marched him south toward the Willis Tower.

Kayla watched, hardly breathing, as another figured slipped out a third floor window of the office tower and slid down a rope in the fading light of the flare. He crouched in the shadow of a column until some rippers passed. He ran into the street in pursuit of Tevy's captors. Kayla couldn't really tell that the hair was red, but the teenage body and the insane pursuit told her it was Elliot. She watched until the flare fizzled out and the city again went dark.

Bobs gave them a chance to pitch Kayla's case. That was the good news. It was hard enough to convince Joyce, but Jeff came on board immediately.

"It'll be like the Battle of the Mountain," he said. "We'll cut the head off the snake."

Bobs wasn't impressed. She sat at the head of the table in her war room and had the younger kids from the Brat Pack serve them sandwiches. Emile and Helen were part of this meeting, and Kayla remembered Tevy talking about them on the bus, how they were like parents to him. In fact, all of the Companions of Bertrand except Barry St. John and Bishop Alvarez sat around the table in the war room, including Julia Chen and Simon Gonsalves, people Kayla hardly knew, even though they led the two armies of Chicago troops from the St. Mike's Cantonment.

Kayla talked at length, but Bobs shook her head even before she finished.

"It's all about the bridges," Bobs said, standing and pointing to her maps. "Even if you could fight across the Franklin Bridge, or Adams, or any of the others, you'd be caught in a crossfire from every office building all the way downtown. Useless massacre to save one guy who's probably already dead. No way."

"It's not about saving one guy." Joyce stood and walked around the table to stand beside Bobs and point to the map in her turn. "If Vlad is here, at the Willis Tower, we should go and get him and get this over with. He's the one bringing troops from California. He's the one doing all the organizing. Kill him and this ripper army will fall apart."

"Love to. But you don't think you'll get massacred?" Bobs met Joyce's eye and Kayla sensed the bad blood and a struggle of wills.

"Wait a minute." Kayla had the seat by the map, and Joyce's finger on the location of the Willis Tower gave her an idea. "It is all about the bridges, isn't it? But what about the lake or circling around and coming up from the south?"

Bobs looked up sharply. "You'd spend a day getting far enough west before you could swing down to the south, let alone start sweeping north again. If your boyfriend's alive, he sure as fuck will be dead by then. Don't you think about the south." Bobs put a finger on the map at the shore of Lake Michigan near the outline of a large building that bore the name CHICAGO ART INSTITUTE.

"The lake thing, though." Bobs frowned. "Never a water person myself, and I don't think Vlad is either. Brat Pack used to get deep into the Loop along the shore and through the park before it became fucking impossible to get across the river. But boats." Her finger traced a line around the mouth of the Chicago River and down the map to the shore near Jackson Drive. "Land here and you've only got about a mile to the tower and the first half is all open park. You won't have any cover but neither will the rippers. After that, it's the concrete and steel canyon."

Joyce nodded as she studied the map. "But surely the rippers don't have so many human troops that they can mount guns in every building and sweep every street. Like you said, we've got them all concentrated on these bridges. They're all up here."

Jeff sat with his boots on the table, a beer donated by Emile in one hand. "Vlad probably doesn't trust his Daylight Brigades. Look how fast those guys in the Mart surrendered to us, even though they'd been told we eat babies or some shit. I hear you've even convinced them to fight for us. My guess is Vlad likes to keep the Daylight Brigades pinned between us and him so they don't get any ideas about heading for the hills and leaving us to fight it out."

"That sounds about right." Bobs studied the map and shook her head. "The tower is going to be fantastically defended though. Vlad's probably deep below his frigging phallic symbol, and you bet he'll have his most trusted humans and rippers at every entrance."

Running feet in the corridor prompted several to draw guns, but it was thirteen-year-old Collin, a runner from the Brat Pack, who threw open the door without knocking, his face flushed and his eyes wide with excitement.

"They broke through...into the river, I mean. I mean they broke through the river into the tunnel. The drill thing! It broke through. There's a foot of water in the basement and it's rising fast."

"The basement of what?" asked Kayla, picturing the dorm of the Brat Pack in the basement of St. Mike's for a moment before she remembered where the drill was located.

"The Mart." Collin couldn't contain his elation. "This is going to flood them out right? The rippers'll all drown."

All eyes turned to Bobs, who stood with an ever-so-slight smile that chilled Kayla.

"Get Webb on the radio and get the bishop the hell in here," Bobs said to Collin. "It's tonight. It's fucking now!" Her fist pounded the table, making all the little flags and toys jump.

She looked at everyone in the stunned room. "Okay, cards on the table. I never gave a shit about those bridges. Who the fuck attacks bridges when they don't have to? It's not like they're on an island." She pointed to Kayla. "You're the only one who figured it out. When you talked about going around and attacking from the south."

Joyce had stepped back from Bobs and crossed her arms. "What the fuck are you talking about?"

Bobs walked to a different map farther down the table, one of the whole country. She had to lean in between Emile and Jeff, and she picked up several little flags off of Malmstrom Airbase in Montana and carried them over to the Chicago map. She placed them just south of the Loop, not far from the Willis Tower.

She looked up at them all, daring an argument.

"People. The Illinois National Guard is coming home. I convinced Webb to abandon Malmstrom and throw in with us. He's been bringing in the Bradleys and Strikers by transport trucks, and they just got here yesterday with lots of supporting troops. Webb's just been waiting for me to give him the word. That's now."

"I can't believe you," said Joyce. "Why the hell did you call us all the way down from St. John's if you have a frigging army?"

"Because I didn't have the army before. That was a deal we worked out after you got on your buses."

Kayla knew that getting in between Joyce and Bobs was a bad idea, but she couldn't help herself. "Then why these attacks on the Mart and the bridges and all? Like you said, we obviously don't need them."

"We needed to focus Vlad's attention. I couldn't have this leak out, and I couldn't have the rippers or the Daylight Brigades find Webb's army by accident. We need surprise and we've fucking got it."

She looked around at them all, her forehead creasing with a frown.

"Don't you see? We're going to win tonight! Tonight we're going to take the Loop. The rippers are gonna be flushed out of those tunnels just as Webb attacks from the south. We're the other side of the pincer. We don't even need to attack! We just hold the bridges and machinegun the rippers as they try to cross. They've got nowhere to go except the lake, and rippers don't do so well on a sunny day on the lake."

"So you were using us as bait." Joyce's bitterness reflected Kayla's feelings.

Bobs again slammed the table with her fist. "You just don't get it, do you? While you and Jeff have been hanging around and screwing up at St. John's, I've been down here making all the tough decisions." She pounded her chest between her breasts. "I'm the one who had to watch millions starve, fighting off good people who didn't have it together. Millions! Do you know what it was like down here? I starved! We all starved and we all fought. It was like being in the middle of a hundred dogs in a dogfight with half the mutts rabid. And you come down here to lecture me about bait? About nuking our enemy?"

The room went very silent, and the look of 'caught' on Bobs' face, one eyebrow raised, indicated that she had said more than she intended.

Jeff spoke first, carefully placing his beer bottle on the table. "I thought you said you'd take it under advisement. I thought we were supposed to talk about this together."

Bobs glared at Jeff. "I did take it under advisement, and advised myself to ignore you pussies and do what needed to be done. By now Vlad knows that he won't be getting any help from L.A. or New York. Nice sunset last night, eh?"

"Sweet mother of God," said Helen, the first thing she'd said since the meeting began.

Bishop Alvarez calmly turned into the room from the corridor.

"Robertta Jean is God's general on earth," he said. "She is winning this war for us."

"By ending the world," said Joyce.

"Joyce, my daughter in Christ. The world ended a long time ago. When did we last hear anything from the Vatican that wasn't ripper propaganda? What about Europe, Africa, or Australia? We already know that several Chinese cities were destroyed with nuclear weapons by their own government eight years ago. The world has been silent. No jets or ships arrive on our coasts to rescue us. They have all gone down to the dogs of hell. The best we can hope for is that some cities survive like ours."

Joyce looked from Bobs to the rest of the people gathered around the table. "We're not needed here anymore. Let's get the hell out of here." She headed for the door, but a call from Bobs stopped her.

"Joyce, if your Raiders really give a shit about Tevy, this would be a good night to go on that raid. The rippers will be completely disorganized, and Vlad will be busy turning his whole army on a dime to fight Webb. When the rippers realize their tunnels are flooding, I'm willing to bet a lot of them will book for the countryside. This is going to be a rout."

"I guess that means Tevy will be just fine by dawn." Joyce turned into the corridor, others rising and heading out to follow with the exception of Gonsalves and Chen. The bishop left in a hurry.

Bobs glanced at Kayla and down to her map and flags and toys. For a moment Kayla thought she caught an odd look from Bobs, one of regret or maybe jealousy. Did she have a thing for Tevy?

"Tevy won't be fine, will he?" Kayla asked.

Bobs didn't lift her eyes from her map. "If I were Vlad and I'd ordered a prisoner for questioning, I'd question the hell out of him until Webb attacks. Then I wouldn't need any more answers. Then I'd know where the real danger was coming from. Then I'd turn to fight, and that prisoner would be useless. I'd give him to my guys for a snack."

Now Bobs did look up, and Kayla was surprised to see concern on Bobs' face. "He was the best of my Brat Pack. I had plans for him. He was going to be the first of a new order in the church. Instead, I'll see that he's listed as a martyr for the cause. Not on the level of Bertrand, of course, not for taking out the anti-Christ himself, but people will remember Tevy."

Kayla turned to go, but she had just reached the door when Bobs again spoke. "So, was he any good in the sack?"

For a terrified moment, Kayla feared she would weep, but her anger saved her and she used it to turn her voice icy cold. She fixed her eyes on Bobs and used words to deliver the most savage blow. "He was fucking great, and so was I."

Kayla caught up with Joyce and the others in front of the steps outside the church, including Emile and Helen. They had stopped to talk to Mabruke, catching him up on the news of the nukes and Webb.

"That explains a lot," Mabruke said. "It seemed strange to me that almost all the fighting was performed by St. John's and my Ericsians around the Mart. The St. Mike's troops did little more than hold the north side of the bridges. We've suffered the most casualties."

"We're getting out of town," said Joyce. "At least some of us. A lot of people came down to stay, and that's fine with me. We'll only need one bus for the trip north."

"I'm thinking it's time for us to leave, too," said Mabruke. "The bishop hates us, and if Bobs now has Webb at her side, her alliance with us isn't so important."

Kayla knew it made no strategic sense, but Tevy had come back for her when the bridge fell into the river.

"So we just all pack up and leave Tevy to die?" she asked.

A white flare burst far to the south, high over the city, and its light was enough to show Mabruke's surprise, even in the shadow the church cast over them. "What's this about?" he asked.

Kayla brought him up to speed as fast as she could while Joyce looked uncomfortable and Jeff lit a cigarette.

"But he's the Dormant Hero," Mabruke said. "Aren't you going to his rescue?"

Suddenly Kayla understood. She didn't need anyone's permission. She was going after Tevy, even if it meant she was risking her own life, even if she had to go alone. She wouldn't live without him, and what if she were pregnant like Joyce had been when Bertrand had died? That would be even worse. Elliot was brave enough to go after him alone in a city full of rippers. She would follow.

"Yes," Kayla said, feeling relief for the first time since Tevy was captured. "I'm going after him."

Mabruke looked delighted, but Joyce looked furious.

"Then you're throwing your life away. Tonight's battle will make the last week look like a picnic. The rippers will have nowhere to go to ground! They'll be like wolves backed into a corner. That's when they're the most dangerous."

"Fuck you. I can throw away my life if I want to. I won't live without him." Her hand pressed her belly. Was there life growing there? She went with the truth. "I may be pregnant."

"What's that got to do with it?"

"I'm not you, Joyce. I won't have a child with him and be left to bring it up on my own. I won't have a ghost for the father."

"Shut up!"

But it was too late. Emile didn't get it, but Helen suddenly put a hand over her mouth in shock. "Oh my God. Little Margaret is Bert's daughter, isn't she? Oh my God. I assumed she was Jeff's."

Jeff gave a pained smile. "See how a man gets a reputation?"

"You guys can't tell anyone." Joyce's panic was evident, but Mabruke was already trying to sooth.

"His soul carried on in others." Mabruke said. "Offspring are wonderful, and when she is of age, I would love her to take the determination, but soul portions are not inherited. She could have a portion of the Angry Captain or the Loving Mother." He waved a hand at Helen. "They're all just as likely as the Dormant Hero." He turned his attention to Kayla. "I'm more concerned about the existing vessel of the Dormant Hero. There must be very few left, because we've never come across another one. I'll come with you, of course. I have a platoon at the cantonment gate. Where do you want to attack?"

"I thought about boats down to the Loop, but I don't really know where to begin."

"I can take care of that." Emile looked drunk and kept giving sidelong glances at Joyce and smiling. "A little Bert. Who knew?"

Kayla tried not to scream at him in frustration, but Jeff saved her. "The boats, Emile?" he asked.

"There's a fishing fleet. Started back in the famines. Come on with me. I know a dozen boats we can use, and their captains are good. They'll land us right at the foot of Jackson, no problemo." To Mabruke: "Bring your guys this way, fast. We gotta move now if we're gonna do it."

They had turned to hurry away, passing the white statue of St. Michael, when Joyce called out. "Wait. Damn you to Hell. Fine. We'll go. At least I'll go."

Jeff finished his cigarette and dropped it to grind it out on the pavement. "Hell, I'd hate to miss a fight, especially when my soul is already down there fighting. I want to talk to the little red-haired hellion. I think he should come up to St. John's so I can make sure Bobs doesn't lop his head off or something."

Kayla ran toward the shore of Lake Michigan, relieved to be doing something, relieved that the Angry Captain and Dependable Rogue were with her, for more and more she believed in the Ericsians 1000 Souls. But she feared failure, because they were missing one of the Trinity. The Dormant Hero. Somewhere, Tevy was down there, dead, alive, or a ripper. But somewhere else Bertrand Allan stalked this city. Joyce had made that clear. Mabruke, Bobs, Emile, and Helen certainly didn't know. Vlad didn't know. Allan was the ultimate wild card. No one could command him, neither ripper nor human.

27

THE DEPENDABLE ROGUE

E lliot had a good buzz on and he wasn't going to let the rippers ruin it, and he sure as hell wasn't going to let them take his best friend to his death. He took a sip of hooch from his metal flask and looked out the window, waiting for the flare to fade and for rippers in the street to be busy with something. A machine gun from the Mart raked this side of river and the rippers took shelter. Perfect. Elliot climbed out the window and slid down a phone cable he had just cut out of the drop ceiling of their floor of the office building. It hurt his hands, because it was only plastic coated wire and it was so thin, but it held his light weight. Jemal could command the Ericsians up there. He knew what he was doing and was really the guy in charge anyway. He'd hold off the rippers until morning.

Elliot hurried down the street, starting in the middle like he belonged there, but moving to the shadows when he saw a whole company marching his way in formation. These were true ripper troops, not civilian conscripts. These must be the guys from California.

A mouse didn't know its warren as well as Elliot knew this city after eight years of spying and scrounging. He dived into a hotel and hurried through the lobby, the restaurant and the far window smashed many years ago by he and Tevy to make this route work.

He had just slipped across the next street when the shadow caught his attention. A ripper was tracking him. Odd. Not raising the alarm or calling out a hunting pack or anything. He must think Elliot would be an easy mark, a meal all to himself.

That would change. Elliot worked his way into a bank, finding his way in the light of a new flare that burst above the city, its white light washing in the high windows. He jumped into the teller's area and turned to place his M4 on the counter, aiming for the shattered window he just came through, but the ripper didn't follow.

Elliot was about to move, when a voice called into the bank.

"My best friend carried an M4 like that. He uses an FN now."

Fuck. The bastard knew he was there.

"What a coincidence. There are so few of these M4s in the country." Elliot really enjoyed sarcasm.

"His name is Jeff Aubert. I believe you know him."

"I think most of Chicago knows him. Why don't you step out and I'll show you how well this gun works? I'm kinda in a hurry."

"Why do you run toward the rippers when everyone else runs away."

"*My* best friend is their prisoner. Look, dude, I know you're hungry and all, but I'm not going to be a free lunch. Your best bet now is to get the hell out of here before I pass a shit load of lead through your brain."

"Yes, I recognized your friend. He came to see me. And you must be the Dependable Rogue. Only he would try to fight through a ripper army for me. He and the Angry Captain of course."

"You're an Ericsian?"

"I'm beginning to think there's something to the 1000 Souls. We haven't much time if we're going to save your friend, and I get the sense that you know a way in to where I want to go. I'm stepping into your gun sights."

The figure, taller than Elliot, stepped through the hole in the glass, the white flare light silhouetting him, although enough light washed around for his features to be visible. For a ripper he kept himself nice—clean new clothes and running shoes. But he still had the alien quality to him, that strangeness about how he carried himself, as if preparing to lunge all the time, even though he stood tall. Elliot could shoot him now, but the ripper seemed familiar. Then he remembered Tevy's story of meeting Bertrand Allan in the woods and later in Chicago in the bunker.

"Vlad's stinking blood. Holy fuck. It's you."

"Quick. With me you'll be safer. I've learned a lot of quiet ways to kill rippers over the years. We have to hurry to catch up. You'll need to find a way into Vlad's tower."

The guy was a ripper for sure, Bertrand Allan or not, and he would be able to kill him in a second if Elliot let his gun down, of that he was certain. The safe thing to do would be to put a bunch of lead through him right now. But that would be noisy, even with all the other shooting going on up near the river, and that would bring all kinds of hell after Elliot, and that would mean Tevy's certain death.

Elliot liked to gamble. A ripper at his side could be totally cool, especially Bertrand Allan. Was he really the same soul as Tevy?

"Okay. Let's go kill some rippers."

As Allan turned in the light of the flare, Elliot caught a grim smile.

"Yes, let's."

Together, they hurried through the city, Elliot leading the way. Two shadows, one young and alive and dangerous, the other dead and very dangerous.

28

VLAD WHO BLEEDS

It had been a food court. Tevy found that oddly appropriate. He recognized some of the brand names: McDonald's, KFC, Tokyo Sushi,
and dozens more, all in a circle around plastic tables and chairs bolted
to the floor. Some of them had been removed at one end to make room
for a long table and maps—a pilfered boardroom table. The maps could
have been Bobs', and it struck Tevy that Vlad brooded over them the
same way Bobs brooded over her toy soldiers. They were trying to see
into each other's heads—a game of chess between two people who had
never met.

Tevy's Winchester, with its holster and his Glock, held down a corner of one of the maps. The place was lit with very dim electric lights,
and for the first time in his life, it occurred to Tevy that rippers didn't
need much light, their eyes always adjusted for dark. That should have
been obvious, but as Helen liked to say, he wasn't always the sharpest
arrow in the quiver—not about stuff like that. She blamed it on his low
protein diet during the famine years.

The stink of blood assaulted Tevy's nostrils, and he wondered in
a detached way if the rippers even noticed it anymore. Bodies hung

upside all through the food court, most of them right in front of the restaurant counters, perhaps some sick ripper joke. Those that weren't dead had only minutes to live, and rippers lined up as if waiting to withdraw cash from an ATM. Tevy remembered lining up with his mother and the sense of impatience yet the certainty that everyone would get what they came for. In this case, blood. A ripper at the front of each line directed the next recipient to the appropriate victim.

Another part of the food court was given over to donors, people who lay on cots as if at the Red Cross, waiting patiently for their pint of blood to drain so that they could leave. Other rippers lined up there. Tevy wondered about the hierarchy: why did some rippers get the live victims, and why did others have to settle for a donation of blood that wasn't coming straight from the source but via plastic tubes and bags?

It wasn't that Tevy wasn't afraid. He was secured spread-eagle to a wooden wheel, and they spun him a few times right away just so that he could see how it worked, and the nausea resulted in the explosive loss of his last meal. But now they'd left him, turned only slightly to one side from vertical, and this respite had given him a chance to come to terms with his death. He knew it was going to hurt. All he could hope for was that he could find a way to enrage Vlad so that he might kill him by accident.

But Vlad was busy. Tall and blonde, his locks flowing down over his shoulders, his clothes black but modern, a dark shirt and studded leather jacket. Black jeans. Black boots. Excellent clothing for stalking in the night.

Tevy passed the time by replaying his night with Kayla. It gave him great comfort that he had been with her, that she loved him.

A ripper coughed and choked wetly. Tevy looked up, surprised that rippers could cough, and several laughed.

"Take it easy there, kid," said one to the cougher. "It's cold, but if you prove yourself, you'll get the real thing one day. Just don't try to choke it all back at once."

Tevy looked over at the cougher. That cough had been a call for attention. Tevy's attention. Radu stood by one of the cots, a pint bag of blood in his hands. He stared at Tevy but his expression was impassive.

What was he trying to tell him? That he was here? That Tevy wasn't alone? That his death wouldn't go unrecorded? Or had Radu converted and embraced his new life as a ripper?

The coughing also caught Vlad's attention.

"Come." He waved a gloved hand at Radu, who put down the pint and hurried over to kneel. "Get up." He grabbed Radu's elbow and turned him to face Tevy. "Is he from St. John's?"

Radu shook his head. "He was sent up with the plea for help. He's one of her runners."

"But he led troops tonight."

Vlad sat in a large office chair, a sumptuous leather creation from an office upstairs, no doubt, and anachronistic in the food court.

"You, Sneak, what's your name."

"Tevy Wexler."

"Never heard of you."

"It's a big world."

"What is that bitch thinking, sending you to take that bridge?"

Tevy would have shrugged, but the ropes bound him too tightly. "She doesn't tell me much, but I think she's coming after you. She needs the bridges to get at you."

"This is what bothers me. She doesn't have nearly enough troops to cut through this city. It would be a bloodbath. Yet still she fights for these bridges. Why?" He tapped his fingers on the table. The drumming stopped and he turned to an assistant. "Send a patrol south."

"South, sir?"

"You heard me. I want a report back in less than an hour, or someone's going to die with their eyes looking at their body from a great distance."

"You." This was to Radu. "Does she have other armies I should know about?"

Radu shrugged. "I never met her. I had just got here before I was turned...evolved."

Vlad stood and approached Tevy, who drew a deep breath. This was going to be the hard part. If he could just die quickly and get it over with, maybe he wouldn't shame himself by weeping or begging.

"She's better than you," Tevy said. "She'll beat you."

"We took a prisoner yesterday, one of the Ericsians. He says you're the same soul as Allan. I find that amusing. I killed Allan, but, of course, you know that."

"I've met him. He's not dead."

The room had been quiet before but now it was deathly quiet. Every ripper turning from their feast to pay close attention to Tevy.

Vlad returned to his chair and sat. "You met an imposter. I tore him limb from limb and gorged on his blood."

"He killed Vlad the Scourge with a grenade and propane explosion. You're the imposter. But Vlad made Bertrand into a ripper before the end. He lives to hunt other rippers."

"The Demon," someone whispered.

"You met an imposter."

But Tevy could tell he had upset this ripper.

Vlad got himself under control. "I need to know all you know about the makeup of Bobs' armies. She's added St. John's and the Ericsians to her usual levies. Who else can come to her aid?"

"I don't know. I don't get invited to high level meetings." But he did know. Had the nukes gone off yet? Did Vlad know?

"You, come here." He waved Radu over to his side. "Kneel." Radu obeyed, kneeling beside the chair like a pet dog. Vlad drew a knife and placed it on his own wrist, slitting it quickly and pushing it to Radu's mouth. "Drink."

Radu drank, at first tentatively, then eagerly. Vlad pulled his wrist away and pushed Radu to the floor. He held up the bloody wrist for Tevy to see.

"I was Vlad the Scourge. Now I am Vlad Who Bleeds."

Radu had a seizure on the floor for a few moments before it subsided to a tremble of ecstasy. Vlad ignored him and addressed Tevy. "Would you like to know that pleasure? I can give it to you. It is better from me than any other ripper in the world. Rippers who drink my blood are immortal, can never be killed."

"I'd sooner eat shit."

"Then you will definitely get some of my blood, you little asshole."

Now Tevy's fear returned. Torture and death were bad enough, but becoming like Bertrand Allan was definitely a fate worse than death.

"I'll kill myself the first chance I get." But then he would go to Hell, wouldn't he? But if he was a ripper he would already be dead, right? So it wouldn't be a sin.

Vlad leaned forward in his chair, one hand clamped over the cut wrist. "Why do humans like you resist converting? It's always been a puzzle to me. Life is so much better when you're evolved."

"Murdering humans."

Vlad pointed at the donators. "In California we don't have to force donations. People give willingly and murders are minimal. It's the new world order."

"I'm old world. I'll never change."

"Oh, you will."

Vlad stood and checked his wrist but it had healed. He drew his knife from the sheath at his belt. "I abhor torture. I have people here who would make you say anything to stop the pain. That's the problem with torture. You can make people say anything, true or false. I prefer conversion."

"Please don't," Tevy said, the panic rising as Vlad approached. "There's nothing I could tell you that's going to make any difference."

"It takes longer I admit, but my blood is so potent with the parasites that your change will be very fast. It might be painful, but not too much. The ecstasy will more than compensate."

"I still won't tell you anything."

Vlad stopped in front of him. "No, not today. But tomorrow, when the hunger takes you, you'll tell me anything in exchange for a pint of blood. I won't be so gauche to offer you a living donation."

Running feet caught Vlad's attention, and a ripper rushed into the room, several others behind him, all looking wide-eyed and panicked. "Sir, we can't raise L.A. or New York, and I was talking to Washington, and they said there was a nuclear flash from the direction of New York, and now Washington won't respond."

"What the fuck?" Vlad turned on Tevy. "What has that crazy bitch done?"

"Nuked your new world order." Tevy turned his head away as if that would help him avoid a blow. His heart beat like it would burst out of his chest. Would it hurt, the death that he was sure was now coming?

"Oh, she's brilliant. What a ripper she'd make." Vlad returned to his chair and slumped down to stare at his map. "Malmstrom. We just about had them beaten down. I should have guessed that she'd get them under her sway." He looked up at Tevy. "So, that's what you would have told me tomorrow. Is that all?" Suddenly, he stood, an unnatural movement, as if gravity didn't apply the same way to him. "I think I have little time. We'll have to go with the old fashion torture. Get Tony in here. I have a job for him."

Tevy began to pray, starting with Hail Marys. Would he shame himself?

"Don't worry," said Vlad. "Before you die, I'll make you a ripper and the parasites will fix the damage."

"NO!" screamed Tevy. "I'll never be a ripper. You can't force me to feed. I'll starve myself, I'll kill myself if I get the chance. It won't be a sin, because I'll be dead anyway. My body means nothing. Nothing. You can kill my body, but my soul will carry on!"

"You're an Ericsian?"

Tevy thought about Elliot and Kayla, about the three of them being the trinity. It felt so right. They were meant to be together. And Kayla was like Joyce, even though they didn't look anything alike. And Elliot was so like Jeff, even though one was tall and blond, the other short and red-haired, and their backgrounds, their lives couldn't be more different.

"Yes. I'm an Ericsian. I'm the Dormant Hero, just like Bertrand Allan."

"Bertrand Allan is dead."

A scream from a dark recess disturbed the food court, and Vlad turned in anger. "Stop your feeding, all of you."

But there was another scream, and a bloodied body slid across the floor to stop at Vlad's feet—a ripper's body.

A man stepped out from the gloom and stopped under a bare light bulb, blood around his mouth but his clothes still clean.

Bertrand Allan.

"Who the hell are you?" asked Vlad. He seemed too shocked for rage.

"I thought you would recognize me, since you tore me limb from limb."

A panicked voice came from the corner. "It's Bertrand Allan, the Demon. I saw his YouTube videos. It's him. It's really him. My God."

Vlad looked prepared to argue, but Tevy spoke up first. "It's him and he's come for you."

"Shoot him." Vlad gave the order quietly, pointing at Allan.

A gunman hidden in the dark recess of the food court did open fire, but not at Allan. The first bullet hit Vlad, causing him to spin and drop.

"I think he's wearing Kevlar," shouted Tevy to the invisible sniper.

Gunfire, the muzzle flashes blinding, erupted from every corner of the room. In the freeze frames, Tevy saw Vlad get hit twice more as he sprinted from the court.

Bullets struck the wheel around Tevy, but Allan threw himself in front, jerking from at least one bullet hit. Rippers ran after Vlad, desperate to escape the sniper, who now started shooting at any ripper in the room. This gave Allan a chance to turn and slash the bindings on Tevy's ankles and wrists.

He slumped like a rag doll, his pins-and-needles arms and legs not responding to commands. Allan tossed him over his shoulder and shouted through the mayhem, "This way!"

The rippers now fled in all directions, expecting an army in their midst. Instead, Elliot ran through the food court, his M4 firing single shots here and there to keep everyone running. Allan led past the table, scooping up Tevy's shotgun as they ran. The three of them rushed into a dark room that stank of mold and wet. There were two doors to the entrance, indicating it was once a public toilet. There was no light.

"Tevy," whispered Elliot. Outside, rippers shouted instructions and gunfire bursts sought an enemy that now hid. "You okay, dude?"

"I'm not shot. I think Allan is though."

"I'll be fine, or no better. It's being repaired as we speak."

"Totally weird." Elliot's voice held awe. "What do we do now?"

Silence.

"Mr. Allan?" asked Elliot again.

"Oh, Joyce would kill me. I've brought us to the Alamo. There's only this way in. No other way out. She was always better at the big picture."

"So we sit tight," whispered Tevy. "Maybe the rippers think we escaped. If you give me that Winchester I can fight soon. I can feel my legs now."

There was a shuffle in the dark, and Tevy felt cold steel pressed into his left hand, and his right hand closed around a familiar wooden pistol grip.

"It's the Winchester 1200, just like the one Emile picked out for you," whispered Allan.

"It is the one Emile picked out," whispered Tevy.

"So we wait and hope they don't find us?" asked Elliot.

"Until dawn. Then I'll help you fight to the surface. After that, you'll be on your own."

"It's our city," said Elliot. "We can disappear like magic."

But two hours later, everything was changed by the flood.

29

VICTORY

Tevy felt the chill of the water first. For the last hour, they listened as the rippers returned to the food court, some shouting orders. Radu must have seen their retreat, because he shouted, "I'll check over here," and approached their door, whispering, "It's me. It's me. Don't shoot." He opened the door just enough to shine a flashlight through and say, "Stay here." Then he left, calling loudly, "Clear."

Vlad must have returned, for his voice, with that Californian accent, called instructions and demanded information. Just when everything quieted down, a voice shouted, "There's a whole army moving up from the south."

There were more shouts, but the same voice rose above all. "No, an army I tell you, with tanks and Humvees and everything, not civvie levies."

"What's that about?" whispered Allan, but neither Tevy nor Elliot knew the answer.

The water was a nuisance at first, just a few inches deep, forcing them to stand. The shouting outside resumed and was quashed by a command from Vlad, allowing one ripper to finish his report. "No, all the tunnels are flooding. That wasn't a crane by the Mart, it was a drill! They drilled through the river and into the tunnel system. We have to get out."

"The tunnels didn't connect here," whispered Bertrand. "They're old. Much older than this building. The rippers must have dug some new tunnels to connect."

Gunfire, distant and heavy, echoed down from above. A gun battle now raged on the main floor in the tower, only a floor above their heads.

"It think there's only about fifty of them," shouted one ripper from a distance.

Vlad issued more orders, most of them about meeting this new threat.

"We have to stop him now, before he crushes this attack," said Allan. "If he dies now, that'll be the nail in the coffin. I'm going to rush him."

"We'll cover you," said Tevy. He couldn't see Elliot's expression in the dark. This would probably mean their deaths, so if he wanted to speak against it, this was the moment. Instead, the sound of a fresh mag snapping into the M4 gave Elliot's answer.

"We go on three," whispered Allan. "Get me to Vlad and then get out. Find a staircase up and don't look back for even a second. Just make sure those troops upstairs don't shoot you. They're not expecting humans down here."

"Good luck," whispered Tevy. His heart pounded with excitement. He didn't want to die, but the chance to kill the nemesis of Chicago was too much to pass up. His death would be a turning point in a major battle.

"One, two, three."

Allan pushed out in the lead. Tevy fanned to his right while Elliot went left, all of them sloshing through ankle-deep water. Tevy held his fire until they had covered half the distance across the food court between their hideout and Vlad. Radu, looking crazed and joyful at the same time, joined their rush, surprising several of his fellow rippers, who didn't expect gunfire from one of their own.

A ripper near Tevy turned, his mouth open in surprise to shout while he frantically tried to draw his sidearm. Tevy shot him in the face, splattering blood and brains out the back of the ripper's head. He pumped the shotgun, turned to the next ripper, and shot him in the chest, dropping him straight down. The M4 fired, and Tevy spared a glance. Elliot stood on a plastic table, aiming one shot after another without regard for his own vulnerable position.

Tevy knew a moment of fear for his friend, but there was little time for emotion. Besides, he had never felt so free. No more fear, and it was such a relief. It was all over, and he could shoot and shoot until he died. It was like the video games of his childhood, before the apocalypse. He fired at another ripper, one closer to Vlad and better prepared, for he shot at Tevy, but Radu crossed in front and took the shot. Tevy's shotgun blast took the enemy ripper in the chest while Radu fell with a splash.

Allan drew the most fire. Even Vlad now drew a sidearm to shoot. Tevy fired at his face but missed; however, it was enough to throw off Vlad's aim. Allan, a knife out, closed with him, tackling him into the water. Tevy stopped with his back to the two as they struggled and splashed, turning to shoot out left and right at rippers who now rushed to Vlad's rescue with guns and knives. The fire of the M4 proved that Elliot was alive and close, but Tevy couldn't spare a glance. A bullet brushed his shoulder, another his leg.

Shouting from across the food court, where the stairs spiraled down from above, caught Tevy's attention, muzzle flashes tracking the pursuit of rippers from above by an invading army. But the rippers attacking Tevy didn't notice this threat. Instead, they skidded to a halt, expressions of horror and fear sapping them of the desire to attack. Tevy couldn't help it. He glanced over his shoulder to see what had stopped the rippers cold.

Allan stood in between Elliot and Tevy, blood coating his mouth and shirt and jeans, his bloody knife in his right hand. In his left hand he held Vlad's decapitated head, high.

"I am Bertrand Allan! The Demon!" he shouted. "I've come for you all!"

The rippers fled, running like rats from a disturbed nest. The panic gave Tevy a chance to shoot, firing at undefended backs. The next danger was the invading army.

Elliot was way ahead of him. "Friendlies!" he shouted.

Tevy saw the white headbands of the Ericsians as they rushed in their direction. "The 1000 Live On!" he shouted. "The 1000 Live On!"

Elliot took up the call, but Allan tossed Vlad's head to the ground, scooped up Radu's crumpled body, and ran the other way, deeper into the dark of the concourse.

Tevy's knees suddenly betrayed him, giving way and forcing him to kneel in the water, gasping and fighting a tremble he didn't understand. It took him a few moments to understand that he had never been free of the fear of death. He had only buried it out of necessity, and now it rose up to choke. He gasped for breath, fighting to be strong, to not shame himself. His kept his eyes on the water, the light of a dim bulb haloing his reflection, blood tainting everything with a diffuse pink hue.

"The 1000 Live On." This time it was gasp, a prayer.

"Tevy!"

Kayla walked toward him cautiously at the head of a squad, her Uzi aimed at his chest.

"I'm alive," he whispered. "I'm alive. I was saved by Bertrand Allan. He really is a saint."

Kayla knelt in the blood and water before him, her own shirt stained red, a fresh cut on her forehead. She stank of sweat and gunpowder and blood. Tevy embraced her and kissed her lips.

"As far as I'm concerned, we're married," he said.

"We're married." Kayla kissed him deeply.

He vowed never to let her go.

30

LOOSE LIPS

Tevy would always remember the next few hours as the best of his life, a short time when he believed good could conquer evil and a better world would rise out of the ashes of the world of his childhood.

They watched from high in the Willis tower, at least ten floors up, as troops swept along the streets, following Bradleys and the wheeled Strikers. Their organization and professionalism awed him. Flares lit the night sky, and the rippers ran from them with little fighting.

At bridges all around the city, rippers fought to escape, but gunfire indicated that Bobs was ready for them, that she had spread her forces to cover all the remaining bridges. Rippers began leaping into the water to swim, but most of them were shot. Bobs was right. This was the night. It was a disaster for the rippers.

Tevy and Kayla slept through the dawn hours, curled together against the chill of the night on a carpet deep in the middle of their floor of the tower. By the time Tevy, Kayla, Elliot, and the Ericsian platoon headed to ground level late in the morning, it was all over. They carefully surrendered to Webb's forces as all of the Daylight Brigades were doing, but when word reached Webb about who his troops had captured, he came to congratulate them and get a tour of Vlad's command center, now so flooded that the plastic tables of the food court were under water, and the boardroom table with the maps had become a raft. Tevy was able to retrieve his Glock from where it still held down a map.

Tevy's first plan was to escort Kayla to her room and fall into bed with her, maybe even sleep some more later, but Kayla wanted to clean up first, and Bobs wanted to see Tevy. He found her in the war room with Gonsalves and Chen, mapping out areas to sweep for hidden rippers. The basement sweeps were to be carried out by Bobs' new Redemption Brigade, the former members of the Daylight Brigade that surrendered at the Merchandise Mart. Bobs wanted them to prove their loyalty to her alone.

When Tevy arrived in the doorway, Bobs looked up and gave him the best smile he had ever received from her.

"I knew if I goaded her enough she'd save your ass," she said. "You guys can go." That was to Gonsalves and Chen. She went to a sideboard and picked up a bottle of wine. "I've been saving this for a special occasion. Sit down and tell me everything."

Tevy sat and accepted a glass with clear liquid that fizzed. It tasted like soda, only without a fruit flavor and not as sweet. He told her of Elliot rescuing him and didn't mention Radu or Bertrand Allan, but Bobs was no fool.

"But who cut his head off then?"

"Another ripper," Tevy said, the bubbles of the drink going to his brain and the exhaustion slurring his words. It couldn't just be the alcohol. He'd only had half a glass. "A ripper who had a beef with him, I guess."

"What happened to him?" Bobs reached forward with the bottle and filled Tevy's glass.

"He booked. The water wasn't too high then, so maybe he got out of the city before the tunnels flooded."

Bobs didn't look convinced. "Pretty strange that a ripper took your side at the last minute."

Bishop Alvarez spared Tevy further interrogation by coming in to congratulate him.

Tevy knelt and kissed the ring, but Alvarez raised him to his feet and kissed each of his cheeks. "Truly, you are blessed by Christ. You will be the first of a new order of the church. But," he said, waving a finger at Tevy and smiling, "you must be celibate. At least until I release you for marriage. We can't let your fighting edge be softened by carnal knowledge."

"Your Excellency." Tevy debated what to say and decided to go for the truth. "I'm honored and all, but I'm not your guy. I'm already married."

Bobs beat Alvarez to a reply. "What!"

Tevy turned to meet her disapproval, his head spinning from the strange wine.

"Kayla and I married this morning. We promised to stay together forever." He turned to Alvarez. "You wouldn't marry us, so we married ourselves after she rescued me."

Alvarez shook his head. "This was not a marriage before God."

"The hell is wasn't." Tevy fought to keep the anger from his voice. "If it wasn't a miracle...an effing miracle...that I was saved and Vlad beheaded, I don't what is. God himself must've made that happen. He wanted Kayla and I to marry."

"Miracles rarely happen, and the intervention of Christ or a saint is required to make them happen. What you should understand—"

Drunken singing interrupted Alvarez, and Emile stumbled through the door, unaware of the sermon he had stopped. "Bobs!" He raised a bottle identical to the one Bobs had opened. "This is the best Champagne! Wow! I mean, this day just keeps getting better."

"Get out and sleep it off." Bobs hardly spared him a glance, her eyes burning holes in Tevy's.

"It's just so great, though." Emile tried to take a drink from the bottle and missed, pouring some down his shirt. "All this time I thought Bert was gone. It's just so great that a little bit of him carried on. I should've known when I saw her face, you know, she's got his nose, same color eyes too." He slumped into a chair at the long table.

Tevy rushed to distract attention from Emile. "Kayla and I are married." He wondered why his words slurred, and he desperately wished he could just lie down.

But Bobs wasn't fooled, and her concentration now centered on Emile. "Who has Bert's face?"

Emile rested his head on his hands on the table, close to passing out, but he looked up with a grin. "The little girl. Funny, I always thought she and Jeff were the couple, him being so good looking and all. Who knew it was Bert? He won her heart."

"Wait a minute. You've seen this girl? Is she here?"

Emile still grinned, unaware of the danger. "Oh yeah, she played with the Brat Pack for a few days before they moved out there to the Mart. Joyce's daughter." His head slumped into his hands.

Alvarez had gone rigid. "Joyce has a daughter by Bertrand Allan?"

He looked at Tevy and raised the crucifix from his chest and folded Tevy's hands around it. "Who is the father of Joyce's daughter? On Christ, who is the father?"

Tevy couldn't think and lying didn't come naturally to him. "Bertrand Allan."

Bobs exploded. "What the fuck? You knew this and didn't tell me?"

"It's none of your business."

"It's all of my business. We're about to make a fucking saint out of him. Saints don't have children."

"We have to get her somewhere secret." Alvarez paced back and forth by the table. "I will establish a convent far from the city. She can be raised there and join their ranks when she's of age. She must grow old and die without offspring. The secret will die with her."

"And what can we do about Joyce and Jeff and him and that drunken lout. Who else knows?" The last was directed at Tevy.

Tevy's stomach heaved, and he feared bringing up the drink right in front of the bishop. He considered and dismissed arguments and pleas, entreaties and suggestions. He knew they were all to no avail. He went with the simplest answer.

"Fuck you."

He made it to the corridor before he emptied his guts.

Kayla got naked behind the blockhouse and Amanda poured several buckets of water of cold water from the well over her. Amanda was almost as excited by Kayla's marriage, and she confided that she intended to have Elliot at the earliest possibility, which was only delayed because, after one fumbling and drunken attempt to remove her jeans, he had passed out on his bed in the dorm of the Brat Pack.

Amanda loaned Kayla a dress, and Kayla twirled once in the light cotton, loving the feel and the freedom. She couldn't wait for Tevy to take it off. She couldn't help but dance a little, in spite of the exhaustion. Everywhere you looked, people danced, cheered, drank, and kissed, mostly in the courtyard by the church, although the whole cantonment was one huge party in the morning sun. Vlad was dead and the rippers that had threatened them for so long were vanquished. Bobs had done it. People sang her name and Webb's. That was the only blemish on the day, that Tevy and Elliot weren't getting their due for their role in ending Vlad's life, but Kayla was sure the record would be set straight in the next few days.

"He must be pretty tired," said Amanda as she fussed over the dress. "Do you think..." She blushed.

Kayla laughed. "I'm pretty bagged, too, so maybe we'll sleep first." She gave Amanda her most mischievous look. "But when we wake up, I'll put him through his paces."

They both laughed. A man from the crowd with a bottle tried to kiss Amanda, but she kneed him in the groin and pushed him away. He laughed and kept going, looking for someone else to kiss. It was that kind of day.

Tevy came out of the church and Kayla had to suppress a surge of disappointment. He hadn't cleaned up at all. In fact, he looked worse than after the medic from Webb's army sewed up his many gashes. Suddenly, Kayla feared his death. He looked so sick. Had Vlad got him after all? Was he dying and turning into a ripper? She ran through the crowd, pushing people out of her way.

"Tevy!" She got to him but didn't embrace him. Vomit mixed with the blood on his shirt. "Are you okay?" She put a hand on his shoulder and it was still warm, and he was standing in full sunlight. These were good signs.

"Oh, Kayla. We have to do something."

"What happened? Tevy, what happened!"

"Emile...he was drunk. He told Bobs about Margaret, about her being Bertrand Allan's daughter."

"Oh, shit. Does she know about him?"

Tevy shook his head and looked as if he might throw up again, but he held it together. "The bishop, the bishop says that she's got to become a nun, that they've got to keep it a secret. That she's got to die without having children herself."

"What? Why?"

"Joyce was right. Allan's to be a saint and this would spoil his...I don't know...his sanctity. Like saints aren't supposed to have sex, I guess, especially without getting married first."

They had a little time but not much. Bobs would move fast on this, but Kayla intended to move faster. She turned to Amanda. "You should come with us. Go wake Elliot. Slap him, throw water on him, whatever you have to do. You drag him to the Merchandise Mart."

"What do I tell him?" Amanda looked bewildered.

"Tell him that Tevy needs his help more than ever."

After last night, that was saying a lot.

Amanda's lower lip firmed up, and she got that detached look she always got when going into battle. "Got it." She ran up the steps of the church.

"Tevy, are you okay? Can you run?"

Tevy nodded, and a little color had returned to his face.

"Good. I'm going to get my guns and ammo and get out of this dress. You run for the Mart and warn Joyce and Jeff. I think they were planning to go tomorrow, but they've got to go now. I'm going with them." Now the big question. "Are you coming with me?"

He looked genuinely surprised. "Of course. We're married."

She ruined the dress by giving him a deep hug despite the blood and vomit.

"Run!" She gave him a quick kiss on his lips.

Tevy ran. He wanted to sleep so badly, but a second wind came to his rescue, and the running helped to clear his head. He weaved through the crowd and had just reached the cantonment gate when he saw a familiar hawkish face and sunglasses.

"Milan! What are you doing here?"

The pilot looked over in surprise, and then a big smile spilt his face. "Hey, if it isn't the guy who saved my life! I am here for the party, of course." His Czech accent was more pronounced than usual, and he slurred his words.

"I thought you were out of action, that your ankle was all messed up."

"Oh no. It was just a light sprain. I have been flying troops in from Malmstrom all week, even with the ankle. I can work the rudder pedals with only a bit of ache." He pulled up the leg of his jeans to show off the tension bandage between his jeans and his running shoe. "It's my ribs that still really hurt, cracked but not broken, but they need every pilot, so I have pain killers. It's the big push on the rippers so everyone must go above and beyond."

"So you're flying another little plane then?" Tevy thought of Margaret. If they could just get her away at least, maybe with Joyce, then perhaps Bobs would let the rest of the Raiders go too.

"Oh no. This is big so we're all going big. They've given me an old Herc, but it is a very good plane. And hey, is not my timing good?" He held up a wine bottle and grinned. "I land with a bunch of troops this morning so I get to join the party here while she is refueling. This is a '12 Cabernet Sauvignon. Probably the last wine from France that I will ever drink."

"I need your plane." Tevy couldn't even pretend to hide his excitement.

"What?" Milan lost all the drunken, back-slapping happiness.

"I need you to fly everyone back to St. John's, all of Joyce's Raiders anyway."

"Impossible, young man. They have no airport up there that can take my Herc, and there is no way I will put her down on that broken highway."

"Then fly us to Duluth. Just get us the hell out of here."

"What is all the rush? We won."

Tevy wanted to scream his frustration. He grabbed the man by his shoulders and shook him. "I'm asking you to save my life. Do this and we're even. Save my life."

"Okay, okay. I'll just let Webb know that I have to make a detour—"

"No! Don't tell Webb. Don't tell anyone. We have to leave in secret. Bad things could happen."

"What things?" Milan's brow furrowed, and he studied Tevy like a man who is worried he's the butt of a joke.

"Just have it fueled and ready. Are you at O'Hare?"

"No, they're saving that for all the bombers and fighters. I'm up on the highway like always."

"Even better. We'll be there in an hour, and we have to go right away. Can I trust you?"

"Yes. I would be drained of blood and rotting if it weren't for you."

"See you soon."

Tevy ran, but he decided to make a detour on the way, really just a change of route. He got a bike from his favorite bike store and rode for the house with the bunker. He drew his shotgun just in case, and made his way down to the basement. The bunker door was closed.

Tevy knocked and shouted, "Mr. Allan? It's Tevy. We need to talk."

The door opened and Allan stepped out. He had changed his clothes and cleaned off the blood of Vlad, but he trembled like a new-born lamb.

"Are you all right, sir?"

"Call me Bert." He sat heavily on the couch. "I've apparently crossed a line into a new level of infection. The parasites are working some new magic or evil. I shouldn't have drank Vlad's blood, but I've been starving for so long."

Tevy wanted to know more, but Kayla had infected him with a sense of urgency.

"Sir, Bert. Bobs knows about Margaret, knows that she's your daughter."

"Does she know about me? That I'm a ripper?"

Tevy shook his head. "No, just about your daughter. Emile got drunk."

"How did he know? Did you tell him?"

"No, I swear, I don't know how he found out. But he knew, and he was drunk and he was happy for you."

"He just killed me." Allan's expression showed his anger. "She was the one good thing that came out of that year. I don't want Bobs to have anything to do with her."

"It's worse than that." Tevy took the armchair but didn't sit back, fearing its comfort while this tired. "She and the bishop, they're not happy. Saints aren't supposed to have children. The bishop wants to start a convent and put her in it. He says she should never have children and should always be a secret."

"Bobs and her publicity machine. Why did she have to make me her martyr? Why does she have to make me a saint?" Allan stood and looked up the staircase in frustration. "I should go to Joyce. Where is she? How long till sunset?"

"Her Raiders are at the Merchandise Mart now. They've made it their base, their blockhouse, but it's only about noon. You can't go for hours."

Bertrand crossed the room in one step and grabbed Tevy's shoulders, much the way Tevy had done with Milan. "Then you have to get Margaret out of here, back to St. John's, far from Bobs. If she tries to stop you, then hold her off until dark. I'll come for her."

The door to the bunker opened further, and Radu pushed into the room, looking weak but alive. "And I will come too," he said. "I love a just fight."

Suddenly, Tevy remembered Radu not running in the woods, Radu warning them, Radu covering for them, Radu running with them in the final attack on Vlad.

Radu hosted a portion of the Dependable Rogue. Tevy was sure, and his conversion to the Ericsians was complete. It just made sense.

Tevy found Joyce and Jeff on the third floor of the Mart, where they'd made a good base for Joyce's Raiders. They had cleaned out useless office furniture and used the dividers to make rooms, all facing the north-side windows, which had been free of ripper and Daylight Brigade sniper fire during the last days.

Most of the St. John's people had stayed in the blockhouses in the city, trying to get to know people and establish themselves in Chicago. They would doubtless be at the party, now looking for potential wives or husbands. Only about forty intended to return to St. John's, and they were all here, packing weapons and ammo and clothes.

"Damn him to Hell," said Joyce when Tevy explained what had happened.

"Kayla says you've got to get out of here today. Now."

Jeff shook his head. He seemed solidly sober, but then Tevy could rarely tell when Jeff was drunk, because he was better than Elliot at hiding it.

"Bobs has got the buses in the cantonment. When I tried to drive one out this morning, I got stopped by her new Redemption Brigade. They said I needed Bobs' permission to take one of our own goddamn buses. Bastards were surrendering to me last week and begging for their lives, and now they only take orders from Bobs."

"We don't need the buses," Tevy said. "I ran into Milan, and he's got a Herc out on the highway fueling right now. I got him to promise to fly us to Duluth. From there we can find another bus and some fuel and drive the rest of the way."

Joyce looked out the window in the direction of St. Mike's. The glass was shot out during the battles, and a cool breeze blew down from the north. Now she looked back at Tevy in surprise. "You're going back with us?"

"I have to. I mean, I'm married to Kayla. At least we married each other, and she's going back, and I told Bobs to fuck off."

Jeff barked a short laugh. "No kidding?"

"I've converted to the Ericsians. I can't stay here if they find that out."

Joyce looked stunned. "My God, you really are like Bert."

"That's the other thing. I stopped by to see him on my way here. At the bunker."

Jeff interrupted him. "You know about the bunker?"

Tevy pointed to Joyce. "She said he'd be in a bunker, and I could only think of one bunker in the whole city, and I know every basement. I've visited him a couple of times."

"Christ, you've got balls." Jeff studied him with new interest. "It's going to be good having you at St. John's."

"Save that for later," Joyce said. "What did Bert say?"

"That if you're not gone by sunset, he'll be coming to get you out."

"We'll be gone."

But the afternoon dragged. They had one pickup truck, a small 4x4, which they could use to ferry gear up to the plane, but before they finished piling it high with all the ammo and weapons they could find, disturbing reports started to arrive. Mabruke had already pulled the Ericsians back to Wright Sanctuary, but he sent a runner to Joyce to warn her that the Redemption Brigade had started bulldozing churches, mosques, temples, and synagogues. All of the cantonments except for St. Mike's were being ripped apart.

"She wants to make everyone move into the Loop, and she's using the celebrations as cover," said the runner, a pre-teen girl with long red hair and long legs for her age. "Mr. Mabruke says he thinks she wants to force them all to convert to Chicago Catholic Church. The Redemption Brigade all had to be baptized at St. Mike's, and all the prisoners Webb took today are going to be, too. She's building an army of her own, and she's already got Webb with her, so she'll be the most powerful force in Chicago."

"Then you guys will be in danger at Wright," said Joyce. Margaret hid behind her mother's leg and peeked shyly out at the runner. Joyce had kept Margaret very close since Tevy's news.

"We're leaving Wright and going very far away to one of our other settlements."

Joyce told her to pass on best wishes, and the runner sprinted for the stairs.

The only good news was that Martin had already left with some people in a van, and Jeff managed to reach him by radio and update him and ask him to prepare the way at Duluth, find a bus and supplies.

Kayla arrived dressed in jeans and her multi-pocketed vest, her battle clothes, carrying a heavy bag of ammo. Tevy's heart leapt at her arrival, because he had been afraid that something would go wrong, that something would prevent her from joining him. They embraced and Tevy craved to meld with her, not just sex, but fuse together as a single human being.

Elliot and Amanda had taken Kayla down to Emile's boiler room under the church and raided the shelves for all they could carry. Elliot had given Emile, both of them still drunk, a lecture about alcohol and the damage Emile had caused with his loose lips. The couple arrived not long after Kayla, burdened with their own backpacks full of ammo.

Shortly afterwards Emile pulled up in his truck, the fifty cal still mounted in the back and Helen riding shotgun. Tevy was happy to see them both, his foster parents, and he received a big hug from Helen. "You did so well, my boy. I'm so proud of you."

"You got a lot of nerve," Joyce said to Emile, who had changed his shirt and sobered, although the bags under his eyes spoke of lack of sleep and a hangover in the making.

"I know. Really, I know and I'm so sorry. But I gotta to warn you. When I woke up there in Bobs' war room, she and Alvarez were having one hell of an argument. He wants her," he pointed to little Margaret, who had gone to Helen for a hug and was now up in her arms, "to go into a convent. She wants a...a quick and permanent solution."

At first Tevy didn't get what he was saying, but Emile's huge guilt, his embarrassment at what he set in motion, gave a clue as to what catastrophe was unleashed. Emile glanced at Margaret to make sure she wasn't looking and drew his finger across his throat. "Bobs called in her Redemption Brigade, the Red Shirts, because no one else would do this."

Joyce shook her head in disbelief, and for a moment Tevy thought she was going to attack Emile. Instead, she turned to Jeff. "I don't care who's packed and who isn't. Fuck everything. We're leaving right now."

It was too late. Tires squealed as vehicles outside skidded to a halt. Men shouted and running feet pounded the pavement. Tevy and Jeff were the first to the window, leaning dangerously far out to look down. 4x4s arrived to join others that had just stopped. Men with blood red shirts jumped out and ran to take up positions. They were well equipped with weapons and ammo, some even had Kevlar vests.

"Shit." Jeff leaned far out the window to look down at the street. "Those are the same Redemption Brigade assholes that wouldn't let me take a bus this morning, and it looks like Bobs has pulled out all the stops for them. Trucks, gas, guns, and ammo."

Tevy never liked Bobs' idea of forming the Redemption Brigade. They were traitors not just to humans, but to Vlad Who Bleeds, their master. These were not people to be trusted at all, clearly willing to switch allegiances at a change in the wind—people of very low moral fiber.

Jeff looked back from the window. "Looks like we're to be arrested."

"When hell freezes over." Joyce hefted her Uzi. "This is still one defendable position. Set up the heavy guns on the third floor, east, south, and west. Everybody else down to the first floor."

Tevy couldn't believe what he was hearing. "We're going to fight?"

"We're just going to keep them back until dark and then we'll slip away somehow, maybe with Bert's help." She pointed at Tevy. "Can you get through their lines to Novak and make sure he's waiting for us?"

It took Tevy a second to remember that Novak was Milan's last name. "I'll be back before you know it."

Getting out was tricky, taking a path he knew under the street, squeezing past a cave-in and up into a wreck of a building on the other side of Kensie that had taken hits from the artillery. Gunfire from the Mart erupted before he'd even reached the Kensie Street Bridge. Luckily, no one was guarding it, so he got onto the highway, running with all he had left, north to Armitage where he found the huge squat plane, its four big propeller engines idle. It was massive compared to the Cessna.

"My God, young man," Milan said when he came down the stairs from the plane, wiping grease from his hands on a cloth. "You look absolutely like death that has been warmed over."

Tevy breathlessly explained that they needed to leave after dark.

"Impossible," said Milan. "How would we land?"

"Martin Morley is already half-way to Duluth. He'll fix it. We're in radio contact."

Tevy gratefully accepted a bottle of water, which he drank in gulps. He looked south back down the highway, summoning the energy for one last run before he must sleep.

"There isn't any way you could taxi this thing closer to us is there?" he asked.

Milan shook his head. "It took us months to get all the overhead signs and lamp posts down to make this our runway." He waved vaguely south. "From here on down there is much in the way, and the road curves and dips. Sorry young man. You can tell Joyce I will wait until midnight, but after that I'm supposed to be landing at Malmstrom. They think I've already left, and I'm very sure that they will be sending people to find out why I'm not doing my job. I'm not waiting around to answer. Webb thinks I'm in his damn army. He would shoot me as a deserter pretty damn quick."

"We'll be here. I promise."

Tevy ran back down the highway as the sun sank below the horizon, sweat pouring from his body, his vision blurring and his heart racing. When he got to the Kensie Street Bridge he could see in the last of twilight that there would be no going back across. Red-shirted men with guns guarded the far side.

Fortunately, their backs were to him, as the guards were clearly intent on preventing people from leaving Chicago. Tevy slipped into the river, grateful of the cool despite the stink of algae, holding his Glock and his shotgun over his head and awkwardly swimming across on his back, using his feet for propulsion. He scrambled up through the brush and climbed out using the railway bridge—stuck permanently up and waiting for gravity and rust to bring it down—as cover. He slipped over the loading docks into the burnt wreck of the Chicago Sun-Times building. The sign high above had survived the fire, although he and Elliot put a few bullet holes in the 'C' when they were still pre-teens.

The report of distant gunfire spurred Tevy to run through the building, following paths he knew that led over and around the hills of fallen drywall and desks and other debris, even squeezing under a collapsed floor to get him into the Illinois Institute of Art. This building suffered even more in the fire, and the ceiling had caved in, but Tevy knew a way up a pile of moldering drywall and a sloping roofing girder that allowed him to clamber up and swing onto the pedestrian bridge. This ran over top of Orleans Street and into the second floor of the Mart. As he had hoped, no one from either side guarded it, because no one knew that the bridge didn't dead end at the wreck of the institute.

From the bridge Tevy's worst fears were confirmed. The gunfire did come from inside the Mart. Joyce was at again war. This time with Bobs.

31

LAST STAND AT MERCHANDISE MART

Tevy crossed the bridge in the dark and felt his way into the Mart. Muzzle flashes guided him down a corridor to the far side. The battle was taking place in the stairwell, or perhaps several stairwells. He found Emile pressed to the wall on one side. His face cut and bleeding, his eyes fierce as he screamed and turned to fire downstairs. A Red Shirt tried to climb over a pile of desks in the stairwell. The man fell to Emile's fire and slipped back down the pile to land beside another corpse. A static road flare burned on the step near the pile, giving a red hue to the white walls.

"How the hell did you get back in here?" shouted Emile. "I thought they owned the first floor."

"I came across the bridge over Orleans."

"Quick, go to the north stair and tell Joyce." He fired down the stairs to keep the enemy from rushing. "These guys are almost as bad as rippers. Bobs told them she'd kill them all if they don't get us. Hurry. I'm running low on ammo, and I'm too old and drunk for knife work."

Tevy hurried back up the stairs and into the corridor, but there wasn't even a bit of light from outside. It was full night. He ran with one hand on the wall, tripping over debris twice, slamming his knees onto tiled floor. More gunfire sent light flashing out a doorway and made the last hundred yards easier.

Joyce and Kayla hunkered behind a heavy granite-topped desk turned on its side. They took turns firing over top and down the stairwell, which was also blocked with a pile of chairs, filing cabinets, and tables.

"Emile wants me to tell you about a way out," he shouted over the gunfire.

Joyce turned sharply. "How the hell did you get back in?"

Tevy explained his route.

"Okay. Go around to all the stairs and let everyone know. In five minutes we all pull back into this hallway and we'll retreat that way. Will they be able to shoot at us in the river?"

"If they know we're there. I'm hoping we can get through before they know."

"I don't like it, but I guess we don't have much choice. Go."

He spared a glance for Kayla, but she was deep in her job, firing only when a target appeared, ducking when fired upon. Tevy had to resist the urge to drag her out of there and take her somewhere safe. He knew she would never forgive him if he did.

Emile took the news with relief, but he was bloodier. Tevy didn't have time to do anything about it. He had just reached the next stairwell when shouting ended all gunfire. Tevy put his head carefully around the doorjamb to find Jeff and Elliot standing with their backs to the wall and their weapons pointing for the ceiling, not aimed.

He was about to ask what the hell was going on when a desk below shifted and Bertrand Allan emerged from the pile of office equipment that blocked the stairway, squeezing though a gap in the computers and filing cabinets and chairs as if being born. He stood and brushed himself off, apparently unaware that he was bleeding from a bullet hole in his shoulder.

Jeff spoke first. "Bert, good to see you dude, but you've looked better."

"No one is coming up this stair." Bert noticed Tevy. "Radu didn't make it. I'm sorry. I think he was happy to go for a good cause."

Tevy wanted to grieve, but he had learned from Mabruke's talks that Elliot and Jeff must have denser souls because of Radu's death. This was a good thing, wasn't it?

"We're going to pull out," Tevy said. He explained as quickly as he could and rushed off to find the fourth stairwell.

They all pulled into the corridor, including about forty people who had still been evacuating from the ground floor. Emile dropped some flares at the east end nearest those stairwells so that they could see any Red Shirts that dared to come up. But Emile didn't join them at a hastily improvised barricade of desks and a countertop ripped from a store. Instead, he slumped against a wall and slid down. Tevy ran back for him and discovered that Emile was beyond help. His breathing had stopped, and the hole in his gut explained the blood.

He closed Emile's eyes, took his rifle, and fled the body of the man who, since Tevy was ten, had been his father. A new rage rose up, not for the rippers that had ended the world, but for the Redemption Brigade. Tevy was no longer afraid to kill humans. He vowed revenge.

Kayla had never been so relieved to see anyone in her life when Tevy shouted into the stairwell, but she couldn't spare him a moment of attention. Another one of the red-shirted bastards was trying to get around the corner to throw a grenade. The last one had detonated a full flight down when it rebounded off the wall and landed at the feet of the thrower. Luck wasn't likely to help a second time.

She fired at the Red Shirt, and he spun away, falling before he could throw. Shouts of "grenade!" from below gave her just enough time to drop the Uzi and plug her ears, crouching down. The blast dazzled her eyes, but it exploded so far down the stairs that it hurt the Red Shirts rather than her. She made a note that grenades work better when lobbing them down stairs rather than up.

Joyce pulled them back a few minutes later, and when they got to the barricade and found Allan had joined them, Kayla was hopeful that they would escape. But then things started to go wrong. First Emile died, and she had to run after Tevy and scream, "Leave him, damn it!"

Tevy ran back to join her at the barricade. Joyce sent Tevy to show others the way out, and Allan stayed with them. A man rushed into the hallway, firing his shotgun wildly as he crossed into a store with broken glass windows. Kayla tracked him even as he vanished into the dark and she fired. In the flash she saw him for a second, still running but with a surprised look on his face. She was pretty sure that she had scored a hit.

"I can't believe Bobs thinks she'll get away with this," Kayla shouted as she crouched behind a desk, painfully aware that bullets could pass through the steel and wood with ease. "You guys are heroes, and people will be pissed."

Joyce shook her head. "I think she's just lost it."

Bertrand spoke, his voice gentle but raised to be heard over the gunfire.

"I should've told you, but if I did, I knew you'd risk everything to kill Bobs."

Even though he was talking to Joyce, Kayla looked over, because she sensed something big. She remembered to watch the corridor, but she continued to listen carefully.

"Told me what?" Joyce's voice had hardened.

"I didn't choose to attack Vlad the Scourge in the Battle of the Mountain on my own. I mean, I guess I could have waited for you guys to rescue me. I don't know, it's all a haze."

"What did Bobs do?"

"She locked me in there with him. Told me if I came out, Terry would shoot me. Told me I was her martyr."

"For fuck's sake, Bert, you should've told me this! I'd never have come down here."

"Yes, you would have, only you would have come here to kill Bobs."

"Okay, you're totally fucking right. I would have."

"Chicago needed her, Joyce. She's the Ruthless General. Only she could stand against the rippers and Vlad Who Bleeds. Only she could pull all the loyalist humans together into a single effort. I didn't want you to come down, remember? Christ, I didn't want to be near her. You're wrong, though." Kayla glanced from the corridor, worried because the Red Shirts appeared to have stalled, which meant they were planning something new. She discovered that Allan was now addressing her. "They'll kill all of you and say you died in a battle with the last of the rippers. Tomorrow you'll all be on your way to sainthood in the new Chicago Catholic Church."

Tevy, Jeff and Elliot rushed up from behind.

"We're all set," said Jeff. "We've got almost everybody across the bridge and heading for the river. He's right. It's our only hope of slipping away."

Allan drew his shotgun from the holster at his hip. "I'll hold their attention here. You go. I'll make my own way to St. John's later."

Kayla knew a moment of hope. Of course, Allan would be nearly impossible to kill. They would get away. She and Tevy would make a life at St. John's. Margaret would grow up, and Bobs would never be able to touch them.

The grenade was too far away to kill, the concussion hardly ruffling their hair, but its light dazzled their night-adjusted eyes. By the time Kayla could focus, over a dozen men rushed into the corridor, running criss-cross back and forth from doorway to shop window to doorway, shooting all the time.

A bullet tore away a chunk of Kayla's ear, but she put the pain away for later, firing and firing, trying to stay with a target as it crossed the hall and not get distracted by one crossing the other way. She needed to change mags when they were only a few body lengths away, but the attackers were down to three, and before she could find another clip in her vest pocket, they were dead. The rush had been stopped.

Kayla risked a look to see if everyone was okay.

Joyce lay back in Jeff's arms, a red hole in her leg, the blood spreading rapidly on the floor. Her face was white with shock. Allan crouched beside her, holding her hand. Tevy sat with an open mouth. Amanda ran up the corridor from the escape route, coming back to help them retreat.

A grenade flashed. Kayla didn't even have to look up to know what was happening: a second rush, even bigger than the first. That's what she would do. Right on the heels of the first, not giving her enemy a chance to reload, knowing they were looking to their wounded. The way they all looked at Joyce. Now they would all die.

Except that Kayla was there and knew what to do, because she was the Angry Captain—the soul that understood close combat, could delegate troops to their roles without concern about whether they were friends or lovers. The universe slowed for her as she computed. Joyce had always said that Bertrand Allan was a bullet. He didn't understand the big picture, but point him in the right direction and pull the trigger and he would do epic damage.

Tevy hosted the same soul as Allan.

Kayla's soul went into a cold state. There were only assets, not people.

She pointed down the hall toward the enemy that she knew without looking poured from the stairwell. She shouted for all she was worth.

"Bert, Tevy! GO!"

Tevy heard Kayla yell "GO" and he lunged up and over the barricade like a horse that has heard the gun at a race. It wasn't till he landed on the far side of a desk that he even understood why she had shouted that order.

Red Shirts charged through the door of the stairwell, firing down the hall so frequently that the muzzle flashes weren't even strobe. The light was continuous. Tevy had two shots left, and the first one went through a man's eye, blowing pinkish-white brains out the back of his head. The second shot went wide, and he threw his Winchester at this man.

Allan crossed in front of him, tossing Tevy his shotgun in the process. It was identical to Tevy's and it fit into his hands as seamlessly as if it were his own gun, only it was fully loaded. Tevy had to lunge to the left to get a clear shot past Allan at another man, but before he could pull the trigger a red hole appeared in the man's forehead.

Pick another target and fire. Make every shot count. Allan crossed in front again and Tevy now understood that the man was trying to protect him, to draw the fire. They raged down the hall, Allan with his Glock and Tevy with the shotgun. Some of the Red Shirts tried to push back into the stairwell, to run from the unexpected fury of their assault. They collided with others and gave Tevy two more easy targets, hitting one man in the side and another in the head, dropping them both with no hope of survival, stopping them dead. They weren't rippers. There were no parasites in their blood to save them.

Now there was a full on retreat down the stairs, and Tevy pushed against Allan, trying to beat him through the doorway. A grenade landed at their feet and Tevy kicked it, sending it bouncing down the stairs with just enough time to dodge away from the fire door. The blast dazzled Tevy and ended the Red Shirt assault.

They stood side by side at the top of the stairs, not far from the body of Emile.

"Come on!" shouted Tevy down the stairs, taunting his enemy.

"WIMPS!" shouted Allan.

They both heaved for breath, and Tevy marveled that a ripper could be winded. That was important to know. They grinned at one another for a moment and simultaneously remembered Joyce. They ran back for the barricade.

―――――

Kayla dropped the mag from her Uzi right after she ordered Tevy and Allan to their deaths and slammed in the fresh mag. She had just enough time to sight a man who would surely kill Tevy. She put a bullet through the Red Shirt's head.

Tevy and Allan were as awesome as Joyce would have predicted. They raged down the hall like a tsunami sweeping all before them. Kayla fired again and again, always going after the ones closest to Tevy.

It wasn't just that he was her lover. Allan was a ripper and could take a lot without dying. After the grenade detonated, when the crisis was over, she remembered Joyce.

Kayla turned to her, still clinical, still the Angry Captain. The bullet had passed through the bone of the thigh, and Joyce was hiding the intense pain admirably, although she vomited suddenly. But Kayla thought of the description of the escape route: across a bridge, climb down a girder, work through the piles of debris of a burned-out building, swim across the river and climb out. Run a couple of miles up a highway. And Joyce would die anyway. There were no ambulances, trauma units, anti-biotics, or even hospitals. Still, they had people who could carry her. Maybe an amputation on the plane could save her.

Joyce tied a tourniquet around her own leg with Jeff's help. She used a ruler to tightened the cord, the sling from her Uzi, and then bound around it to keep it in place. It would mean the death of her leg, but it would keep her from bleeding to death in minutes. She looked up at Kayla as she finished. "Get them out of here."

"What?"

Joyce spoke in short sentences, the pain raising a sweat on her forehead and making her as pale as a ripper. "I'm finished. I'll just slow you down. Get them out of here now and save Margaret. They would have shot us all in the river anyway if they had figured out we were gone, or they'd have chased us up the highway in their trucks. This way I can hold their attention here until you're all across. After that carnage," she said, nodding toward Tevy and Allan as they ran back, "they'll be afraid to attack. I can buy you maybe an hour. Go!"

But Kayla didn't understand. They could all make a run for it. They could carry Joyce.

But Tevy did understand.

As he knelt in front of Joyce, he remembered his father shoving him deep into the closet, his mother blowing him a kiss while she was loading Granddad's old .38 Smith and Wesson. He retrieved that gun from the burnt wreckage of the home of his childhood a month after their deaths. He hugged the burnt skull of his mother for an afternoon until Elliot found him and helped him bury the bones of Tevy's loving parents in the back yard.

"You're a good mother," Tevy said to Joyce.

She understood, and he helped her take hold of her Uzi.

"We can't leave her!" yelled Kayla.

She didn't get it, and Tevy only had a moment to educate her. "This is what loving parents do!" Tevy discovered that he wept even as he shouted at Kayla. "This is what they do. They die for their children. They die."

He grabbed Kayla by the arm and pulled her to a standing position. Elliot and Amanda stood too. They got it.

Allan again sat holding Joyce's hand. He looked up to Kayla. "I'll stay with her. Tevy's right. It's your only chance of sneaking across the river. You have to go before they try again."

Jeff still sat behind Joyce, cradling her in his arms. He looked up at Tevy and Kayla. "Say hi to Barry for me. I can't go anywhere without these two, anyway. I'm staying. Go and toast me when you get to St. John's. Check the footlocker in my room. There's a half full bottle of single malt scotch: Balvenie Doublewood. Twelve years old. It's really good."

He slapped a fresh mag into his FN, that science-fiction looking rifle.

Tevy had to pull Kayla, but she came with him. They left the Trinity to their fate.

32

ESCAPE TO ST. JOHN'S

Tevy hoped that leaving the three to die would be the last tragedy of the night, but he got through the Sun-Times building and over the loading docks to discover that Helen had been left alone at the edge of the river, holding Margaret, who wept quietly, because she knew her mother wasn't with them. She also apparently knew that silence was essential. It reminded Tevy of his last days with his parents, when he had learned that silence meant life.

The Red Shirts on the bridge hadn't heard people splashing across the river because the gunfire from the Mart riveted their attention. Helen had been left behind in the panic. A strong crescent moon was on the wax, but that wasn't much light to see by, and Tevy's eyes had yet to adjust to the dark after all the muzzle flashes and explosions.

"Let's go," whispered Tevy.

Helen nodded and stepped into the river with the little girl. The water seemed colder to Tevy than before, and it stung all the hurts that he didn't even know he had earned. It wasn't until half way across that a new disaster made itself evident. Helen suddenly shoved Margaret at him, the girl bravely not screaming in the panic that she must have felt as her head went under the dark water. Tevy grabbed her arm and pulled her to the surface, rolling onto his back so that he could carry her on his stomach.

"Helen," he whispered. He shoved Margaret over to Kayla and reached for Helen, finding her hand deep. The cool water closed over his head as he fought to pull her to the surface, but she turned oddly in the current and suddenly her foot kicked into his stomach, separating them forever. He lost her body in the dark. It wasn't hard for him to understand. Helen didn't want to slow them down on the highway, and she was very old and couldn't run. The river took her from him. Another Companion of Bertrand lost to save his daughter.

They ran up the highway, lightning flashes from the windows of the Mart proving that the battle still raged, until it was lost to sight. Milan had started the Hercules's engines, and once they were on board, he shouted instructions for closing the door. Well into the flight, Tevy joined Milan in the cockpit, the dials space age to him and reminding him of a flight simulator he had intended to learn when he was finished *Call of Duty*. But the world had ended.

As they neared Duluth, Elliot, looking pale and frightened, came up to the cockpit.

"What happened?" asked Tevy.

Elliot shook his head. "I dunno. I was just falling asleep and suddenly an army walked over my grave, a total heebee jeebee, but on steroids."

Kayla joined them, also looking shaken. "My soul just got denser," she said. "I think Joyce just died."

Elliot looked at her in awe and looked back to Tevy. "Is that what happened to me? Did it happen to you?"

Tevy shook his head. What could he say? Exhaustion ended the discussion, and they all went back to sleep.

Milan was able to land at Duluth thanks to the radio and Martin Morley on the ground, who engineered a fast and furious effort to provide two long rows of bonfires to guide them into the runway. Milan abandoned the Hercules there. "Webb will court-martial me for this. I must throw my lot in with you fellows."

Martin had also located a bus at the depot, and he and his mechanic had it working by dawn. Martin even found a bulldozer and a tractor-trailer to haul it. The run back up to St. John's was easier than the trip down, although without the bulldozer it would have been impossible. The rippers had stubbornly blocked the highway with cars and trees, usually where the road passed through a deep cut in the Canadian Shield rock so that they couldn't drive around.

St. John's had changed since their departure. Barry St. John, ever the contractor, had begun a long stone wall around the building. The rippers had attacked one night, perhaps because they heard rumors of the bus convoy and figured that the Keep was weak. They had driven a truck at the front doors and nearly succeeded in ramming it through into the great hall. Only the heavy steel doors and a steady hail of gunfire had foiled the attack. The stonewall would encircle the building and have medieval towers, gun slits, and a double gate with a portcullis as well as iron doors.

"I'd love to make it of poured concrete," Barry had said to Tevy when giving a tour. "But there's no operating concrete plants. I've had a tough time even scrounging mortar. Had to send crews as far south as Thunder Bay, raiding every concrete plant and hardware store they could find."

Tevy and Kayla took a room together, and Margaret took up residence with them. She knew who saved her in the river, and she latched onto them. They became her foster parents. Amanda and Elliot took another room. Both couples told everyone they were already married, but they did take the time a week after their arrival to dress in the best clothes they could find and have a joint wedding reception. The forty from St. John's that they escaped with all came, and Barry St. John lavished them with ammunition as wedding presents. He and his wife took care of Margaret that night. The newlyweds opened Jeff's Balvenie and drank a toast in his and Joyce's and Bertrand's honor. It was really good. Even Tevy enjoyed it.

Six weeks after their return, Tevy found his shotgun sitting in the middle of the highway. There was no doubt in his mind that it was his, for he knew every groove in the wooden pistol grip, every scratch on the barrel. He had lost it at the Mart, throwing the empty gun at a Red Shirt.

Tevy took a big chance that night.

He waited until Kayla and Margaret slept soundly before he slipped out of bed and downstairs. There was a fire exit at the back of the tower and he pushed his way out, taking a deep breath as the door closed behind him, locking him out for the rest of the night. He couldn't help but feel relief, for while he knew this was a better place to raise a family, he missed his city, and he felt claustrophobic in the Keep. He craved those missions when he and Elliot would scout deep into the Loop, killing rippers surprised to find humans out at night and hunting.

The highway was lit by a full moon, one so strong that the trees cast moon shadows. Tevy walked in the center of road until he reached the place where he had found his shotgun, a crossing of two roads, an intersection with a dead traffic signal light. He sat cross-legged on the asphalt and breathed in the cold air of his new home, trying to understand the woodland sounds, getting used to the scent of pine and spruce. It was cold enough that the mosquitoes had slipped away, so he was comfortable and patient and he loved the stars.

He didn't have to wait long. A figure approached, walking up from the south, his hands out from his sides to show that he carried no weapons. He made no greeting, no claims of coming in peace. The man simply walked up and sat cross-legged in front of Tevy, staring at the asphalt between them.

It was Bertrand Allan.

He looked less emaciated than at the battle at the Mart. His clothes were new. He was clean. Yet, his head shook slowly back and forth as if denying memories.

"I couldn't save her," Allan said at last. "I couldn't save my love, my Angry Captain."

Tevy didn't answer because there was no answer. He didn't even want to imagine having to watch Kayla die in battle.

"I couldn't save my best friend. I couldn't save either of them. I couldn't save anyone."

This, Tevy could answer. "You saved your daughter."

Allan still looked at the asphalt, not meeting Tevy's eyes, but now he nodded. "Yes. We saved her. Who's taking care of her?"

"Kayla and I. Margaret chose us, I think because we saved her at the river when Helen drowned."

"Helen drowned." It wasn't a question, and the numbness of the statement was more disturbing than screaming and crying. "Margaret chose you because Kayla is familiar to her. Her very soul has Joyce written all over it."

They sat in silence.

Finally, Allan looked up and met Tevy's eyes. "She made me drink," he whispered.

"Drink...blood?"

"Jeff was dead. She was dying. I think maybe even I was dying, I'd been shot so many times. The Red Shirts had run away, but we knew they would be back soon. She begged me to finish her and get away. She begged me to drink her blood for strength and run. She was very near the end."

Tevy didn't know what to say, so he said nothing.

"All these years I resisted the temptation, starved on ripper blood and animal blood, forever hungry, forever craving. Even now, I can practically hear the blood rushing in your veins, calling me."

For a moment Tevy regretted not drawing his shotgun and having it ready.

"I gave in because she was right. I drank my lover's blood, the first living blood I've ever had, and it was incredible. Malcolm was right. It's way better than sex, better than drugs or drink or anything. And I didn't stop there. I went crazy. I drank from the Red Shirts. By dawn I was stronger than ever. All my hurts had healed and I found refuge in the bunker. She saved my life even as she died."

Now Allan began to shake, a quiet sob that chopped off. Tevy feared for the man's sanity, but he let time pass, sitting face to face in the dark until well after midnight. Finally, Tevy reached out and placed a comforting hand on Allan's knee.

The man, the ripper, looked up from the ground.

"Rippers can go dormant," Allan said. "I want to go dormant. I'll live for Margaret, in case she needs me some day, but not day to day. Build a cairn right here, right in the middle of the road. Build a vault, a grave, under it. I'll occupy it and I'll sleep. Wait till she's an adult and tell her about me and her mother and show her the cairn. If she needs me, she can call for my help. I'll always answer. But I swear this to you: I will never drink living blood again. Never."

33

MONUMENT TO A HERO

B arry helped Tevy craft the monument, finding the right stone, cutting it and carving it with tools they looted from a monument factory in Thunder Bay. Kayla drew the design with Margaret's input. A cross for the religion that now worshiped Bertrand as a saint. They entwined it with a triangle, representing the Battle of the Mountain where he lost his humanity—and the trinity: Bertrand, Joyce, and Jeff.

Barry held a funeral for the three, and all of St. John's Keep attended. The next year on the anniversary of their escape from Chicago, Tevy, Kayla, and Elliot laid a wreath at the monument. Amanda had been too sick with her pregnancy to join them.

They made it a tradition to lay a new wreath every year on that day.

Tevy always whispered, "Rest in Peace. We are here. We are good. We are safe. We are strong. We are complete. We are the Trinity."

ACKNOWLEDGEMENTS

There are so many people to thank. Mark Alliksaar, a technical instructor and cliché checker; Mark Downie, a dedicated fan and honest beta reader; Rebecca M. Senese, fellow writer and fellow e-rebel; all of *The Fledglings Writers Group*, for years of work, especially Karen Danyluk, who devoted time to copy edit this edition; Matt A. Baker, a careful editor; Michael Custode, for great artwork of the first edition and the awesome image of the monument at the end of this book; Barry Currey, for the gripping cover of this edition; Dr. Margaret Docker, Associate Professor, University of Manitoba, and Melanie Fogel, former editor of *Storyteller Magazine*, who both patiently taught this physics graduate grammar and writing, something sorely lacking in my university curriculum. Many thanks to Dooley, my Dependable Rogue. And most of all thanks to my wife - my toughest critic and staunchest supporter.

Thanks also to all my charter fans. Your emails and reviews about *Sacrifice the Living* (initially released as *Apocalypse Revolution*) let me know I was on the right path and encouraged me to keep going.

Special Thanks to You

The final thank you belongs to you for reading this book. I write books that I enjoy reading, and I'm delighted that you made it not just to the end, but to these acknowledgements. I'm honored. I hope you enjoyed **GENERATION APOCALYPSE** as much as I did.

I would love to hear from you. Visit me at **beyondtheslushpile.com** or send an email to **mike@michaelandremcpherson.com**. I'm on Facebook (Michael Andre McPherson) and Twitter @mcpherson_ mike. If I've moved you to prose, please write a quick review. Tell your friends, tell your family, make a point of bringing up the book in casual conversation. You get the idea.

Thanks so much - the 1000 Live On!

BUT WAIT! THERE'S MORE!

Keep going for a sneak peak of what's coming next.

HERETICS FALL

by **Michael Andre McPherson**
Book Three of *1000 Souls*
pectopahbooks.com
Publishing in 2014

PROLOGUE

Just when she thought she and Mom were going home, the Redemption Brigade came for them. Margaret didn't understand who they were at the time because she was only seven, and up until that day she had always assumed that all humans were friends, could never hurt one another or shoot one another. Only the rippers were evil. Only the night needed to be feared.

Margaret enjoyed their adventure to Chicago until that day, seeing the huge buildings and playing with the kids of the Brat Pack at St. Mike's. They were the orphans of Chicago, and for a few days while her mother was off killing rippers, Margaret stayed with them and their sort-of mom, Helen, a really old lady who smiled a lot, and their sort-of dad, Emile, a smelly fat guy who laughed a lot and showed them how to shoot. He even let her take a turn with a small handgun. She missed the target, a board with a bunch of circles painted on it leaning up against an empty old house, but he gave her two more tries, patiently instructing her on how to hold the gun until she hit the second circle.

The church was amazing. She'd never seen carving and painting like that. Some guy in a black robe came and told the children all about God, but Margaret had already been warned by her mother and Uncle Jeff not to mention the 1000 Souls, that these Chicago people weren't believers yet and were afraid of Ericsians. Margaret also found it weird that while they were near anyone from Chicago, she was supposed to pretend that Kayla was her mom. After some big battle her mom won, they moved away from St. Mike's and into a huge building, the Merch Mart it was called, but she wasn't allowed to go exploring through the empty stores or offices, and there were no other kids there, so it was really boring. All she could do was look out the windows at the big city that spread all around them, miles and miles of empty buildings. One night flares popped high and there was a lot of shooting around the bridges over the river, but she only watched it for a few minutes before Uncle Jeff found her by the window and took her to the safe ammunition room on the north side of the Mart to sit with a couple of others and stuff bullets into magazines. She was very good at it, one of the fastest.

While all this was exciting, she was homesick for the familiar crowds of St. John's Keep and the open fields and forests of Canada. Everyone in Chicago seemed very tense up until the party day, the kissing day. That was the best and worst day of her young life.

She was old enough to know that they'd won some big battle with the rippers, that they were all dead. She thought that meant every ripper in the world was dead, that the war was over for good. People danced and hugged and kissed in the morning light in front of the church. She hugged and kissed each one of her new friends in the Brat Pack, and she was especially pleased when Collin, the big boy, a full thirteen years old and a messenger to her mom, gave her a kiss on the forehead and an awkward hug. She treasured that memory for years. She loved him.

But her mom was all worried and angry about something. They rushed from the party at St. Mike's back to their camp in the Merch Mart and started packing crazy fast.

"We're going to go on a big plane," said her mom. "We'll be back home the day after tomorrow."

But the Redemption Brigade arrived in their trucks with their guns and surrounded the building, wouldn't let them out, told them to surrender.

Margaret had heard a lot of gunfire in her young life, but never in daylight, and never a battle between humans. There was nowhere for her to hide like in St. John's, where they always sent them into the mine if things got really scary. Even the ammunition room wasn't safe because windows facing north were hit with bullets too. They could only tuck her into a corner of a corridor behind some filing cabinets, where she filled magazines as fast as her little hands could jam in the bullets. People rushed out of the haze of gun smoke and grabbed full clips from her in panic, dropping off their empties. Some people were dragged past her back from the barricade with bullet wounds, some dead. Helen, the nice old lady who took care of the Brat Pack, stayed with her until dark. Her mom joined them for a moment, blood running down her cheek from a cut, her face a thunder that warned Margaret not to dare to argue.

"Helen's going to take you to the big plane. I'll be right behind, okay, baby? Just remember Mommy loves you very, very much. Be quiet with Helen though, okay? No crying. These evil ass...the Redemption Brigade, the bad people, mustn't know that we're sneaking away, okay? And some are on the bridge at the river. You'll have to swim, but nice and quiet, okay? Quiet as a mouse." Her mother gave her one last desperate hug and smeared her blood on Margaret's cheek when she kissed her.

Helen carried her through the wreckage of a building in the dark while all the gunfire only got worse behind them in the Merch Mart. They crossed a narrow footbridge and had to slide down some piles of broken building to the ground because the stairs were gone. She got a lot of scraps and a nasty cut, but she kept silent as her mother asked, telling herself to cry on the inside. When Helen reached the river not far from the bridge, she stopped and waited. Margaret assumed they were waiting for her mother to catch up.

Kayla and her new boyfriend joined them instead, and they all slipped quietly into the cold water together, but something went wrong. Margaret's head went under and she couldn't breathe. Suddenly Helen pushed her into Kayla's boyfriend's arms. He carried her out of the river, but Helen just disappeared in the dark water. It was too bad. Margaret liked her.

The plane was huge! She'd never seen anything so big. Kayla called it a Herc. It wasn't really comfortable inside though because there were only benches to sit on, but there was a lot of space for running around. Kayla told her it wasn't really a passenger plane, that it was for stuff.

They made her sit while the plane took off, but once it was in the air Margaret went looking for her mother. She walked up and down the benches, checking each face carefully a second time as if she might have missed her by accident. Uncle Jeff wasn't on board either. She even went up to the cockpit, but only Milan, the man who always brought candies for the kids when he flew into St. John's, was driving the plane. He turned from all the controls and smiled at her, but it was a sad smile.

Margaret walked very slowly passed everyone back to Kayla, slowly because she didn't want to believe that her mother wasn't on the plane. She stood in front of Kayla, who had tears on her cheeks. Kayla wiped them quickly when she realized Margaret was standing in front of her.

Margaret didn't ask. She didn't have to. She just stood in front of Kayla and waited to hear the worst.

Kayla shook her head. "I'm sorry, honey. I'm so, so sorry. Your mommy's gone. She was killed by the bad guys." She pulled Margaret into her lap.

They wept together. Even Kayla's boyfriend, Tevy, wept and patted Margaret's shoulder many times, promising that they would take care of her forever. Kayla tried to clean the blood from Margaret's cheek, but that was her mother's blood. Margaret never let anyone clean that blood, but it wore off anyway, severing her last connection to her mother. Margaret finally let herself fall asleep, hoping that it would all be a bad dream, that her mother would wake her from her bed in their room at St. John's.

She woke when the plane landed and wept some more, but they had to hurry onto a bus and headed out even before sun up. Kayla told her to go back to sleep, but before she drifted off a little fire took hold in her soul, an anger, a rage. It grew while she slept.

She woke in the afternoon, the sun on her side of the bus making her hot. She remembered a question that she desperately wanted answered, a question the angry Margaret wanted answered.

"Who killed Mommy?"

"The Redemption Brigade," said Kayla.

314

"Bobs," said her boyfriend at the same time.

Margaret whispered those names to herself again and again during the long drive home. "Bobs and the Redemption Brigade." She stared out at the forests sweeping past, her head pressed against the bus window so that she could see better in the bright sunlight. "Bobs and the Redemption Brigade."

She vowed that when she grew up, she would kill them all. For Mommy.

Eight Years Earlier

When the best looking jock from her old high school phoned Bobs and asked her out on a date, she knew the end was near. The signs had been there for a while.

Her first year at DePaul University had been great. She met new friends, shunning anyone from her high school, and they had introduced her to the rec center and a weight loss program that focused on exercise rather than dieting. Not girlie aerobics but useful exercise: karate, running, swimming and boxing. She particularly liked boxing because most of her opponents took one look at her five-foot nothing height and blonde hair and totally underestimated her ability. In six months she had shed the extra weight that earned her the description of "chubby" or "full figured," depending upon whether it was a creep or one of her friends talking. She also shed the Goth look, because it was making a comeback big time.

They were in every club in the city now, these pasty-faced freaks who referred to people like her, people with school and jobs, as "Day People." At first Bobs felt sorry for them, because there would only be two or three hunched over a table talking and not drinking, looking with envy at the dance crowd. But as more and more started to take over the clubs and the dance floors, still not drinking but all apparently totally wacked on ex, Bobs changed her mind. They weren't looking on in envy as she had at many high school dances: they looked more like they were hungry.

If that wasn't weird enough, the campus got in a tizzy about the Chicago Ripper, and suddenly Bobs wasn't one of the few women in karate. They flooded the class, all of them convinced they could take on a serial killer action-hero style. Bobs knew better and would've joined a gun club if there was one, but she had to settle for archery, and that's where she met Terry.

He was gangly and nerdy and loved first person shooter games. He was the anti-jock, and he owned crossbows. But you can't walk around the city with a crossbow, so Bobs started the paperwork to get a gun, but new laws had come into force, and even though they were the subject of a supreme court challenge, it looked like she'd graduate before she'd be allowed to purchase any gun.

She and Terry stopped going clubbing when the fires started. They were coming home late one night in June when they saw a burning house and ran toward it, expecting emergency vehicles to come rushing to the scene. Instead they watched from across the street as a crowd stood on the lawn shouting to the owner, taunting him to come out to meet them or burn with his house.

Bobs was no chicken-shit, but when a Goth-like guy in the crowd turned their way, she knew their lives hung in the balance.

"Run," she whispered to Terry. He didn't have to be told a second time.

They stayed in after that, gaming on the console in his basement, his parents stunned and happy that he had a girlfriend even though they weren't more than just friends. She knew he had the hots for her, and a couple of times she caught a glimpse of a bulge in his jeans that suggested wood, but she didn't want to go there now—-not with anyone.

But hiding in the basement didn't change the fact that the city was going to Hell.

Every morning on the walk to her summer job at the Athletic Center at DePaul, she found another burnt shell of a house somewhere along her route. At first the usual emergency vehicles attended after sunrise: a half dozen fire trucks, an ambulance or two and lots of police vehicles. But as June progressed into July, fewer and fewer fire trucks would clog the street around whatever house had been torched. One morning, a lone fireman with one truck and one hose poured water onto smoldering ruins. He nodded to her as she passed, and she suddenly felt like she was part of a shrinking club: Day People.

News of the Chicago Ripper was replaced with news of the new housing crash and the stock market crash and the strikes and lay offs as the economy crumbled, and her parents spent the evenings discussing the markets, totally absorbed and totally as clueless as ever. Even though Dad was a financial planner and Mom an economics teacher, they'd bought their current home and an "investment property" way back at the peak of the market, just before the first housing crash. They missed the second peak too and instead ended up sitting on both houses right through the second crash. Bobs had little faith in their prescience.

But she did trust Terry's. When he said there were many rippers, thousands of rippers, she believed him. When he said they were vampires, she didn't laugh, but she reserved judgment. He showed her a YouTube video shot at a protest rally at a McDonald's of all places, where a guy, Bertrand Allan, stood on the counter and preached that there were vampires, that you couldn't trust the police, that everyone should organize into community defense groups and stop living in isolated houses. It was just so ridiculous, so freaking impossible even if it kinda fit the facts. She just wasn't ready to believe that a cliché out of a horror movie really existed.

Until Steve Harrison called. Jocks don't call chubby Goth girls they haven't seen in over a year and rarely noticed during four years of high school. Wormison, she and her friends referred to him amongst themselves for no other reason than he was a bit of a prick and they all wanted his attention. Bobs answered her cell because she was working the reception desk at the rec center and it was totally dead. Even the traffic out on Sheffield was light, and that was weird for mid-week near evening rush hour.

He chatted like they were old friends, calling her Roberta because he didn't know that all her close friends called her Bobs, a nod to her full name: Roberta Jean Roberts—Bob, Jean Bobs. Harrison told her about his summer after graduation at his parents' lake house, apparently an endless series of parties and debauchery. He raved about his winter spent backpacking through Europe, spending most of the time in the south of France or in Italy, although he had oddly made a long side trip into eastern European countries like Hungary, Bulgaria and Romania.

Then he dropped the bomb.

"So we should hang out. Hit a club or something and get to know one another a little better. How bout tonight?"

With that proposition, Bobs became a believer. She always thought he was a parasite on society, and now she was convinced that he wanted more from her than just sex—that, he could get from any skank. But she was also convinced that a wrong word now would result in her family home burning down after dark.

"Wow!" she said. It was so easy to fake enthusiasm. She just pictured how any of her friends back in high school would respond to such an invitation from Harrison. "That'd be so totally great but I have to work till nine, and I promised my folks I'd have a late dinner with them. They're putting in long hours these days with all the absenteeism and all, so we don't see much. How about tomorrow?"

This was a total ruse. He was surprisingly put out by a 24-hour delay for someone who hadn't spoken to her in a year, hardly at all really. Bobs' suspicions of his motives only deepened. She never had to let a guy down before, and the stakes had never been so high. Her gut told her that if she did this wrong she was dead.

She bailed from work at five and hurried over to Terry's. They ate pizza, not delivery because that was impossible to get now, but frozen pizza baked in the oven. They debated what to do, not just about Harrison, but about the vampires. It was near midnight when Harrison called for the second time. He said she should check the alley behind her house, the one that served her parents' detached garage. Said he didn't want this to happen to her, that he'd tried to save them, but it was too late. Said he could make her invincible.

She wanted to run straight home, but Terry saved her, holding her close for the first time, not because he was trying to bang her, but because he knew she would die if she ran into the night. She struggled and even punched him, but the initial panic subsided and he let her go. Bobs picked up a game controller and sat down to start killing on-screen zombies. Terry was right. There was no point in running to save dead parents. She went cold, ice cold, and fought to a record score.

They found her parents just outside the garage in the morning sun, the Volvo keys still in her mother's hand, her dad's briefcase on the ground beside him, their throats not just slashed, but with big chunks cut out. There was surprisingly little blood.

Bobs didn't waste time calling the police. That McDonald's guy, Bertrand Allan, had been totally right. There were vampires all over Chicago, and you couldn't trust the police because they were in on it. Terry helped her bury her parents in a shallow grave in her backyard, and she got the priest from St. Mike's, Father Alvarez, to say a few words. He didn't seem surprised that her parents were murdered or that she chose to bury them close to home without the usual family funeral. As she stood over their graves, she knew she should weep, should feel an absence, but the coldness that had settled over her soul last night as she killed game zombies had not gone away, would never go away. It wasn't about revenge. Her head was totally clear. She knew what she had to do simply because it needed to be done. She was passionless.

"We gotta organize the neighborhood and build an army," she said to Terry as she tossed aside her shovel and wiped the sweat from her brow.

They fought the rippers together over the next two years, and Terry was always her go-to guy, the guy who got things done and never questioned her judgment or hesitated to follow her orders.

When he lay dying of pneumonia during their second winter, when people were dropping like flies from disease and starvation, she held his hand to the very end. He must've known it was coming, for he opened his eyes and said, "We tried, Bobs. We tried to save the world."

For the first time since it all began, Bobs wept—huge wracking sobs. It wasn't just that Terry had been her occasional lover, he'd been her rock, her center, the guy who'd been prescient and dependable while her parents had been clueless and got themselves killed, leaving her alone to face the apocalypse, the end.

She didn't let go of his hand, even as he drowned in his own bodily fluids, even as he drew his last gasping breath. When his chest stilled and his heart stopped, Bobs kissed Terry's cold lips and made a promise.

"Don't worry, dude. I'm gonna take over Chicago. I got a plan. I'm going to save the world. I got nukes. I promise, I'm gonna rule the new world, and I'm gonna kill them all."

AUTHOR BIOGRAPHY

Michael Andre McPherson earned a bachelor's degree in physics from the University of Toronto, but soon found his true love of writing after a trip to Afghanistan.

Working in the film industry for more than ten years, McPherson's assignments ranged from production managing low-budget independent films to camera assisting on Hollywood blockbusters. He has since left the film industry and now co-owns a multimedia software development company.

McPherson's short stories have been published in *Storyteller Magazine* and have won various awards in the Bloody Words Mystery Convention's short story writing contest. His story "Working with Psychos" won first prize in the 2006 Great Canadian Story contest, while he placed third in the James Patrick Baen Memorial writing contest for his short story "Acclimatization." He is currently hard at work on his 1000 Souls series.

McPherson lives in Toronto with his wife and three children.

Want to know when Book Three is available for sale? Visit pectopahbooks.com.

1000 SOULS: THE SERIES

Book One
SACRIFICE the LIVING
The End is Now
Published: 2011

Book Two
GENERATION APOCALYPSE
No One Dies of Old Age
Published: 2012

Book Three
HERETICS FALL
Hell Hath No Fury
Published: 2014

Book Four
VAMPIRE ROAD
Journey Home
Published: 2011

Book Five
JACKY'S WAR (Working Title)
Anticipated Release Date: 2015

Buy the books, connect with the author and sign up for exclusive bonus offers: pectopahbooks.com.

What soul do you host? Find out at 1000souls.com.

www.ingramcontent.com/pod-product-compliance
Lightning Source LLC
Chambersburg PA
CBHW030017180626
46810CB00001B/75